It's Me Again is the third and fourth volumes of Donald Jack's highly successful Bandy Papers, a series which grew out of his prize-winning first novel, *Three Cheers for Me*. The series records the hilarious adventures of Bartholomew Bandy, a Canadian pilot in the First World War. Bandy's career continues its crazy course as he pits his wits not only against the Germans, but also against his senior officers, his adjutant, a vindictive pigeon, and that temperamental new invention—the parachute.

As the war draws to its close, Bandy's adventures take him home to Canada, where his reception as a war hero is very short-lived; and to Russia, where his talent for disruption is seen at its best in the Bolshevik revolution.

Donald Jack is an English writer who moved to Canada in 1951. He is well known in Canada and the United States for his plays, films, and TV scripts. The Bandy Papers has earned him international recognition as a humourist.

ALSO BY DONALD JACK

Three Cheers for Me
That's Me in the Middle

IT'S ME AGAIN

by Donald Jack

PaperJacks LTD.

Markham, Ontario, Canada

A CANADIAN

PaperJacks

One of a series of Canadian books
published by PaperJacks Ltd.

IT'S ME AGAIN
THE BANDY PAPERS VOLUME 3

This PaperJacks edition represents the two volumes, IT'S
ME AGAIN VOL. 3 and ME AMONG THE RUINS VOL.
4 which were published by PaperJacks in 1976 and these two
titles have been combined and represent the entire Vol. 3
of THE BANDY PAPERS first issued in hardcover by
Doubleday.

Doubleday edition published in 1975

PaperJacks edition of Vol. 3 and Vol. 4 published in 1976

PaperJacks combined edition published in 1977

This PaperJacks edition includes every word contained
in the original higher-priced edition.

PaperJacks editions are published by PaperJacks Ltd., 330 Steelcase
Road, Markham, Ontario L3R 2M1

CONTENTS

IT'S ME AGAIN

Me, in My Staff Car

On my way back to the front, I ran over a general.

I drove on for another hundred yards or so, stopped the car, thought for a moment, then backed up, and pulling carefully alongside him, called out, "Sir? Sir? Can you tell me the way to my squadron?" And told him the number.

After all, he was an Air Force general, so he was bound to know.

He didn't seem to be concentrating too well that afternoon, though. As a matter of fact, he was busy counting his teeth.

I don't know why he was sitting there in the gravel adding up his teeth, unless it was some form of disorientation brought on by being struck a glancing blow by a large Vauxhall just as he was stepping out of his château for a breath of fresh gunpowder. But there was no doubt that, with staring eyes and peculiar, fumbling gestures, he was running his finger tips shakily over his front teeth, as if checking to see if they had come loose, or were busy rattling about back there like nicotine-stained dice.

I hadn't seen shock take this particular form before, and I started to get quite interested in his dental *arpeggio* —until it occurred to me that he might not be well-disposed towards me when he recovered his senses.

It wouldn't be any use my explaining, either, that it was his fault for getting in the way. I knew enough about the military by then to know that if there was one thing a senior officer hated, it was an explanation.

The unfeeling decision to leave him sitting there in the gravel, using his teeth as an abacus, was quickly put into practice when I saw a red-tabbed major emerging from the french window at the side of the château. As the Vauxhall was already in reverse, I hurriedly let up the clutch and backed down the driveway—the château was so posh it had peacocks strutting around the grounds—and, after a short drive, got back to the main road and hurried onward, roughly in the direction of Amiens.

My third tour of duty at the front didn't seem to be starting out any more promisingly than had either of the others. To begin with, the early-morning steamer had taken four hours to cross the Channel, to avoid a lurking submarine, and by the time I'd disembarked, the squadron chauffeur, a cheeky-looking cock with wattles, had had time to visit every *estaminet* in Dieppe. The result was I'd had to put him in the back seat and drive the staff car myself.

I'd told him off, of course, in a dignified, restrained manner, as befitted my position. I had even considered charging him for common drunkenness. But it would have been a waste of time, as he was incapable of taking anything in, or even of finding out where the loud voice was coming from. So, as I said, I just bundled him into the back and took the wheel myself. This inspired many curious stares, and a loud remark from an Australian sergeant to the effect that if all the brass hats stayed as blotto as that, maybe there was a chance we'd win the war after all.

I guess he thought the reeking, huddled form in the back seat was a staff officer.

By George, though, that chauffeur got an earful as soon as he was *compos mentis* again, about ten miles short of our destination.

"You made me run over a general," I said, as he climbed, blood-shot and feeble-fisted, into the front seat, his loose cheeks swaying about in a nauseating fashion. "It was your fault. I think it's been a very poor show, Witcomb," I said. That was his name, Witcomb.

Things didn't look any more promising at the squadron, either. It looked dismayingly well organized. As the open staff car emerged from the French mist, a motorcyclist, who seemed to have been keeping watch, roared away from the guard hut and up a narrow avenue lined with Normandy poplars. Simultaneously, a couple of ack-emmas dressed up as sentries marched up to the gleaming white gate and swung it aside on well-oiled hinges and saluted energetically as the chauffeur winced past holding his headache together with both hands and steering with his knee.

The Vauxhall throbbed to the end of the tree-lined driveway, bearing its precious cargo of sandals, wood, silks, ebony, silver-backed clothes brushes, Bibles, dandruff remedy, monogrammed pajamas, toilet paper, a boiled ham, and me, huddled horse-faced in the back, peering out at my new domain with all the arrogance of a two and sixpence a week tea-boy on his first construction job.

At the top of the avenue stood a spacious house with a roof of red pantiles. In front of it, numerous squadron signs and tulips had been planted. Off to one side, a small, symmetrical mountain of coal.

The coal had been whitewashed.

As I wrenched my eyes from the whitewashed fuel, I started slightly. I'd noticed several thousand men lined up, a few feet away.

They were standing at ease, in perfectly positioned and ordered ranks, for as far as the eye could see—about 290 feet, in that mist. As the car lurched up, a powerful-looking captain, in a creaking Sam Browne and spotless boots, about-turned in foot-stamping gardee style to face the throng, and as the car reached him he uttered a shrill scream.

11

For a moment, I thought we'd run over his bunions. But apparently he was just issuing an order, for the ranks of airmen in front of him immediately presented arms, slapping their butts with a precision highly uncharacteristic of air-force groundlings. Even in the dull light, their bayonets shone as if forged from sterling silver.

What in heaven's name was going on? I twisted round and gaped over the back of the Vauxhall to see if Field Marshal Haig or Generalissimo Foch was approaching. But there was nothing but a few withered snowdrops. Even they seemed to have sprung to attention.

As I stood up in the back seat for a better view, the captain looked me over for badges of rank, or at least for some air of authority. Finding neither, he enquired guardedly, as if meeting imposters was a familiar experience, "Major Bandy, is it?"

I nodded dumbly. Whereupon he flung up his arm in a Sandhurst salute, complete with the regulation finger-quivering. "Captain Malt, Recording Officer and P.M.C. Sah!"

A beefy-looking chap with huge, pink hands and two campaign ribbons on his perfect regimental tunic, he held the salute until I had reinserted my eyeballs and somewhat weakly returned the salutation.

A bored major with a ginger mustache strolled forward. He and Malt looked up at me expectantly.

I realized I was still standing up in the car, and that my jaw was beginning to slacken again, as I gaped along the ranks of riggers, fitters, lorry drivers and motorcyclists, blacksmiths, tinsmiths, coppersmiths, carpenters, armorers, cooks, and clerks.

I scrambled down, straightening my cap and fumbling for my orders.

"May I present Major Reeves-Goring," Captain Malt shouted. "Major Bandy, Major Reeves-Goring!"

We shook hands, and as the major checked my orders,

I tried to smooth the wrinkles from my travelling raincoat. It was the worst-looking garment I owned. Well, I hadn't expected anything as formal as this.

There was worse to some. After indulging in the regulation chit-chat for a minute or so, Captain Malt suddenly belowed in my ear-hole, "Sah! Would you care to inspect the men?"

A moment later, I found myself walking dazedly along lines of frozen-eyed airmen and officers, with Malt following precisely three paces behind, his boots crunching heavily on the gravel.

The major, meanwhile, had moved over to supervise the unloading of the staff car. I thought it was very kind of him to see to my luggage that way—until I realized he was throwing it out to make way for his own gear.

He seemed in a hurry to be off. I couldn't blame him in the least.

"You! Your puttees aren't straight," Malt bellowed at my neck.

I started to reach down guiltily, before remembering that I wasn't wearing puttees.

"Sarnt, take that man's name and numBAH!" Malt shouted, glaring ferociously at the unfortunate airman, whose puttees were indeed a good eighth of an inch out of true.

As we reached the end of the last rank, several hours later, I said wonderingly, "Very smart. Very smart indeed . . ."

"Thank you, sah. Now may I introduce you to your pilots?"

It was quite a shock when I saw the pilots drawn up as well. It was the first time I'd ever seen active-service pilots on parade. To make matters worse, Captain Malt introduced me as formally as if I'd been the Prince of Wales.

The pilots didn't seem to think much of it either. Dressed in the usual variety of dark-blue, khaki, and light-blue uniforms—naval, regimental, R.F.C., and R.A.F., they stared sullenly ahead. I failed to take in a single name.

After the inspection, there was a tense pause. For an awful moment, I thought they were expecting me to lead the squadron in a stirring rendition of 'The Cobbler's Song,' from *Chu Chin Chow*. However, after another calculating glance at me, Malt dismissed the parade without further ceremony.

The airmen promptly marched off in column of four in the direction of the hangars, which were barely visible along the south side of the field. But I watched the pilots, as they moved off silently toward a large tent that was sagging dispiritedly behind a splintered barn. They looked utterly defeated.

"That's the officer's mess tent," the major said.

"Oh ar."

Reeves-Goring paused to frown at the chauffeur, as the latter fumbled several tons of war booty into the staff car.

"Come on, get on with it, Witcomb. I haven't got all day."

"Sir."

Witcomb looked pretty defeated too. He looked as if his brains had been scooped out and replaced with Dundee marmalade.

Reeves-Goring turned back, stabbing a thumb through the bright-green trees beyond the mess tent. "The officers' Nissens are over there, at the edge of the wood. Your quarters, of course, are in the house. Malt will show you around, if that's all right, Bandy. I'd do so myself but I want to get to Boulogne tonight."

Malt stood respectfully nearby, surreptitiously looking me over. He spent some time over my features. I wondered if my face was dirty. The Vauxhall had thrown up quite a bit of filth whilst detouring around Amiens on sundry muddy cart tracks. The chauffeur had avoided Amiens because there was still a great deal of disorder in that city, following the massive German attacks that had started on March 21.

"Anything else you want to know?" the major asked, looking pointedly at his watch.

Anything else? He hadn't told me a thing, so far. I opened my mouth to say so.

"The paperwork's well in hand, I can assure you of that," he continued. "The brigade commander is a stickler for efficient paperwork, as Malt will tell you."

"Good. It's 5F1s you fly here, isn't it?"

"Correct. We've just finished converting from Spads."

"What do you think of them? I've heard they're death traps."

"They're very reliable aircraft, whatever the pilots say," the major said stiffly. "Incidentally, you don't want to pay any attention to the officers, Bandy. There's been a few casualties lately. Nothing much out of the ordinary, of course, but they're in rather a miserable mood just now, as you probably gathered. Still, as long as they're dealt with firmly. They appreciate firmness."

"M'yes."

"Look, I'm in a hurry to get off, Bandy," the major said. "You were late arriving, you know. Captain Malt will tell you the rest. He's a very good man, very efficient and hard-working. You couldn't do better, I can assure you of that."

"Oh, fine."

"A word of advice," he said, as we walked over to the loaded staff car. "Keep a particularly close eye on Lieutenant Carson. That's A Flight deputy-commander. He's a real Bolshie. I'd have got rid of the blighter in another week, I can assure you of that."

He climbed into the back of the car beside his silver-mounted dressing case, his roasting jack, his portable bath, and his adjutant, who was driving down to the main gate to see the major off.

"Well, good-bye, Bandy," he called out over the spluttering of the motor. "Sorry to rush off like this, but you know how it is with the leave boats. So, I leave you in Malt's capable hands. Right, then. Good luck."

Pretty bewildered, I watched him and Malt go off, with their heads together.

As they disappeared into the poplars, I looked around glumly. Nearby, a little airman with an appealingly ugly face was shifting about anxiously.

"I'm your batman, sir," he said hurriedly, stiffening to attention. "Smethurst, sir. I've taken your luggage upstairs, if that's all right, sir. Shall I go ahead and unpack, sir?"

"M'yes. I'll just have a look at the squadron office first."

The ground floor of the house was entirely taken up with offices, the kitchen, and the sergeant-cook's room. In the large room to the left of the hall, two tidy clerks were working at trestle tables. They sprang to attention when I walked in, their chairs sliding back over the polished parquet with scarcely a sound.

The place seemed to be filled to the brim with paper.

Behind the partition that divided the room was Reeves-Goring's office. Mine now, I supposed. It contained a real office desk and a real office chair, as well as a real armchair and a real carpet, to cover the squeaks and groans in the hardwood floor. There was also a side table, on which piles of Army forms were neatly arranged. Two of the walls were almost completely covered in charts, plans, a notice board, aircraft silhouettes, pilots' maps, and large-scale maps of the front.

Beyond the desk was a french window with a view along the eastern edge of the airfield.

"Spacious, isn't it?" I said to the young corporal, who had somewhat hesitantly followed me in.

"Yes, sir." He snapped to attention. "Corporal Tomlinson, sir. Your personal secretary."

"My what?"

"Secretary, sir. Least that's what Major Reeves-Goring called me."

"*Tiens.*"

"Yes, sir. I used to be an aero engine fitter, but Captain Malt brought me in here because he heard I could type-write, sir."

"And can you?"

"Sir?"

"Can you typewrite?"

"Yes, sir. I learned from my sister," Tomlinson said, looking as if he wished he'd never met his sister.

"M'm." I looked through the window at the deserted airfield. "No flying today, I see," I said, somewhat super-fluously.

"No, sir. Too foggy."

"M'm."

I followed the batman upstairs to the living accommodation, to find the most lavish quarters I'd seen outside of a corps H.Q. There was not only a well-furnished bed-room but an adjoining sitting room, complete with chintz curtains lined with blackout material, a splendid side-board, and a gramophone with a stack of records beside. I glanced at the top record: 'I've Always Got the Time to Talk to You.'

"What very nice rooms they've given me," I said to the batman.

"These are Captain Malt's rooms, sir."

"Oh."

Mine were almost as nice. By standing on the extreme right of the sitting-room window, I was able to obtain a splendid view of the fog.

Malt returned from the main gate a few minutes later and asked if I'd care to take afternoon tea with him, in his rooms.

"I think I'll take a look round first, Captain, er, Malt," I said firmly.

"It's all set up, sah."

"I still have to get my bearings, you see. And—"

"Should be thoroughly stewed by now, sah."

"Who should?"

"Always insist on the tea being thoroughly stewed, Major. I'm sure you could do with a spot of tea first."

"But it'll be getting dark soon, and—"

"We have Eccles cakes today, sah."

"Eccles cakes? Well . . ."

So we had tea and Eccles cakes in his sitting room, served by the officers' cook, a puffy-faced sergeant named Bixby, with eyes like a couple of raisins plucked from his own Eccles cakes and embedded in hollows of spare dough.

I suspected the sergeant was serving us personally in order to size up the new C.O., for he hung around for several minutes, fussing with the crockery and listening carefully to my inane remarks, until Captain Malt dismissed him with a wink, a blink, and a nod.

"You seem to do yourself proud, Captain," I said, looking around at the luxury.

"Can't complain, sah, can't complain. When you've had to rough it the way I've had to, you feel you're entitled to a spot of the old home comfort."

"You were in the trenches, were you?"

"Quartermaster's store, actually."

That was before he joined the R.A.F., he explained. He had been with the squadron ever since Reeves-Goring took over. "We were at school together," he said casually, leaning over to dig a currant out of the seam of his flies. He nibbled it fastidiously.

"Ah. Thought you two looked kind of pally."

"Before Reeves-Goring, Major Soames was the C.O.," he said. "It was he who originally formed this squadron, back in 1915. He's now the commander of our particular brigade."

"Soames is?"

18

"Yes. First-class chap, you know. Independent income. Loves the piano."

"Does he play well?"

"Naturally he doesn't play himself. He has one of his men do that."

Malt wrapped his large, pink paws round his tea-cup, and asked casually, "Do you know him?"

"The pianist?"

"Brigadier Soames."

"No. Why?"

"Thought you might have got this job through knowing him, that's all. I mean, you must have had some sort of influence."

"How d'you mean?"

"Well . . ." Malt looked embarrassed. "You know. Understood you'd left the Air Ministry under something of a cloud."

Captain Malt had obviously heard of the Fallow speech.

"Anyway, I don't suppose the brigadier will hold it against you—provided you don't stir things up. Good man, you know. Fine administrator. Relative."

"A relatively fine administrator?"

"Eh? No, I mean he's a relative of mine. Cousin."

"Oh."

He held up his empty cup to see if the tea-leaves had formed a suggestive picture. "So naturally he takes a particularly keen interest in my squadron," he said, giving me another sly glance, to make sure I'd got the point, that it would be as well to keep in with the brigadier's relative. "Got a pip of a wife," he added.

"You must miss her a great deal, Captain," I said glumly.

"I'm talking about Soames's wife, old man."

"Oh."

Très sexy," he said, blushing slightly. "French, of course." He lowered his voice. "Don't mention this to anyone else though, will you?"

"There's nothing particularly shameful in being French, is there?"

"I'm talking about my connections, Major. Wouldn't want people to think I was trading on the family relationship, or anything like that."

I nodded approvingly and pushed back my chair in a significant sort of way; but Malt was pouring himself another cup of tannin. I pretended I'd merely been making myself more comfortable.

"No, I'm not married," he went on, massaging his thigh with his free hand. "Wouldn't leave me much time for my hobby, would it?"

He seemed to expect me to answer, so I said dutifully, "You have a hobby, have you?"

"H'm? Yes, I'm a bit of a collector, in my own small way."

Match boxes, I thought. Now I'll have to spend another half-hour looking at his bloody match boxes. Or horse brasses.

"Had an interest in the subject for quite some time now," he went on, patting his plump stomach. "Most of my collection's at home, of course. Worcester. I'm just an amateur, mind you. Gifted amateur, I suppose you might say."

He moved over to the sideboard and placed a thick, wrinkled forefinger on top. "Managed to pick up a few items over here, matter of fact," he said, looking proud but, for some reason, rather jittery. "You, ah, you really want to see my collection?"

"Oh, sure."

He hesitated, coughed, then opened the two end compartments of the sideboard and stood back, pink with pride and anxiety. "There they are. These are just a few samples, of course. As I said, I've quite a considerable number at home, including several crested examples."

I stared dumbly into the sideboard. It was filled to the brim with chamber pots.

He removed one of them and showed it to me. It had a blue eye painted on the bottom. Curving round the eye were the words,

> *Use me well and keep me clean*
> *And I'll not tell what I have seen.*

"That's the one I use;" Malt said, "on special occasions."

"Yes," Malt said, as we squelched through the trees after inspecting the officers' Nissen huts, "it's an interesting study. They've unearthed an astonishing number of Roman chamber utensils in Britain, you know. Chill climate must have had an effect on the Roman bladder—suppose that's why they made so many. I have two Roman pots. Both broken, unfortunately. But it's my main ambition to own one of the Empress Josephine's musical pots."

"Musical chamber pots?"

"Had a music box incorporated in it. Tinkled a tune every time she sat on it."

"Not 'The Marseillaise,' I trust?"

"Eh? Why not?"

"Well, every time it played, she'd have to stand up again, wouldn't she?"

Malt was still regarding me a bit mistrustfully as we passed the house again on our way back from the hangars. A party of men in the charge of a corporal were busy weeding a flower bed in front of the house.

"The major's pride and joy, those tulips," Malt said. "That flower bed was the one thing he hated to leave behind."

"It's a splendid display," I said. "But, tum, are we overstaffed or something?"

"Eh? All these men, you mean? No, they're just on punishment. Corporal! Major Bandy thinks you're doing splendidly. Keep up the good work."

21

"Sir."

As we continued onward toward the barn, I glanced back and saw the corporal deliberately kick one of the flowers in the crotch. When he saw me looking at him, he knelt down quickly to apply a field dressing to the wounded tulip, or possibly a splint.

The squadron was situated immediately to the east of the tiny village of Montonvillers, six miles northwest of Amiens. There were several squadrons in the area, including 48, 84, and 209 squadrons at Bertangles, all within walking distance. But ours, Malt said, was the smartest of the lot.

Certainly it had one of the best locations I'd ever come across, with the bright green woods on the east side of the spacious field, which we shared with an S.E. 5a squadron, across the way.

The men's sleeping quarters and mess tents were in the far corner of the airfield, as were the store tents, workshops, and transport compound. Along the south side were four spacious Besseneau hangars, and my heart sank when I saw the ugly great beasts that were huddled miserably inside them. I'd heard a good deal about the 5F1, and it wasn't favorable. The cockpit opened from the middle of the top wing, so the pilot's head stuck out into the open in a terribly vulnerable way, forming an easy target for enemy machine guns. Moreover, if the plane overturned—and every pilot overturned at least one aircraft during his career, it was practically an Air Force regulation—his neck would obviously be the first component to snap.

"It's a decidedly Hunnish-looking bus, isn't it?" I said uneasily.

"Between you and me," Malt said, leading me to the officers' latrines, "the pilots certainly haven't accomplished much with it." He lowered his voice to a croaky whisper as we inspected the canvas structure, with its open compartments, and the toilet lids all standing to attention.

"With one or two exceptions, like Captain Kiddell—he's A Flight commander—the pilots are a pretty poor lot, if you ask me. In fact, the last time the brigadier was here, he practically accused them of having wind up."

Oh, Lord, I thought. Apparently Colonel Treadwell hadn't been doing me a favor at all when he got me this job.

As we turned away, I caught sight of another structure, at the edge of a hayfield beyond the barn.

"What's that?" I asked, and started toward it.

"Just my personal toilet," Malt said shortly, and turned aside, obviously expecting me to follow.

But I was much too busy drinking in his personal toilet. "Good heavens," I said.

It was a solidly constructed edifice among the trees, approached by a neat path bordered with whitewashed stones. It had a decorative wooden moulding around the Gothic doorway. The moulding was faultlessly painted in green and gold. Atop the pointed roof was an ornamental iron weather vane in the shape of a cock. The barnyard variety, that is.

"My goodness gracious me," I said faintly.

I walked slowly toward it, suffused with awe, greedily taking in each lavish detail: the decorative curlicues at each corner of the roof, the little stained-glass window in the side, the spotless antique bootscraper at the door, in the shape of a Saxon serf, the polished Yale lock, the extra keyhole below it, the perfectly lettered sign planted in the manicured grass plot that read, RECORDING OFFICER *Out of Bounds to All Other Personnel*.

"This is really a toilet?"

"Course it is. I told you."

"It's . . . it's absolutely magnificent," I breathed.

"It serves."

"Do you . . . do you think I could possibly see inside?"

"Well . . ." He looked down. I think he was checking

to see if my boots were clean. "The pilots are expecting us, Major."

"If I didn't see the interior first, I . . . I don't think I could go on, Malt."

The idea didn't seem to appeal much to the adjutant. However, after a few more agitated objections, he reluctantly brought out his key-ring; but then hesitated again, and said, "Don't know why you're so interested in somebody else's toilet, Major. Doesn't seem very, well, wholesome to me."

"I can't help myself. Please, I must see inside."

"Oh, very well," he said, sounding quite disturbed by my unhealthy attitude. He opened the door.

"Oh, Malt," I said.

A polished brass oil lamp hung from the ceiling. A Victorian pot cupboard frowned in the corner. There was a complete set of Balzac, with deckle edges and uncut pages. On the wall, a picture of Sir Douglas Haig, the Commander-in-Chief.

"Oh, Malt," I said again. I realized I'd removed my cap.

"A carpet," I whispered. "Bookcases. Real toilet paper. Stained glass."

And in the middle, a real pedestal toilet. A toilet? A symphony in porcelain, with an exquisite fluted bowl surmounting an ecstatically smiling sea creature.

"It's . . . it's . . ." I breathed.

"It should really have a syphon cistern, of course," Malt said breathlessly, his face pink with pride and worry. "But there was too much of a problem involved in conveying the water here, so I have to flush it by hand."

"By hand? You mean you put your hand in and sort of—?"

"No, no. With a *bucket*," Malt said, looking revolted. Then: "It's J. Bolding and Sons' most famous design, of course. *The Dolphin*."

"A dolphin. Of course, it's a dolphin. Supporting the bowl. A *smiling* dolphin."

His toilet even had a lid, of polished mahogany, hinged to an ornate bracket.

"Do you think . . . do you possibly think . . . ?"

"It's just for my personal use, of course," Malt said quickly. "I did have an arrangement with Reeves-Goring, because he flew it over for me, from England. But—"

"*Flew* it over?" I faltered, my mind reeling at the thought of an airborne lavatory. Had Reeves-Goring sat on it all the way across the Channel perhaps?

"Would you mind if I closed the door now, Major? It's misty outside. Don't want the furnishings to get damp, you understand."

As he carefully locked the door again, he said, "You do understand, don't you—it's my personal property. Nothing to do with the Air Force whatsoever."

"Yes . . . no . . ."

"Fine. Just wanted to make it clear where I stood, that's all."

"Or sat," I mumbled.

"Beg your pardon? No, I mean, I just wanted the situation to be quite clear, that's all."

"It's getting clearer every minute," I said.

"Atten-hun!"

It was sour and muggy inside the big mess tent behind the empty barn. I got a quick impression of a handful of scruffy seats, trestle tables, a bumpy floor of brown grass, and a makeshift bar surrounded by disheartened expressions.

As we entered, the officers rose with an alacrity inversely proportional to their status. The last to rise was Captain Kiddell, the only other Canadian in the squadron.

"Captain Kiddell's our biggest Hun-getter," Malt said in the unnerving silence. "How many is it now, Kiddell?"

"Nine."

"Very good. M'm, very good. Yes, I've heard about you, Captain," I ejaculated, then winced because I'd spoken so loudly and with such insincere emphasis. I'd been making a great effort lately to reduce my voice to a more gentlemanly volume, as I understood that my normal projection was capable of menacing the foundations of even the stoutest edifice. And the tent was far from stout. In fact, when I spoke I'm sure the canvas bellied slightly.

I must have winced quite noticeably. Kiddell stared. He probably thought I was developing a twitch before I'd even taken over.

"Yeah," he said. "We've heard all about you too, Major."

"Well, now you can hear my side of it," I said, looking around with my mouth half open, ready to join in the hearty laughter.

There wasn't a titter. I wondered uneasily if maybe they *did* know all about me.

"The major's very impressed with what he's seen so far," Malt said. "So let's give him all the help we can, shall we, to make sure this is not only the most efficient squadron in the Air Force, but the one with the best fighting spirit."

This was also greeted with a leaden silence. I turned hurriedly to the keenest face in the vicinity.

"How, uh," I began. "How long have you been with the squadron?"

"Too long," the lieutenant said. He had an American accent. "Matter of fact, Major, I'm applying for a transfer."

"M'm, that's a good start," I said distractedly. "Why is that?"

The American, Orville France, started to say something, but then looked away and shrugged. "They're keen on us moving over to our own service, that's all," he said.

I became aware that a rather frightening-looking 1st lieutenant was staring at me fixedly. His thin, intense face was pockmarked with gunpowder grains, and his lips were ferociously twisted. They had been damaged by shrapnel, and improperly repaired.

"And, uh, who are you, Lieutenant?" I asked timidly.

He took his time about answering. "Just another piece of cannon fodder," he said in a grating voice. "Carson."

So this was the man the C.O. had warned me about. The former C.O., that is. I must remember that.

"He's my deputy," Kiddell grunted. "You were given his name at that goddam parade, but I guess you've forgotten." He moved over to the rickety bar. A couple of 2nd lieutenants made way for him respectfully. "You care for a drink, Major?"

"No, thanks. I don't drink."

He didn't look surprised. "Funny," he said. "I had an idea you didn't drink. Don't know how I got the idea, but there you are. I said to myself, 'Gee, I bet the major doesn't drink either'."

"The bar's nearly out of booze anyway," Orville France said. "As usual."

"I laid in a good stock only last week," Malt said. "You fellows drink too much, that's all. You ought to take a leaf out of the major's book."

"What book is that?" Carson asked, baring his teeth. *"Mother Goose?"*

After a while, the pilots began to mutter among themselves again. I caught the eye of a good-looking captain sitting by himself at one of the trestle tables. He had a half-filled tumbler of whiskey in one hand and a pencil in the other. He looked at me guardedly for a moment before lowering his eyes to the paper on which he was sketching.

I moved over, trying to saunter casually, but feeling as if my knees had seized up.

"I didn't quite get your name either, I'm afraid," I murmured, sitting opposite.

"Derby, sir. I'm B Flight commander." He put his forearm casually over the paper as he leaned forward to indicate his companion. "Lieutenant McKindle, my deputy; and this lad here is Ringan-Smith."

I liked the look of John Derby. He had high, square shoulders and a nervous face with bloodshot eyes. He wore a wary expression, as if he expected me to start making improper advances at any moment.

His deputy, Jock McKindle, complemented him perfectly. He wore a perpetual, Scottish-type scowl.

"And, uh, how do you find the new 5F1s, McKindle?" I asked.

"I usually find them doon by the hangars."

"No, I mean, how are they in combat?"

"Combat? What combat?" Kiddell said contemptuously. "We've done nothing but trench-strafing for weeks."

"How are they to fly, then?"

"Ye canny see the horizon over that great, ugly snout."

"It stalls like a wet hen."

"You can't see a goddam thing going on below."

"The wudder's too sensitive"—this was Lieutenant Monty Murgatroyd—"and the wadiator's wonky."

"There's no room to move with those bloody Lewis guns swinging round your head."

"In short," Carson grated, "they glide like a brick, the oil system's a failure, the magnetos are no damn good, there's no protection for the pilot if they turn over, the radiators wouldn't cool a Zulu's tit, and whoever thought of putting in the fixed Lewises ought to be flung over the White Cliffs of Dover by a Japanese Sumo wrestler."

"But apart from that they're all right, are they?"

Murgatroyd gave me a quick glance. Kiddell stared.

"You mean you haven't flown one?"

"No."

"Christ." Kiddell turned his back and stared morosely into his glass, and muttered, not quite inaudibly, "Another goddam penguin for a C.O."

A penguin was a pilot who had retired from war flying.

I turned back to Derby, trying to see what he was

drawing. It seemed to be a sketch of a feeble-looking horse, dressed in regimental uniform. "And, uh, who else is in your flight, apart from you three?"

"Nobody else at the moment. I've lost the rest."

"Lost?"

"Two were shot down yesterday by ground m.g. fire, and the other lost his engine over Bray."

"Oh."

"The major said Ringan-Smith will have to join the flight tomorrow," Derby said casually, but looking at me directly for the first time.

Ringan-Smith wore the R.A.F. khaki uniform. He looked about seventeen.

"I see. How long have you been out, Ringan-Smith?"

"About two weeks, sir."

"Two weeks? How many hours?"

"Nearly thirty, sir."

"Twenty-six," Derby said.

"I'm really looking forward to going over the lines," Ringan-Smith said.

Everybody had fallen silent again. Though they were careful not to look at me, I had a feeling this was some sort of a test.

After a moment, I got up and started to stretch, but stopped half-way through it. I must have looked as if I were about to break into the Highland Fling.

"Well," I said, my jaw muscles rippling manfully as I suppressed a number of yawns, "I guess I'll see you all at dinner, eh?"

The heavy silence continued as I stiff-legged it to the tent flap. "Perhaps, uh, we'll be able to get to know each other better then."

"I wouldn't count on it," Carson said loudly, as I went out.

I saw what he meant when dinner time arrived. Apart from Malt, Captain Peters, the armament officer, and myself, there were only three other officers present. The rest had gone to a small French restaurant in Flesselles for dinner.

It was a pretty pointed snub, though I tried to convince myself that it was the cooking that had driven them away. Sergeant Bixby's pork chops, for instance, tasted as if they'd been basted with wallpaper paste.

I hoped my dear friend Dick Milestone, who had applied for a transfer to this squadron from Home Defence, would get here soon. I felt very friendless and alone.

I felt even more friendless and alone next morning, when I lined up with the rest of the squadron to greet the officer commanding the 5th R.A.F. Brigade. He had close-set eyes and the regulation mustache, but was otherwise that great rarity, a thin general. A thin, *limping* general.

"I've heard that voice before," he said in a high-pitched voice. He turned to his major. "Where've I heard that voice before, Dennison?"

"I don't know, sir."

"Well, I've heard that voice before," he said quite agitatedly. "I couldn't possibly forget a voice like that."

"It wasn't me, sir," I said shrilly. "It couldn't have been me. It was . . ."

"Who couldn't?"

"Unless—unless it was at the Air Ministry," I cried. "Yes, that's where it was, sir. You must have heard me at the Air Ministry."

His brow clouded with doubt. "I don't know . . . I don't know . . ."

I did, though, I *thought* he'd looked a bit familiar as he limped down from his staff car, exhibiting his teeth.

Tiptoeing Through the Tulips

I'd no idea there was so much office work involved in running a squadron. In five days, I managed only one trip over the lines, during which I distinguished myself by bombing an empty crump hole with pinpoint accuracy.

The rest of the time, I hardly had a chance to stick my nose out of the house, I was so busy negotiating with stores and aircraft parks and supply depots, organizing the training of new pilots, passing on the operations orders from Wing Headquarters, filling in forms, writing up, checking, or initialling all kinds of records, logs, and registers, dealing with and passing on reconnaissance and low-bombing reports, handing out punishments for infractions of discipline, sending sympathetic letters to next of kin, making tours of inspection, and in general handling so many forms, chits, receipts, orders, and vouchers I couldn't help suspecting that Malt was heaping me with chores to prove how hard *he* was working.

In any event, I found myself almost completely desk-bound, while Malt bustled about, busily doing very little work as far as I could make out, but giving the impression that it was he who was holding the reins of power, while I was there merely to sweep up the horse cobs.

"Why do I have to check all this stuff anyway?" I asked one drizzly morning. "We have an awful lot of clerks; why can't they handle it?"

Immediately I wished I'd phrased that remark differently. Malt was always seizing on stray comments of mine and re-employing them to my disadvantage. For example, he would almost certainly tell the staff later that I had described them as an awful lot.

"Major Reeves-Goring managed all right," Malt said in the tones of fatherly indulgence he'd adopted in his dealings with this sulky new C.O.

"Did he manage to fly as well?"

"Oh, yes. He often went up to check the weather."

"Well, I want to fly a lot," I whined.

"Brigadier Soames doesn't encourage his commanders to fly, Major."

"Well, I don't care," I mumbled, drawing a ring on the desk with a forefinger. "Anyway, surely you ought to be looking after all these details."

"Of course, sah," Malt said heartily. "After all, that's what I'm here for, isn't it? To buffer you against all the complaints, take the minor cares and worries off your shoulders, and relieve you of the trivial responsibilities. By the way, don't forget to put in for another pad of W.3348s, will you? You never know when they might come in handy. Oh, and here's Corporal Tomlinson's application to go back to his old job as a fitter. You'll have to turn it down, of course. We can't spare him from the office."

I looked up defiantly. "Unless, of course," he added, "you want even more paperwork on your hands."

As I obediently wrote "no" on Tomlinson's request, there was a droning sound from the airfield. I got up to look longingly through the french window. A couple of Scouts were curving across the wet sky and turning in to land, their streamers fluttering. I pressed my nose against the glass and watched as they bumped down, sending up fountains of spray from the waterlogged grass.

The SE squadron across the field had not flown all morning, but Wing, on Brigade orders, had phoned through earlier on to insist on our machines making a trench reconnaissance in the Albert region. Four aircraft of C Flight had gone out a couple of hours before, under low clouds.

I cranked my head sideways to peer toward the east, but no other aircraft appeared.

Two or three minutes later, C Flight's commander, Captain Blackbourne, and his deputy, Monty Murgatroyd, entered the squadron office next door to make their verbal reports and fill in the appropriate forms.

Blackbourne and Murgatroyd were former Royal Naval Air Service pilots, and usually wore their naval uniforms in the mess. Both had very expensive accents. In fact, I understood that C Flight was known as the Upper Class Flight. A third member, Charles ffoliot, was the son of the British ambassador to China or Japan, or somewhere mysterious.

"Where's the rest of the flight?" Malt asked them. Blackbourne had taken two new men across the lines that morning.

"Fire from the ground got one of them," Blackbourne said. A nerve below his left eye was twitching away merrily. "We don't really know what happened to the other chap."

Murgatroyd, who lisped like something out of *The Boy's Own Paper,* said accusingly to Malt, "We were the only people up today. We should newer have gone out in we'wer like that."

"Brigade's orders, I'm afraid," Malt said sympathetically. "Isn't that right, Major?"

Actually, Malt had taken that particular call and passed it on, but what else could I do but agree?

"When did you last see the other pilot?" I asked.

"We lost him in a rain squall somewhere east of Albert," Blackbourne said, still addressing himself to Malt, as Murgatroyd morosely examined a rent in the crimson lining of his tunic.

Malt said he'd ring up a battery on that part of the front, to find out if they'd seen anything of the missing

33

pilot. "Oh, by the way, Pash," he said, after the pilots had completed the paperwork, "if anyone wants the tender to go to Flesselles this evening, it'll be quite all right. Pass it on, will you?"

"Most of the fellows can't afford to eat any more this month," Blackbourne said shortly, and tramped off with Murgatroyd toward their damp Nissen.

I hurried around the partition, to get back to my desk before Malt did. But he got there first.

As he settled himself at my desk, he looked up at me triumphantly, his large hands folded over his stomach. I paced up and down in front of him, like a caged mole.

"By the way, can't we do anything about the food here?" I asked. "It's not very well prepared, is it? I mean, maybe the pilots wouldn't eat out so much if, well, if—"

"You could, of course, forbid the officers to go out in the evening," Malt said expressionlessly.

"No, no, I didn't mean that. I meant—"

"Yes, perhaps it would be a good idea to compel them to eat in the mess. Shall I draw up an order to that effect, sah?"

"I didn't mean that. I just meant—Well, *esprit de corps,* and all that. It could be improved slightly, I thought. I mean—"

"You don't wish me to forbid them to eat out?"

"I . . . no, of course not," I said, summoning up an image of myself being guillotined, and my head dropping into the basket, the eyes staring up at the sky in a somewhat victimized sort of way.

But, darn it, I wasn't going to give up that easily. Nobody was going to walk over me—at least, not without wiping his boots first. I ceased pacing, and faced the desk squarely.

"And another thing," I began.

Malt must have seen the determination in my face. He stood up.

"The mess fees—they seem awfully high, Captain. Don't you think—"

But apparently Malt had risen only to leave the room. He was already disappearing around the partition.

"Oh, Tomlinson," I heard him call; then, a moment later, conspiratorially: "I'm sorry, but the major's turned down your request. Look, Tom, why don't you try again in about a month. I'm sure I'll be able to persuade the major to . . ."

I looked out the window. Rain began to slaver down the glass. After a few minutes, I took up my old raincoat and went around the partition. The two clerks stood up. "Sit down, sit down," I snorted. "There's no need to spring up like gollywogs every time I make an appearance."

As I tramped away through the drizzle, I heard one of them neigh. There was a stifled outburst of giggling.

This is no use at all, I thought, as I settled myself in the drafty latrines for a good think. In a remarkably short span of time I seemed to have deteriorated from an experienced character actor in the drama of life to a supernumerary in a Plautus farce.

I couldn't help wondering if it had anything to do with my New Year resolutions. I'd been brought up in an Ottawa Valley household so pious and Spartan that if you slept in later than six A.M., you were considered to be teetering on the verge of Roman degeneracy. However, soon after my arrival in Europe in 1916 as a pi, Spartan, and elderly (23) sub-lieutenant in the Victorian Light Infantry Regiment, I'd begun to succumb to the fleshpots of Salisbury, Maidenhead, and places like that, to such an extent that within eighteen months I was reeling around with the worst of them, swearing, smoking, and smashing the mess furniture in the traditional R.F.C. manner. Moreover, affected by the Church's apparently wholehearted approval of the slaughter, I had almost entirely given up reading the Good Book—or even the Bible.

By January of this year, though, I'd begun to feel thoroughly guilty about my backslidings. At first I'd tried to fill the void by peripheral disciplines. As part of my New Year resolutions, I'd given up smoking, swearing, drinking, and imagining naked women. (My erotic imaginings hadn't been too convincing anyway, as, until my marriage, the month before, I'd never seen any naked women except in the pathology department of the medical school I'd attended, and they didn't count, being pickled.)

However, my spiritual needs, whatever they were, had not been entirely fooled by these appeasements, and on my way back to the front I had decided to go one step further and behave from then on with a sense of true Christian humility. I felt ashamed of the enjoyment I'd received from maddening my superiors and disorientating just about everyone else, with this great, blank face of mine and whining North American drawl. I determined once and for all to crush the bellicose hobgoblin in me that seemed to awaken the moment its host's comfortable insecurity was threatened by harmony of any sort.

Things didn't seem to be working out too well, though. The squadron, which had had its hopes raised by the change of command, seemed now to have sunk even deeper into the slough of despond. I was being manipulated by my adjutant, bullied by Wing, chortled at by my clerks, and ignored by my pilots.

If only Milestone were here, I thought, shivering as a shower of rain blew into the canvas enclosure and pattered on my bare kneecaps, to explain why it was that, whenever I tried to behave decently in this rotten army, I immediately began to fade away, like a great, blank-faced Tinker Bell.

It looked very much, I thought, as if I'd have to start backsliding again.

The wing colonel greeted me with something less than enthusiasm, though we had known each other for quite a while. He was my old C.O., looking just as fussy, plump, and bulging as when he had commanded the Camel squadron back in 1917.

"What are you doing here?" he hissed, as I joined him in the otherwise deserted wing mess, shortly after lunch. "I'm having enough trouble with the brigadier without you pestering me as well. Go away."

"Brigadier Soames is here? At Wing?"

"He's been harassing me all morning about one thing or another," Ashworth said in his thin, peevish tones. Lowering his voice, he glanced around in a hunted sort of way. "Incidentally, just what've you been doing to him?"

"Nothing," I said quickly. "I haven't done a thing."

"Well, he's beginning to develop that teeth-gritting look that senior officers often get when you're around. He's been asking all sorts of questions about you," Ashworth muttered, fumbling about in his lumpy pockets for one of his dozen or so pipes. "Dashed strange questions some of them are, too—like were you in the habit of making vicious, sneaking attacks on your superior officers, things like that. When I told him jokingly about the time you accidentally crashed your Camel on top of your former battalion commander, he looked very queer indeed."

"Gee, I wish you hadn't told him about that," I muttered.

"I only related it as a good story. But he seemed to find it extraordinarily significant, for some reason. Just what have you been up to, Bandy? You didn't strafe his staff car when he went to visit you, did you?"

"Certainly not. I don't know how you could suspect me of such a thing, Colonel."

"Well, he seems to be harboring some pretty profound suspicions about you. And that political speech of yours hasn't exactly prejudiced him in your favor, either."

"He knows about that, too?"

"Course he does, man. Who doesn't?"

He was referring to the speech I'd made the previous March at an inferior sort of English public school by the name of Fallow. Carried away by the enthusiasm of the boys, I'd gone much further than I'd intended in analysing the strategy of the British commander in chief, Sir Douglas Haig. By listening fairly carefully to my own words, I'd discovered that he had no strategy at all. He was merely seeing how many men he could kill off in as short a time as possible.

Unfortunately, the occasion had been unusually well attended by the national press, and the journalists, almost as deluded as to my real importance as I was, had reported the speech at length. There had been quite a fuss about it, and as a result I'd been flung out of the Air Ministry and posted to a band of suicidal cyclists.*

"All in all," Ashworth said, "you haven't exactly made a very good start in your command, have you."

"M'm."

"What do you want, anyway?"

I braced myself for what I knew would be a difficult interview. To put it off as long as possible, I asked, "By the way, does Brigadier Soames have Mickle with him?"

"Who?"

"Lieutenant Mickle. You know, Soames's personal secretary?"

"Oh, him. Yes. Why?"

"I'm looking forward to meeting him," I said.

I wanted to meet Mickle partly because of all the gossip about him. Apparently the brigadier hoped to be first on the post-war market with his memoirs, and learning that he had under his command a writer who had written a couple of biographies, Soames had hit on the idea of employing that man as his portable Hansard. So now Mickle spent much of his time sorting, editing, and typing the

* See Volume II of The Bandy Papers: *That's Me in the Middle.* Doubleday, 1973.

brigadier's biographical material, and taking notes of everything Soames wished to pass on to posterity.

Or nearly everything. Sometimes the brigadier would amend his own thoughts as if already seeing them in print. "Rephrase that when you have a moment, Mickle," he would say. And often he would have his immortal words struck out completely, to such an extent that his injunction, "Don't put that in, Mickle," was becoming quite a catch phrase in the Air Force.

"Is that all you came here for?" Ashworth snapped. "To enquire about Mickle?"

"Oh, no. I . . . I just wanted to ask him something, that's all," I said vaguely. "No, it's about all this low bombing and machine-gunning we've been engaged in since the March attack."

"Well? What about it?"

"It'll have to stop, sir, that's all," I said respectfully. "If you don't mind."

He seemed a trifle slow on the uptake that afternoon. It was several seconds before his face began to turn a sort of purplish color, as if some Chinese torturers had been at work on it, stripping off skin here and there.

"You what?"

"All this low work will have to stop, sir."

"You . . . you think it'll have to stop, do you?"

"Yes, please."

"*You* think it'll have to stop."

"Right away, Colonel, if that's all right."

"Who the devil," he asked, "do you think you are? You . . . you come in here—without an appointment or anything—"

"Well, you won't come to us, will you, sir? So I have to come to you, don't I?"

The colonel never visited our squadron if he could help it. Apparently he found the experience a bit numbing.

He did quite a bit of spluttering for a while. However, after he got his pipe lit, he calmed down long enough for

39

me to summarize the effects of our low bombing and compare the results with the casualties.

"You must admit it's a pretty poor balance sheet, Colonel," I said.

"The brigadier believes in keeping up a continuous pressure against the enemy," Ashworth snapped, glaring at his pipe. It had gone out again. "And that's all there is to it."

"Well, it's obvious we can't go on this way, Colonel. The pilots are drinking themselves insensible nearly every night, they're in such a state of nerves. Even I'm twitching a bit, and I've only been out three or four times. I mean, I'm quite willing to do low work when there's a big push on—"

"Are you indeed? How very good of you."

"When we're really helping the infantry. But what are we accomplishing now, apart from making life only slightly more miserable for the enemy, and ruining the squadron in the process? It's not good enough, Colonel."

"Don't you tell me what's not good enough," he said, but not very heatedly.

Thus encouraged, I went on tactfully, "I mean, don't think I'm accusing you of being callous about all the lives you're wasting, sir. I guess it's just that you brass hats don't understand the extent of the sacrifice you're demanding. I mean, I realize it's not *really* your fault that the whole atmosphere of the times seems to envelop you and your kind in, what shall we say—hierarchical insensitivity?"

The colonel seemed to have used up his day's ration of apoplexy. He merely walked over to the fireplace and leaned his forehead against a piece of marble and thudded his head against it two or three times, but not too hard. "Oh, God," he muttered. "It's starting all over again . . ."

"I mean, give the pilots a chance, Colonel. Even balloon-busting is better than being continually shot up from the ground."

"Oh, stop whining, Bandy," Ashworth moaned, still cooling his forehead against the marble. "I can't stand it when you whine. Anyway, I've already pointed all that out to the brigadier, without result."

"I'll speak to him, then."

"No, no, don't do that, Bandy," Ashworth said quickly, fumbling agitatedly for his Swan Vestas. He lowered his voice and glanced around in considerable perturbation. "As a matter of fact, isn't it about time you were leaving? Yes, that's a good idea; you go home, now, Bandy, or— or it'll be nearly dark by the time you get back." The colonel had driven into a mine crater one night whilst returning from a celebration at a Bristol Fighter squadron. He had been wary of nocturnal travel ever since, and assumed that everybody else now shared his distaste for night driving.

"Well, all I can say is, if we don't do something soon, we might as well disband the squadron and send the pilots to the Salvation Army," I said. "We really must have a decision, Colonel."

"What decision is that?" a voice said from the rear.

We both jumped as if a miner's drill had just broken through to the surface from directly below.

The brigadier was just coming into the mess, followed by a whimpering entourage.

"We were just discussing a few minor problems, sir," Ashworth said quickly. He turned to me and gave me a slight shove. "Right. Well, I won't keep you, Major," he said. "Off you go, then. Good-bye. Good-bye."

"What problems?" Soames asked. Then: "Oh, it's you," he said, looking at me with considerable dislike.

I regarded him without much affection too. I still rather resented the way I'd run over him with my motor car.

I waited alertly, half expecting him to start quivering all over, the way he'd done at Montonvillers.

Instead, he smiled.

Utterly relieved, I gave a respectful bob and smiled

back, thinking that maybe he wasn't such a difficult person after all.

Turning to his entourage, he said heartily, "You haven't yet had the pleasure of meeting my newest squadron commander, have you? Apart from you, Dennison, of course. You've encountered him, haven't you?"

"Yes, indeed, sir."

"This, gentlemen, is Mr. Bandy. The name is no doubt familiar to you all? No? Surely you've heard of the Air Ministry's spokesman and commentator, and the C-in-C's principal military adviser?"

As Ashworth found a match and sucked the flame agitatedly into the bowl of his pipe, the various red-tabbed officers stared rudely at me. There was only one lieutenant among them, a short, Napoleonic-looking bloke of about thirty. So that was Mickle, eh? He was holding a notebook.

"Yes, we have quite a celebrity in our midst," Soames was saying. "Our Major Bandy is famous throughout the British Isles, don't you know, for his political and military insight." He moved closer to the empty fireplace and stood with his back to it. "And his penetrating analysis. Or should I say *ba*nalysis?"

Everyone smiled appreciatively. Make a note of that, Mickle, I thought to myself.

"This is quite an honor," Soames said. "You must give *us* the benefit of your advice too, Bandy, on how to win the war without casualties. Can't let the civvies have your words of wisdom all to themselves, now, can we? Tell us what mistakes we're making. Pray set us right."

I looked down and drew a circle on the floor with the toe of my left boot.

"Don't be shy," Soames went on. "Speak up, man. Do tell us where we're going so frightfully wrong."

As he rose up and down, his heels crunched on a stray cinder.

"What, nothing to say? Why this extraordinary reticence

all of a sudden? Cat got your tongue, has it, Major?"

"Perhaps he's lying fallow at the moment, sir," a staff captain said.

"Ha-ha. Very good. Very good indeed, Captain."

The captain blushed and brushed his mustache with the back of his forefinger. In the background, Colonel Ashworth slowly disappeared in a cloud of smoke.

"Though personally," Soames went on, crushing another cinder with his heel, "I'd be inclined to place the emphasis on *lying* rather than on fallow. What?"

"Yes, sir."

Soames smirked across at Mickle to make sure he'd got that bit, then went on, "Strange, though, that in spite of our Mr. Bandy's extraordinary impact on national affairs, he should have sunk to the command of a mere squadron. One should have expected him to attain the rank of, at the very least, a general officer commanding. Imagine Bandy as our G.O.C., Dennison. Isn't that a thought to send *frissons* of pleasure down your back?"

"It's quite a thought, sir."

"It is, isn't it? But what's this? Still nothing to say, Bandy? Nothing to contribute to the general weal?"

He opened the small, quite prettily shaped lips below his straggly mustache to continue, but, on an afterthought, turned to his secretary and said, "Oh, make a note of that, Mickle. We might have a play on words, with that word *weal,* don't you think? Meaning 'well-being' and also in the sense of a bruise or welt. In the latter sense it's particulary applicable to our Mr. Bandy."

"Yes, that's very good, sir," Mickle said, making a note.

"Yes, I think it's a particularly appropriate literary flourish in this case." He turned to me again. "Well, Bandy? We're still waiting, you know, with bated breath, for some enlightening remarks. Speak up, man, don't be reticent."

One or two members of his entourage were beginning to shift about embarrassingly. Perhaps sensing this, the brigadier suddenly abandoned his light, bantering tone, and his voice turned brisk and businesslike.

"Yes, well, what was this problem you came to see Ashworth about?"

The colonel's anxious face appeared dimly through the smoke. "The major is concerned about the state of his squadron, sir," he said quickly.

"Is he indeed?"

"He feels the continuous low work is having a deleterious effect on morale, sir. And I . . . I must admit he does have a point, sir."

"M'yes," I said. "I just feel, sir, that—" I stopped, wondering why everybody had jumped; then recollected that this was the first time they'd heard my voice. "Uh . . . I just felt it would be good for the squadron if we could go onto offensive patrols for a while. Apart from any special jobs that might come up, of course."

"That's the way you feel, is it?"

"Yes, sir."

"And after your presumptuous attack on the military leadership at Fallow, you think I should be concerned about the way you feel, do you?" Soames said pleasantly.

"It's for the squadron as a whole, sir. It's not much to ask. We just need a little time to recover, that's all. The pilots—"

"Oh, la. It's your pilots you're concerned about now, is it?"

"Besides, the Dolphins are more in their element at high altitudes, General," I said, trying to curry favor by addressing him as if he were a real general.

"You're saying I don't know my business either. Is that it?"

"Oh, no, sir."

"Oh, no, sir," he mimicked. "Well, in my opinion, Major, your squadron doesn't seem to be in its element at *any* altitude. When they show some signs of having real offensive spirit—"

"But, sir, how can we build up any offensive spirit if we're having 50 per cent casualties—"

"Don't interrupt me! How dare you interrupt me when I'm addressing you! Who the hell do you think you are," he cried, in a passion, "strolling in here like Lord Muck, and telling me how to run my brigade! By God . . ."

After a spot of deep-breathing exercise, he strode toward the door. "I don't wish to discuss the matter any further," he said.

"Sir, it's urgent that—"

"I said I don't wish to discuss it! You'll bloody well do what you're told," he shouted.

He turned in the doorway, the skin white around his close-set eyes. "There was no morale problem before you arrived, Bandy! There was never any problem with Reeves-Goring in command. Just obey orders, that's all you have to worry about. *You will continue to bomb and machine-gun the enemy until further notice.* Is that understood?"

I looked at him. For some reason, this upset him even more. He clenched his hands, and the white area started to spread all around his mustache.

"Is that understood?" he screamed.

"Yes, sir," I said.

When I got back to the squadron, I found the usual large party of defaulters working on the flower bed in front of the house. I called the men together.

"Men," I said, clapping my hands together so sharply that one of them dropped a spadeful of manure onto his boots. "I have a hard day's work for you. Soon as you've done it, you're let off further punishment."

I told them what I wanted done. Affected by the reprieve from the dreaded flower bed, and by the sudden uproar from on high, they hastened off, whispering excitedly. I strode onward into the house. A group of pilots, led by Captain Derby, were just shuffling out of the office, muffled to the eyebrows in their heavy flying gear.

"Where are you off to?"

"To the trenches, Major. Where else?"

"What's the job?"

"Usual low work. Why?"

"I'd like to see you in the mess tent first, please. The patrol's off for an hour or so."

The pilots looked dumfounded. Malt, who was writing something at one of the trestle tables, looked up sharply.

"What d'you mean, the patrol's off?" he demanded. "Wing's ordered—"

I went up to Corporal Tomlinson. "Tomlinson, I have a job for you. Get it done today and you can go back to your fitting, or whatever it is you used to do. I want all this stuff taken out of the house and dumped in the barn."

"All what stuff, sir?"

"All this. Tables. Chair. Records. Files, paperwork— the lot. Everything *in* the house *out* of the house."

"Just what do you think you're doing?" Malt demanded.

"Leave my office carpet and the armchair," I said to Tomlinson, "but take everything else, including that partition, and all that rubbish on the walls."

"Just the stuff in these two offices, sir?"

"All the office stuff in the house. Every scrap of paper in the place."

"And just where do you think we're going to work?" Malt shouted.

"In the barn."

"The barn? But it's filthy in there!"

"I've organized a party of men to clean it out." I pointed to the two squadron office clerks. They were listening open-mouthed. "*You.*"

It was thrilling, the way they scrambled up, banging their thighs against the trestle tables.

"Good news for you men. I'm letting you off clerking for the rest of the day."

They began to grin.

"Instead, you're going to cart all this rubbish to the barn, under Corporal Tomlinson here. Then you can change into work clothes and collect forks and buckets and a wheelbarrow, and repair to the *fumier* outside the barn."

"The what, sir?"

"The French dunghill. I want it moved away from the barn. We can't have French dunghills sitting outside the new squadron office, now, can we? It might give people the wrong impression."

Malt elbowed his way over, his face red. "These are my clerks, not laborers."

"It'll be a nice change for them." I turned to Derby. "Derby, I want to see all the pilots in the mess tent in thirty minutes. Pass the word, will you?" Derby continued to gape. "Quick-quick, man, quick-quick."

The pilots stumbled out, looking as if a Minnie had burst nearby. Tomlinson asked hesitantly, "Did you say I could go back to my old job, sir?"

"As soon as you get all this stuff out of the house."

Tomlinson grinned all over his face. He took a deep breath. *"Right,"* he said. He turned to the gaping clerks and shouted, "Come on now, you two, what're you waiting for, the eight-fifteen to Cheetham Hill? Get this stuff out of here! Every bit of paper, every bloody typewriter and filing cabinet in the place. Come on, now, jump to it, you dozy lot!" He seized an armful of papers and files, and slapped them against the chest of one of the bewildered clerks. "Go on, man, what're you waiting for? Get on with it!"

A bunch of yellow Army forms slipped from the man's grasp. One of them curved gracefully through the air and glided to rest against Malt's foot.

"Just a minute," he shouted.

"Oh, and Malt. You can clear out those two rooms of yours upstairs, too. I shall need them. And you tell that pal of yours, Sergeant Bixby, I shall want his ground-floor room as well. I want him out of there in one hour."

"Gentlemen," I said, talking as I strode into the packed mess tent half an hour later, "we're making one or two small changes around here, as from now. As you've probably heard, the barn is where the new squadron office is to be."

Malt came into the tent, breathing heavily. In the distance we could hear the flower-bed corporal and his bodies already at work in the barn, skylarking, shouting, and sloshing water about.

"You want the house to yourself, is that it?" Carson asked. "Too distracting for you, Major, with all those pens scratching away?"

"I'm handing the house over to you. From today the house is the officers' mess."

There was an astonished murmur. Several of the pilots glanced covertly at Malt. The adjutant was gripping the tent flap as if preparing to tear it to shreds. "We'll see about that," he shouted. "I'm calling Brigade right this minute."

"Okay. Your cousin, the brigadier, was at Wing a couple of hours ago. You'll probably be able to reach him there."

Carson, ever alert for confirmation that the war was a plot instigated by international financiers, profiteers, and old school chums, said sharply, "Cousin?"

"I'm telephoning right this minute," Malt said, rooted to the ground.

"The brigadier is his cousin? Where'd you get that rubbish?" Carson asked.

Malt glared at me as if I'd betrayed his trust, as I suppose I had.

"He told *us* he was Reeves-Goring's cousin, not the brigadier's," Carson said.

Malt continued to cling onto the tent flap. I looked at him curiously for a moment, then turned back to the pilots.

"Well, anyway . . . Next, I understand you've had to get official permission every time you've felt like joyriding, visiting other squadrons, or even practicing at the ground targets. That's a load of excreta, gentlemen. From now on, you can take your machines up any time you like, without asking permission from anyone. That particularly applies to the new men."

When I next glanced at the tent entrance, Malt had disappeared. I took a deep breath, and lowered my voice. "Now: I've had a word with the brigadier about all this trench-strafing."

There was a tense silence.

"He said we'll have to continue with it."

The pilots looked as if it were no more than they'd expected. Derby sighed, Kiddell shrugged.

I put my hands in the pockets of my old raincoat and flapped the coattails cheerfully.

"Well, we can't disobey orders, of course," I said. "That's utterly unthinkable."

"Naturally," Carson sneered.

"However"—I flapped my coat again, "we're having no more of this stooging up and down over hosts of machine guns, looking for likely targets and a ticket to eternity. From now on, you get rid of your bombs quickly, and from a reasonable height."

They all looked at each other. "What's a reasonable height?" Kiddell asked.

"Not less than two thousand feet."

There was a brief barrage of exploding breath.

"But we couldn't even hit a Zeppelin shed from two thousand."

"Nevertheless, that's the minimum bombing height until further notice.

"As for machine-gunning," I continued, over the hubbub, "from today we're going to fire at the trenches only to warm up the guns—and you can do *that* from two thousand feet, too. After that, we go on normal patrols.

"So there you are," I said. "From this moment, I'll be very annoyed indeed with any pilot who gets himself killed by ground fire.

"Finally, no new pilot will cross the lines until he's spent a full month in formation flying, firing at the ground targets, bombing practice, familiarizing himself with the countryside, and hedge-hopping."

"That's crazy," Kiddell said. "It'll only leave seven or eight pilots for O-pips."

"Then the war will have to be fought by those seven or eight, that's all."

There was quite an uproar as I left the tent. As I emerged, Malt hurried up.

"I'm the recording officer of this squadron," he said, his voice trembling. "I won't be treated this way."

A couple of clerks staggered past. They were loaded with boxes, and looked very discontented indeed.

When I didn't say anything, Malt went on shakily, "I'm not working in that filthy barn, and that's all there is to it."

"How about your toilet, then? Maybe you could work in there."

"I don't think that's the least funny, Major."

"Oh, and don't forget—I need those two rooms of yours."

"You were serious about that?"

"I was thinking of putting my flight commanders in there, so I'll be obliged if you'd move out by six tonight, Captain."

"But those are *my* rooms! I've always had them!"

"Not any more."

He clutched at himself. "I won't," he said. "I'm not. I'm not moving out." I looked at him. "Well, I'm not."

Actually I'd never intended throwing him out of his rooms. I'd made that threat for bargaining purposes.

"Oh, all right," I said, as if he had overwhelmed me with telling arguments. "You can stay."

Malt panted with relief.

"But in return," I said, "for not insisting, I'll expect several concessions from you, Malt, beginning with the parades."

"What about them?"

"From today, there'll be a Monday morning camp inspection, and that's all. No more parades."

"What? That's—that's completely out of the question. I'm not having this squadron ruined just . . . just because you don't understand how we do things here!"

"M'm. Anyway, after today, no more of this parading, please. You'll announce it yourself, will you? Or shall I do it? Yes, maybe I ought to tell the men."

"I'm in charge of that!"

"Good. I'll leave it to you, then."

As Malt stood there, looking as if his whole world was collapsing around him, Sergeant Bixby hurried up, and tugged at Malt's sleeve.

"Hey," he said. "What's going on? They're throwing all me stuff out of me room. What's the big idea?"

Malt whirled and bellowed at the top of his lungs, " 'ere, who d'you think you're talking to? Who d'you think you are, you, you *pastrycook!*"

Bixby recoiled.

"I'll give you just two minutes to move out!"

"But where'll I go?"

"You can go to hell for all I care!" Malt shouted, and stalked off.

"Back under canvas, Bixby, old boy," I said. "Don't worry, you'll soon get used to the earwigs.

"Unless, of course," I went on, clasping my hands behind my back and gazing at the sky, "you'd prefer a transfer? The reason I ask is, we've had a request for a volunteer for a particularly rewarding line of work. With your qualifications, Sarge, I think you'd be the perfect man for the job."

"What job is it?"

"It's a roving burial party. Good pay, plenty of exercise, free transport, excellent opportunities for travel and seeing new faces, and I think I could even swing a promotion for you. How does that sound?"

He didn't seem to like the sound of it at all.

"Well, you think about it, okay?

"And," I added, "I'll think about it too, every time I sit down to a meal."

I nudged him jovially. "Get it, Bixby old bean?"

Milestone

Some days later, Wing telephoned. I took the call in the hayloft, feeling quite proud at the way I'd completely overcome my well-known fear of the telephone.

"Hello, hello," I said, gripping the receiver as if it were a struggling python.

There was a tinny ejaculation at the other end, then a faint voice said, "Bandy?"

"Yes? Yes?"

"Bandy," Ashworth said distantly, "why do you always have to bellow like that into the phone? You don't have to scream, man, as if you were calling down to the engine room in the middle of a tornado. You're supposed to let the telephone do the work."

"Oh?"

"It's not a long, hollow tube, Bandy. It works by . . . by electricity or something."

"Yes, sir. Anyway, whajawant?"

"I'm not all sure, now, my head's ringing . . . Oh, yes. Have you got your map handy?"

He sounded decidedly unfriendly. I could understand that. For several days we had suffered no casualties, but on the other hand we hadn't accomplished much either. I was beginning to wonder if the brigadier wasn't right after all, that the squadron really was fit only for trench sorties and whitewashing coal.

"Ready? There's a call in from our part of the line. They're having trouble with an enemy observation balloon." He gave me the map references. "Get onto it right away, will you?"

I'd already heard about that kite balloon from the SE people across the way. They'd been trying to shoot it down for three days now, and had lost a man on it the day before.

"Is it up now?"

"Course it's up now. Why do you think I'm calling?" Ashworth snapped. "So get a move on." And, presumably to get his own back, he slammed down the phone as hard as he could.

Orville France was sauntering from the mess. "Just the man I was looking for," I said. "How'd you like to tackle a balloon with me?"

"Sure. When?"

"Right now. I should warn you, it's well protected."

"Aren't they all?"

"This one more than usual, I've heard. It must be doing important work."

"That's all right, Major. I've always wanted to get a balloon. Hate those goddam things, sitting up there like they owned all the real estate in sight."

"All right. Grab your sidcot and meet me down at the hangars."

As we waited for the Vickers to be loaded with Buckingham incendiary, I explained what we'd try to do. Orville began to look quite interested.

Much of Orville's frustration stemmed from the fact that though he had shot a Pfalz to pieces on his third patrol, he had had little opportunity since to indulge his propensity for cheerful violence.

That was one reason I was taking him on this trip. Like so many American volunteers in the British service, France's aggressiveness seemed to be in direct ratio to his prospects, which were good indeed. If he survived, he would one day take over the family firm, which manufactured a product called *Snibbo*. I wasn't sure what that was, but, according to Orville, half the population of the United States was beginning to consume it in prodigious quantities.

"So you'll take it from underneath," I concluded, "and I'll come in high, and feint."

"Sure hope I don't faint as well."

"You'll have to fly right down on the floor, Orville. It's a new tactic, but I think it'll work."

"If it doesn't, you can rely on me to send a nice, sympathetic letter to your wife, Major," he drawled. "Or maybe I'll call in person. I hear she's quite a frail."

"One more thing, Lieutenant France," I said formally. His smooth, boyish face turned serious. "Yes, Major?"

"What the heck," I asked, "is Snibbo?"

Orville looked at me wide-eyed. "You can't mean it," he faltered incredulously. "You're from that side of the Atlantic yourself, and you've never heard of Snibbo?"

"Well, I . . . I led a rather sheltered life . . ."

"For gosh sakes, Major," he said, walking toward his plane, "you sure must."

He was still shaking his head in stunned disbelief as he pumped up pressure and waited for the corporal-mechanic to swing the prop.

The first time I clambered into Mr. Sopwith's latest product, I had been appalled. In contrast to the simple, uncluttered Camel, the cockpit of the 5F1 Dolphin was jammed with apparatus. The war's first multigun fighter, the Sopwith Dolphin had two Lewis guns mounted overhead, pointing forward and upward, and two synchronized Vickers guns partially buried in the cowling. The butts of all four guns encroached alarmingly on the pilot's *Lebensraum*.

Below these jutting butts was an ironmonger's nightmare of wires, cables, levers, wheels, dials, gauges, indicators, clocks, and switches. And if there weren't enough projections, bars, and loading handles already, to smash your face against, the cockpit was surrounded by raised steel tubing to which the great top wings clung for dear life. In the Camel you could be up, up, and away in two or three minutes. It took about five minutes to get *into* the Dolphin.

I think it was the airframe designer that had really finished it off in the esteem of the pilots. The wings had a decided backward stagger—the lower wing sticking farther forward than the top wing. If there was one thing pilots mistrusted it was an unconventional design, and with that bulbous, pugnacious nose and the lower wing stuck forward, and the cockpit in the middle of the top wing, it was most certainly unconventional for a scout. It looked damned dangerous even when it was on the ground.

The first time I brought the machine bouncing in for a shamefully hamfisted landing, I complained to Derby, "The prop doesn't even revolve the right way. My feet didn't know which way to turn."

The Dolphin was everything the pilots said it was. It stalled too readily, the radiators were inefficient, the magnetos were faulty, the view downward was disastrous, the geared Hispano-Suiza engine was totally unreliable, and the plane was a killer when overturned. After a dozen flights, and after I'd removed the port Lewis gun—like the rest of the pilots, I retained the other for shooting two-seaters up the backside—I thought it the most delightful plane I'd ever flown.

The kite balloon was visible for miles, flaunting itself over the mauled landscape just west of Bray. The solitary Dolphin, with me sticking out of the top wing, sped past, well to one side, at about six thousand feet, as if it had not the slightest interest in the gasbag.

The balloon didn't seem too interested in the plane, either—feeling a little overconfident, perhaps, after foiling so many attempts on its life during the past few days.

Black Archie bursts smudged the air round the plane. However, an R.E. 8 a mile or two farther east seemed to be getting most of it.

Pretty soon, Archie lost interest entirely in the Dolphin. That was pleasant—until I remembered that this some-times indicated the presence of an enemy scout in the neighborhood. I looked around sharply, but saw nothing but the Harry Tate, and a few Camels frisking about over Fricourt.

I circled some distance behind the balloon, not too happy about the weather. It was perfect—for the balloon observer. He could see for miles. Orville would have to nip in very smartly, if he was to get to the balloon before they hauled it down.

Below, the sun ferried itself across the Somme River, paused, then jumped into a waterlogged shellhole. I raised my goggles and peered over the side, wondering if I should have taken the low road myself. If the plan worked, the man coming in from below would be the one to get the balloon, if anyone did; but he would stir up a good many machine-gun nests in the process. On the other hand, the man above would attract most of the heavy Archie, and the Archie that surrounded a balloon was a particularly unpleasant form, called flaming onions.

On the other hand, flying close to the ground wasn't as dangerous as flying at one thousand feet, where I'd be, much of the time. On the other hand—

Running out of hands, I squinted to the west, wiping an eye that was beginning to water in the chill slip-stream, and almost immediately caught sight of Orville's plane. It was just darting over the front-line trenches. I couldn't see his shadow. He must be darned low. He was travelling full out.

I waited until he was half-way across, then put the stick onto my right knee and winged over toward the balloon, resisting the impulse to speed up. I didn't want to make the attack seem too determined. I wanted them to delay hauling in the balloon. I braced myself for the flaming onions.

These came up in groups of eight, floating up slowly at first, then passing with an unnerving rush. In a few seconds, there were hundreds of them, their bile-green tails twisting. I turned aside before the balloon was in range.

The KB seemed to be hesitating, as if the ground crew couldn't decide whether I was serious or not.

As I turned away cravenly, the ground machine guns opened up. Several holes appeared in my port wing. I flung the bus about brutally, at the same time twisting my neck to watch the receding balloon. My ears popped with the changing pressure.

Orville was just skimming over a slight rise in the ground less than a mile from the balloon. He was flying so low his wheels seemed to be riffling the stagnant waters of the battlefield.

They didn't see him until it was too late. Just before he threatened to slice himself into No. 5 best bacon on the cable, he zoomed. I didn't see his Vickers firing. But, then, he wasn't using tracer.

He'd plainly taken the defences by surprise. They'd been too busy watching me. He shot up the cable, and continued up to five hundred feet, flicking the right way up as he completed his half loop. Hardly a shot was fired at him.

For some reason, nobody was shooting at me, either, though I was still dawdling along at only one thousand revs.

For a moment, nothing happened. I was just turning back, thinking that Orville had missed or that his guns had jammed, when an orange flame flickered from the gasbag.

The observer had his leg over the side of the basket. Not more than a second later, the balloon turned into a great stain of black and orange. The observer jumped. As he dropped, the line snatched open his parachute.

I banked vertically, only just missing him as he floated

safely the few hundred feet to the ground. As I straighten-ed again, more holes appeared in my top plane.

The top plane? How on earth were they managing that? I hadn't been flying upside down, had I?

I gawked around. There was a biplane only twenty feet behind.

It was such a shock, my hand jerked spasmodically on the stick. The Dolphin heeled over just as the other plane fired again.

No wonder my ears had been popping. He must have been taking pot shots for the past two minutes. And I hadn't even known he was there.

I supposed I'd saved myself accidentally with all that twisting about around the balloon, and by the fact that he was such a terrible shot. All the same, even the rawest pilot could hardly have made so many mistakes in such rapid succession: watching somebody else at work instead of keeping an eye on my tail, flying slowly over Hunland, not looking where I was going, failing to take in the sig-nificance of those holes in the wing.

The biplane, a sky-blue Albatros, turned and fired again from the side. Instinctively—it was as well my instinct was working, my brain certainly wasn't—I turned toward him and zoomed as he passed overhead, flipped right side up, all this in a couple of seconds, and dived after him.

I caught up with him twenty feet above the ground. Splintered trees rushed by, upturned faces blurred past. The Albatros had given itself no room to maneuver. It remained within easy range, forty yards. I started to press the levers.

Then I remembered I was carrying Buckingham.

He continued to jiggle about in the ring sight, the pilot looking back over his shoulder. He had his mouth covered with a scarf. I could see the hole of his open mouth through the rippling silk.

I couldn't bring myself to use incendiary bullets on him and set him on fire. Unlike the balloon observer, he couldn't escape from a fire. Besides, that kind of bullet caused awful wounds. Besides, if you came down behind enemy lines and they found incendiaries, they were likely to put you in front of a firing squad.

So I just stayed on his tail, following him easily as he dodged about. The Dolphin was a good deal faster than the Albatros and far more maneuverable.

When he realized he was only a mile or two from our lines, he risked a desperately steep bank to the right, his wingtip almost dragging through a field of barbed wire. I kept going, watching as he straightened out and sped away, looking back over his shoulder. I waved.

Milestone arrived on Tuesday, May 14, irritated and exhausted after three days at No. 1 A.S.D., Marquise.

"They had me on the range practically the whole time I was there," he snarled. "What the hell use do they think ground machine-gun practice is, for a scout pilot? Bloody fools."

However, after dinner and a few whiskies, he recovered his spirits and we settled down to a delightful reunion.

"I must be mad, volunteering for the front again," he said, sprawling in the best armchair. "Especially as the first ghastly sight I see is you, looking like God's gift to the Temperance Movement."

"Just to show how wrong you can be, I'll have a beer."

"Good Lord."

"Waiter? A ginger beer, please. A *double*."

Milestone grinned and looked around. "Food's not up to much, is it," he said. "Pretty impressive mess, though."

A few days before, I'd persuaded the pilots, not without difficulty, as they had gotten out of the habit of exercising their initiative, to raid an R.E. supply depot on the other side of Amiens. This was only after I'd tried in vain to requisition supplies through the proper channels. We had returned with two lorry-loads of loot, including some hardwood that was supposed to have gone to some general's château. As a result, the squadron carpenters had been able to put in a splendid, twelve-foot bar, complete with shelves for the bottles and glasses, and a foot rail.

What with that, the former office armchair and carpet, and part of one wall decorated with the propeller and black cross cut from a two-seater that Blackbourne had forced down behind our lines a couple of days previous, the place was beginning to look quite homey.

"A piano, that's what we need naixt," McKindle said. "The brigadier has a piano, so I don't see why we should-ny have wan."

"God, no," Milestone said quickly, "or Bandy will play it."

"He said he was a dab hand at the ivories."

"Dab's the right word. He plays like a duck."

"Come, you exaggerate," I quacked. "Anyway, you're just envious because your only talent is for patting your head and rubbing your stomach at the same time."

"It's more than you can do."

"I can wiggle my ears."

"So can a horse."

The other pilots looked curiously at the fresh-faced lieutenant with the lazy blue eyes and cynical, down-turned mouth. Milestone was one of the four survivors or so of our first squadron. This was only partly a matter of luck, for the first sentiment I'd heard him express was the determination not to give his all, or even a small part, for King and Country, if he could possibly avoid it.

Nevertheless, he was a good deal more effective than many a pilot who had gone out full of patriotic fervor. He was certainly on the credit side, with six or seven victories, partly made up of halves and quarters, where he had shared kills with other pilots. As a matter of fact, I intended making him a flight commander as soon as a vacancy occurred.

"I saw your wife just before I left," he said. "Knowing how mad you are about chocolate, she managed to scrounge half a dozen bars for you. I have them in my bag somewhere, if I haven't eaten them."

"How is Katherine? Utterly desolated, I hope? Pining and wasting away in my absence?"

"Never seen her look so happy. Doesn't miss you a bit."

"Well, I got three letters yesterday saying she does, so there."

"Then you'll know her family's moving back to town in August? If they can get possession of their Kensington house from the Rousseau Society."

"I thought it was the Friends of Borneo who were occupying it at the moment?"

"No, Rousseau. Back to nature, and all that. Man is born good but has moral pollution thrust upon him. Personally I've never liked old Jean-Jacques, after what he did to his kids. He said because they were illegitimate they would be legally underprivileged if he kept them; so he put them in a foundlings home."

"Katherine did mention that her father had looked over the London house and had come home looking a bit depressed."

"No wonder. I went along with him, actually. They've made a frightful mess of the place. Illiterate slogans on the walls, dog dirt, torn wallpaper, broken glass, and copies of *Discours sur l'inégalité des conditions* scattered everywhere."

It was grand to be yarning again with Dick. Quite apart from the fact that we'd come through some of the worst fighting of 1917 together, he had been one of the few people to support me steadfastly after the Fallow ordeal.

I was about to tell him confidentially that he would have only a short period as Tail-end Charlie before he got his flight, when one of those queer silences fell over the mess—the kind of mysterious hiatus between surges of talk that some foolishly superstitious people say occurs only at twenty minutes past the hour. I looked at my watch and saw I was right: it was exactly 9.20.

It was just like Carson to drip his venom into that wound of time. From the depths of the silence, he said:

"I feel like killing somebody."

Milestone twisted around in his armchair and stared, open-mouthed. Carson had been drinking about the same as usual, heavily. As usual, he wasn't showing it, except in a kind of vicious elation that flushed the pallor of his gun-powdered face.

After a moment, Charles ffoliot said in that bored way of his, "You don't feel you've slaughtered enough people, darling, during all those low-level attacks of yours?"

"I suppose I've killed quite a few from the air," Carson said. "But that's not the same thing. I want to kill somebody up close, with personal feelings involved.

"I wonder," he mused, "if I'd feel guilt and anguish, or just more of the same: indifference?"

"They could use you in Russia," Blackbourne grunted.

Carson's eyes sparkled like ground glass. "Yes, it must be a very rewarding experience, being in Russia just now," he said. "Killing off all the officer-class, the financiers, the diplomats, and the middle-class parasites." He looked spitefully at Charles ffoliot. "And ambassadors.

"Still," he went on, "I expect we'll have the chance when the war is lost, to establish a socialist paradise. I wonder who I should go after first? Lord Derby, perhaps."

There was an uncomfortable silence, until Monty Murgatroyd said, "How about the Bwigadier, Carson? Nobody would miss him."

Milestone and I were still yarning away at midnight. As we strolled toward the Nissen huts, artillery fire flickered eerily through the trees, and once the ground trembled as something big went off at the front.

"What flight am I in, by the way?" Milestone asked.

"What flight do you want to be in, Dick?"

"I don't think I want to be under Kiddell. From the way he talks, he sounds as if he takes too many risks."

"M'yes."

"And that deputy of his, Carson. God. What kind of a war has he had?"

"He earned his M.M. charging a machine-gun nest single-handed."

"Just as I thought. He's mad. And he only got the Military Medal for that?"

"Well, you know how they are. An officer would probably have got the V.C., but a lowly private, as Carson was at the time . . . Besides, there are rumors that it was he who'd shot the C.S.M."

"He shot his own sergeant-major?"

"Yes. After the sergeant-major had charged him for failing to return the rum ration that had been issued to the platoon just before it was wiped out."

"Do you think it's true? About shooting the man?"

"Carson says it is."

Milestone stopped dead and stared at me. "He admitted it?"

"Oh, yes."

"Christ. Then I definitely don't want to be in A Flight. Where does he come from, a loony bin?"

"Worse. Eton."

"Garn." Milestone had been at Eton in the dim days before the war.

"No, actually he claims to be from the slums of Northern Ireland. He enjoys regaling the Honorable Charles ffoliot with his gay Belfast experiences, involving murder, rape, incest, and overeating."

"Sounds worse than Ottawa," Dick said.

"Anyway, don't worry about Carson. He's going to Number One General at Boulogne tomorrow, for surgery on his face. Apparently he's been waiting for two years to have his lips tidied up."

"They ought to tidy up his mind, as well."

Milestone leaned against a tree and lit a cigarette.

"And listen," he said, "what's wrong with that adjutant of yours?"

"Malt? Oh, he's just a bit huffy because he has to do all my work while I'm out having a good time over the lines."

"Why is he so privileged?" Dick asked, picking a shred of tobacco off his tongue.

"Privileged?"

"That stately pleasure dome of his. His personal bog."

"He was related to the former C.O.; I guess that had something to do with it."

"You know," Dick said, "that lavatory of his rouses my very worst egalitarian instincts."

"Same here. I've been having all kinds of mean thoughts about it."

"Why should he have a regal edifice like that, when the rest of us are having our bums frozen in the open?"

"Right." We turned our heads to watch a flare that was drifting down about a mile away. The air turned an oily green. I saw that Dick was grinning.

"I say," he said. "Do you think we should do something about it?"

"Machine-gun it?"

"Set fire to it?"

"Bomb it?"

"Put it out of bounds to all adjutants?"

"Hide it?"

"Remove all the bolts so when he pulls the chain the sides fall down?"

"Drag it away and leave it outside Brigade?"

We started to snigger and chortle childishly.

"I've got it," Dick exclaimed. "Haul it up into the trees with a block and tackle—"

"Then give him cascara—"

"And a very long rope ladder."

We fell about among the trees, holding onto each other.

"Why don't you shut up out there," a voice hollered from the nearest Nissen hut. "We're trying to sleep."

After a moment, Dick whispered, "Course it wouldn't be much fun for anyone walking underneath, at the wrong moment."

"No . . ."

Bombers droned overhead. There was a series of hazy flashes, followed by a loud bumping from the direction of Bertangles. The enemy had been bombing the airdromes over there for the past three nights, but for some reason they'd left us alone. Perhaps they didn't think we were worth it.

"Gosh, it's good to have you here, Dick."

We reached the hut that Dick was to share with Derby, McKindle, and a new Canadian pilot by the name of Smith. The last-named was sound asleep when Milestone tiptoed into the hut.

He shook the pilot. "Hurry up, Smith," he said urgently, "or you'll be late for the dawn patrol."

Smith, a tall, gangly fellow with a placatory sort of face, got hurriedly out of bed, his eyes gummed with sleep, and started to hop around with his slacks over his ankles.

A Decidedly Hunnish Bus

"Switch off, petrol on."
"Contact."
"Contact."

The massive 220-h.p. engine started on the third swing and bellowed furiously, puffing out clouds of oily smoke.

I adjusted the throttle compensator, yanked on the CC gear handle, then, after checking the switches and instruments, clutched the circular grip protectively to my stomach to keep the tail down, and ran up the engine.

We were going out on a high patrol that afternoon—officially. The Dolphin had at least been restored to its proper position as a high-altitude scout.

After distrustfully testing the B.T.H. magnetos, I twirled the tailplane incidence wheel, then looked enquiringly along the line of aircraft. Three pale faces gazed back over the tops of the wings: Derby, McKindle, and Milestone. I raised my arm, then gestured forward stiffly, the way I'd seen the U.S. Calvary do it in a marvellous Wild West moving picture.

The mechanics, who had been waiting patiently during the long running-up, whipped away the chocks and got out of the way fast as the four machines bellowed, pawed the ground, then began to pound across the grass to the far end of the field, swinging their heavy noses from side to side and flicking their tails.

I swung the Dolphin into position, checked the instruments once more, then pushed forward the throttle. The brutish-looking bus surged forward. The tail came up immediately, rudder flicking. There was quite a lot of vibration at first; then, as the plane gathered speed, it calmed down. The controls tautened. The wheel bounced, then the ground fell away. The bulbous nose lifted and rose steeply over the Nissens and the trees at the east side of the field.

Up to two thousand feet in what seemed like seconds, the plane no longer a bull but a fairy, darting and flashing in the late afternoon sun. I circled. The last Dolphin was just taking off, its fuzzy shadow drifting obliquely over the grass. I couldn't see the other two aircraft anywhere. The sky was empty.

Then suddenly they were behind me, wobbling into position on either side, and about twenty yards back.

A couple of minutes later, the fourth machine joined up—Milestone—and we resumed the climb. And what a climb. Exhilarating. The horizon was only just above the jutting edge of the lower wing, yet the air-speed dial showed nearly 100 m.p.h. Ten thousand feet in eleven minutes.

At fifteen thousand we set out toward the lines, still climbing.

It grew fiercely cold. I was glad of the magnificent fleece-lined leather coat Katherine had given me the day I left Burma Park. With no rotary engine to spray it with castor oil, it should last for months, assuming I did. I was also wearing her mother's old fox fur. Mrs. Lewis hadn't been the least surprised when I'd asked for it. Milestone, though, had laughed himself silly when he first saw it clinging to my throat, with the peeling snout tucked into the collar and the two brown eyes peering glassily over the top.

I didn't care. It was splendidly warm and comfortable. Monty Murgatroyd wore a girl's silk stocking round his neck and mouth, but it couldn't have been half as warm as my old fox fur.

Nine minutes to the front line, still climbing. The fighting in the Somme had died down by then, and there was little of interest going on so far below, apart from occasional puffs of yellowish-grey smoke among the trenches that fissured the landscape from horizon to horizon.

There was plenty of activity aloft, however. Swarms of British machines were in the air that afternoon. There were also quite a few Huns, dotting the empyrean as high as eighteen thousand feet. But, for the nonce, they seemed content to keep their distance.

We had a peaceful twenty minutes of wandering back and forth over the lines before Archie grew annoyed and started to paint the scene with black smudges. Milestone, at the rear, seemed to have lost his instinct for knowing when to take evasive action. As a result, the German gunners began concentrating on him, hoping, no doubt, that his evasive tactics would send him crashing into one of the other aircraft.

The more he pranced, the more hotly they pursued him with their bursts, and soon he was positively drenched in Archie, which was surprisingly accurate, considering that we were now at nearly twenty thousand. Archie must have been practicing lately against Bristol Fighters and other high-flying merchants.

I made a rude gesture at Dick—just as an Archie bellowed nearby. That wiped the snigger off my lips, all right. It had not only been horribly close, it had exploded directly overhead. I couldn't understand how it had got there without passing through me first. I felt myself, then looked over the plane to see if there were any large holes anywhere. But there weren't even any punctures from the shrapnel. Peculiar, that.

Feeling invulnerable again, I beamed around, overjoyed at the view the Dolphin afforded. Apart from a small area of sky obscured by the drum of the stripped-down Lewis, the view above and on all sides was unobstructed.

I sang. What a magnificent plane it was, and what a splendid life.

Those clever Sopwith designers had concentrated most of the weight between the wings, making the controls so sensitive that the slightest twitch of the hand grip had the plane flitting all over the sky, just like its brother, the Camel.

A few minutes later, though, after its first burst of aerial elation, the Hispano-Suiza developed an intermittent vibration, and the instruments refused to hint at the cause. So I was careful not to go too far over.

However, after a while the engine seemed to settle down all right, and we turned east again, to stalk a flight of Albatroses. We'd been wallowing through the rarefied air trying to use our height advantage against them now for twenty minutes, but without being able to get into the right position. They were after a pair of Harry Tates that were busy exposing plates over the German back areas. The R.E.8s were escorted by a whole squadron of Camels. Every time the Camels tried to climb after them, the Albatroses turned away. But they kept coming back.

I noticed that whenever the Camels snapped at them, the Albatroses always turned north. So we positioned ourselves some distance to the left, keeping the clouds between us and the Huns, and also between us and the ground, so that Archie wouldn't alert the six Albatroses to our presence.

It took time, but finally the Huns came over, and drifted about below us. I pushed the loading handles of the Vickers to the top, then fired a short burst, to warm the guns. A faint stutter from each side indicated that the others were doing likewise.

I adjusted the radiator louvers, feeling shivery with excitement, and hung over the side, watching until the e.a. were directly below. They were so preoccupied with the Harry Tates, they obviously hadn't seen us at all. I waggled the wings and dived, and dropped onto the Albatroses just as they were turning back again.

They split up hurriedly, but they were too late. One of them grew rapidly larger in the Aldis. I pressed the levers. The Vickers chattered. The Albatros reared up, then flopped over and fell away in a series of graceful, swooping glides. Another started across the sights. I fired again quickly, in short bursts, holding him on rudder, and saw the tracer wisping along his fuselage. Then I had to pull up sharply to avoid colliding with a Dolphin.

A quick glance around to make sure the other Dolphins were safe, then looked over the side. I couldn't see the first machine I'd fired at, but the second was going down smoking. It hurtled straight through the Camels, narrowly missing one of them. The Camels bobbed about excitedly.

Another trail of black smoke stained the sky. At the end of it, a flaming Albatros. And I could see another Hun spinning, obviously out of control. The remaining Albatroses had disappeared.

A moment later, Derby, McKindle, and Milestone joined up again. All four of us hung over the side, watching the planes as they fell. It looked as if we'd destroyed half the enemy flight. The fight had lasted no longer than twenty seconds.

In fact, we learned later that four of them had been seen to crash. Derby and McKindle had accounted for one each. That was what height advantage could do for you.

A few minutes later, the R.E.8s turned for home. As we still had half an hour to go, we continued the patrol. Feeling peckish as well as exhilarated, I fumbled out one of Katherine's chocolate bars and took a bite; which was a mistake, for I almost choked on the stinging rush of saliva. For about half a minute, I could scarcely breathe. It was difficult getting enough air as it was. We were back at 19,500 feet.

As the sun swelled tumorously and drooped onto the horizon, we turned for home, thinking we'd finished work for the day. But when we were about half-way to the lines, a dot appeared ahead. It grew rapidly larger, and turned into a wide-winged observation machine.

We started to climb still higher. The two-seater kept straight on, probably not expecting us to reach its exalted height in time. It didn't know Dolphins, though. We were level with it while it was still half a mile away.

The two-seater—recognizable now as an L.V.G.—kept on, the pilot presumably trusting to our combined speed of 200 m.p.h. to get him past before we had a chance to do any damage. Once through us, a steep dive would probably carry him well out of range.

I preferred to let the other pilots do the work whenever possible, while I kept an eye on things aloft; but in this case the Hun was dead in line with my plane, so I hunched forward to peer through the Aldis. He was approaching rapidly, still climbing. There was time only for a quick burst with the stick back. Then he was past, swishing by about fifty feet overhead. I tried an Immelmann turn. The Dolphin mushed and fell sideways. The L.V.G. flashed into view, disappeared, then jerked into view again. It had gotten away.

No, it was smoking. There was a burst of flame. The L.V.G. continued in a shallow glide, flames licking around the engine.

I didn't see any more. My own engine quit. Without warning, it suddenly vibrated, squealed, then stopped dead.

I banked sharply westward again, startled by the sudden hush.

I was not unduly alarmed, however. There was plenty of air left.

How far to the lines? About four miles. Nothing to worry about. I knew the Dolphin's capabilities by then.

On a 100-m.p.h. glide it sank less than three thousand feet per mile.

The other three planes were now flying alongside. Three sets of goggles turned interestedly toward the stationary propeller. I adjusted the dive to keep at an exact 100. Without power, the Dolphin felt like an entirely different aircraft, heavy and sullen.

Archie hadn't yet noticed I was in trouble, so I edged the stick back a fraction, looking over the instruments. No oil pressure. Plenty of fuel left. Fat lot of good that was. And it was a bit irritating, the way the Dolphin's *élan* had seeped away. The controls were sluggish, the nose heavy as lead.

Ten thousand feet. The sun was just disappearing below the horizon, leaving a great band of hazy pink sky. The enemy support trenches were drifting underneath.

Archie grew more enthusiastic when he saw one of the planes was in trouble. The other scouts spread out and started twisting about, diving under some of the bursts and banking around others. A stray pair of Camels came over for a look, then darted away again, so as not to share in all the clouds of hate. Very unselfish of them. Just for fun, I rolled.

A Dolphin edged over. Derby raised his goggles to peer at me, probably thinking that all that rarefied air had affected my brain; so, just for the heck of it, I rolled again, keeping the heavy nose well down, as I'd nearly stalled the first time.

The trenches zigzagged underneath. After a scatter of parting shots, Archie fell silent. Below, a stand of splintered trees hatched the earth with long shadows. The air grew pleasantly warm again, and hissed soothingly through the bracing wires.

After a while, the Doullens road appeared. That looked like Talmas on the left. Too far north. I banked gently away, waving to the others to go home.

After some hesitation, two of the Dolphins sped away, but 'E'—Milestone—continued to drone alongside. As the plane dragged itself heavily across the sunset, I started to look around for a suitable landing site.

At its present altitude, there was a fairly good view over the cowling and the steel cross member. I'd travelled much farther than I'd expected to. It was a pity I couldn't glide the last four or five miles. That would have been quite an accomplishment, gliding home from such a distance.

The plane was about six hundred feet up as it turned over the road from Naours to Flesselles. The ground on all sides was unpromising: mostly ploughed land with small stands of trees. So I circled back to the road. The wind was perfect, blowing straight down the road.

But what a lump the Dolphin was, without power.

I sideslipped ponderously over what the Europeans would consider a forest—back home we'd think of it more as a woodlot—and lined up with the dirt road, a darkening line in the fading light. It disappeared below the jutting Vickers. The road looked narrower than it had seemed from higher up. Fortunately there were no hedges, just a shallow ditch on one side. It was deserted.

A touch of rudder to follow a mild curve. Sink. Back with the stick. The Dolphin thumped onto the road, banged noisily through a pot-hole, and slewed as one of the wheels crossed a groove. A nervous jiggle on the rudder. The plane straightened, and rumbled to a halt.

As I climbed out stiffly, Milestone dived and whizzed past, waggling his wings. He continued onward without turning back. The roar of his engine faded, until his plane was just a silent shape rising over Flesselles.

A few minutes later, a French peasant in a billowing blue smock pedalled up on a bicycle.

I stepped expectantly into the road, wreathed in Francophile smiles. The peasant cycled carefully around the

74

plane and continued onward, without even looking up from his handlebars, as if the presence of a large warplane in the middle of the road was an everyday occurrence.

"Huh," I muttered. "The hell with the Entente Cordiale, then."

I sat down again on the kilometre post, marvelling at the typical phlegm and stolidity of the French. The evening hush settled again. Even the guns were stilled. A nightingale pierced the dusk with its song.

It was half an hour before the next vehicle came along. By then it was nearly dark. For a moment, I thought it was the squadron car. But, no, it was coming from Naours, the wrong direction.

The slits of the headlights appeared out of the woods a hundred yards up the road. It looked like a staff car. I hoped it didn't contain a general. Generals were inclined to be impatient, and there was no hope of getting the car past until help arrived from the squadron.

The open car drew up a few feet from the Dolphin's tail. I walked over to it, then stopped in some confusion. The back seat was occupied by a lady.

A very attractive lady, too, as far as one could tell in the twilight. She had a travelling rug over her limbs.

She didn't seem to be in the best of tempers, though.

"What's the matter? Why are you blocking the way?" she asked sharply, with only the smallest trace of an accent.

I essayed a gracious, courtly bow. "Sorry to hold you up, Marm," I said, "but I've come down with a dud engine."

She looked ahead at the airplane, her lips parting as she raised her head.

"Help should be along in a few minutes, Marm," I went on, putting a foot on the running board, and optically pawing her redoubtable bust. It was safe to do this, as my eye sockets were safely in shadow.

"I have a long way to go, *M'sieur*. Can't you move your airplane into the field?"

"It's kind of heavy, Marm."

"The corporal here could help."

Her fat, lazy-looking chauffeur looked quite relieved when I said, "It'll take three or four men, I'm afraid."

"It's too bad," she said, untying her hat with an irritable tug—it was secured under her chin by a ribbon—and throwing it angrily onto the seat beside her. "I will be late getting to Paris. I think it is very unfair of you."

"M'm. Sorry."

She dug around in her handbag and drew out a cigarette case. Selecting a cigarette, she closed the case with a loud snap. A match flared in the semi-darkness, revealing a broad but far from serene brow.

Holding her skirts to one side, she stepped down from the car and began to pace up and down, puffing furiously.

She was the first woman I'd ever seen smoking. In the open, too.

She turned sharply to her chauffeur. "Can't you drive around the airplane?" she demanded.

"Ploughed land, Ma'm. And it's a bit muddy at the edge, there. We'd get bogged down."

"I'm afraid that's so, Marm," I said.

"Will you please stop calling me that 'orrible name," she said, stamping her foot. "If you must talk to me, please call me *Madame.*"

"Very good, *Madame,*" I said, quite enjoying her display of temper.

"Why did you have to land your stupid airplane in the road anyway?" she stormed. "Why didn't you crash it somewhere sensible?"

Her chauffeur, who seemed to be used to her tantrums, sighed faintly, nestled his head into a more comfortable position, and closed his eyes.

The squadron car arrived just as the last glow faded

from the sky. It brought two men to guard the machine until the mechanics could work on it next day.

Unfortunately, after the plane had been pushed into the field, the lady's car refused to start.

Her chauffeur puffed, panted, and cranked. The car sat there in the dark, unmoved by his exertions.

"Ah, no! Damnations! I'll never get to Paris at this rate!"

My chauffeur, Witcomb, was obviously enjoying the other's hard work. After a moment, he slouched up and reached for the starting handle. " 'Ere, let me try," he said.

"Be off with you," the other chauffeur mumbled—or words to that effect. "I'll look after it."

"You aren't doing it very well, are you, cock. You sure the ignition's on?"

The two chauffeurs started to argue in the dark. "Give up that bloody 'andle, I tell you."

"I'll give it up all right, mate. Right up, handle and all."

" 'Ere, watch it."

"Except you'd probably enjoy that."

" 'Oo are you shoving, you sackful of lard."

"This is my tool, you get your hands off it."

"I wouldn't touch your tool wiv rubber gloves, knowing where it's probably been."

"I'll have you up for molesting a corporal."

"Come, come, boys," I said. "Let's not have any unseemly wrangling. I'll do it. I have a way with motor cars." I felt around for the crank. It was being gripped at both ends. "Come on, release the handle, men."

"Did you hear what he called me, sir?" Witcomb cried.

"It's nothing to what I'll call you if you don't let go, you horrible pair. *Will you let go?*"

A three-way tug-of-war then ensued. The other men, the guards, started to titter.

"Oh, for God's sake," the lady said disgustedly. "Are we going to be here all night?" At which the three of us released the handle simultaneously, and it took us another two minutes to find it again, in the dark.

The motor still refused to fire. "I guess we'll just have to tow your car to the squadron, Marm—*Madame,*" I said at length. "We'll fix it there—unless you want us to tow you back to where you came from?"

"No," the lady said sharply. There was a tapping sound. She was drumming her fingers on the mudguard.

"I suppose," she said finally, "I will have to wait at your squadron until the car is mended."

"I don't think we're allowed to entertain ladies, Marm. It's a military establishment. I wouldn't be setting a very good example if I brought home a strange lady."

"I am not strange! How dare you call me strange. I am just a little *distrait,* that's all."

"Ah."

"Then what are you going to do about it? Just leave me here in the wilderness, alone and unprotected?"

"I wouldn't mind taking her 'ome," Witcomb murmured.

My heart began to thump like billy-ho. "I believe," I said slyly, "that there's quite a good restaurant along the road, at Flesselles. Perhaps you'd care to wait there for your car while we, yum, have dinner together?"

Feet shuffled in the darkness. The mechanics and chauffeurs must be listening with considerable interest. I was glad they couldn't see my face.

"It's the very least I can do," I added, taking deep breaths of French dust, pollen, and thistledown, "for all the trouble I've caused you."

"Well," she said at last, briskly, "I suppose I have no other choice. All right. I will wait there until the motor car is mended."

"Ah, splendid."

"On one condition, *M'sieur.*"

"What's that?"

"That you remove that ridiculous fox fur from around

78

your neck, I am certainly not entering a restaurant, even a village restaurant, with a man who is wearing fox furs."

I wasn't sure, but I think now she was smiling.

On the way there in my car, she suddenly leaned over and touched my hand, which was illuminated by the dim headlights of the car we were towing.

"I'm sorry if I was in such a bad temper, *Monsieur* ... ?"

"Bandy."

"It had nothing to do with you, you see. It was my husband. We had a quarrel."

"That's too bad."

"He wasn't at all pleased when I turned up at his château."

She hesitated, then: "It was an impulse, you understand. I thought he would be glad to see me." I felt rather than saw her shoulders rise and fall. "I should have known better."

She must, I thought, be the wife of a quite senior officer, to be able to travel so freely in the war zone.

"But he was so cold and stuffy, as only the English can be. I was very hurt. So I insisted on leaving, to teach Arser a lesson."

"Arser?"

"First he is angry because I arrive. Then he is angry because I leave. He is very unreasonable, my husband."

"Arser? Is that really his name?"

"Yes. Arser Soames."

"Arse—You mean Arthur—Brigadier Soames?"

"But yes. Do you know him?"

"Yes," I said. "Oh, crumbs."

Busy Philandering

The Maison d'Or in Flesselles was a whitewashed cottage that had been converted into a restaurant. Blackout curtains hung across the passage just inside the front door. Beyond it was a small, candle-lit parlor crowded with tables, where a few pilots from another squadron and a group of artillery officers were seated, murmuring and sipping red wine. A sallow-faced girl was collecting their empty plates and smiling reservedly at the attempts of the officers to converse with her in French.

They all stiffened and fell silent as Mrs. Soames entered. She glanced around casually, as if she was quite used to turned heads and admiring glances.

As she selected a corner table, the serving girl stood gaping for a moment, then hurried out to the kitchen, from which came a susurration of French, the clop of horses' hoofs, or possibly pot-lids, and a very nice smell indeed. A moment later, a woman in a black dress hurried in, wiping her hands on her apron.

After a flustered greeting, she took our order, but continued to hang around, lighting extra candles, wiping the oilcloth, rearranging a chair, and looking as if she'd have liked to feel the material of Mrs. Soames's brown dress. (The other officers looked as if they'd have liked to feel her dress, too.)

"You are from Amiens, perhaps, *Madame?*" the proprietress ventured.

"Paris, *Madame.*"

"Paris!" The woman went into raptures. "You visit perhaps your husband?"

Mrs. Soames nodded, and tossed the hair from her eyes with a lazy shake of her head.

The other *madame* looked at me for the first time. "*Monsieur* is a very lucky man," she said, smirking all over her chops.

I waited for Mrs. Soames to point out that this was not the husband she had been visiting. Instead, after raising her eyebrows at the proprietress, then turning to regard me gravely, she said with a perfectly straight face, "Yes, he is lucky, isn't he?"

I stared at her in some confusion. A lot of confusion, in fact.

"Ah, *Monsieur* is a major," the proprietress exclaimed as my sleeve came into view. "You are not, by hazard, the strange new *chef* at Montonvillers?"

"Eh? No, I'm not a chef, I'm a pilot."

"You are not, then, the one who wears an English fox?"

"Oh, yes, he's the one," Mrs. Soames said.

The proprietress gazed wonderingly at my blank countenance. Mrs. Soames's eyes flashed in amusement.

"You should have told her," I whispered after the *madame* had gone reluctantly back into the kitchen.

She took out her gold case and rapped a cigarette on it. The artillery officers and pilots stared even harder.

"You are ashamed, then, to be mistaken for my husband?" she asked lazily.

"No, certainly not," I said, a hot flush settling over my noble brow, which I promptly buried in the tiny, hand-written menu. "Nobody could possibly be ashamed to be in the company of such a gorge—such a beaut—such a —I wonder what they have for pudding?"

She dragged in a professional lungful of smoke and leaned back, holding the cigarette as if it were a teeny javelin. "So you are Major Bandy," she murmured, studying me carefully. "I've heard my husband talking about you. You were involved in some scandal or other, I think?"

"Oh, it was just because of a sort of speech I made, that's all."

"It wasn't over a woman, then?"

"Oh, no."

"No, I forgot," she said, making a face. "Your English scandals are never about women."

"M'm." To change the subject, I said, "Your English is very good."

"I learned it in America."

"Still, it's really quite good."

"Thank you. I was married to an American. I've been married twice, you see."

"Good grief."

Her first husband, she said, was an aviator and aero-engine designer. The marriage hadn't lasted long, however, for he had been killed in an air accident in 1915. She had married Soames late the following year in London, when Soames was Assistant Director-General of Military Aeronautics.

At the moment, though, she was living in Paris, in an apartment that Soames, who had considerable private means, was renting for her.

As I listened, I felt more unsettled than ever. It was that lazy, slightly hoarse voice of hers. It was the most exciting and sexy voice I'd ever heard.

Even before I said good-bye to Katherine, I'd been wondering how on earth I'd be able to hold out, sexwise, until my next leave. And here was I, aflame with illicit passion after only three weeks.

Nevertheless, I was determined to control the carnal man. So I made an effort to listen to what she was saying, rather than how she was saying it.

By now we had the dining room to ourselves. Mrs. Soames became aware of this, and stopped suddenly in the middle of a description of her American travels, and said, "But here I am talking all about myself, and you have hardly spoken a word."

She leaned forward impulsively. "You know," she said, "I adore pilots."

"Jolly good."

"One of my friends is Charles Nungessor. He has over thirty victories; isn't that marvellous? Do you know him?"

"I know of him, *Madame*."

"Marm, *Madame*. I am not an old woman," she pouted. "Why don't you call me Marguerite?"

"Right. Sure thing, Marm—Mam—Marguerite," I babbled, covering my lap with the skimpy oilcloth.

Mrs. Soames seemed to have forgotten about getting to Paris. She was lighting yet another cigarette, "Yes," she said languidly waving away the smoke, "if you're ever in Paris, you must meet Nungessor. I'll introduce you if you like—unless he's in hospital. He is always injuring himself in accidents. I really don't know why you pilots don't wear parachutes."

"Parachutes?" I said, in some astonishment.

"Yes, parachutes."

"Oh, that's not done," I said.

"Why not?"

"Well, parachutes are for air displays and nonsense like that," I said. "No decent pilot would dream of wearing one."

"Our French aviators don't wear them either. But I think it's ridiculous," she said. "Nungessor, for example, would have saved himself so very much pain. After all, you give them to the men in the balloons, don't you?"

"Well, you see," I said, feeling more at ease now that we were talking shop, "it's different with airplanes. It's a matter of altitude, you see."

"Altitude? I don't understand, *Commandant*."

"Parachutes," I said, steepling my fingers judiciously, "aren't any good at higher altitudes."

"Oh?"

"Well, it's obvious," I said with an avuncular smile—even though she was several years older than I. "Jumping out at high altitudes inevitably results in panic, or at the very least, broken limbs. It's a well-known fact."

"Oh, is it?" Mrs. Soames—Marguerite—said, squinting at me through the smoke.

"Of course. Quite apart from the danger of not being able to breathe, or move your limbs."

"Surely you wouldn't want to move them," she said, "if they were all broken."

"They certainly wouldn't get *me* wearing a parachute," I said stoutly, "and that's how all the other pilots feel."

"Yes, our French flyers seem to feel the same way."

"Another thing," I said. "If you were travelling at high speed—a hundred miles an hour or more, you wouldn't be able to get out of the aircraft anyway. Because of the air pressure."

"Oh, I see."

"And even if you could get out—well, say you were at fifteen thousand feet—you'd come down faster and faster, you see, through all that thin air. As a result, the parachute would get torn to absolute shreds."

"I suppose you know all about that, because of your scientific training," she said, ever so respectfully.

"Well, I didn't actually take aerial dynamics when I was a medical student," I said modestly. "But I did study anatomy, so I have some idea of what the human body can stand up to."

She nodded thoughtfully, holding her cigarette between thumb and forefinger. "All this panic, and falling faster and faster through the air with broken limbs," she murmured. "That wouldn't apply to a girl, of course?"

"Of course," I said, smiling. Then, blankly: "Eh? Why a girl?"

"I just wondered," she said lazily. "Because I saw a

84

girl jump from fifteen thousand feet, and she seemed all right when she got down."

"What? You mean in a parachute?"

"Of course. It was an American girl, called Tiny Broadwick."

"Oh?"

"I watched her make a parachute jump when I was in America, in . . . nineteen fourteen, I think."

"Oh," I said. After a moment, I picked up the carafe and put my eye to it and looked inside, to see if there was any wine left.

"Well, they . . . they do say that mature women are sometimes much tougher than men," I mumbled.

"This girl was about fifteen at the time," Marguerite—Mrs. Soames—said.

"M'yes . . . well, there you are," I said, sounding rather like Malt in one of his denser moments.

I looked up with relief as the front door opened and a current of cool air drifted through the dining room, which had suddenly gotten terribly hot and stuffy.

My chauffeur was peering through the blackout curtain. He saw us and came over, saluting casually.

"Is the lady's car ready yet?" I asked hopefully.

"No, that's what I come to tell you, sir. They're still working on it."

"How long will it take?"

"Least another couple of hours, they fink."

I looked at Marguerite, waiting for another outburst of temperament. But all she said was, "What's the matter with the car?"

Witcomb came to attention and said formally, "It's the ignition system, Modom." But then he relaxed and put his scarred knuckles on the table. "You see, the gudgeon pin 'as been rendered out of compression by the auxiliary camshaft, Modom. You know, where it joins the secondary coil, or tappet. We've 'ad to remove the exhaust stroke from the inlet manifold to get at yer differential, see?"

"Oh, dear, that does sound serious."

"Yerse, Modom, certainly does."

"But have you tried connecting the timing chain direct from the helical gears to the needle valve of the carburetor?" Mrs. Soames asked. "That should work just as well, don't you think?"

Witcomb's face turned brick red. Later he blamed me for not tipping him off that Modom had once been married to one of them American mechanical geniuses.

Feeling mean, I let him suffer for half a minute before looking at my watch and exclaiming, "Odd's teeth, it's nearly eleven."

"Is it?" Marguerite didn't seem to mind about the time any more. She pouted thoughtfully for a moment, then: "I'll have to stay here, then. Oh, but my travelling case."

Witcomb said sulkily, "I still 'ave Modom's luggage in our car, if that's any 'elp."

Mrs. Soames smiled at him charmingly. "Bring it in, then, will you?"

Witcomb went out, slightly mollified by the smile, and returned a couple of minutes later with a suitcase and a hatbox.

Meanwhile, Marguerite was negotiating with the proprietress. At the prospect of a paying guest, the other's face lit up, then clouded, then looked thoughtful, then crafty, all in a matter of seconds.

"There is the girl's room, of course," she said reluctantly. "It will be somewhat inconvenient, but possibly she could be persuaded to sleep somewhere else . . ."

"Will twenty francs be all right?" Mrs. Soames asked.

Judging by her expression, the proprietress would have thrown out her aged grandmother for a sum like that. "Follow me, *Monsieur,*" she said, gesturing at the luggage.

I picked it up and followed them through the kitchen and up the back stairs, assuming she merely wanted a

responsible male to okay the arrangements for the brigadier's wife.

The back bedroom was tiny, but clean enough. A worn
mat covered the pine planking. A brass bedstead crouched
arrogantly under the sloping ceiling.

"Ah, yes, this will do splendidly," I said heartily; then,
turning doubtfully to Marguerite: "I mean, will it? Is it
all right?"

She tested the bed—it uttered a faint groan—and nodded indifferently. The proprietress fussed around, straightening the lace on the bedside table, adjusting the blackout
curtain, closing the cupboards, and pouring a pint of
drowned spiders into the washbasin. The sallow-faced girl
edged in sulkily and started to collect her nightwear.

"I'm sure that *Monsieur* and *Madame* will be very comfortable," the proprietress said, giving the bed a final
caress, in what seemed to me a decidedly lascivious fashion.

"Yes, splendid," I said heartily. "This will be just—
what?"

The woman was backing out, smiling encouragingly,
her hands clasped around the empty water pitcher. The
sallow girl had already flounced out.

"Hey, just a goldurn minute," I said.

"We'll bring some fresh water for to wash, in just a
little moment," she said. *"Bonsoir, Madame. Bonsoir,
Monsieur."* And she slapped the door shut before I could
jam my foot in the opening.

I looked around in rising panic. Marguerite was sitting
on the bed, looking at me with an expression that in the
circumstances seemed disgracefully unconcerned.

"I *told* you you should have explained," I hissed. "Now
look what you've done."

She took out a comb and went to work on her tresses.
"You can explain when she comes back with the water,
if you wish," she said.

"I know, but somehow it's never that simple," I said crossly. "It would've been much easier to have disillusioned her when the misunderstanding first arose."

"Disillusioned?" Marguerite raised her eyebrows. "I am a disillusionment, *Commandant?*"

"You know what I mean. What I mean is, it's my experience that misconceptions have to be misunderstood right at the beginning, or—that is, these kind of mistakes have to be ironed out immediately or the situation gets terribly wrinkled, and, and, is what I've found. Why, only a few months ago I found myself in a situation not unlike this very—situation. A hotel bedroom I found, found myself in, containing not just one woman but three, nearly all with husbands who arrived at a very inopportune . . ."

She raised her eyebrows, interested.

"Yes, well, we won't go into those women just now," I said firmly, shifting my weight from one foot to the other and moving sideways, as if trying to tamp down a row of carrot seeds. "Let's stick to the point. The point is—"

"Pass me that nightdress, will you?" Marguerite said lazily, pointing to her suitcase.

I took out the nightdress, still talking in firm but reasonable tones. "I mean, all it needed was a simple explanation back there in the dining room. Like, 'Oh, no, you've got it all wrong, this is not my husband, this is just a fellow who was blocking my passage earlier this, this . . .' Or: possibly you might have uttered a light, trilling but incredulous sort of laugh," I said, shaking the nightdress vigorously, as if it were full of sawflies. "Or," I went on in my measured tones, "if that wasn't enough, a simple statement to the effect that you'd been having trouble with your motor car, and I had gallantly offered to bite you— offer you a bite, that is—to eat, that is, while the mechanics fiddled with your differential. Or—"

"Do you have to flap that nightdress about quite so much, *Commandant?* Or are you sending up Indian smoke signals?"

The door was flung open and banged noisily against the wall. I turned eagerly to explain the situation, but unfortunately it was the sallow girl, and she was obviously neither the right person to listen to explanations, nor in the mood to do so.

Nevertheless, I started to babble while she was putting down a new pitcher of water on the bedside table. She paid no attention.

"Wait!" I cried. "Attongday!" And reached out a restraining hand. The girl looked wide-eyed at my clutching fingers, and shrank out into the passage, apparently under the misapprehension that one woman wasn't enough for my bestial appetites. At any rate, she backed out hurriedly and scuttled off down the passage as if pursued by satyrs.

Meanwhile, Marguerite—Mrs. Soames—was making queer, snuffling noises with her face averted, most unladylike. However, when she turned back her face was carefully expressionless again.

"Would you like to wash first, or shall I?" she asked.

"What? What?"

She twisted round on the bed until her back was toward me again. "But first, unfasten my dress, will you?"

"How can you sit there so calmly," I whispered desperately, doing my carrot-tamping act again—until I realized that the floorboards were, as a result, creaking rhythmically underfoot. The thought of *Madame* the proprietress overhearing a rhythmic creaking from the bedroom froze me to the planks.

"Do something," I hissed.

"I'm waiting for you to do something," she responded. "Or are you just going to click there all night like a metronome?"

"If you are," she said, getting up and raising her arms to unfasten the dress herself, "I might as well turn in."

"No, no, you can't turn in! The situation has to be *revolved!* I'll—I'll have to go down and tell her. Yes, that's what I'll do."

"She'll think it very strange that you've waited all this time to tell her," Mrs. Soames said. A bare, slightly plump shoulder appeared. She held her dress to her, her fingers spread across her chest, and regarded me gravely.

"You're right. It's far too late, now. Well, I'll just have to sneak out when she's finished tidying up down there." I could hear sounds of movement from downstairs, and a clash of dishes.

"Unless you climbed out the window," Mrs. Soames suggested.

"The window! You're right, the window," I said thankfully. I started toward the black-out curtain, but stopped dead again when the floor creaked—rhythmically. "Blow out the oil lamp, will you?" I whispered, sounding as hoarse as her, now. There was an oil lamp burning on the bedside table.

"Are you sure I can trust you in the dark, *Commandant?*"

"What? Course you can!"

"I don't know. You've been behaving rather agitatedly."

However, she turned down the lamp, and watched as I pulled aside the curtains and looked out.

Damn. The squadron car was directly below, with Witcomb sprawled in the front, his boots over the side of the car.

"Oh, this is ridiculous," I whispered. "Why don't I just walk downstairs and—simply walk out? I could just give her a sort of, of forgetful smile as I went past, as if I'd forgotten something."

"Your nightcap, perhaps? Or your bedsocks?"

"Yes, exac—listen, this is no time for jokes," I hissed heatedly. "I have my reputation to think of, not to mention my, my . . ." I looked out the window again. The gutter was only a few feet up. Maybe I could get away over the roof?

Mrs. Soames suddenly seemed to get tired of the whole business. "Look, Bart'olomew," she said briskly.

"Shhh!"

"Shush yourself. Look, just do as you said. Go downstairs and just walk out. You're an officer, you don't have to explain anything." There was a frightening rustle of clothes. More and more of her gleaming skin appeared. "Now I'm going to bed. Good night, Bart'olomew."

The bed uttered a hollow groan as she sat on it again, and started to unfasten all sorts of hooks and things. That did it. I hurried to the door, opened it, scampered along the corridor, and creaked downstairs on tiptoe.

The proprietress was just putting her broom away for the night as I walked into the kitchen, shoulders back and head held so high my dampish hair was practically cleaning the ceiling. Remembering Mrs. Soames's advice not to get involved in complicated explanations, I merely acknowledged the woman's stare with a brisk nod and the words, "Just stepping out for a moment or two. Forgotten something, you see. And being a bit full-up after your delicious dinner, *Madame,* I need a brisk canter to settle the . . . And then there's the car to see to, you see."

She looked a bit puzzled.

"Also, I must have a word with my chauffeur, you see. Also—"

"You are not staying with the lady, *M'sieur?*"

"Um, well, actually, no." I took a deep, shuddery sort of breath. By now I'd inhaled enough extra oxygen to last me through the next dozen high-altitude flights. "You see, the fact is, she's not, well, the actual fact is, to be frank, she's not really my, yum, wife, you see."

"But what has that to do with it?" she asked indignantly. "That is no reason to abandon her in such a manner."

"Ah," I said. "Ah. Yes. Well. There you are," I said, and after a final brisk nod, turned and seized the knob of the door, and fell into the cellar.

That's Malt, Just Out of the Picture

After a month of sweeping and scrubbing, the barn still smelled pretty evil, but everybody except Malt seemed to have settled down all right.

I'd invited the adjutant to share the hayloft with me, but he was still behaving so churlishly I wished I'd established him in the cow stall below. I compromised by putting the office partition between us so I wouldn't have to look at his face.

I suppose I could have gotten rid of Malt easily enough, as the position of squadron commander seemed to carry with it powers rivalling those of an oriental despot. The trouble was I found Malt so intriguingly sneaky and false, so mean, petty, rigid, smug, and orthodox that I was reluctant to part with him. I felt that his eccentricities gave the squadron character.

All the same, I had to be constantly on guard against any reassertion of his hidebound hegemony, against any attempt on his part to increase the clerical staff, the mess fees, and the tension, or to sneak in extra ceremonial under the guise of pay parades, sick parades, kit parades, or snap inspections.

His attitude toward visiting pilots was a typical example of his stubborn resistance to everything that was orderly, decent-minded, sensible, intelligent, and progressive, ie., to everything *I* thought was best.

I didn't realize what he had been doing until one evening a D.H.9 force-landed on our airfield. I met the pilot as he was storming from the mess, snorting indignantly that he would take care not to have a dud engine near *this* squadron again.

When I asked what was wrong, he said the adjutant had insisted on charging him a mess fee to cover the liquor he'd imbibed.

So I settled down in the mess for another vicious hand-to-hand encounter with my adjutant.

"The food and drink have to be paid for somehow, sah," he said contentedly, working his thigh over with his fist.

Malt was always feeling himself in this fashion: rolling his biceps with his finger tips, squeezing his waist, kneading his neck, gripping the roll of fat over his stomach in both hands, slapping his behind affectionately, or even rolling his buttocks in separate clockwise and counter-clockwise movements, that sort of thing.

"It's a mess committee rule, sah, and that's all there is to it," he said stolidly.

"It violates all the rules of hospitality, Malt. I think you should do something about it."

"You're dictating to the mess, are you, Major?" Malt said, looking significantly at the pilots.

"No. But—"

"The rules have to be obeyed, sah, and that's all there is to it."

The argument went on for so long that several of the pilots got up and went to bed. Malt remained obdurate.

"As long as I'm President of the Mess Committee, I shall continue to enforce the rules without fear or favor," Malt said, folding his large, pink hands comfortably over his stomach.

"M'yes, I guess you're right, Malt," I said weakly. "We can't afford to make exceptions."

"I'm glad you see it my way," Malt said, now smirking at me in quite a kindly fashion.

"How much do you charge the colonel and the brigadier and their staff when they visit us?"

"Eh? Malt laughed indulgently. "We could hardly charge them, now, could we?"

"You don't charge them?"

"Course not."

"Why not?"

"It's obvious," Malt sighed, looking at the others in a long-suffering way. "They're our wing and brigade commanders."

"What's that got to do with it?"

"If you can't see that," Malt said, shaking his head pityingly and smiling at Captain Blackbourne. "I mean, no one in his right mind would dream of doing that."

"*I* would."

"Yes, well, there you are," Malt said, as if he'd scored a telling point.

"After all, Malt, you said there could be no exceptions."

"I meant—"

"So you'll have to charge the colonel and brigadier and all the rest of them next time they come, won't you? You'll have an opportunity any day now, by the way. The b.g. is due to visit us again, soon."

Malt raised his voice. "I can't do that," he said, "and you know it."

"It's okay, I'll do it. I mean, darn it, the very last thing I want to do is flout your rules, Malt."

Blackbourne stuck out a foot, tilted it over, and examined his toecap for scuffmarks.

"You wouldn't dare," Malt said after a moment.

"Dare? There's nothing to dare. I'll just tell them I'm following your rules, Reginald."

Malt stared at me fixedly, gripping his left buttock. After pinching and rolling it around for several seconds, he started to say something, stopped, looked toward the blacked-out window, then abruptly turned his back and marched out, fiery-faced.

94

After sleeping on it, though, he must have regained some sense of proportion, for next morning he sauntered up casually and said that if I felt that strongly about such a pettifogging matter, he'd see what he could do about amending the rules, if I was all that concerned about a few miserable francs.

I didn't by any means dislike old Malt, even if he was something of a pest. At least he wasn't supercilious, like some regulars of his ilk. In fact, I quite admired his ease of manner when dealing with other ranks, and his ability to talk to them in their own language. I thought he had that rare gift among officers, an intuitive understanding of the men.

I was quite disappointed when I learned that his linguistic slumming came naturally to him. It hadn't been so very long before that he'd been another rank himself.

"I met him at beginning o' t' war," the batman told me. " 'E'd been int' Boer War, and 'ad re-enlisted in 1914 as a corporal. Though he was a sergeant-major when I met 'im at Aldershot."

"Really?"

" 'E doesn't know I've recognized 'im, so don't let on I told you, mind, or 'e'll 'ave me posted to an even worse squadron than yours, Major."

"I shouldn't have thought," I said acidly, "that Reeves-Goring would have stood for having a former sergeant-major as a cousin."

It took Smethurst a while to understand what I was talking about. " 'E's not the major's cousin," he said scornfully, sitting in my armchair to adjust his puttees. " 'Is father was the Reeves-Gorings' farm agent."

"He's the son of a farm agent? He's not related to Reeves-Goring *either?*"

"Course not. I know, because old Mr. and Mrs. Malt turned up at barracks one day, from Worcester, to see their son in 'is natural 'abitat. 'E weren't too pleased to see them, neither. 'E 'ad them out front gate so fast, his dad's hairpiece flew off, and the barracks cat ran off with it."

The adjutant's connections seemed to be growing steadily less influential. Any day now, I expected to learn that he wasn't even Mr. and Mrs. Malt's boy, but had been left on their front doorstep by an Albanian organ-grinder.

I had endless quarrels with Malt. In many of them, he emerged the victor, mainly because I was flying more and more frequently, now, and simply didn't have time to argue.

Typical of the way he took advantage of me was the occasion when a visiting pilot from a Camel squadron asked his friend Middleton if he could do a few circuits and bumps in one of our machines.

It was the first time he'd flown a Dolphin, but the visitor believed that a pilot who could fly a Camel was capable of flying anything.

He managed to take off all right, but when he came in to land he couldn't get the tail down. Seeing the trees and Nissen huts rushing toward him, he had to smash the throttle forward to get off again. Three times, he attempted to land, but his tailskid utterly refused to score the ground.

I was busy talking to the carpenters when a flight sergeant came running up to tell me about it. I got there in time to witness the fourth attempt. The Camel pilot dropped in neatly enough, his wheels bouncing and tittuping over the grass, but once again he had to open up, to stagger alarmingly over the woods.

A crowd of pilots and mechanics had assembled near the hangars. "I forgot to tell him about the tailplane incidence control," Middleton said, his handsome face creased with anxiety. Middleton wasn't so much worried about his friend as about the machine. It was his bus, and brand-new.

The Camel pilot was apparently unfamiliar with this feature. His tailplane was still adjusted for take off but not for pancaking.

Anyway, while I was trying to work out how to inform the pilot about the control wheel, Malt marched up and, hardly glancing at the distressed aircraft, started pestering me about the ground staff being out of condition and insisting that something should be done about it.

"Yes, yes, Malt, leave me alone."

"That's all right then, is it? A cross-country?"

"Yes, yes," I said, and turned back to Derby, with half a dozen impractical suggestions as to how to get the plane down in one piece.

The result of this preoccupied exchange was that on the following Saturday, a very wet day indeed, Malt paraded the already overworked ack-emmas in full pack, and sent them off, cursing and swearing, across ten miles of sodden countryside.

As for the other problem, of the tail-up Dolphin, it was Orville France who came up with the solution. He had us all lie down on the grass, and proceeded to arrange our forms so as to spell out a two-word message.

The Camel pilot got the message all right, and rolled to a silent standstill on his next attempt. He looked pretty crestfallen and apprehensive when he climbed out to face me; with good reason, as I was exceedingly annoyed at having had to curl up, head to tail with Monty Murgatroyd, in order to form the first letter of the words we'd spelled out in the wet, prickly grass: SWITCH OFF.

As a result of that sneaky gambit of Malt's, I decided to pursue my latest brilliant idea with more than usual determination.

For, one day, I had the splendid idea of promoting Malt's toilet to the position of squadron emblem.

I was so excited at the idea, I rushed to Malt straight

away, with the proposal that he donate his sculptured masterpiece to the mess.

He was so impressed he could hardly speak for several minutes.

"Put my toilet in the mess?"

"Not to actually use, Malt, but for purely decorative and symbolic purposes. Think of it, Malt! It could be a really worthwhile addition to the ante-room!"

"You're mad . . ."

"I promise you it would be treated with the utmost respect, Malt. We could have quite a dignified ceremony. A short service from the wing padre, perhaps. And I'd make a really dignified speech, Malt. I'd say, 'Gentlemen, our honored adjutant has been graciously pleased to donate his most precious possession to the scout pilots of this squadron,' or something like that. 'Gentlemen,' I'd say, 'I give you the squadron's new emblem: J. Bolding and Sons' masterpiece: *The Dolphin.*'"

"Never."

"Can't you just see it, Malt—Reginald? Why, people would come from far and near just to see your toilet. It would be—"

"I've never . . . I've never heard anything like it in my life," Malt said. He had gone quite pale. "I think it's the most outrageous . . . only *you* could think of something like this."

But the more I thought about his toilet, the more determined I was to acquire it. I went after him whenever I had a spare moment; in his rooms, in my rooms, in the barn, the mess, the hangars—I even took to hanging about outside his embellished privy, like a Piccadilly tout.

"Oh, don't be so stubborn, man," I cried. "It's for the good of the squadron as a whole, can't you see that? Anyway, it's a shame to hide anything so beautiful away from the eyes of mortal men! Don't you see, Reginald, it'll give the squadron character, an', an' *distinction*. Like

56 Squadron; 56 is famous for its orchestra, right? The one that Major Bloomfield has built up? Don't you see, Malt—Reginald—you could make this squadron equally celebrated!"

"I don't wish to discuss it any more, and that's all there is to it," Malt said, his voice all shaky with emotion and stuff. "And if you pester me any more about it, I'll complain to Headquarters that you're victimizing me. I mean it. I mean it."

"You surely can't refuse to make this minor concession for the well-being of your own squadron, surely?"

"It's not my squadron any more. The way the men slop around with their hair almost touching their ears, and unpolished brasses, and hardly even saluting any more. They're slovenly, and nothing's painted or whitewashed no more—"

"The aircraft are well looked after—"

"—and they seem to think they can do just what they like—the whole place is a bloody disgrace," he shouted, and went on in this fashion for some time, working himself up to the point where he finally bawled, "And if you don't watch out, yew 'orrible man, yew, I'll do somethink real drastic, I can assure you of that!"

"Like what, Reginald?"

"I'll, I'll put in for a transfer, that's what I'll do!"

"Oh, no."

"I will. An immediate transfer!"

"That's terrible, Reginald. Gosh, I don't know what we'd do without you," I said, appalled. "Honest, things just wouldn't be the same, Reg—or, Reggie, is it? It would be awful. I'd hardly be able to carry on, hardly.

"But, tuh . . . assuming you *did* transfer, Reg—you'd have to leave your toilet behind, wouldn't you? In that case—"

"Major, I wouldn't leave you so much as a turd," Reggie said, trembling all over by now, as well as squeezing, massaging, palpitating, and kneading himself like mad.

I was about to reprove him for descending from the high plane of our discussion to this uncharacteristic vulgarity, but suddenly stopped and stared at him thoughtfully instead.

I had just understood the reason he was always manhandling himself in that fashion.

Until that moment, I'd assumed that his indecent assault on himself was just a mannerism, like the way Orville France was always pushing his lips in and out, as if osculating with invisible frails. For the first time, it occurred to me that this tactile revelry of Malt's was symptomatic of insecurity. That he was constantly feeling himself in that manner to reassure himself that he was really there— that he existed as a meaningful society entity.

Poor devil. As if it *mattered* that he was only the paltry son of a farm agent. As if it *really* bothered us *elite* types that he was merely an insignificant, lower-class *parvenu*.

After that, feeling sorry for the no-account fellow, I made only one further attempt to win him over to the cause of truth and beauty, plumbing division. His answer, I thought, was exceedingly childish.

"Go to hell!"

"Now, Reginald."

"And you're never getting it," he bellowed, his voice cracking. "Never, never, never, never!"

It was obvious that I was wasting sweet reason on him. "Look," I said coldly, "let's stop beating about the bush, Reg. I want a plain answer. Are you prepared to give up that 1882 Bolding masterwork or not?"

"I'm not telling you again! I'm not telling you again!"

"I see. I see. Well, if that's the way you feel, Malt."

"And you're not going to terrorize me the way you've terrorized everyone at Wing, either! You'll never get it, never, never—"

"All right, all right! Keep your rotten old toilet!"

"I will, don't you worry."

"You don't have to keep on and on about it. I can take a hint. Keep it."

"Don't worry, I am."

"Huh. It's not all that marvellous, anyway," I said. "It's just a piece of old porcelain anyway. Who wants your rotten old lavatory, anyway?"

As if Malt wasn't bad enough, I also had the pigeon to contend with.

About half a dozen of them had been roosting in the barn when we first moved in. Since then, all but one had moved out. The exception was a badly groomed specimen that had refused to budge from the beam above the hayloft where I had my desk.

This pigeon had none of the docile manners of the Anglo-Saxon variety. In fact, there was something really upsetting about the way it had taken to staring down at me as I sat muttering and grumbling at my desk. To make matters worse, it had bags under its eyes, and there was also something wrong with its cooing apparatus. Instead of producing the standard peristeronic moan, it sounded as if it were constantly swallowing material that was too bulky for its gullet, or as if it were gargling with sump oil.

However, as long as it continued to perch well to one side, where the cross beam met one of the rafters, I was content to let it stay. Recently, though, it had begun to edge farther along the beam that ran spanwise over the hayloft, coming closer and closer to the point directly above my desk.

"I think that pigeon's out to get me," I said to Milestone with an uneasy laugh.

"Rubbish."

"It is. It's quite definitely been working its way farther along the beam."

Dick studied the pigeon for a moment. "Dispatch it, then," he said.

"And make pigeon pie, you mean?"

"No, I meant entice it down with a few tasty morsels, then quickly attach a message to its leg, and dispatch it to Ramsgate."

"It's a French pigeon, Dick. It probably doesn't know the way to Ramsgate."

"Send it to Dunquerque, then, and let it take the boat."

"I don't know what I could use to entice it down with, anyway. Certainly not with any of the food Bixby cooks."

"I have it," Milestone said, brightening. "Snibbo."

"You have some Snibbo? What's it like?"

"I don't mean I have any. I was just suggesting that's what you could entice it down with, if you could get some."

"Perhaps the pigeon doesn't know what Snibbo is."

"H'm, yes, that could be a problem," Dick mused. "It wouldn't know whether to eat it, wear it, smoke it, or sit on it."

Dick was perched on the corner of my desk in the hayloft. He was a bit subdued that evening, despite the fact that the squadron had just won another resounding victory.

We had flown every available aircraft on a squadron show in the afternoon, and the superior performance of the Dolphins had taken them high above two layers of about thirty Pfalz. There had been a right slaughter. Pfalz scouts were outclassed by Camels, let alone Sopwith Dolphins. Ten had been claimed, and artillery spotters confirmed that eight of them had dived, flamed, or spun into the ground around Etinehem, with only one casualty on our side, the first in nearly two weeks—ironically, a pilot who had just completed the month's practice designed to protect him from just such a premature fate.

"I wonder what we'd do if we lost eight machines in one fight," Dick said. "Poor devils, there must be gloom and *Angst* in that Hun mess tonight."

I wrenched my gaze from the pigeon and said, "This

102

squadron's had its fair share of gloom and *Angst*— whatever that is."

"Yes . . ." He slipped off the desk and walked across to the barn wall, and peered through a gap in the planking. We could hear the pilots yowling and rowing in the mess a good hundred yards away.

"By the way," he said, "I didn't thank you for picking that Hun leader off my tail. You're really quite a shot, aren't you, Bart? You can't have fired more than ten rounds."

Hs slouched back to the desk, hands in pockets, shoulders hunched. "God, I'm sick of this war," he muttered.

"Cheer up, Dick. Think of it as an adventure."

He tilted his chin, looking at me bitterly for a moment. But then he smiled wryly. "I must say you've been one of the bright spots in this war for me, Bart. I've watched your career with the kind of fascination a bacteriologist must experience as he watches something growing in a petrie dish."

"You think of me as a bug, do you?"

"You're getting talked about again, did you know? Going round in that ridiculous fox fur . . . bullying your own colonel . . . locked in a life-or-death struggle with your adjutant. The men don't know what to make of you, either. They've never come across a C.O. who joins in their football games and takes illegal bottles of whisky to them in the hangars."

"Well, they sometimes have to work long after midnight on those Hispano-Suizas," I said defensively. "On five shillings a day, too."

"Bart?"

"H'm?"

"Have you ever thought about what you'll do after the war?"

"Can't say I have. Why?"

"Maybe . . . well, maybe we could do something together. Something connected with flying."

"I've never thought about after the war."

"I don't see why we shouldn't. The war can't last all that much longer. It looks as if the Huns are whacked—in the air, at least. And they've dangerously over-extended themselves on the ground. It can't last forever.

"Why not?" he said enthusiastically. "I don't think we've anything to worry about, now. I've enough experience to look after myself. And I know nothing will ever happen to *you*," he said, just as the pigeon shuffled the last few steps, fluffed out its feathers, closed its eyes ecstatically, and moved its bowels straight onto my best regimental uniform.

"It's good luck," Dick said.

The next time I saw it shuffling overhead, I flung a flying boot at it. The pigeon flapped in momentary panic to another beam, while the boot sailed down to the main floor and thumped one of the clerks between the shoulder blades.

He blinked up at me in a stricken sort of way.

"Sorry," I said, peering guiltily from the hayloft. "It was the . . ." I gestured toward the roof.

"You've never forgiven us for whinnying at you, have you?" the clerk said.

"No, no, you don't understand," I called down. "It's—"

"We've moved that French dunghill twice, and we've worked really hard," the clerk said, his chin quivering like anything, "to make the barn nice and homey for you. I mean, surely we've expiated our sins by now. I mean . . ."

"I tell you it was the pigeon."

"A pigeon couldn't possibly have thrown a heavy flying boot like that," the clerk said. "I mean, if you aren't satisfied with our work . . ." He stopped, overcome by the sheer injustice of it all.

Having got the range, the pigeon did it again, two

nights later, spattering the squadron log and a letter to Katherine in my best handwriting.

"That does it," I said, my voice echoing in the dim, empty barn. I marched grimly over to the mess, and up the stairs to my room, and dug out my automatic pistol. That bloody bird had ruined nearly two hours' work.

I snapped a bullet into the breech and started for the door. But now that I had the gun actually in my hand, it was hard to sustain my indignation. Damn it all, I thought, it's only a pigeon, even if it does have bags under its eyes and makes choking noises like British generals at a political conference.

It all began to seem rather petty and undignified. Finally, I put the pistol away and started unbuttoning my tunic, yawning exhaustedly and wondering how I could get rid of that pest, short of giving it a lead suppository. Perhaps I could mount an air-raid klaxon up near the ceiling. I could press the buzzer every time the pigeon came too close. It would soon get tired of a klaxon blaring in its earhole every time it made a wrong move.

The only trouble was, I'd never get any work done, I'd be so busy watching the brute. Perhaps, I thought as I prepared for bed, I could put up some kind of tent or canopy over the desk? But working under a tent, like a disoriented Bedouin, would look rather eccentric, surely? And the last thing I wanted was to be thought eccentric.

I was in my jammies before I remembered that I'd left a candle burning in the barn. And with all that dry timber
. . .

I got wearily out of bed again, fumbled around for my filthy raincoat and boots, and wended my way back to the barn; and I was just about to lurch inside when I heard a scraping noise from within, followed by a muffled curse.

Wondering who could be about at this time of night, I stuck my head cautiously through the doorway, and was just in time to see Captain Malt raising the hayloft ladder and placing it against the beam above my desk.

He was clutching half a loaf of soggy bread.

As he tested the ladder to make certain it was secure, a nasty suspicion began to form.

There was an agitated clatter of wings as he climbed slowly and carefully to the beam high overhead. Under cover of the noise, I skittered along the wall to a point below the hayloft. As Malt had taken the ladder, I stood on a desk and gripped the edge of the hayloft and drew myself up, breathing through my mouth.

He still hadn't heard or seen me. He was too busy grunting and muttering and saying, "Shoo, shoo," and he hung up there—laying a trail of breadcrumbs.

That was what the sod had been doing: enticing the pigeon farther and farther along the beam by laying a trail of breadcrumbs to a point directly above my desk.

The bugger! He had been encouraging that damn bird to shit on me!

Late the following morning, Dick came up to the hayloft to ask if the rumor was true: that Malt had applied for an immediate transfer.

"H'm? Yes, I fear so," I mumbled, hunching in a preoccupied way over a *Combats in the Air* report. "I tried to dissuade him, of course, but . . ."

Milestone looked at me cynically.

"How did you manage it, Bart?"

I told him about Malt's pigeon-enticing act the night before. Milestone almost fell through the rotting side of the barn.

"I wouldn't have put it past him to have dipped the breadcrumbs in syrup of figs, either," I said resentfully, "to inspire it to even greater heights of intemperance."

"Oh, stop, stop," Dick moaned, holding his diaphragm.

After several deep breaths, he said faintly, "So you ordered him to apply for a transfer, is that it?"

"Oh, no, that was his own idea entirely."

"But why? Just because you'd caught him out?"

"Well . . . actually it was over something else."

"What?"

"Well," I said, a shade guiltily, "you see, while he was up there, draped over the beam about twenty feet above the floor, I, well, took the ladder away, you see."

"You what?"

"And wouldn't let him down until he'd agreed to donate his, you know, thing—to the mess."

"His thing?"

"You know. His fancy toilet."

Dick stared at me for a moment, then: "So you've got it after all . . ."

"M'm."

"You know," Dick said wonderingly, "I never really realized it before, but you're a pretty ruthless bastard when you're opposed."

"Whajamean? I gave him a perfectly straightforward choice, didn't I?"

"Some choice. Give up his pride and joy, or hang up there for eight hours, like a potbellied bat."

Coming Back from a Patrol

On June 6, we received orders to try to discourage the new German two-seaters that were photographing the lines from hitherto unchallengeable heights.

We'd been after them three or four times already, without success. As they were most active at midday, B Flight took off at eleven, as usual, and circled to maximum altitude before heading for the lines.

After we'd been mushing back and forth at air-gasping heights for half an hour, Derby gave the dud-engine signal and turned for home. McKindle also seemed to be having trouble maintaining revs, and Milestone and I had to keep inching back on the throttle so he could keep up.

In case McKindle's Hispano packed up for good, we kept fairly close to the lines. Just as we were turning west for the tenth time or so, a Halberstadt emerged from the clouds below, flying in the same direction.

As it crossed a gap in the clouds, German Archie put up a couple of warning bursts. The observer looked around, saw us, and leaned over to his pilot. The Halberstadt flew on, calm and confident.

By then, we were diving and firing. The observer fired back, coolly and without haste, his tracer coming uncomfortably close. I got him in the Aldis, but the Vickers loosed off only single shots, so I got out of the way hurriedly. By the time I'd finished working the loading handles, the two-seater had disappeared into the cloud, followed by McKindle.

The cloud stretched for about half a mile; then there was another gap. Guessing that the pilot would alter course inside the cloud, I circled over the spot where he had disappeared, and, sure enough, he emerged half a minute later, heading in the opposite direction. I put the wing over and dived. Milestone followed, and opened fire on the right.

The crew were obviously experienced customers. The pilot split-arsed so skilfully that I couldn't keep him in the sights for more than a split second at a time, while the observer kept up an alarmingly accurate fire. When his tracers started to waver between my propeller blades, practically, in a kind of reverse synchronization, I broke off and dived underneath, to try to bring the fixed Lewis gun to bear, from a safe spot. The Halberstadt promptly banked until the observer could see straight down my throat. After a quick burst to hold his attention while Milestone attacked from above, I skipped out of the way.

Milestone must have upset the Halberstadt pilot, for he suddenly dived. Milestone charged after him. The two-seater pulled a sharp, banking turn a thousand feet below. The Dolphin kept on going, leaving a faint trail of exhaust smoke.

No. Good Christ, it wasn't exhaust. He was on fire. Flames seared back from the engine, and the fuselage caught immediately. Seconds later, the whole machine was blazing, from greenish nose to red-white-and-blue tail.

The dive increased. The Dolphin rolled slowly, almost casually, as it hurtled down to perdition.

I caught a glimpse of McKindle hurrying up. I dived at the two-seater again, hunched forward to look wide-eyed through the Aldis. Tracer wisped past. A strut splintered, holes appeared in the wings. The Vickers chattered. I took my thumb off the levers and zoomed, then dived again, firing as the black holes of the cockpits jerked into the view-finder. The pilot slumped, and the two-seater went into a flat spin, like the seed of a Manitoba maple.

McKindle joined up, hanging over the side, looking down the great twisted pillar of smoke that was supported at the bottom by the flaming remains of Milestone's Dolphin.

Snapshots

Intellectual pilots are a rarity, and intellectual adjutants are practically a contradiction in terms. Captain Sylvius Hibbert was both.

"Oh, God, what have they sent us now?" Derby whispered as the new adjutant stuck his head out of the carapace of his shyness for the first time and held forth during dinner on the relative merits of Mottl and Richter as interpreters of Wagner, on Diaghileff ("Such a revelation after the cardboard Victoriana of Covent Garden, don't you think?"), and on Nijinsky's impertinent behavior toward gravity: "His levitation is such," he told Kiddell, "as to inspire in one almost a sensation of discomfort."

"Yeah," Kiddell said.

However, Hibbert was one of the many persons at the squadron who greatly improved with acquaintance, in spite of his passion for Wagner (who was, after all, a German). A slight, twenty-three-year-old with sandy, thinning hair, a gently ascetic face, and a ruined leg, he once trapped me in his sitting room for what seemed like twenty and a half hours, forcing me, through his deferential mien, to listen to all—or part of—or twice—the Wagnerian tetralogy, on his phonograph. That didn't include the time he spent explaining the odd activities of Fasolt and Fafner, Froh, Fricka, and Freia, Woglinde, Wellgunde, Brünnhilde, Flosshilde, Gutrune and Gunther, three Norns and a gnome—or was it three grottos and a Valkyrie?

His deference toward me was born the fourth day after

his arrival, when, learning that I was a pianist of note, in fact several notes, he said, "Incidentally, the use of that phrase to learn the lines of the stave, E, G, B, D, F— *Every Good Boy Deserves Fun*—is pretty trite, shouldn't you say? It's not even especially true. Surely a bad boy also deserves fun—and is more likely to have it. No, one feels that if one has to have mnemonic—memorizing— assistance, for something as simple as E, G, B, D, F, why not something a little more apposite, like Emasculated Goats Bleat Decidedly Falsely, or Elderly Generals Become Depressingly Featherbrained."

"M'm," I said. Then added, somewhat testily, "Incidentally, I'm perfectly well aware of what pnemonic means." Which was true. It was one of the long words I was acquainted with. (The others were cacchinate, obviate, and peristeronic—of or pertaining to pigeons.)

Whereupon, Hibbert had become most humble and apologetic and, instantly assuming that because I was familiar with the word pnemonic, I must be equally at ease with the rest of his poly-syllabic vocabulary, had been lavishing it upon me ever since, confident that we were now in total communication, like a Bertrand Russell conversing with an Alfred North Whitehead; though, in fact, I didn't know what he was talking about three quarters of the time.

And when, one evening, he was waxing enthusiastic about modern French art and I happened to mention that I owned a painting by one of the artists he was mentioning, Matisse, his respect for my mental capacity was immediately matched by his admiration for my aesthetic sensibility. Naturally I didn't mention that the Matisse painting had practically been forced on me at a giveaway price by an impecunious Russian called Rodominov, who had had to throw in an old samovar to clinch the deal.

To everybody's surprise, Hibbert turned out to be an unobtrusively industrious and efficient adjutant; and when he was elected P.M.C., there was an immediate improvement in the messing arrangements. After tutting, whiffling, goggling, and ejaculating over Malt's accounts, he made changes that enabled the mess fees to be reduced from ninety to sixty-five francs a week. This made him exceedingly popular. And when a signal was circulated around the squadrons asking if any first-class cooks were available, Hibbert drew up a glowing testimonial to Sergeant Bixby's abilities and posted him forthwith to the officers' mess at H.Q., where he subsequently became famous for his bread puddings.

Hibbert's most enterprising action was to acquire the culinary services of a woman from the village, a Madame Masson. As a result, the food improved so enormously that instead of fleeing from the dining room to scour away the taste of the food with raw scotch, the pilots, with glad stomachs and soul-soothing cigars, began to linger on even after the port was served. The port, made, I believe, in Birmingham, was the one part of dinner that Madame Masson could do nothing about.

"Well, at least it's better than Cuban wum," Monty Murgatroyd said.

We had a visitor in the mess that evening, a rather stolid U.S. Army major with an astonishing number of medals, considering he'd been in Yurrup for only three weeks.

"Wum?" he asked.

"Yes. You know, old bean. As in Jamaica wum. I watched them make it in Cuba, once. They mix it with all kinds of dweadful foweign objects, you know: spiders, mice dwoppings, and so forth. Delibewately, as faw as I could make out."

"You've been to Cuba?" Orville asked.

"He was a gun-runner there," Blackbourne said, beaming proudly at his deputy.

"He was what?"

"Well, they wewe always having upwisings and things,

113

you see, and there was a lot of money to be made in arms," Monty said. "I must have supplied about five diffewent sets of webels with Mausers and ill-fitting ammo —until they incarcewated me in Havana jail."

We all gazed at Monty in astonishment.

"Get away," Derby snorted. "France is the furthest you've ever been from the playing fields of Eton."

"Eton? Deaw old chappy, I've hardly even been to school, let alone Eton. I had a simply marvellous tutor when I was a pip-squeak, who quite spoiled me for further education. Though I did go to Fallow fow a year, when I was fourteen." He regarded me politely. "I believe you'we acquainted with that school, awen't you, Major?"

"M'yes. I didn't last quite a year, though. In fact, they threw me out the day after I arrived."

"Oh, come on, Monty," Charles ffoliot said in his bored voice. "How could you have been a gun-runner in Cuba? You're only about nineteen."

"Twenty-five," Blackbourne said.

There was a surprised murmur. "Twenty-five? He can't be, not with a face like that."

"My face never seems to learn fwom expewience," Monty said regretfully.

"That's how he got away with so much," Blackbourne said. "Tell them how you got out of that jail in Havana, Monty."

"Oh, it was easy, weally. I just blubbered."

"Blubbered?"

"Yes. I'll show you." And Monty's long, smooth face slowly collapsed, until he looked like a filleted missionary. His lips and chin began to quiver, tears rained down his pink cheeks, and a heart-rending boohooing racked his slender frame.

"Blubbewing has got me out of an awful lot of difficulties," Monty explained, once the shrieks of laughter had subsided. "The guards in the pwison couldn't beaw it, you see, and one of them went to His Bwitannic Majesty's Ambassadow and Plenipotentiawy, who bailed me out on the understanding that I would join up the moment I wetuwned to England. It was 1914, you see."

"And did you?"

"Of course," Monty said, affronted. "I would hardly bweak a solemn pwomise, would I? Mind you, I took good care not to go home fow another thwee years. But I certainly joined up the moment I *did* get back."

Everybody listened, fascinated, as his past history unfolded like a soiled banner. His mother having remarried, he had run away to sea at the age of fifteen and promptly run slap into a Colombian revolution. His ship's captain had arranged for a band of revolutionaries to raid the ship's gun rack while the captain's back was turned, presumably for some pecuniary consideration. Not being apprised of this fact, Monty and the third mate had resisted the boarding party, killing one of them. The centralist forces had rewarded Monty and the mate with commissions in the Colombian Navy. This was just as well, as their own captain had thrown them off the ship when he learned what had happened.

Unfortunately, the Colombian Navy—a nineteenth-century gunboat—had foundered before Monty and his friend could report on board. By this time, the government's gratitude had cooled, and the two of them had found themselves stranded in Bogotá with only about eight or nine million pesos between them. ("There was a certain amount of inflation in Colombia at the time.") They had managed to sign on with a New York-bound freighter, but conditions on board had been so bad that they'd been forced to steal a lifeboat and make for Florida. It was this boat, suitably repainted and renamed (*The Skylark*) that Monty had subsequently used to ship old rifles and ammunition to his dishonest broker in Havana.

As we moved to the ante-room and ordered drinks, the U.S. major whispered, "That Lieutenant Murgatroyd

—we sure don't have anybody like that in our flying service. How'd he ever get past your selection board?"

"Blubbered, presumably."

The major looked at me for a moment, then: "And that friend of his—Foley, is it?"

"ffoliot, yes."

"Is he all right? I mean, you know?"

"Oh, yes. He's one of our best pilots."

"Yeah? But he called me darling."

The major became aware that the pilots were arranging themselves in a line and raising their glasses toward the bar. He hastily raised his own, and turned smartly in the same direction, perhaps thinking this was another ceremonial toast to the King.

When he saw the toilet, with its graceful, fluted bowl surmounting the sculptured coils and grinning visage of the dolphin, his glass slipped from his hand. He managed to catch it, but his knuckles got pretty drenched in Johnnie Walker.

The toilet had been reposing there above the bar for some time now. At first, the pilots had regarded it quite offendedly, as if they thought I was trying to tell them something about their past accomplishments. However, as their successes mounted—Kiddell alone had brought down six aircraft since its ceremonial installation—this defensive attitude had slowly given way to one of acceptance, and finally to considerable pride when pilots from other squadrons began to drop in to admire it. It was completely accepted even before Derby began to raise his glass to it after dinner in a formal toast to the king of toilets (thus establishing one of the R.A.F.'s most enduring and least publicized traditions).

As the major averted his eyes from the misplaced sanitary appliance, Derby came up to him, his arm linked through Hibbert's.

"I hear our esteemed brigadier is visiting us in a couple

of days," Derby said. "He once commanded this squadron, you know."

"Yes, I know."

"Did you know that he wiped out the squadron twice, in about six weeks?"

"Where'd you hear that?"

"Hibbert, here. He was with this squadron back in 1915. Go on, tell him, Hib."

"You shouldn't exaggerate, Derby," Hibbert murmured. "He didn't wipe it out—not entirely, anyway."

I knew from Hibbert's records that he'd spent most of 1916 in hospital and had not flown since; but I must have missed the bit about his being a former member of the squadron.

"What happened?" I asked.

"Go on, tell him, Hibbert."

"Well . . . we had the Vickers Gunbus then, and it was just too slow for shooting up trenches, and, well, Major Soames, as he was then . . ." He stopped, looking unhappy. Hibbert didn't enjoy gossiping, except about the lives of the French poets, particularly Verlaine.

"Go on," Derby urged.

"Well, Soames insisted on strafing from a hundred feet or less . . ."

"And they lost every single pilot, and then very nearly every single replacement, in about six weeks." Derby finished triumphantly.

Hibbert leaned over at an angle, to take the weight off his bad leg. "It's certainly true that when I arrived, there was only two left among the replacements, but . . ."

"Is that when you were shot down, Hib?"

"Yes."

"H'm. Well, there's never been a shortage of aggressive C.O.s," I said diplomatically.

"I wonder if that's why Soames had always had it in for this squadron," Derby mused, "and why he seems to resent our success so much. Because we're a reminder of his own criminal regime."

"Steady, old man," Hibbert murmured.

"And here was I thinking it was just old Bandy's face that was upsetting him so much."

A discreet move away from this slander brought me close to the U.S. major. He was badgering Orville France again. Orville had been trying to avoid the visitor all evening.

"Look, France, you put in a request for a transfer. Right?"

"But I'll end up flying Spads, or Nieuports again, sir."

"What's wrong with them?"

"Nothing, sir. But they're not in the same class as the Dolphin."

"Hell, man, I've told you there's a promotion in it. Haven't you any ambition?"

"Sure. But—"

"Say, listen, Major," I said, leaning on the bar at an important angle. "I'd like to ask you something."

The major looked irritated but answered politely enough, "Yes?"

"Tell me—what do you think of parachutes?"

There was a massed groan from the pilots.

"Oh, no."

"Lord, he's off again."

"Parachutes?" the major said, as if it were one of Hibbert's new words.

McKindle explained in a long-suffering sort of way. "For days," he told the major, "he's been chewing our ears off on the subject. Aye, and paistering the curr-nel aboot ut as well."

"I haven't been paistering the colonel at all," I said shortly.

"No? Well how is ut he'll no even speak tae us any more, on the tailyphone?"

"That's only because he has this absurd phobia about

118

the telephone," I said curtly. I turned back to the visitor. "Anyway, what do you think, Major? Why shouldn't pilots be given parachutes?"

"No aviator worth his salt would dream of wearing a parachute," the major said, and turned back to Orville. "Look, France—"

"Why not?"

"What? Why not?" The major refused to take his gimlet eye off Orville. "Apart from anything else, it's just not practical."

"How?"

Orville said quickly, "I don't see why it's not practical. After all, the kite-balloon guys have them, why not us?"

Several of the pilots looked at him irritably. All week, Orville had been as scornful of the parachute idea as everybody else.

But, of course, Orville was just seizing the opportunity to change the subject.

"It would be cowardly, wearing a parachute," a new pilot said disdainfully. "It's an officer's duty to ride his plane down."

"Even with, say, the wings torn off?" I asked.

The young pilot shuffled his feet, pouting defiantly.

"For God's sake, parachutes are for stuntmen," Derby said. "They're all right for pleasing the crowds, but not for real flyers."

There was a murmur of agreement.

"Anyway," he added, "you can't wear them in an aircraft, they take up too much room. So I don't know why you keep on about it."

"No pilots wear parachutes," Kiddell said. "Not the Germans or the Austrians, or the British, French, Italians, Americans—nobody does."

"We should just go on killing ourselves unnecessarily?"

"It's just not done, that's all," the new pilot mumbled sulkily.

"No, wait a minute," Blackbourne put in smoothly.

"I've been thinking about it. Bart's not entirely talking through his hat, you know."

"Oh, for Chrissake," Kiddell said. "Don't you start, Pash."

"I suppose," Blackbourne went on thoughtfully, "that just because nobody's using them doesn't mean it's not a good idea, theoretically. I must admit I wouldn't feel too unpatriotic, jumping by parachute from a disabled plane." The new pilot looked at Blackbourne in a shocked way. "But there are just too many practical problems, Bart. As Derby says, apart from anything else, they're far too bulky. There's little enough room in the cockpit as it is, without a dashed great sackful of silk on your back."

"Right," the U.S. major said.

"I don't know," Orville said cheerfully. "They've licked plenty of other problems in this war. I don't see why they can't do something about them being so bulky."

"It is rather surprising we don't use them," Hibbert said hesitantly, rubbing his leg, "when you think about it."

"But you can't *use* them in aircraft," Derby said stubbornly.

"They've been using them for years," I said.

"So you say," ffoliot said, yawning.

"It's true, small f. I've been looking it up. I've told you about that American girl. She's jumped hundreds of times, apparently."

"A stunt."

"The first man to jump, another American, Albert Berry—I gather he was an army man—jumped from a Benoist pusher as long ago as nineteen twelve."

"There you are, see?" Orville cried. "People have been flinging themselves out of planes for five years. So why aren't they being developed and improved—and used?"

There was a silence. After a moment, Orville turned to the major and said, "Uh, about the transfer, sir."

"Yeah," the major said. He hesitated, then: "Yeah,

120

well, look, maybe you better stay where you are, France. You . . ." He cleared his throat. "You seem to be settling down pretty good, and . . . Well, maybe it wouldn't be right to move you just yet," he said, his expression plainly indicating that he considered Orville had already spent too long with the British to be rehabilitated.

It was true enough that I'd brought the subject up with Wing a few times, at first over the telephone, then in person when the colonel refused to pick up the instrument any more.

"I'm perfectly well aware it's possible to jump from aeroplanes," Ashworth shouted as he hurried across the lawn at Wing H.Q. "But there hasn't been the slightest demand from the pilots for parachutes. The very opposite, in fact. They simply won't have them. And will you please stop running behind me like the back end of a pantomime horse!"

"But that's a matter of education, sir," I whined, still following him. "They didn't want the Bristol Monoplane or the Tripe, or several other unconventional—"

"Stop treading on my heels, dammit! Now look what you've done—one of them's come off!"

"We've resisted far too many unusual designs, Colonel —*and* brilliant ideas."

"Major Balls, I'm going to my room now, for my nap," the colonel said, as he scurried into the house. "Call me if—"

"The thing is, they just weren't advertised properly, that's all."

"—if anything important comes up, will you?"

I pattered after him, across the lounge.

"It's a matter of education, sir," I went on. "The idea of this life-saving device being sissy has simply grown out of prejudice, conservatism, ignorance, superstition, insensitivity—"

"God damn it, there goes my other heel!"

"—and misguided tradition, Colonel," I said, as he ran down the corridor toward his room. "But all we need, sir, is a little pub—"

There was an echoing crash in the corridor.

"—licity," I said, trailing off a bit, as he had slammed the door in my face.

I went out into the garden again. Luckily his window was open. "And another thing, sir," I called through, being careful not to tread on the bindweed, spotted cowbane, and bladder campion that grew in profusion below the window, "if parachutes are impractical at the moment, it's only because nobody's bothering to make them otherwise. I understand the problems are relatively easy to solve, mostly a matter of—"

There was a wild cry from inside the room. A moment later, the colonel's favorite teapot came sailing out the window, followed by an old copy of *The Wipers Times,* a tooth mug, a picture of his wife, and, for some strange reason, a pair of suspenders, or braces as I believe the colonel would call them—though at the moment he seemed too busy raving and stamping his foot impotently in there and uttering shrill cries of hopeless rage to call them anything.

Two or three days later, we had another visit from the brigade commander.

Most of the pilots were absent when Soames arrived with his pet major, three or four other staff officers, and his biographer. There'd been a binge in the mess the night before, to celebrate another victorious day's work, and most of the furniture had been smashed. To replace it, a high-spirited party under Captain Derby had gone out in the tender that wet morning, to loot one of the front-line villages that was gradually being reduced to rubble and firewood by the artillery bombardment.

Soames seemed rather put out by the casual reception: just Hibbert and me, and some wilting tulips. I suppose he'd gotten used to Malt's rather more formal receptions.

"Where the devil is everybody?" he asked sharply.

"Hard at work, sir," I said enthusiastically, flapping the raindrops off my old raincoat. "Hard at work."

He tugged viciously at his mustache as if trying to straighten it, hesitated, then: "Yes. Well. Let's not waste any more time. Let's get on with it," he snapped. He shot a glance approximately in my direction and sneered, "That is, if the major here doesn't mind getting his raincoat wet."

"Not at all, not at all," I riposted. I was in a particularly witty humor that morning.

"No. Rather needs a good scrubbing anyway, shouldn't you say?"

As he and his band strode toward the barn: "Well, I see you've been adding quite a bit to your score, Bandy," he sneered. "I suppose you'll expect me to congratulate you for taking time off from your proper duties?"

"Thank you very much, sir," I said, as if he *had* congratulated me.

He snorted and lashed out with his stick at a poor, inoffensive daisy.

"Actually, the work's well in hand, sir," Hibbert said loyally.

The brigadier didn't deign to answer, but looked more peevish than ever.

As I pottered along among the red-tabs, I looked around for the brigadier's personal secretary. He was bringing up the rear. I dropped back to have a word with him.

I'd been looking forward to this conversation with Lieutenant Mickle for weeks. I had it all planned and rehearsed. First a brief introduction, designed to put him at his ease.

Accordingly, I sidled up to him and cleared my throat.

"You're Mickle, aren't you?" I said in a friendly way.

"Yes, sir."

"I don't think we've met formally, have we? My name's Bandy."

"I know."

"You used to be a writer, I hear."

"Yes." (Luckily this carefully planned conversation didn't depend on Mickle's being loquacious. He was perfectly entitled to be as monosyllabic as he liked.)

"You once wrote a couple of biographies of Parry and Stanford, I believe. That's how you got this job with the brigadier, isn't it?"

"Yes."

"That's very interesting. I once played a piece by Parry on the piano. Or was it Stanford?"

"I don't know."

"But listen, what on earth made you want to write about a couple of inferior composers like them?"

He glanced at me expressionlessly as we splashed through the rain. "My wife is a Stanford," he said.

He had his hand stuck in his tunic. I thought he was trying to look Napoleonic, until I realized it was because he was holding his notebook under there, to keep it out of the rain.

Having put him at his ease, I now proceeded to the second stage of the carefully planned exchange.

"And tell me, Mickle," I said, barely able to keep a snigger of anticipation at bay, "you're married, aren't you? Any children?"

"Five." (I already knew this. He *did* have five children. That was important.)

"Ah. Well, nice chatting to you," I said, and started to move away. Then moved in again, for the kill. "Five children, eh?" I said, my mouth twitching. "And is it true what they say, in that well-known English expression?"

"Is what true?"

"That *many a mickle makes a muckle?*" I said loudly; and opened my mouth, ready to laugh.

He just looked at me as if I had gockies sticking out of my nose.

Obviously no sense of humor.

"What the hell is this?"

I started, dragged away from my musings by the sound of the brigadier's voice.

After he had inspected the squadron office-*cum*-barn, he had looked more discontented than ever. But he had said nothing until he walked into the first of the Besseneau hangars.

"What the hell is this?" he repeated shrilly.

Because of the rain, C Flight's aircraft were all crowded under cover.

"What, sir?"

"This paintwork, damn you!" he shouted. "What the devil d'you think you're playing at, Bandy?"

"Paintwork?" I enquired. "You mean the paintwork on the aircraft?"

I'd had bright yellow panels painted on the fuselages of the Dolphins, with vertical blue stripes superimposed: two for leaders, one for deputy leaders.

Well, the Germans could paint their buses any color they liked, so I didn't see why we couldn't make our aircraft a little more distinctive as well.

I gathered, though, that the brigadier didn't agree.

"Tarting up the equipment this way! What the hell d'you think these machines are—bloody billboards?" he shouted, and went on in that fashion at some length, his pale eyes all bloodshot and his mustache all knotted.

I couldn't understand why he was gibbering so frightfully. I knew of at least one other squadron, 213, that had sloping red, white and blue bands on its aircraft, to identify flight commanders and deputies. I'd been inspired to emulate them one morning when some joker (Derby, I think) had tied large pink bows on my streamers, making me so conspicuous that Camels, S.E.s, D.H.s and French 1½-Strutters had come hurrying up from all directions to take a look; and on arriving back at the field, the commander of the squadron opposite had strolled across to ask if I'd care to borrow his hair net.

"Are these modifications authorized?" Soames stormed.

"Authorized? Certainly. I authorized them."

"This is defacing War Department property; you realize that, do you?"

He didn't know the half of it. I'd also coaxed the metalworkers into fabricating yellow spinners to streamline the propeller bosses. Luckily they hadn't yet been fitted.

"Well, these markings are much easier to see than streamers, you see. I thought—"

"You thought! We've had a damn sight too much thinking from you, Bandy," Soames shouted, his face bloated with fury; and he continued to rave for some time, apparently indifferent to the presence of several other ranks.

Perhaps he hadn't noticed them. They were certainly doing their best to hide.

I listened interestedly to the brigadier's diatribe, nodding appreciatively now and again at some of his more telling points. My understanding nods, though, seemed to enrage him still further. Soon he was positively shaking all over with an almost berserk fury, as if missing on half of his mental cylinders.

"And stop nodding and humming as if I were merely giving you the grocery list, God damn you!" he screamed. To make matters worse, he caught sight of his personal biographer. Mickle was busily recording his masters intemperancies. "Don't put that in, Mickle," he screamed. "What the hell d'you think you're doing? Who the bloody hell told you to take all this down?"

Mickle blinked his rather prominent eyes a couple of

times and faltered, "But sir, you said I was to write every-thing down this afternoon, in case a *bon mot* or witticism escaped your lips, you said, that you might wish to pass on to poster—"

The general hurled his swagger-stick at the luckless lieutenant. It narrowly missed the staff-major and smacked against the canvas wall of the hangar. "I'll tell you when to write, you miserable scribbler!" he shrieked. "Get out of my sight! Go on, get out!"

As Mickle hurried out of the hangar, Soames rounded on me again. "As for you, you wretched, bloody man . . ." He was gasping for breath. His brigade major turned away and stared out into the rain. "As for you, just get that gaudy mess covered up immediately, do you understand? I want the cockades restored by tomorrow morning, do you understand?"

I thought perhaps I'd better mollify him a bit, especially as I had something important to discuss with him. "Well, all right," I said. "If you really think it's not such a good idea, naturally I'll have the panels painted over, if, if you really insist, sir. I mean, the last thing I want to do is anything detrimental to the, you know, Air Force. So if you're *absolutely* sure you don't think it's such a good idea . . ."

The veins stood out on his brow like corduroy pants.

"Yes, well, I'll see to it right away," I said hurriedly. "Oh, Sergeant?"

As the brigadier lurched out of the hangar, the sergeant whispered, "What about the spinners? I was going to fit them this morning."

"Better wait until he's gone," I whispered back.

"You still want them fitted?"

"Sure. Why not?" I said, looking at him with surprised eyebrows. "He didn't say anything about not having them, did he? He was just talking about the panels, you see."

Perhaps it was just as well that Soames didn't go into

the mess that morning. He was obviously not in the mood just then to appreciate our squadron emblem. He went from the hangar straight back to the staff cars.

"Are you sure you won't stay for lunch, sir?" I asked. "We're having steak and kidney pudding today."

He wouldn't answer.

"And chocolate mousse too," I said.

He turned his back and glared blindly down the tree-lined avenue, breathing with some difficulty, his fingers crooked in the shape of a throat.

"Besides," I said, "I wanted to discuss something, sir. Parachutes, actually."

He turned, still trembling. "What?"

"I wanted to ask why nobody's ever thought of issuing flying crews parachutes, Brigadier."

"Parachutes?"

"Yes. After all, the balloon observers get them, why not us?"

"Are you serious?"

"Certainly," I said, raising my eyebrows. "I've already taken it up several times with the colonel."

"Yes? And what did he say?"

"Well, frankly, he was a bit taken aback at first. But only because it's a new idea, Brigadier. But that doesn't alter the fact," I went on reasonably, "that it seems a considerable gap in our organization, not having them. You know, I didn't realize it before, but Hibbert tells me we've had parachutes since shortly after the French Revolution, Brig."

Soames winced exhaustedly. Perhaps the French Revolution was still a sore point with him.

"And it seems kind of remiss of us not to be using them in aviation, after all this time. I mean—"

He walked away. I hurried after him. "No, but listen," I said, plucking at his sleeve. "I gather they have several workable designs in the United States that nobody over here has made any attempt to investigate. And then there's

128

the British Guardian Angel, that's said to be very promising. Well, sir, I thought that it's scandalous that nothing seems to have been done about it. I mean, it must cost hundreds of pounds to train pilots, and surely it's only common sense to protect our investment, even if not for humanitarian reasons. I mean—"

The brigadier scrambled into the back of the leading staff car, his mustache getting frightfully twisted up again.

"I mean," I said, putting my foot on the running board, "I know balloon parachutes are too bulky for aircraft use, but this Guardian Angel design is said to be entirely feasible for aircraft. If you could give me official permission to investigate the situation, Brig, I'm sure—"

"What the bloody hell are you waiting for," Soames said hoarsely to his driver. "Hurry up, drive on, for God's sake . . ."

The car jerked forward. My foot scraped along the running board and thumped against the tool box. I removed my brown shoe quickly before it got entangled in the rear-wheel spokes. The car turned toward the poplar'd driveway, skidding frantically in the gravel.

"Stop!" Soames shouted. The car jerked to a stop. He turned, his face a really unhealthy hue.

"Oh, yes," he said, "I heard all about that conversation you had with my wife, about parachutes." He stopped, realizing that everybody was listening with more interest than ever. He gestured violently. "Come here."

I trotted up hopefully. He lowered his voice, his eyes looking like bathwater whorling down two plug holes. There was a yellowish sort of foam at the corner of his mouth. "Yes, it was very good of you to entertain Mrs. Soames the other day," he said, his voice trembling. "Very gallant, rescuing a lady in distress. Even fixing up a room for her. You moved out first of course, didn't you? Didn't you?"

"But of course I don't expect the truth from you. But I'll tell you this, Bandy. If I ever hear of you being gallant again that way, I'll, by God, move heaven and earth to ruin you. I promise you that."

With a final, murderous look, he gestured viciously at the driver, and the car skidded off into the downpour, followed by the other staff car, with its white-faced occupants.

I watched him go, plucking thoughtfully at my lower lip.

I was wondering if that was the reason he was in something of a snit that morning. Because he was a trifle jealous of his wife?

That's Carson, on the Left

On the fourth of July, there was a local attack organized by the Australian General Monash, an onslaught on a three-mile front. Ten Aussie battalions and four American companies took part, supported by over seventy tanks.

The attack was against Hamel and Vaire Wood, an area I knew uncommonly well, for I had fought over it with the 13th Bicycles only a few months before. Our squadron was given the job of beating up as much noise as possible, by flying a few feet up along the line of advance, the purpose being to drown out the grindings of the new Mark V tanks.

Monash was one of the efficient generals, and it turned out the first truly successful battle I'd ever taken part in. As we soared over Vaire Wood at about four in the morning, with the smoke from exploding gas shells and rockets cancelling the sky's first attempts at dawn, we caught glimpses of the enemy running about in confusion, still wearing their respirators. The tanks had taken them completely by surprise.

In front of Hamel, we saw twinkling lights from several machine-gun nests. I waggled the wings and fell toward them almost vertically, firing long bursts. The other planes followed, diving and zooming in all directions, and in seconds a confusing web of tracer was being spun all over the flare-lit sky. Curiously, some of the tracer rebounded from the earth and curved away in lazy parabolas, before fading into the murk.

131

As I levelled out after a third strafe, a wheel suddenly appeared over the port wing. I stared stupidly at it, as it drifted toward my head. I looked up. *Jesus Christ!* A Dolphin thirty-six inches overhead, its propeller flashing almost within the arc of my prop.

It was a violently convulsive reflex that shot the stick forward, only a split-second before the other machine started to bank. My bus fell on its back and went into a vicious flat spin. I was almost on the ground before I got it the right way up again, the wires shrieking, the wings groaning, and my teeth chattering.

It was sunrise before my teeth met again on friendly terms.

By then the battle was over, and lines of grey prisoners were starting to snake back toward Villers-Bretonneux.

Just as we were turning for home, the sky suddenly filled with parachutes.

For nearly half a minute, I really thought that narrow escape had unhinged me. The parachutes looked quite ethereal, the rising sun drenching their white canopies in heavenly pink. Then, as the Dolphin roared past one of them, I recognized its all too substantial cargo, the familiar WD boxes with the rope handles.

After four years of repeated failure to bring up supplies through support trenches in time to reinforce the forward troops before the inevitable counter-attack came, it had finally occurred to somebody to employ a piece of equipment that had been available to them since round about the time that old Charlotte Corday so rudely disturbed Marat at his ablutions.

Carson was back. He'd spent three weeks in hospital in Boulogne, having his face cleaned up and operated on. He walked aggressively into the mess late one afternoon with his head swathed in bandages.

"Hello, Carson."

"Hello, Carson. You back?"

The reception was not exactly hearts and flowers. There wasn't a soul in the squadron Carson hadn't offended at one time or another.

He'd taken his Bolshie outlook to hospital with him, too, with a vengeance. It was said that he had clashed several times with the specialist who'd fixed up his face. We'd heard about it from a visiting pilot, who said Carson had caused an uproar at No. 1 General by making some pretty insulting remarks about the surgeon's competence.

"Pompous bastard," Carson grated through his green-tinged bandages when we asked him about it. "Swanking to the matron about the important people he knew, and how good it was of him to take time off from his Harley Street practice to give us brave boys the benefit of his surgical talents. I told him that as far as I was concerned he was just a superior sort of mechanic, and I'd judge whether he was as incompetent as the rest of the fraternity when I'd seen the result of his handiwork."

"Jesus," Kiddell said, "somebody's going to spread-eagle you on a gun carriage one of these days."

"When do the bandages come off?" Ray Middleton asked, touching his own handsome features as if for re-assurance that they were still in place.

"Next week, they said. But the hell with that; I'm tearing them off in a couple of days. Waiter!"

"Sir?"

"Whisky!"

"Sir."

"Well, what's been happening while I was away?" he asked, looking around arrogantly. "Anyone dead, maimed, or otherwise sacrificed on the altar of international finance?"

He turned his vicious brown eyes on me, the greenish bandages over his lips fluttering as he spoke. "I hear you've been picking off a few more unhappy Huns, Bandy. Is that right?"

He wasn't wasting much time resuming his former

hobby of pricking me to see how much hot air escaped.

"I also hear the brass have taken us a stage further in losing the war, God bless 'em."

He was referring to the latest German attack, in the Chemin-des-Dames sector. Field Marshal Haig, or Marshal Foch, or both, had been convinced that the next onslaught would fall on the front north of the Somme, against the British. So naturally the Germans had attacked in the south, against the French.

It was another catastrophe, like the March attack. The French commander in that area, a certain General Duchesne, had crammed practically all his men into the front lines, down there in the Joan of Arc country—Compiègne Forest to Rheims. Apparently, nobody had told Duchesne about the brilliant new German tactics of infiltrating past strong points and pressing on regardless, leaving the mopping up to the follow-on troops. Or, more likely, they'd told him but he had refused to listen.

The result was, the Germans were now back where they'd been in 1914, on the Marne.

"Maybe they'll get to Versailles and wipe out Supreme Headquarters," Carson said hopefully.

"Jesus, Carson, don't you want us to win this war?" Kiddell snapped.

Kiddell didn't like Carson at the best of times, Also, he was still in a bad temper after missing an opportunity that afternoon, because of a Number Two stoppage, to shoot down a Pfalz. Then, on the way back, his engine, on which he had personally lavished hours of attention, had suffered a connecting-rod failure. He had smashed his beloved Dolphin so badly on landing that it had had to be trundled back to the aircraft depot on a lorry. He still had a bruise where his forehead had met one of the gun butts.

"I'm hoping we lose," Carson snarled, "to bring our own revolution that much closer."

"You could be shot for talking like that."

"That's why we will have a revolution, Kiddell, because of answers like that. Anyway, at least I know now who I'll go after first. That surgeon, with his Lord This and the Duchess of That, and his condescending smirk."

Two mornings later, as I was strolling toward the barn with Hibbert, a cry of fury howled through the trees. As the bellows of rage went on and on, we ran toward the Nissen huts beyond the barn to find about a dozen pilots, some in flying gear, others in pajamas and dressing gowns, clustered at the door of one of the huts, peering cautiously inside. They were all whispering excitedly.

I pushed through, and went inside. After the brilliant morning sunlight, it took several seconds for my eyes to adjust to the gloom.

Kiddell was standing, half-dressed, at the door. Middleton and France were still in bed, sitting bolt upright, staring at Carson.

"Look what that bastard has done! Look what he's done!" he was shrieking. "Oh, my God, my face!"

Carson had just unwound his bandages. As he turned his livid face away from the mirror, I started back. There was a scrunching sound as I ran over Kiddell's bare feet. He was too shaken to feel a thing.

The surgeon had fixed Carson's face, all right. He had picked it marvellously clean of gunpowder grains.

He had also sewed a wide, fixed, cheerful smile onto Carson's lips.

Looking a Bit Lopsided

"Captain Blackpool, isn't it?" the G.O.C. said, from the head of the table.

"Yes, sir. Blackbourne, actually."

"Blackbourne, that's what I meant. Navy?"

"Yes, sir."

"Yes, I thought you had the look of the Navy about you. Perhaps it's that naval uniform you're wearing. Not one of the Dorset Blackbournes, are you?"

"Well, my father lives in Devon, actually, when he's ashore."

"Of course, I meant Devon. Well, let's hope the admiral is ashore when you go home on leave in a few days, Blackbourne."

"Leave, sir?"

"Oh, didn't I tell you? Leave is being resumed in a few days, now the emergency seems to be over."

A gratified murmur ran round the crowded dining room.

"And I don't think I'll be committing an indiscretion, Blackbourne, if I mention that you'll be one of the several people in this squadron going home with a D.F.C."

There was another buzz from the pilots, and smiles from the red-tabbed visitors. "Good old Pash," somebody called.

After a few more words with a glowing Blackbourne, the G.O.C. looked down the table at Orville.

"Let me see, now, you're . . . ?"

"Lieutenant France, sir."

"Ah, yes, the American. Entente Cordiale, eh? Britain and France—Lieutenant France, that is." Orville smiled dutifully. "Six, isn't it?"

"Sir?"

"You've brought down six balloons in the last month. No need to look surprised, my boy. I read all the reports, you know," the G.O.C. lied gruffly.

His G.S.O.1, Lieutenant-Colonel Treadwell, picked up a champagne glass and twirled it casually in his strong, brown fingers. He had obviously briefed the old man well, on all the right things to say. The G.O.C. was certainly saying them. It was the first time he'd visited the squadron, and the pilots were plainly enchanted with his apparent knowledgeability, as well as his easy informality.

"Well, Bandy! Created quite a mess, haven't you?"

I pushed my pudding dish over the wine stain in the table cloth before realizing that he was referring to the dining room.

"Almost as good as ours, isn't it, Andrews?"

"Certainly is, sir."

The G.O.C. nodded. "Though we rarely have champagne as good as this. Veuve Cliquot. Where did you get it?"

"Our enterprising adjutant here, Captain Hibbert, made a special trip to Rheims for it," I said, touching my swollen cheek tenderly. I'd woken up that morning with a toothache.

"Ah. Poor beleaguered Rheims. Hibbert, eh? You're the chap with the collection of bedroom utensils."

"I believe you're thinking of the former adjutant, sir."

"That's right. I was." The general turned back to me. "You don't seem to be eating much of this excellent food, Major."

"It's my tooth, sir. It's giving me heck."

"Oh, I see. I thought your face was a trifle lopsided, but I didn't like to say anything, in case . . . Toothache, eh? That's too bad."

"It's all this office work," I muffled, sounding as if I were trapped in a warehouse filled with cotton wool. "It seems to be having a somewhat deleterious effect on my molars."

"Somewhat? Your right cheek is a good eight months preggers," Charles ffoliot drawled.

Woofer Smith leaned forward, looking earnestly sympathetic. "Don't worry about it, though, Maje," he said soothingly. "I'm sure it'll go down after a while. The thing is not to worry about it. Try not to think about that awful swollen flesh of yours."

I looked at him viciously. Besides being so maddeningly comforting, Smith was always using the most enraging words in the language against you. Words like *flesh, pot, scanty, sullen* and so forth. Even normally imperturbable Pash Blackbourne had flinched and seethed the other day when Smith, sympathizing over Pash's slightly expanding middle, had employed the worst Middle English word of all: *girth*.

Really, I don't know how the early Anglo-Saxons had been able to stand each other, using words like that practically the whole time. Not to mention their disgusting four-letter words. Why hadn't they employed decent, upright terms derived from Latin and other respectable sources?

As for Smith, I was beginning to suspect that he was employing this etymological aggression deliberately, to unsettle his peers. I was rather hoping he'd be shot down, soon.

I realized that the G.O.C. was talking again.

"Sorry, sir . . . ?"

"I was saying you ought to see a dentist about it."

"Oh, no, that won't be necessary," I said quickly. "It'll go away, sir."

"Make a note of it, Andrews? Major Bandy—teeth."

"No, no, don't put that in, Mickle," I moaned.

The general turned his face away to avoid the sight of my cheek, or to hide a smile. "What's that chap's name in Paris. They say he's quite good. That American. Robinson, that's it."

"No, I don't need a dentist," I whimpered. "Honest, it doesn't bother me one bit."

"Fix it up, will you, Captain? Can't have young Bandy here looking so dashed asymmetrical. Keep expecting to see him fall over with a crash, what?"

"But," I said. But the G.O.C. was now addressing Treadwell in a loud whisper.

"Really don't know what Arthur's talking about," he said. "Seems to me things are going quite well. Quite well." He darted his head in another direction. "Ashworth!"

Colonel Ashworth started, dropping some Camembert into his port.

"Thought you said the food here was abominable, Ashworth. Think it's rather good myself."

Ashworth mumbled something about being pleasantly surprised himself.

"Delicious, in fact. A splendid dinner," the G.O.C. said. "With, if you'll forgive me saying so, Bandy, with the possible exception of the pudding. Your French cook certainly has a way with the veal, not to mention the lobster salad—never tasted anything so good in me life. But I feel she doesn't quite have the reverent approach that our English cooks bring to this particular dessert, or achieve the 'sweet harmony' of the time-honored constituents. No, I'm afraid she hasn't entirely succeeded in obtaining the proper fibrous quality of the one, nor the uneven consistency of the other."

"No, I don't think Madame Masson quite understands prunes and custard," I mumbled.

After blessedly short speeches from the visitors and an amusing reply from Pash, the pilots trooped eagerly into the ante-room, and waited to see how the general would react to the *décor*.

However, he must have been briefed about that, too,

for after everybody had been served, he turned to the toilet and raised his glass.

"The Dolphin," he intoned gravely.

There was a gratified rumble from behind the long line of raised glasses, and a communal gurgle.

"May it continue to be flushed with success," the G.O.C. added, and smiled around almost bashfully at the loud response.

As he and his entourage settled themselves in the armchairs near the french window, the evening sun came up like footlights, casting spiky shadows over the bright green grass of the airfield.

"Very comfy indeed," the G.O.C. said contentedly, looking around at the new furniture and carpets, Derby's framed cartoons on the wall opposite the propeller and black cross, and the beautifully carpentered bar with its ranks of gleaming bottles.

The general's aide leaned forward. "Cigar, Bandy?"

"No, thank you. I have my pipe," I said, drawing it out and showing it off proudly to the throng of staff officers.

Colonel Ashworth looked interested and asked to see it. He probably thought I was flattering him by imitation; but it was just that I like the look of myself with a pipe clenched between my manly teeth. I'd been studying the effect in a mirror for several days now, trying to get just the right—puff—degree of authority and cogitative—suck —sagacity. As soon as I looked sufficiently strong and silent, I would purchase some tobacco to go with it.

Ashworth peered closely at the trade mark on the stem. " 'Briar Rabbit' " he read. "Never heard of it. Must be a new make." He slipped it absent-mindedly into his pocket.

"Er . . . ?" I smiled, holding out my hand. He dropped a spent match into it.

The noise level rose as more drinks were passed around. The pilots were in a boisterous mood, still celebrating the previous day's work. The squadron had brought down a record twenty-one e.a. without loss, though three of the pilots had crash-landed, including Carson. His engine had been riddled with bullets. He had overturned in a shell crater.

He was still looking a bit dazed, though it was possible this was caused at least as much by his altered appearance as by the crack-up. The fixed smile that the surgeon had worked into place was such a cheery grimace that strangers had begun to react quite positively toward him. Only that morning, when he had turned it in the direction of a replacement, the pilot had shaken Carson's hand so warmly that Carson hadn't the heart to utter his usual response: "It doesn't matter what my name is, you won't live long enough to learn it by heart."

It was only when you looked into his eyes that you saw it was the same old Bolshie underneath.

It had been interesting to see the general's reaction when he was introduced to Carson. Like everybody else, the G.O.C. had responded to the surgeon's sabotage with an instant warm smile of his own. It was only when Carson drew closer and the G.O.C. was faced with the disturbing contradiction between Carson's up-turned lips and his venomous gaze that the general's own beaming smile had faltered and turned to one of disoriented uncertainty, as if he'd just embraced someone he thought was near and dear, only to find he had a paranoiac transvestite in his arms.

But even Carson was becoming affected by his own optimistic rictus. At least, so far he had not spoken a single mutinous word to the red-tabbed visitors. It was almost as if that beautiful smile was beginning to seep, willy-nilly, into his soul.

As the G.O.C. relaxed in the best armchair and chatted with a group of pilots, Ashworth sidled up to me in his usual state of irritable anxiety.

I thought he had just realized that he had purloined my pipe. I held out my hand with an understanding smile.

"What?"

"Er, my pipe, sir?"

"What're you on about now?" he said testily. "What have pipes got to do with it?"

"Do with what?"

Ashworth held his brow. I started to hold out my hand again, but then gave up. After all, it was a pretty cheap pipe.

The colonel regarded me twitchily for a moment, then said abruptly, "By the way, I've put you in for a D.S.O."

"Have you? Thank you, sir."

"Though I wish you wouldn't go up quite so often, Bandy. I mean, all this flying is all very well, but squadron commanders don't grow on trees, you know. Though admittedly the brigadier seems to have changed his tune lately. All of a sudden he seems anxious for you to do as many offensive patrols as possible. Keeps ringing up to see if you've been—to see how you've got on."

"M'm," I said.

"Anyway, never was a D.S.O. better earned," Ashworth said, with a burst of forced heartiness.

"Ta," I said.

"Yes." The colonel hesitated, then drove his hands nervously into his already distended tunic pockets. "It's a mark of our esteem as much as anything else," he said, letting off esteem with rather an effort. "In recognition of your, uh, concern for the smooth running of the machine."

"What machine?"

"The Air Force machine, of course."

I gazed at him blankly, wondering what he was havering about.

"And for your reticence and, and loyalty," he added, almost choking on the last word.

I began to understand. "Ah," I said archly. "You're hoping I don't bring up a certain subject, eh?"

"H'm?" He looked terribly innocent. "What subject?"

"Parachutes?"

"Parachutes?" He emitted a cracked laugh, dribbling slightly. "What on earth makes you think I'm thinking of parachutes?"

"I'm glad, because that's just what I wanted to talk to you about, sir."

Abandoning his terribly innocent act, Ashworth said bitterly, "Yes, I hear you're going round pestering the balloon people now."

"Just to have a closer look at the things sir, and see them in action," I said. "But the ones they use aren't suitable for aircraft. They're packed in whacking great conical containers attached to the balloon basket."

Ashworth faced me squarely. "Look here, Bandy," he whispered, "you'll very much oblige me if you'll let the subject drop, for one evening at least. I don't want you pestering the general with all that nonsense. I absolutely forbid it, do you understand?"

We became aware that Colonel Treadwell had moved close. He was looking up at the ceiling as if it had no right to be there.

"Why is it nonsense?"

"I want your word you won't mention the subject, do you understand? I know you. Once you start, you won't let up until you've driven the G.O.C. half-mad with that dreadful loud voice of yours."

"One needs a certain projection," I said distantly, "to make oneself heard above the Army uproar."

"And treading all over his feet and everything. I won't have it, Bandy. He has enough on his plate without you worrying him with your ridiculous ideas."

The G.S.O.1 lowered his eyes and regarded me thoughtfully.

"I've read your notes to Ashworth on the subject," he said. "Tell me, Bandy, why did you feel you had to send me a copy?"

I hesitated, then said cautiously, "I wasn't sure the brigadier would pass it on, otherwise."

"Well, I can tell you this," Ashworth said. "Soames is livid about it. I really don't understand you, Bandy. You seem determined to go out of your way to upset the brigade commander."

Treadwell took my arm in a grip like an Eaton's Patent Combined Anvil and Vice, and drew me out of the anteroom and into the hallway.

Ashworth followed, looking as if he'd given his favorite nephew a lollypop, only to have the little blighter stick it in Uncle's ear-hole.

"When I got you this job," Treadwell said, fixing me with his fierce eyes, "I thought I'd made it quite clear you were not to make a nuisance of yourself again."

"But I'm not," I said, raising my eyebrows—then hastily lowering them again. I knew by now that this gesture had a particularly upsetting effect on superior officers. "I'm just pointing out a strange gap in the defences, that's all."

"You believe all that nonsense about the need for parachutes?"

"It's self-evident, surely?"

"Until you started, it wasn't self-evident to a single other pilot, flight commander, squadron commander, or administrator in the entire Allied air forces," Treadwell said in a bandsaw voice. "Just what makes you think you know better than any of them?"

A mess waiter squeezed past and effaced himself into the dining room.

"It's not a matter of knowing better," I said respectfully. Colonel Treadwell had a force of personality that had been known to silence a conference room full of generals, admirals, and even a minor Treasury official. I certainly wasn't getting on the wrong side of *him*. "It's simply a matter of common sense," I said thinly, but stoutly.

"You're the only person in the war with any common sense, are you?"

144

"Oh, I wouldn't go that far," I said with a modest smirk. "But it's obvious, isn't it? Everything that's said about parachutes could just as easily be said about safety belts. The only difference is that safety belts have been accepted and developed and used, and parachutes haven't. And why haven't they? For no reason, far as I can see, other than thoughtless prejudice on the part of the Air Force, and blind insensitivity on the part of the military equipment and supply departments."

As Ashworth was starting to make some rather queer noises, I lowered my voice a trifle, and moderated my tones to ones of light banter and sweet reason. After all, I didn't want to sound critical or unreasonable or anything. I particularly prided myself on my sense of proportion.

"It's just that the more I think about it, the more peculiar and suspicious it seems," I went on. "I mean, when you consider that people have been parachuting safely from aircraft for six years—an American started it in nineteen-twelve, Hibbert tells me, from a Benoist. In Missouri, it was. Mind you, this American chap had to climb down out of the cockpit first and get dressed, and struggle into his parachute whilst standing on the axle of the plane, which can't have been too safe, mind you. And then there was this girl, Tiny Broadwick—I heard about this from a Mrs.—a certain French lady who actually saw her jump, in nineteen fourteen. Apparently it was her father—not the French lady's father, I mean Tiny's father—who developed a pack that didn't need to be attached to the plane; it could be worn quite comfortably by the person jumping and—

"Anyway," I said, taking a deep breath, "the question is, why hasn't any further work been done on parachutes, that's what I want to know. I mean, we've gone from hunting rifles in aircraft to multi-machine guns, from hand-bombs to four-hundred pounders, from hand signals to wireless, from eighty to three-hundred horsepower engines —but what's been done for the safety of the pilot? Or are we just content to go on throwing away highly trained men the way the Army has been doing in the trenches for the past four years, and, and, and—that's all I have to say," I said, in rather a lame finale.

It seemed to have gone terribly quiet in the ante-room next door. Only a couple of minutes before, there had been quite a buzz of talk and laughter, but now there was hardly a murmur.

We heard the G.O.C. clearing his throat. He started to murmur gruffly. Out in the hall, Treadwell, who had been staring at me in a surprisingly unfriendly way considering how much he loved and respected me, said through his teeth, "You're a bloody pest, Bandy. By God, there's no other word for it, a stubborn, fanatic, horrible bloody pest. What the hell always makes you think you're right and it's everybody else who's out of step? And just what do you think you're accomplishing with all this nonsense, going round firing memos in all directions, worrying other squadron commanders to try to get them on your side— oh, yes, I've heard all about it—what good do you think you're doing, other than making a fool of yourself?"

Ashworth shook his head and sighed hopelessly. Now that Treadwell had taken over the responsibility for being bad-tempered, Ashworth looked much more cheerful.

"Damn it, man," Treadwell said, trying to sound restrained, "once again—do you think we wouldn't have done something about it long ago if it had been possible?"

"But sir, it's been possible to supply the infantry by parachute for several years. But nobody ever thought of it until that Hamel attack, did they? All I'm saying is, it should be just as easy to do something about all the R.A.F. casualties. Or are parachutes only available for dealing out ammunition, but not for saving pilots?"

Treadwell's nose turned white at the tip.

"Also," I said quickly, "the German Air Force is proving they're feasible."

"What?"

He burned holes in me with his eyes, then turned to the wing commander. Ashworth was looking at the floor. He was trying to lever up a splinter from the parquet with the toe of his boot.

"Who told you that?"

"I heard about it only a few days ago from the pilot of a Bristol Fighter squadron. I went over to check, Colonel. Several of their pilots saw the German jump by parachute from his plane. And get down safely behind his lines.

"And I've heard of a similar incident from another squadron, and rumors of another."

After a moment, Treadwell said quietly, "I suppose you can give me names, dates, squadron numbers?"

"Yes. You didn't know about it, sir?"

"No, I did not." He turned to Ashworth. "Did you?"

Ashworth nodded, still proding the floor with his boot. "We've had three reports in the last two weeks. We passed them on to Brigade."

The two colonels stared at each other. Both of them looked away at the same time.

"I was wondering why it's never been mentioned in Comic Cuts," I said. "Somebody hushing it up, are they?"

The way Treadwell looked at me, I began to wonder if perhaps he might not adore me as much as I'd thought.

As we entered the ante-room again, everybody looked away, as if they'd just caught us coming out of a bordello. There was a somewhat awkward silence for a moment, then the genial voice of the G.O.C. sounded from the far end of the room.

"Yes," he said, rising. "Well, Matthews, I suppose we should be making tracks, what?"

There was a rustling and scraping as everyone scrambled to his feet.

"And I don't mind telling you that we now look on this squadron as one of the most effective on the Western Front." The pilots glowed. "And I'm more than pleased at your pride and confidence in the Dolphin. As you know, it's not looked on with much favor in some quarters, but I've always maintained it has the makings of a first-class scout, so I'm particularly happy that you, along with 19, are showing what can be done with it. So, thank you again, and keep up the good work, and the very best of luck."

As he and his entourage and the pilots, who were looking quite emotional with pride, straggled out to the staff cars, I tugged anxiously at Treadwell's sleeve.

"Sir," I whispered hoarsely. "About that subject we were discussing."

He looked at my hand on his sleeve. I let go quickly.

"Discussion?" he said. "Is that what it was?"

A muscle twitched in his cheek. He continued to regard me unblinkingly, like the president of a court-martial contemplating the sentence for a particularly enterprising pervert.

"When it becomes known that the enemy are beginning to save the lives of their pilots in that way, we'll surely have to do something about it then, won't we?"

"You propose to let it be known, do you?" Treadwell said, in his Dangerously Calm Voice.

"I wouldn't like to be responsible for suppressing evidence, Colonel," I said, as pointedly as I dared.

His eyes burned into mine. I had the devil of a job meeting his steely gaze. In fact, my eyes began to water, to such an extent that I feared he would think I was getting all emotional about it. I hoped that wasn't the reason he turned on his heel and hurried over to the staff car without another word; because he thought that, like Monty, I was about to break into great, heart-rending blubs to gain my point.

"It's been a pleasure meeting you, gentlemen," he said.
148

He telephoned the very next day, though, and as usual came straight to the point.

"I've had a word with your brigade commander, and that particular end of it has been cleared up. Apparently one of their people failed to pass on the information to us, because of some clerical foul-up."

"H'm."

"What?" I heard him breathing through his nose. "Anyway, I've discussed it with my boss, and he's just been onto the D.G.M.A. in London. A new mark of an established parachute is scheduled for testing in England in two or three weeks. The G.O.C. has requested them to speed things up. The Director-General has promised to see what he can do."

"That's good, sir. Thank you for letting me know."

"Are you satisfied now, Bandy?"

"Yes, I think so," I whined. "As long as they're going to work on it with any real degree of urgency, that'll be quite a good start, sir."

"After all," I said, "I want to be reasonable about this, Colonel Treadwell. I mean, there's nobody in the world who's more tolerant and easygoing than me, as you know. It's just that your typical military mind has such a habit of thinking like a snail, you see," I explained, "and making the resulting tardiness seem like a virtue. You know, sir—in the name of caution, circumspection, and giving due delib—"

But he had hung up. In fact, it sounded as if he'd hung up with a sledge-hammer.

Me, Among the Peacocks

These mild lobbyings of mine had a dreadful result.

Twenty-two hours after Treadwell's call, I returned from a squadron show to be told that I was to report to Brigade H.Q. forthwith.

I wasn't at all pleased. H.Q. was a long way off, and I had a worse toothache than ever after all that high-altitude maneuvering. Also, we'd lost a new man, a keen, nineteen-year-old Canadian by the name of Bolt. He seemed to have been suffering a baulky engine, but though I'd twice signalled him to turn back, he had continued to wallow about a couple of hundred feet below, trying to keep up.

After I'd spent one and a half hours maneuvering the squadron into position above two flights of Albatri, a queer-looking Hun bi-plane of an unfamiliar design had nipped out of a cloud and closed on the solitary Dolphin, so we had to go to his aid. Whereupon my guns jammed, the two enemy flights escaped, and Bolt was shot down anyway.

When we got back, I gathered the pilots together in the barn and said some pretty harsh things about selfish pilots who wanted to die for their country without allowing anybody to make a profit on it. "You're a liability if you continue on with a dud engine, and I've enough to think about without worrying about idiots with underdeveloped senses of self-preservation."

It was only when a rotten timber fell from the roof, and a herd of field mice thundered out of the barn in fright, that I realized I was shouting.

The pilots looked pretty taken aback, except for Woofer Smith, who patted me on the shoulder afterwards and said, "Don't you worry, Maje. I, at least, intend to go on preserving myself indefinitely."

The bugger thought he was reassuring me. In fact he was getting me down so much that when I'd said, "If there's anything wrong with your bus—go home!" I'd very nearly added, "All except Lieutenant Smith."

Well, he was really getting on my nerves with his infuriating comfort. Like the previous night, when I'd snapped at him and he had merely smiled indulgently and encouraged me to get all the bile out of my system. He quite understood that it had to have some outlet, and if it made me feel any better to take it out on him, I was just to go ahead—get rid of my bile.

Bile, that was the latest of his hateful words. I was seriously thinking of not waiting for some obliging Hun, but shooting him down myself when nobody was looking. Except he'd probably go down shouting, "That's the stuff, Maje! Get it out of your system!"

Brigade H.Q., which I'd visited once before under inauspicious circumstances, was a fine château in the Pas de Calais, set in spacious grounds surrounded by ornamental iron railings, the splendor of the entranceway somewhat marred by the presence of a Nissen guard hut, a flagpole, and a canvas latrine.

The château had been rented from a peacock-breeder. Soames had prevailed on the owner to leave behind a few samples of his stock for decorative purposes, on the understanding that he would be personally responsible for them. They included six hens and a single male, a rare hybrid with purplish-black wings.

I was able to obtain a close look at it because, as I roared up on my motor bike and jammed to a stop in a flurry of gravel, it came swanking over to see what all the racket was about, the last rays of the sun illuminating its tail feathers in a glorious, breathtaking display of color.

"Piss off," I said.

I was directed through the open french windows at the side of the house, and found myself in a sumptuously furnished chamber, with an Aubusson carpet, oil paintings of upper-crust ladies dallying with effete-looking swains, and a handsome upright piano that neatly complemented the symmetry of the tall windows on each side of it.

I'd heard about that piano. It was a personal possession of Soames's, who allowed only one member of his staff, a sergeant, to play it, and only when the brigadier himself was present. The sergeant was a former concert pianist who had originally been conscripted into the R.A.F. as a dishwasher.

What with his personal pianist, his personal biographer, and a lawnful of peacocks, Soames obviously fancied himself as a Florentine-type patron.

The room glowed with silverware, mahogany, and red-tabs. Several of the people the tabs were sewn to, twisted in their seats to stare at me as I stumped in, wearing a dispatch rider's helmet and a scowl. Being in a thoroughly mean mood, I put my foot on the armrest of a Riesner chair to remove my bicycle clips, before asking its occupant, a full colonel, where I could find Soames.

The colonel's face went all red and swollen. He said fiercely, "What the—just who the hell d'you think you are, sir?"

"Bandy," I snapped back. An elderly major nearby woke with a start and ducked, as if a whizz-bang had landed.

The colonel subsided almost at once. "Oh. Oh, yes." After looking over my oil-stained tunic—I hadn't had time to change it—he went on almost placatingly, "You're not going in to see him like that, are you, old man?"

Before I could reply, Lieutenant Mickle glanced in through the far doorway, saw me, and came over, looking more than ever like a demoted Napoleon. He informed me that the brigadier general was waiting for me, and would I follow him, please?

I'd expected to find Soames in another of his incoherent, quivering furies after being caught out in a "clerical mix-up." To my surprise, he was not only calm as sump oil, he was positively brimming over with affability.

As he fussed about, personally settling me in the best chair in his office, his close-set eyes seemed to fuse into one pale Cyclopean orb filled with what seemed remarkably like elation.

I looked at him open-mouthed, my childish petulance slowly draining away into my socks.

"I'm sorry to bring you this distance at such short notice, Major," he said in the clipped, brass-hat manner. "Your adjutant said you were leading a squadron patrol when I called. A successful one, I trust?"

"We lost a new man—"

"Splendid," he said, obviously preoccupied with other thoughts. "And you did well personally, I imagine?"

"Mostly, these days, I just try and keep an eye on things from above—"

"Splendid," he said again, quite gayly, running his fingers over his polished desk as if practicing an *arpeggio* on his beloved piano. "Your concern for the pilots does you great credit, Major."

He cleared his throat. "I suppose," he said with a jauntiness that was only slightly forced, "that's why you're so concerned about parachutes."

I stared at him. He was actually bringing the subject up himself.

He leaned back, finger tips still on the desk, and I was

sure there was a smile there, somewhere, under his mustache. "And that's why I've called you in, Bandy," he said. "First of all, to let you know that I've now seen the light."

"You have? What light?"

He looked away, at a row of bound field manuals. "Colonel Treadwell had a word with me on the subject— as a follow-up, apparently, of a conversation he had with you. We . . . we had a heart-to-heart talk about it, and as a result I'm now completely in favor of speeding things up."

"The production of parachutes? That's great, sir."

"Yes, it is, isn't it? And a lot of the credit must go to you, too.

"I must admit," he went on, with almost charming ruefulness, "that I've found your persistence perhaps a trifle upsetting at times, Bandy. I wouldn't be entirely frank with you if I didn't say that." His fingers rippled again over the desk. "So if I've seemed a trifle irritated with you on occasion, you must put it down to pressure of work. I assure you that whatever annoyance I may have shown, *au fond* I have as much personal regard for your, your qualities as everybody else at H.Q. seems to have."

It was so close to an apology I felt I had to reciprocate. "I quite understand, sir," I said warmly. "I must admit I've been quite concerned."

"Concerned?"

"That your hypertension on those occasions might become a precipitating cause of intercranial pressure."

"What?"

"You know, sir. Apoplexy."

"What?" The brigadier seemed to be getting tense again. I hastened to calm and reassure him.

"I took some years of medicine, you see," I said, relaxing in the best armchair, and crossing my ankles contentedly. "And I got quite anxious when I thought about it, sir, so it's a great relief that your apparent aneurism, stertorous breathing, rigidity, and so forth, were merely signs of overwork. The symptoms as every schoolboy knows, are often similar to apoplexy, you see.

"But I guess," I added comfortingly, "yours were just passing vascular spasms."

"Passing vascular spasms. Yes," the brigadier said, in a suppressed sort of way. "However, as I was saying—"

"You haven't been having any mental confusion lately, of course?"

"As a matter of fact, I . . . I'm having some right now."

"In that case, you should be laid flat and rolled over, sir."

"Laid flat? Rolled over?"

"On your side, sir. You know, so you won't swallow your tongue and stuff. Actually your face—Do you have any false teeth?"

"Do I what?" he asked, his voice rising so markedly I thought he'd crossed his legs and trapped himself.

"In that case, your teeth should some out, Brigadier. In fact clinical re-education might be called for," I said, feeling really at ease now, and proud that I was remembering so much from those distant days at the University of Toronto. "The patient usually has to be encouraged in the re-use of the mental faculties, you see. That's why I mentioned—"

I stopped, because ominous symptoms were reappearing. He was now quite pale and sweating, with trembling hands and stertorous breathing, and everything. Also, he was starting to take great mouthfuls of his mustache.

I wondered if my amended diagnosis might not have been too precipitate. He really did look a likely prospect for apoplexy, now I looked at him more closely.

However, he managed to regain control of himself, though with something of an effort. After wrenching and plucking at his collar for a minute or so, he said shakily, "Yes. Anyway . . . where was I, Mickle?"

See? Mental confusion.

155

Soames suddenly realized that Mickle had been recording the whole conversation in shorthand.

"Don't put that in, Mickle," he said despairingly. "Just from where we . . . strayed off the subject. Where were we?"

"You had just seen the light, sir."

"What?"

"Parachutes."

"Ah, yes. Parachutes, Yes. Parachutes. Yes. Well," He took a deep, shuddery sort of breath. "After discussing the situation with Treadwell, I had a splendid idea, Bandy. You know what it was?"

"No, sir?"

"To supplement these home trials with a spot of additional testing of our own. Under— what were my actual words, Mickle?"

Ready for his cue, Mickle flipped over a few pages of notebook. "Under simulated combat conditions," he read out.

"That's it. As a result, Bandy, I've ordered a few samples of the latest version of the parachute to be flown over. They should be here tomorrow, in fact."

"That's wonderful, sir. Would I be able to watch the tests over here?"

"I can do even better than that, Bandy. The problem was, you see, to decide who was to make the actual trials. We don't have any experienced test personnel over here, of course. Well, it's your obsession that has led to the present situation, isn't it? It seems to me that as you're the one who is pressing most enthusiastically for their adoption, you ought to be the one to get the credit."

"C—credit?"

"For seeing that the parachute receives a triumphant work-out."

"You mean—?"

"Yes. After all," Soames said, looking really overjoyed again, "what more appropriate person could we use to test the parachutes than the man who has done so much to champion their cause?"

"You mean . . . *me?*"

"You, Bandy. I want you to jump from a great height. Right here at Brigade H.Q. At fourteen hundred hours on July thirteenth."

Left Dangling

I was so looking forward to the parachute trials, I lay awake most of that night thinking about them. I was so excited, that my tooth, finding itself ignored, gave up aching entirely.

My heart futted away like an early Bleriot whenever I imagined myself treading on the atmosphere, with nothing between me and strawberry jam but a few pounds of Chinese silk. It would be another remarkable experience to add to the Log Book of Life. After all, a girl of fifteen had done it. Dozens of times. Gosh, I was really looking forward to it.

But when I looked out the window at five in the morning, imagine my feelings when I saw it was pouring with rain. It looked as if it was on for the day, too. The tests would obviously have to be cancelled.

I was so disappointed I was hardly able to sing in my bath that morning.

"Take the pistons out of my kidneys,
The gudgeon pin out of my brain
From the small of my back take the crankshaft,
And assemble the engine again,"
I sang, apparently a trifle loudly, as Smethurst had his hands over his ears. But there was a definite note of *tristesse* in my noble baritone.

"Looking forward to t' Paris trip, are you, sir?" Smethurst asked as he brought in my dry towel, my loofah, my hot-water mug for shaving, my toy battleship, and my

Dr. Chereful's Patented Pink Powder for the Relief of Perspiring Extremities and Ant Repellant.

"Hardly, my good man," I said gravely. "After all, I am booked for the dentist, which, however much laughing gas he uses, is no chortling matter, I can assure you, even if he is an American dentist, who are, I am told, particularly effective in their profession, not least because of their willingness to embrace the very latest equipment available to the profession for the—" I stopped, realizing I was babbling a bit.

I was still looking acutely disappointed when I went down to breakfast. Hibbert and the armament officer, Peters, were the only ones up that morning. I'd passed the word to the batmen not to bother rousing the pilots, as there was obviously not going to be any flying that day.

"They could do with a day off," said I, eating like a horse. "Why don't we organize a tender for them? They could go to Boulogne."

"It'll clear up this afternoon," Hibbert said.

"No," I said decisively. "Take a look at those clouds, Hib. It's on for the day."

"I think we'd better hold off on the tender until noon, anyway."

"Whatever you say, Hib old bean. But you'll see. It'll be coming down in bucketfuls all afternoon."

It stopped raining at 11.30. By noon, the hangars were steaming in the sun.

"God-damned filthy sodding European weather," I said viciously to Hibbert on my way down to the hangars. "You can't rely on it from bleeding minute to minute."

My Dolphin, D.4141, stood in morose solitude in the middle of a green puddle. A couple of mechanics hurried up as I climbed in. I gave the radiator a kick in passing.

Hibbert limped up to the fuselage and said hesitantly, "You haven't yet told me where you're going, sir."

"D.H.9 squadron, near Frévent," I snapped.

"When will you be back?"

"I probably never will be back," I said shakily, fastening the safety belt.

"I'm sorry to bother you, Major, but after all, it's my duty to know where you are."

I sat there for a moment, thinking about it. Soames had hinted that the G.O.C. was anxious not to attract too much attention to the trials, as they weren't being held under strictly official auspices. He had asked me not to discuss them with anybody until they were concluded. But he surely couldn't have meant I wasn't even to inform my own adjutant?

So I muttered, "I'm making three or four parachute jumps, in the vicinity of Brigade."

"What?"

"For Soames."

"You're going parachuting?"

"No need to look like that, Hibbert. It's an extremely reliable parachute, from all accounts."

"But . . . you've no experience."

"All the better. It'll show that anyone can do it if they're forced to."

Hibbert was shifting about in a flustered way. He took off his cap, ran a hand through his thin, sandy hair, and put his cap on again. "But why you?"

"Well, I've been badgering everyone on the subject for ages, so I'm the logical choice, aren't I?"

"I don't like this at all, Bart."

"Haven't I said repeatedly that parachutes are the answer to all the casualties? Well, this is my chance to prove it."

I wiggled the controls morosely. This was to make sure that all control surfaces were free and unlocked—though I probably wouldn't have noticed if an elephant had been sitting on the tail.

"Besides," I added, "Soames said if I didn't do it, somebody else would have to. Anyway, I want to, and that's all there is to it."

160

"Yes, but . . ." Hibbert's studious face was all scrunched up. "But why all the secrecy? Why didn't you tell me before? Is it official?"

"Course it's official," I snapped, signalling to the mechanics.

"Switch off, petrol on," the corporal mechanic called out.

"I was talking to Wing only half an hour ago," Hibbert said quickly. "They never mentioned this. Do they know about it?"

"Will you stop badgering me!" I shouted. "I've told you where I'm going, and that's all I have to do. Now just, just get on with it," I said, pumping up enough pressure to inflate a kite balloon. "Switch off, petrol on!"

"Contact!"

"Contact!"

In front of the plane, the corporal held hands with the other mechanic, in a pally sort of way. The latter leaned back gracefully. With his free hand the corporal swung the propeller, held back by his mate so he wouldn't overbalance into the whirling blade.

The engine banged into life and started beating noisily. I inched back on the throttle. As the mechanics grabbed the chock lines, Hibbert moved away slowly, until he was clear of the tail. I opened up, looking at the rev counter, throttled down, and waved, in a hurry, now, to get away.

The mechanics hauled away the chocks and scampered to the wingtips to guide the plane around. I opened up again, and bumped away over the grass, feeling ashamed at shouting at old Hib that way, especially when his cap blew off in the slipstream and went skittering into a puddle.

He was still shaking it as the Dolphin roared past fifty feet away, the wheels sending up a gauze of spray that arched vivid rainbows over the grass.

They may not have known about the parachute trial at

Montonvillers, but they obviously knew all about it at the D.H. airdrome. Several pilots, who had just risen after the previous night's bombing trip, looked at me in some awe as I came into the mess with the C.O. half an hour before we were due to take off.

The C.O. had volunteered to fly me personally.

His name was Greaves, and he had lost several lower teeth in a crash-landing. What with that and his somewhat prominent upper teeth and deep, droopy mustache, he looked remarkably like a bull walrus that had lost too many battles for walrus mates.

"You will have a drink before the . . ." he began in dismal tones. The way he said it, it made you suspect that the word he'd left out was *catastrophe*.

"I sure will. Two, in fact."

Greaves had been briefed by the brigadier personally. Soames and company, he told me, would be watching the trials from the lawn of the château. The brigadier wanted three jumps, or four if there was time, from different altitudes: fifteen thousand, eight thousand, and three thousand, and possibly fifteen hundred. The jumps were to be made under simulated combat conditions, that is, another machine would accompany us and engage us in a mock dogfight. "So the plane will be splitarsing about quite a bit beforehand," Greaves said morosely.

"But I won't be able to get out if you're splitarsing."

"Oh, don't worry, I'll level off long enough for you to fling yourself into the void."

"Oh . . . good . . ."

"Except for the third jump, my old. You're supposed to do that while the old bus is in a steep dive. But don't worry, I won't make it too steep."

" 'M'kew," I said, pouring a third scotch into my empty tank.

"The idea is, you see, that you're getting out after a losing battle with another aircraft."

I pointed through the window at a long line of D.H.9 bombers. "Can those things dogfight?" I asked unsteadily.

"Oh, yes, they're pretty spry when they're not loaded. When they're bombed up, that's another story. They won't go above fifteen thou, or much more than seventy, with a full load on."

"Good Lord. How do you manage to survive?" I asked, not caring about *his* problems in the least.

"Often wonder ourselves, my old. Mostly because we hardly ever reach the target. The exhaust valves usually burn out before we're half-way there."

I squinted reprovingly at the bar waiter. He was starting to advance and recede rhythmically. I thought of telling him that this was no time to practice the mazurka, but his C.O. didn't seem to mind, so . . .

"Anyway, as I was saying," Major Greaves said, "they've marked out a field close to Brigade H.Q., where I'll land the bus after the drops. There'll be spotters with field glasses on the roof of the château to follow your descent, and they've provided a car to take you from where you fall to earth back to my plane for the next trip."

"I wish you wouldn't use terms like that—fall to earth —an', an' about flinging self into th' void."

"Ah. By the way, have you had lunch?"

I drew out a flask. It gurgled faintly. "I've got it with me," I said.

The parachutes were heaped on a trestle table at the entrance to one of the D.H. hangars. A large, hairy lump formed in my gullet as I gazed at the untidy-looking sacks.

"They're the Guardian Angel type," Greaves said. "I knew a chap who was killed testing one of these. Mind you, they've improved them quite a bit since then . . . I believe."

I looked around the empty hangar, dully surprised that there was nobody there to give skilled help or advice. I thought they'd have lent us a manufacturer's representative, or at least some fairly knowledgeable person from Martlesham Heath. But they hadn't even sent a seamstress. It all seemed rather casual to me.

However, the procedure seemed simple enough. The Guardian Angel was a bulky back-pack with shoulder straps and a canvas strip called a static line, wound in position over a releasing buckle. It was the automatic type. All one had to do was attach the static line to the floor of the aircraft by a clip, jump, and hope for the best. It was up to the static line to pluck the canopy out of the parachute sack.

The major himself helped me on with it. "Rather you than me, my old," he said. "This'll teach you to go around hurling the old swill into the wind. Wouldn't get me wearing one of these. Takes up too much bloody room, for one thing."

I couldn't help thinking the same. The pack bulged way out, from shoulder to waist. I looked like a Quasimodo—with vertigo.

Also, the parachute was a lot heavier than it looked. When Greaves let go, I nearly fell over backward.

It was even worse in the rear cockpit of the major's D.H.9. I could hardly raise the flask to the level of my mouth.

"God, I'll need an axe to get out of here," I said shakily to Greaves, who was stowing the other three parachutes into the bomb bay.

"Don't worry about that, my little cabbage. At fifteen thousand, you'll soon contract in the cold."

To make matters worse, I was facing rearward. Somehow that position didn't seem entirely appropriate for an escaping scout pilot, somehow.

It was worse still when Greaves took off and climbed steeply over the huts and hangars. I didn't enjoy being flown by others at the best of times, but to be dragged backward at a steep angle, with a disorienting view of a wiggly rudder and a totally unfamiliar view of terra firma, was even more upsetting. I'd polished off half the contents of the flask by the time we reached seven thousand feet.

I was rather hoping the plane would live up to its reputation before the dreaded moment arrived, but the rotten bus behaved perfectly that afternoon. The D.H.9 was quite an attractive aircraft, with its neatly faired nose and wide, graceful wings, but it had one shortcoming: it had been senile from birth. I'd heard a lot about it when I was at the Air Ministry, and had flown it once myself, at Martlesham Heath. I couldn't understand what had prompted the Air Board to order it into production, for it wasn't half as good as the plane it was designed to succeed, the D.H.4.

The Air Board, though, like so many similar bodies of civil servants, benighted knights, and other people whom the government owed a favor, had been responsible for some mighty queer decisions on almost as many occasions as they had failed to come to any decision at all.

On the ground, I'd been sweating like a toilet tank. By the time the biplane was clattering noisily through twelve thousand, I was thoroughly chilled. I couldn't move about properly to keep the blood pulsating around the old system. But I blamed my half-frozen state on the fact that I wasn't wearing my fox fur. I'd left it behind, partly because Brigadier Soames seemed to have enough doubts about me without my flouncing up to him in fox furs; and partly because the fur was starting to get disgustingly matted, what with all the oil, sweat, and chocolate I'd dribbled onto it. Several days before, John Derby had complained that it was turning putrid and had called in the wing doctor and tried to persuade him to issue a death certificate.

It was a bloody perfect day for parachuting. The sky was cloudless, the visibility unlimited. I became aware that the rudder was bent sideways and that the horizon was tilted at a nauseating angle. We were circling, still gaining height though we were already at fifteen thousand.

I gripped the side of the cockpit and peered into the void. Then recoiled and snatched at my flask again. The château was directly below. It was the size of a piece of confetti, or confettum.

God, I couldn't do it. I'd have to tell Greaves right away. "Look, old chap, I've changed my mind. I don't think I'll go overboard after all, if you don't mind. You see it's this, this tooth of mine. It's been giving me heck, you see. Look, why don't we just send my tooth down by parachute, that'll be nearly as good. I mean, it's such a large, heavy tooth, I'm sure it wouldn't mind taking my place . . ."

No, it had to be a sensible reason. "Greaves, by Jove, I've just remembered," I'd say with a carefree laugh, but one loud enough to be heard over the craven howls of the Puma engine, "I have no head for heights, old man. Funny, I never noticed it before, but I'm afraid you'll have to go down to a more reasonable speed and altitude, say five miles an hour at six feet? Oh, and another thing, there's this letter to my wife that I've forgotten to post. Actually, it's not so much a letter as a will. I—"

The plane lurched wildly. I clung to the sides. The movement was so violent I was sure my eyes had fallen out and were swaying about at the end of the optic nerves.

The sky was falling, the sky was falling. I clung onto the fuselage so tightly the glue started to ooze from the plywood. Another plane flashed past. The 'enemy' D.H.9.

It disappeared. The horizon jerked about, then hung straight up and down. The other plane appeared again, jiggling below the tail. The earth was standing on end. We were half-way through a loop. Greaves had gone mad —looping a bomber.

It seemed capable of looping very tightly, though. The earth lunged overhead. The flask slipped from my bosom and started to shoot upward. I let go the sides to catch it. I caught it all right. Suddenly I had no fuselage to hang onto. It disappeared completely.

One second I was being crushed through the cockpit floor. The next I was executing a perfect loop-the-loop; the only trouble was, I wasn't doing it in a plane.

I was out in space.

It was true what they said. My whole life flashed before me, like an incredibly fast talking picture show, yet somehow with each scene being projected at the most leisurely pace imaginable: mother thrashing me sadly, because I'd stolen brandy balls from Mr. Hackforth's general store; giving away my prized possessions when I thought I was going to die: policeman's whistle, 140 marbles, my rock with a vein of fool's gold, part of an old rubber douche that I'd used as a peashooter; then saw myself reciting Latin in the one-room schoolhouse—in love with the schoolmaster's wife, who had fat legs but a kind face; my cousin trying to drown me in a firkin of molasses; my first dissection—I could even smell the formaldehyde.

The almost casual tug of the static line seemed to come hours later, though it couldn't have been more than a second after the plane disappeared so treacherously. Almost immediately, a violent wrench at the shoulder harness. The ground whirling, fifteen thousand feet below. The horizon turning like a compass needle in a spinning scout. A wild pendulum act, gradually slowing.

And then, just a gentle rush of thin air.

I looked up groggily. Shivering shroud lines spreading outward to the rim of the silk canopy. The glint of the plane, far away.

It seemed that I was parachuting.

I'd done it. I was *parachuting*.

By Jove, all the old arguments were utter nonsense! The blast of the wind had not knocked me unconscious. I was able to breathe the thin air with as much ease, or difficulty, as at twenty thousand feet in a Dolphin. I was able to move my arms and legs, and they hadn't been shattered at all. And there had been no uncontrollable panic, like they said. There hadn't been time.

There wasn't even any sensation of falling. The only sound was a hollow, rushing noise as the breeze blew over my gaping cake hole.

I closed my mouth with a clop.

I was still gripping the flask. The little, cup-shaped cap had gone, but the stopper was still in place. I removed it and took a swig in mid air. And beamed.

It was marvellous. Marvellously peaceful after the din of the engine and that sudden, ghastly splitarsing. I looked down, and started snickering at the sight of my flying boots dangling down there over the green patchwork quilt of the land—what?—ten thousand feet below?

I was already a third of the way down.

Gosh, it was easy to parachute. All you had to do was . . .

But, for the life of me, I couldn't work out what the method was. I was sure I hadn't stood up and jumped; I was sure of it.

Let me see. I was sitting there minding my business while the pilot took evasive action. Then he had dived, and completed the first half of the loop—

H'm. M'yes. Now I knew. I'd been so preoccupied with making sure that the parachute harness was tight, and the static line securely fastened to the special ring in the floor of the cockpit, that I'd forgotten to fasten the safety belt.

I hadn't jumped. I'd fallen out.

Parachuting was splendid, there was no doubt about it.

As a boy I'd often jumped from considerable heights, or they'd seemed considerable then: from the massive beams in Mr. Baxter's barn, down onto the hay; from a cliff, thirty feet above the Ottawa River; from a hilltop down onto a sloping hillside of sand. Always there had been that deliciously unpleasant sensation somewhere to the left of the bladder. But now, as the fields infinitesimally expanded below, there was no sensation of falling at all, at all. A tight harness, a steady wind up the nostrils, nothing else.

I looked around. It was better than any view from a plane. Olive fields, chocolate-colored loam, greenish-grey woods, red tiled roofs. The white château. And there was the English Channel, glittering in the distance. I could even see a ship, zigzagging.

There was a whirring noise. One of the D.H.s dived past, throttled back. The other, the attacking plane, also came over for a look. It waggled its wings as it curved past, several hundred feet away, the pilot's and observer's goggled faces turned toward me.

I raised the flask to them, then took a swig, smiling from ear to ear. They both waved back.

After circling me a couple of times at a safe distance, they started to climb again, the engine sounding thin and high-pitched in the sparkling air.

There was almost no wind, except vertically. I was swinging a bit as the air grew denser. Or rather, it was more of a cork-screwing motion. I wondered why that was.

I felt thoroughly elated as I gazed down at the château. It was about two miles to the north. I could see tiny groups of figures on the lawn in front of the house, and a couple of men on the roof. As the parachute swung lazily lower, I could even tell that one of the men on the roof had a bad cold—or maybe those outsize hankies he was holding to his nose were signal flags.

I took another swig, then started chortling and giggling and waving the flask about joyfully, at the thought of having a beano in mid air.

The rushing air grew perceptibly warmer, Above, the edge of the canopy was fluttering as the air spilled out of it.

I was at nearly one thousand feet before I remembered

the iron railings that surrounded the château grounds. They had arrow-shaped spikes every few feet. I wouldn't want one of those up my, my nose. I looked down, but it was all right, they were well to the north.

I was going straight down onto open ground. Apart from straggly lines of hedge and an overgrown quarry, about a mile farther east, that was filled with greenish-black water, there was nothing but grass and a few scattered trees below. I couldn't help feeling impressed by my remarkable timing and marksmanship. I was headed straight for the largest, flattest field of all.

The ground was rising faster, now. It was only then that I thought about how I was going to land. How were you supposed to do it? Really, there ought to have been at least one experienced man around to tell me these things. Were you supposed to crank your legs as if bicycling, or stiffen them against the impact, or what? The field was spreading out. I was falling much faster than I'd thought. Quick, what was it that balloon observer had told me? Go limp. That was it. Loosen the legs. Pretend you're drunk. That was a good idea. I'd pretend I was drunk.

The ground was rising at quite a speed. It was an effort not to tense in anticipation of the shock. Level with the tops of the trees over there. A second later my knees were sunk into my stomach and I was an untidy heap in the grass, feebly fighting off the cloud of silk as it settled on top of me.

I was gasping for breath and feeling as if somebody had been using my stomach as a butter churn. But I was down. I had made it.

Whatever his faults, Soames's organization was always efficient. A staff car, driven by a sergeant with an army signalman beside him, followed by a lorry containing the airmen who had been detailed to retrieve the parachute, arrived so promptly I hardly had time to polish off the rest of the scotch.

Thirty minutes after I'd thumped down, I was rolling up in the staff car to the grass strip adjoining the château grounds, where Greaves's plane was waiting.

Greaves was lolling against the fuselage chatting to a mechanic as I drove up in triumph. The only other people present were some Tommies who had wandered over from a nearby rest camp to see what all the hullabaloo was about.

Except there was no hullabaloo. "Where's the welcoming committee?" I said. "Mean to say I've risked lice and limb and nobody's here to congratulate me?"

"I expect they're all busy congratulating themselves," Greaves said, jerking his head toward the château, "and dishing out D.S.O.s to each other after your splendid effort."

"Huh," I said, and fell out of the car.

The sergeant driver helped me up politely.

"Bandy, my old, I believe you're blotto."

"Cer'nly not. Um, um just pretending. That's how you're supposed to land, see? You pretend to be drunk, Gleaves."

"I see. Well, are you ready for the next jump?"

"Ready, willing, and able," I cried wittily. But as Greaves heaved the pack onto my back, my legs started to buckle. The mechanic came over to help, but they weren't too efficient about it, he and Greaves. I rather suspected they'd had a few, they were staggering about so much.

"Come, come, men, stop messing about," I ordered.

"It's like harnessing the elements," Greaves panted. "For God's sake, man, stop trying to help. We can manage."

By the time they'd finished, I was hot and sweating with the effort. Some Guardian Angel this was. I felt like the young man with the old man on his back.

As I clung onto a wing strut, Greaves studied me in that grave manner of his.

"I say, Bandy, wouldn't you like to take a breather first?"

I drew myself up and said, "Ready, willing, and able, Greaves old bean. Enough of this silly-shallying. Let's get on with it."

Somehow they got me lashed down in the rear cockpit again, watched by the Tommies, who were wearing the kind of limp, skeptical expression that other ranks always seemed to wear when attending a concert party. I waved to them. "Hulloa, chaps," I called out, hiccuping so loudly that Greaves thought somebody had started the engine without him.

"Incidentally, that was pretty dashed clever," Greaves called over his shoulder, as we circled and climbed once more above the château.

The motion of the aircraft and the effect of flying backward was beginning to make me feel a bit sick. "What was?" I croaked.

"That idea of yours. Getting out while the bus was upside down. Quite took me by surprise."

"Oh. Oh, that. It was nothing, really . . ."

"It was bloody original, my old. I'm damn sure nobody's ever done it that way before. How are you going to do it this time—hacksaw your way through the cockpit floor?"

"Oh, I think I'll do it the conventional way this time," I said, gazing down blearily to make sure they'd fastened my safety belt.

Fifteen minutes later, we were again simulating combat, at eight thousand feet. I felt queasier than ever, and was quite looking forward to plonking myself into the void for a bit of peace and quiet. This time, all that emptiness below was not the least disconcerting. As the other

172

D.H. broke off the fight and turned away, Greaves shouted, "I'll try and drop you straight into the grounds this time. Ready?"

I stood up groggily and put a foot over the side, remembering not to get the other entangled with the static line.

"Now! Good luck!"

I swung the other leg over and pushed off. This time there was the old, familiar falling sensation, amplified by nausea. I felt myself falling forward.

Not wishing to be hanging head downward when the parachute opened, in case I was snapped in two when it opened, I waved my arms wildly, and was more or less vertical when the first tug came, followed almost immediately by the crack of the canopy.

It was a perfect jump. Again the pendulum effect. By the time Greaves's plane was a couple of miles away, I was swinging quite slowly and gracefully.

It was good to be away from all the noise and the awful splitarsing, and I began to feel better almost immediately. The other D.H. came over for a look, much closer this time. So did a couple of S.E. 5a's, out of the west. They were probably new machines being ferried to Candas. The pilots seemed interested. They circled me all the way from six thousand to two thousand feet—one of them kept searching the sky overhead, as if looking for my kite balloon.

Greaves had calculated the drop remarkably well. Probably his bombing experience. The middle of the château grounds was directly below.

There was quite a mob in the grounds, by now, many of them staring up through field glasses. I caught the flash of a lens, and felt rather self-conscious about being scrutinized in this manner, as if I were some sort of military objective. At this range, they could probably see the cavity in my tooth.

The parachute settled down a bit as the lawn swept up. I was clear of the onlookers, but as I dangled down through three hundred, a peacock emerged from where it had been up to no good in the bushes, and spread out its tail shamelessly.

I suddenly realized I was drifting toward it.

I expected it to hurry back into the shrubbery as soon as it saw the beast of prey overhead, but the idiot just stood there and gawked. I started to wave and shout. "Gerrout of it! Go on—gerraway from there!"

It continued to preen. I was only twenty feet up. I yelled at it again, waving my arms. It gaped—open-beaked—looking rather like Witcomb. I fell on it.

Soames was the first to arrive, but he didn't even look at me. He was staring, bulge-eyed and panting, at the heap of plumage.

"Oh, my God," he said. "It's the male. It would have to be the male . . . Hundreds of quid worth . . ."

He turned on me. "You bloody fool," he shouted, as the others ran up. "It's the prize male! You've landed on my cock!"

I was so unnerved by this *contretemps* that I was at three thousand feet before I had recovered enough to feel resentful.

"Well, it wasn't my fault," I said, pouting over my shoulder. "It was that stupid peacock."

"It certainly was, my old," Greaves called back.

I twisted around suspiciously. He sounded as if he were laughing.

"My God," he went on, "I wouldn't have missed this for the world. I'll be able to dine out on this story for months."

Little did he know just how much he would have to tell.

"You're a great man, Bandy," he shouted. "I believe now everything they say about you."

There was no doubt about it. He was laughing out loud.

"What? Anyway, he ought've corralled his stupid birds. He ought've been more careful, the careless swine."

"Course he should, Bandy, my little cabbage."

"Well, I'm not paying for his prize bird, whatever he says. He'll have to compensate the owner all by himself. I'm not paying. It was purely an accident."

After a while, Greaves lost interest in my mutinous mumblings, and scanned the sky for the other aircraft. Cumulus clouds were forming at the top of the heated columns of air, another thousand feet up.

"He didn't even congratulate me on a perfect jump," I said. "Fact, he almost seemed disappointed I hadn't done myself in already."

"Where the hell's that other bus?"

Suddenly it was on us, diving vertically from a cloud. Greaves flung his machine around again, as if it were a Camel. He certainly was a damn good pilot, in spite of his slow, heavy-hearted talk. When the other plane finally got behind us, he kicked the D.H. into a spin.

As he pulled out in a shallow dive with the engine throttled back, he waggled the wings once more, and twisted round and shouted, "Carry on, Bandy. Good luck again."

I released the lap belt. It was certainly a good cockpit to get out of. They'd removed the observer's machine gun but had left the Scarff ring, which was useful for holding onto while I stuck a leg over the side.

The leg started lashing angrily at the plywood side of the fuselage, as if it were in a bad temper.

Carefully moving the other leg around the static line, I perched on the port side of the cockpit, being buffeted by the slipstream, and leaned into the gale, and jumped.

The wind snatched at my flying coat, the skirts rattling like a machine gun. The umbilical cord tying me to the aircraft snaked out and tightened almost instantly, dragging the parachute out of the pack. As the parachute opened with a crack, the cord broke.

That was as it should be; but what happened next was definitely not part of the procedure. The canopy exploded wide open before it was clear of the aircraft. A second later it had snatched at the port stabilizer. It clung on, wrapping the stabilizer in violently flapping silk.

I found myself being dragged through the air behind the airplane at three thousand feet, parallel to the ground, at 80 m.p.h.

Seconds whipped by before I was able to grasp the situation. I was caught, trapped. And what was even more frightful was that the canopy, with my weight on it, was hauling down on the elevator. The plane was going into an uncontrollable dive.

There was nothing I could do, even if I'd been able to think clearly. It was difficult to think clearly while you were spinning first one way, then the other, whilst being snagged on an aircraft now travelling at well over 100 m.p.h., and with the speed and the spinning effect increasing every second.

Half the canopy was pregnant with the shrieking wind, the other half bunched, rattling, around the tail. I couldn't see Greaves, but I could imagine him easily enough, hauling desperately on the stick, probably very nearly as disturbed as I was. The wind was howling in the bracing-wires.

The plane continued to dive steeply. The ground was only fifteen hundred feet below.

It hardly mattered, as far as I was concerned. Even if old Greaves got the plane out of the dive, sooner or later he'd have to land, and that would be the end of me. With luck, I'd be unconscious by then. The whirling land and sky was already darkening. The spinning effect was causing me to lose consciousness.

Only a few hundred feet to go, now. The inclined plane of the ground was shooting up. It got even worse. The plane started yawing violently, and sideslipping.

Almost indifferently, I understood. Greaves was attempting to jerk the parachute canopy off the stabilizer, hoping the sideslipping would draw the canopy off sideways. At least he was still thinking. He was a cool customer, all right. However, he had only a few seconds left. The sky was greying out, the ground rushing past. My thoughts were about Katherine. It was funny the way I'd begun to love her really passionately only after we'd gotten married. I understood it was usually the other way round. I felt so sorry for her, because she'd lost every one of her childhood friends in the war, and now her last and only friend had gone west as well. But at least she'd have that Rolls I brought back from the Somme, and that painting by Matisse. She loved it. Heaven knows why. Terrible daub.

The parachute was free.

Suddenly it was free. It had torn itself loose. The D.H. engine, beating dimly again, quickly faded. I was hurtling down independently.

The sideslipping had worked. At least Greaves was safe. But the canopy was ripped, so I was no better off. Though there was some braking, I would still hit the ground at fifty miles an hour, at least.

An overgrown cliff face shot past. Then the impact, and darkness. So this was what death was like. Rather like drowning.

Goodness, I *was* drowning . . . It was real water, of a particularly thick and disgusting composition . . . I flapped my limbs feebly, without much thought. When, a couple of aeons later, I came to the surface, I found I'd fallen into a quarry.

It was three quarters of an hour before two cars and three lorries arrived at the quarry, just as I was climbing over the top, covered in green slime.

"My God," Greaves said. "The creature from ten thousand fathoms." And then he did something rather embarrassing in front of all those mechanics and signalmen and staff officers. He embraced and hugged me, without saying another word.

That's Me, and That's the Eiffel Tower

I understood that Paris was seething with bitterness over the continued Allied reverses, that pacifist activity was widespread, and that defeatist sentiment was being eloquently expressed, not just in the salons, boulevards, and quays, but in the newspapers as well.

It certainly wasn't being expressed in the café opposite the Gare du Nord, though. *"Quelle joie de vivre,"* I trilled, stretching luxuriously, after the long car ride. *"Quelle bonheur, quelle vie magnifique,* and stuff."

"Blimey, Guv, you'll be breaking into a pas dee dux in a minute," Witcomb said.

We had made an early start that morning so as to experience as much of the city as possible in the time available. Even my molar was in a fairly good mood. The closer it got to the City of Light the less it ached, until by the time we'd finished a second breakfast in the café, I was seriously thinking of cancelling the dental appointment and just making the most of my first day off in over two months.

Appropriately enough, it was also my twenty-fifth birthday.

"And what are you going to do this glorious fourteenth of July, Witcomb?" I asked, as I sprawled all over the café, watching the civvies strolling across the square in the brilliant sunlight. It was the first really hot day of the year.

"I'm repairing to the nearest 'ore'ouse," Witcomb said, "and I'm not coming out for twelve bloody hours."

"Disgusting."

"Yerse," Witcomb said with reverent anticipation.

"Well, I'm not having a poxed-up chauffeur," I said. "So if you catch anything, you'll just have to go back to your old job in the cookhouse."

"You don't 'ave to worry about that, Major. They're clean 'ere, you know. It's them bidets, see? First time I saw one of them things I thought it was a footbath. 'Ere, that's funny, I thought. The froggies don't seem to mind never 'aving a bath, so why are they so particular about their feet?"

He got up and stretched. "Well, I'll be off, then," he strained. "I'll bring the car back to the rileway station over there at ten tonight, right?"

"If you think you're taking my car to a whorehouse, you're very much mistaken," I said. "*I'm* taking it."

"*You're* going to an 'ore'ouse too?"

"Certainly not. I mean, I'm having it."

"Where are you 'aving it, if not in an 'ore'ouse?" Witcomb asked, winking at some workingmen at a table nearby. Then: "Oh, all right, you can 'ave the car. But look after it, mind. Where *are* you going, Major, just in case I 'ave to come and carry you 'ome?"

"Look who's talking. Well, let me see, now. I believe they still sell old books along the Seine. I think I'll browse around there, first."

"Books?" Witcomb looked at the workingmen again. As they appeared to be interested, he addressed them again, with a wealth of Anglo-Saxon gesture. "Books. 'E's in Paris for the first time in 'is life," Witcomb told them, "an 'e's going to look at books. Cor luv a duck."

And he lurched off into the crowds, swinging his wattles hopelessly from side to side.

Having been told all my life about the gaiety of Paris and its inspired art, music, and mistresses, I suppose it's possible that I was importing a fair proportion of the *joie* myself. But as I strolled along the sunlit thoroughfares, the very air seemed to sing an objective hymn to the nobility of the senses. Everything was entrancing and fascinating: the texture of the walls, crumbling and aesthetically stained, the unfamiliar scent of the tobacco, the open-air markets (live cats, dead rabbits, brass cages, cut flowers), the taste of the wine, the feel of the cobbles underfoot, the liveliness of the signs advertising Vermouths and can-can dancers, the carefree hooting and parping of the cars, and above all the lively faces of the people as they promenaded along the dark green river, or loitered around the bridges, waving and calling out to the boatmen in the cargo vessels, or clustered around the booksellers, arguing good-naturedly.

"We are here since sixteen hundred fifty years," one old couple told me, gesturing proudly at a mile of stalls along the Seine. "Mong Joo," I responded, *"vous ne semblez pas aussi vieux que ça."* But they didn't get my little joke.

"Alors," I continued, coughing slightly, "I am searching for books on the subject of parachutes." And they were kind enough to direct me to a stall about half a mile farther along the river, from which I obtained a comprehensively illustrated history of French under-clothing, but unfortunately nothing on the other subject. I checked about two dozen stalls all together, and drew a variety of shrugs and tolerant smiles at my interest in such arcana.

So I had to spend the rest of the morning filling in forms and breathing the dust of the National Library. The closest I came was an illustration of Leonardo da Vinci's parachute design, which might just conceivably have been the cause of Mona's smile.

My main hope now was Katherine. I'd written to her three or four weeks before, to see if she could dig up any material on the subject; though if the French, with their long-established interest in aerial matters, had neglected the corollary subject of parachutes, it wasn't very likely she'd find anything useful in England.

It was beginning to look as if everybody *was* out of step except me.

My delight in the city persisted even after being gypped out of nine and a half francs during lunch at a sidewalk café on the Champs Elysées.

I suspect it was my uniform that inspired the waiter to charge me ten instead of the usual half a franc for a glass of wine. I was wearing my sky-blue air-force uniform, which was positively drenched in gold braid. The cap alone looked as if it belonged to the commodore of some particularly ostentatious yacht club. I received salutes from a Belgian colonel, two high-ranking Russian naval officers (old style), half a dozen pensioners, about two hundred gendarmes, and even a couple of poilus; which helped to still all but the occasional pang of fear that stapped me vitals whenever I thought of the dental appointment in the Rue Morgue, or wherever Robinson's office was. I'd made a note of it somewhere. I hoped I'd lost it.

The open admiration of the ladies, who strolled past the tables on the Elysées in scented streams, was also a very pleasant distraction, until an octogenarian gentleman with the red ribbon of the Legion of Honor on his dusty frock coat informed me that their interest was purely, or not so purely, professional.

"You mean they're Ladies of the Night? But it's daylight. Besides, they're so well dressed."

"They should be, Monsieur. They charge enough," the old gentleman said indignantly. "Why, only yesterday— then, that is another matter."

It was then the idea occurred to me to call Mrs. Soames. Naturally there was no logical line of thought there. I just wanted to find out what else she could tell me about parachuting, that was all.

After all, why not? She'd invited me to call on her whenever I was in Paris. And I was in Paris, wasn't I?

It was nearly three in the afternoon, however, before I managed to pluck up the courage to look her up in the directory in a postal bureau.

"Is Madame Soames there, please?" I enquired (remembering at long last that the telephone was not a long hollow tube, but worked by electricity or something).

"Who calls?" a man asked. At least I think it was a man, though it may have been a female concierge with a throat condition.

"Monsieur Bandy—Bart."

"She is not at home, Monsieur Bandybart. I am sure of it. Is it another complaint about *Madame's soirées?*"

"No, I don't think so."

"This is not *Monsieur* the Advocate?"

"No, just a pilot."

"Ah. *Madame* adores pilots. I will bring her to the telephone immediately."

A minute later, that disturbingly hoarse voice tickled my left eardrum. *"Allo?"* she said, sounding as if she'd just got up.

"It's me, Mrs. Soames, Bartholomew W. Bandy," I said in English, suppressing an urge to bellow. "How are you? I'm fine, thanks. I just happen to be in Paris, and I thought I'd give you a ring. Well, actually I just don't happen, I came here on purpose."

"To see me, Bart'olomew?"

"No, to see a dentist, actually. An American dentist, name of Robinson. I'm seeing him later this evening, but I'll be available until then, if not after. I—"

"Oh, dear. I'm so sorry, Bart'olomew."

"It's all right. Dentists don't bother me, Mrs.—Marguerite," I said with a light trill.

"I mean, I'm afraid I won't be able to see you today. My husband is in town. In Versailles, to be exact, but we're going out for the evening."

"Oh. Oh. That's all right, then, Mrs. Soames. Just thought I'd say hello. Hello. Well, good-bye."

"Wait. You are here tomorrow?"

"No, I have to get back."

"You should have telephoned earlier, Bart'olomew. We could at least have had lunch together. As it is . . ."

So that was that. I replaced the telephone receiver, and with a light carefree smile on my swollen face, I sauntered off in the direction of the Place Maubert, where I'd parked the car, but first glancing around the cathedral.

This, of course, was the famous Notre Dame, the exquisitely decorated thirteenth-century cathedral where Quasimodo had hung out. I was especially entranced by Discornette's delicate scrollwork, the felicitous flying buttresses, and particularly the two magnificent transept rose windows, with their flashing blues. I was similarly inspired by the light, airy west front gallery, from which one could obtain a magnificent view of the Sainte Chapelle, the Church of St. Augustine, and the . . . I should have called Marguerite before lunch, I suppose, instead of putting it off until the day was more than half spent.

Still, it didn't matter. Where was I? Oh, yes, the view from the gallery . . . Besides, I was a married man, now. I was sure I'd be able to hold out until I could be of one flesh again with Katherine. Though, as I said, that had absolutely nothing to do with it. I'd only wanted to ask Marguerite about parachutes, that was all, as she seemed to know quite a bit about the subject.

Anyway, now I'd be able to spare a few minutes for the Louvre.

"Excreta" I said, and lashed out with my black shoe at the nearest bird market.

There were about a hundred cages ranged along the sidewalk near the cathedral, containing fowl, songsters and various other kinds of dickey bird. As my foot thwacked against the slats, an ornithological hubbub arose from the beady-eyed occupants. Budgerigars, canaries, magpies, hens, ravens, tumbler pigeons, larks, and parrots broke into an uproar of squawkings, whistlings, flappings, and flutterings. So did the beret-crested bird dealer.

"Socialist assassin," he shouted after me, shaking his fist. "Sadist of birds. Species of cucumber."

Well. All I had to look forward to now was the dentist.

The dentist's office was on the ground floor of a crumbling house off the Boulevard St. Michel, on the south side of the river. A wood-and-frosted-glass partition separated his office from the waiting room, which was unoccupied except for about half a dozen huge, high-backed chairs. They looked as if they'd been ejected from Notre Dame on account of arrogance. There were crosses carved in their high, oaken backs, and also designs that looked suspiciously like wreaths.

This didn't exactly send my morale soaring. Nor was I particularly encouraged by my first sight of the dentist. I could see his shape wavering across the frosted glass of the partition. I watched the impressionistic scene with considerable uneasiness. There appeared to be something of a struggle going on through there. A lot of arms were waving about frantically, and possibly even legs. The dentist seemed to be trying to cope with an upended patient with convulsions, unless he was practicing on an unruly squid.

Suddenly remembering I'd left the engine of my Dolphin running, I turned to leave. But the dentist must have heard me clawing at the emergency exit, for he straightened and called through the glass, "Don't go away. I'll be through in ay few minutes."

From the tone of his voice I got the impression that he was quite used to losing his patients, even before he'd got them into the chair.

Thirty minutes marched past in columns of four, grinning toothlessly. The air in the waiting room was hot, heavy, and saturated with the sharp, frightening odor of cocaine.

After that first glimpse of Robinson at work, I kept my eyes turned away from the frosted glass. But this didn't help much, as I was forced to listen to a good many painful gasps and sighs and death-rattles and things, and worst of all, a steady, encouraging drone from the dentist. He sounded as if he were administering last rites.

Sweat trickled down my legs. It felt as if flies were crawling over me. Whenever I shifted position, there was a rasping sound, my trousers unsticking themselves from the medieval chair.

Finally the dentist emerged, ushering out an amazingly intact-looking client. He seemed surprised to find me still there.

"Let me see," he said. "You're . . . ?"

He waited. But I was too busy counting the spots of blood on his white coat and shivering in the heat.

"Major Bandy, is it?" I nodded spastically. "Ah, great. I'll be with you in ay moment, Major," he said cheerfully.

After rifling the patient's wallet and sending him back into the world, Robinson regarded me optimistically, his plump, yellowish face and bald dome polished with sweat. "I hope you weren't trepidatious, sir," he said, dabbing his steaming scalp with a cloud of cotton wool, "about any torturous ejaculations you may have heard from my inner sanctum." He put a hand on my shrinking arm and squeezed it in an encouraging way. "It was me making those sounds, Major. It's the last residue of an attack of muscular spasm, you see. I get these attacks every now and then. It's all this bending over people, I guess. Goddamn nuisance, though, having it. Like yesterday, when I got a twinge just as I was driving a needle into this lady's gums. I had to grab hold of something to stop me sinking to my knees. You know how it gets you, when

186

you have a muscular spasm. You get a stab in the back, and there's nothing you can do but slowly sink to your knees until the attack passes.

"Anyways, I grabbed hold of this dame's necklace, and broke it. She wasn't too pleased about that, I can tell you. Lucky they was only imitation pearls. She was just a streetwalker, anyways. Some reason, I get a lot of *poules* as clients. I guess they think it's kind of chick and swave to have their teeth fixed up by an American dentist."

I suddenly realized he had maneuvered me next door and that I was already ensconced in the chair. I stared wildly at the array of instruments on the napkin-covered table. The brute had placed them in full view of the patient.

The drilling apparatus was also horridly visible. It looked as if it had been purchased from the bankrupt stock of the Ratchett Screw and Gear Company. But worst of all was the sight of a pile of teeth in the far corner.

They were leering up at me out of the fluff and dust. I was up and half-way through the frosted glass before I realized they weren't teeth at all, but the imitation pearls that he or his concierge had swept aside but failed to remove from the sight of mortal men.

"You know, young man," he said, as he stuck several fingers and a knuckle or two into my mouth, "you ought to have all your teeth out."

"Ah blog, ah nost ah bahg!"

"Huh?"

"I said, Oh, God, they're not all bad, are they?"

"No, but, well, you know, it would save you a lot of trouble in the future. Besides, I need the practice."

He picked up a small hammer and started to ring my teeth as if it were his ambition to play the xylophone. "That's the one that's giving you the trouble, right? I can tell because of all them beads of perspiration that's suddenly dotted your brow. M'm, that's a bad one all right

187

. . . have to come out, of course . . . And there's this molar here, tha'll have to be excavated. This one. Feel that probe?"

"Arghatch!"

"That'll need filling, Major. That's quite ay crater. Filling that with gold might be as good an investment for you as a hundred shares in the Stutz Motor Car Company. Well, I'll drill that one first—eeek, eeek!"

For a moment, I thought I'd bitten him. But it was just another of his muscular spasms. He clutched his back with one hand and held onto the drill stand with the other, saying "eeek" and slowly sinking below the level of my terrified gaze.

He'd reached his knees, and mine as well, before he was able to pull himself up the drill stand, hand over hand. "Goddamn spasms," he grunted, wincing. "More they hurt, the more you tense up, and the more you tense the more they goddamn hurt . . . I better get to grips with that molar before I end up helpless on my goddamn back . . . Just give me a minute to get the treadle going . . . Kind of like working a Singer Sewing Machine, ain't it, Major?"

A heart-rending groan burst from my dank lips as the drill vanished into the nearest cavity. It felt as if he were using a sharpened egg beater. The dentist frowned, then went on, "Don't mind me, Major, I always like to chat while I'm working. The perfesser at the dental school I attended in Salt Lake City said it was important to distract the patient as much as possible before they saw all the blood. Matter of fact, he was pretty good at distracting us students as well, especially the time in Pathology when the prof fell into the tank of formaldehyde, you know, where they kept the bodies. He had ay hell of a job getting out, too. He had to keep pushing cadavers aside, you know, and he was spluttering and gasping and screaming quite ay bit before he finally clambered out. He was never quite the same after that . . . Fact, he developed some kind of crazy suspicion that one of the students he'd flunked had pushed him in, a guy called Augustus G. Timberlake, Junior, who had to get out of dentistry as a result . . . Believe he's a geologist now . . . Close your mouth a bit, will you? Jeez, Major, I wish you wouldn't keep rolling your eyes like that. You're not nervous, are you? I mean, if you're like this for a simple filling, what you gonna be like for an extraction? Maybe you better have gas."

"Ahg."

"Huh?"

"Yes, yes, please. Gas, I'd like that, Mr. Robinson," I whimpered.

"Yeah, maybe you better have a whiff of N_2O for the extraction before you eeek-eeek!"

He clutched at his back again, emitting bursts of blasphemy, and his knees slowly buckled. As they did so, the drill clattered against my teeth. I could feel large bits of something swimming about in the saliva that immediately started to dribble over my lips in a veritable Niagara Falls of spit, soaking my bib through and through. The pieces felt like the remains of several perfectly sound teeth, and perhaps even a few shreds of tongue.

I wished to God I'd never come to Paris. I should have just tied some piano wire around the infected molar and attached the other end to a passing Dolphin.

Finally, after squirting ice-cold water onto several exposed nerves, he turned to a little wooden cabinet and, still eeeking out his imperfections, took out the largest available filling.

"There now, that wasn't so bad, was it?" he asked, after he'd leaned on me to press the ingot home.

I gazed at him bitterly, feeling faint from loss of saliva.

Now he was wheeling forward a pair of scarred cylinders. After fiddling with the knobs, he sniffed the mask, then listened to it, as if it were playing Irving Berlin. Then he clamped the mask over my face as if in a hurry to blot out the sight of my haggard face and accusing eyes.

"This'll only take a few minutes," he murmured, glancing at his watch. "Jeez, I better hurry, I'll be late for dinner. Just breathe normal. Look, I said normal, man. Major, for Crysake, will you let go my arm? You trying to break my wrist or something? That's better. No, no, don't hold your breath, Crysake, what good'll that do? That's it. Relax. Breathe in and out. In and out. All right. How's that? Okay?"

I mumbled something but couldn't quite catch what I'd said. Beyond the dentist, over by the window, there was a thick cobweb, wavering and flicking in the heat. It seemed to be in the shape of a rope ladder. I wondered why the spider had done that, woven a rope ladder instead of the usual spiderish strand. "It's because I have ay muscular spasm," the spider told me.

The sun was slanting through the window. It was so bright, I closed my eyes. The dentist's voice receded. He sounded as if he were speaking from the far end of the Paris sewers. Then I was sure I heard Mrs. Soames's voice. A moment later, she was flying slowly through the Notre Dame buttresses in a coal barge. She was throwing army blankets to the pedestrians below. One of them turned into a woollen parachute. She jumped out and drifted down, showing her garters.

A cathedral choir hummed and hawed. The sound turned into a loud buzz. Then my cheek was being slapped, gently but a trifle impatiently. "Okay, now, Major, okay? That's it. Here. Drink. Spit. No. Spit, not dribble. That's it. How d'you feel?"

"Fine," I mumbled, holding my head and wondering why I had no feeling in my fingers. They didn't seem to belong to me.

Then I realized they didn't; they weren't my fingers, they belonged to the dentist. He was supporting my head.

I was in the waiting room again. There was some incomprehensible conversation buried under a loud, humming sound. Somebody tucked my head between my knees. I giggled feebly at the sight of an unfastened fly button. "Guess it's the heat," I heard the dentist say. ". . . look after him," a woman said. "You're all right now?" That was Robinson. "Oh, sure, I'm fine, thanks," I said, feeling sick as the tip of my tongue disappeared into the gaping hole where the offending molar had been.

Mrs. Soames's face swam into view. She was really there. "Mog . . . Mog . . . Mogereet," I mumbled. "I'm very glad you're still here, *Commandant*. I felt sure you'd have gone, by now."

"Actually, I think I'm going to go at any moment . . ." "I came to see if you'd like to escort me this evening after all, Bart'olomew." Her voice sounded cool, formal. "Arser telephoned to say he couldn't come after all. The conference is lasting longer than he expected. He's staying the night at Versailles. But perhaps you won't feel like going to a recital, after . . . ?"

"No, I'll be delighted to escort you, Marguerite," I said gallantly, but spoiled it by tittering. I don't know why; I wasn't feeling the least amused.

I stood up. There was a slight concussion. The windows rattled. I thought at first it was Big Bertha bombarding Paris again. But it was only me, staggering against the wall.

Suddenly we were outside, in the street. Somebody scented was holding an arm. I think it was mine. I was surprised all over again to see Mrs. Soames. "Fancy meeting you here," I said. She was wearing a dark-red evening gown.

We floated over the cobbles. They were greasy in the evening heat. Our shadows were twenty feet long, and rather unsteady.

"Did you say you had a car, Bart'olomew?"

"Did I? Yes, that's right," I said. "It's brown, with

flutes." I giggled again. I'd meant it had a fluted hood. Or fluted bonnet, as it was an English car.

"Perhaps we'd better not go . . ."

"No, honest, I'm okay now, thanks, Marguerite," I said. As she had her arm around me, I put an arm around her. "I love you, Marguerite," I said, feeling simultaneously sick and exhilarated. "You're so beautiful and calm. Don't much like your husband, though. He's not beautiful. Or calm."

"He doesn't like you much, either," Marguerite said, not the least offended. "Is this your car? Perhaps I'd better drive, *hein?* I'm not a very good driver, but all the same I think it would be safer."

"You're quite safe with me, my dear," I said, and started as somebody laughed villainously.

As she sat frowning at the dashboard, I leaned over and kissed her, and was overjoyed when her lips pushed back against mine. "I love you, Marguerite. Isn't it ridiculous?"

"It has a self-starter? Ah, yes. What a fine car this is. It will be very nice to turn up at Madame de Hautcloque's in such a car. Why is it ridiculous, *cher Commandant?*"

"I've only been married a short time. I love Katherine. I love her whole family. I can't possibly be in love with you as well, now, can I? That would smack of amorous inflation."

Amorous inflation. I liked that. I used it again. "Amorous inflation," I said.

"Of course not."

"Of course not what?"

"That you can't be in love with me, Ooops, that's reverse, isn't it?"

"All the same, I've been thinking about you constantly ever since we met. How adorable you are, Marguerite. Listen, let's not go to the recital. Let's go to stead in bed—bed instead," I amended, amazed at the things I was amending. "Oh, Marguerite, if you only knew how difficult it is, since I first tasted the joys of connubial bliss. I can hardly think of anything else. Except flying, administration, maintenance, and things like that."

"I know you've certainly been thinking a lot about parachutes," she said. "You've driven my husband almost crazy, you know, with your little notes and messages. He starts to rave and gibbet every time your name is mentioned. Bandy—you only have to say the word and hey presto, he starts to gibbet. Or is that not the right word?"

"Gibbet? No, that sounds about right."

Marguerite drove fast, used the horn exuberantly, and shouted something rude at a cab driver. I don't remember much about Madame de Hautcloque's house, except it was large. Our hostess was a bustling society lady with wobbly arms. She had a large vaccination mark on her right arm. She greeted Marguerite with a theatrical embrace and was extremely impressed with my uniform. She kept making flattering remarks about the Portuguese Army, for some reason. She may have thought I was some exotic generalissimo. She was gay, charming, graceful, filled with compliments, suffused with smiles.

"She's furious," Marguerite whispered, wearing a malicious smile. "All the best people have failed to turn up, because of the Boche long-range guns."

Accordingly, Madame de Hautcloque's salon was packed with nobodies: writers and people like that. I was introduced to a good many of them, but retained the names of only three: a couple of strange American ladies, who seemed to have something to do with the Red Cross, and a middle-aged composer. I remembered him because he kept squeezing Marguerite's waist and whispering scandalous suggestions in her ear. On one occasion, when she sat in an armchair, he kneeled on the padded armrest to continue his verbal love-making, with his big nose only inches away from hers, and with his face almost upside down. But I wasn't jealous. He quite plainly didn't take himself any more seriously than Marguerite did.

She smiled and chatted to him fondly, not the least flustered by his inverted attentions.

As for the American ladies, the smaller of the two was not particularly noteworthy, except for the absorbed interest she took in her nails. For the entire time she was there, she hardly stopped polishing them, with quick, nervous movements.

Her companion, however, quite dominated the large alcove in which she had installed herself. She was dressed in sandals and a corduroy skirt, her knees widespread beneath the thick brown material, presumably for maximum air circulation in the stifling heat. In spite of the heat, she wore an ample, though shapeless, jacket. Above this was thrust a powerful head, on the front of which a strikingly direct face had been moulded.

Madame de Hautcloque had introduced her as "One of the most distinguished members of our *émigré* society, a lady I'm sure needs no introduction. Monsieur le Général Banda, may I present the celebrated writer and connoisseur of the arts, and patroness of many of our greatest painters—Madame Stein."

"Miss," said the monolith in corduroy.

"Gertrude Stein," her companion added, as if it were important for us to know her first name.

"Ah! So you're Gertrude Stein," I said, bowing unsteadily. I still felt woozy, after all that gas. "This is indeed an honor, Miss Stein," I said, kissing her finger tips. I'd never heard of her.

Then the lady was talking matter-of-factly, though in gloriously sonorous tones. "Your brow is pale," she said. "Your brow is pale and pale is your brow that is pale and beyond the brow is your paleness. So much paleness is pale that is brow that is pale where the paleness is but where there is brow there is brow that is pale where the paleness is. The brow is where the paleness is that is pale but the paleness that is pale is pale but where the paleness is is where the brow is the brow. And beyond the brow is the pale. And a pale is a pale is a pail is a bucket, and the bucket is beyond the pale."

"Er," I said, perhaps a shade inadequately.

Showing My Teeth

Even though Marguerite must have known that I hardly knew what I was saying, and ought logically to have dismissed my loving words as the gibberings of a gas-besotted birdman, in fact she behaved as though I had declared myself on bended patella after days of clear-headed deliberation. My amorous behavior in the car established such a warm intimacy between us as to sustain itself throughout the evening, right up to the moment when I said good-bye to her at the front door of her place in Montmartre.

At least, I'd intended saying good-bye, as Witcomb must already be waiting for me at the Gare du Nord. But she unlocked the door and went inside as if she expected me to follow.

So I lurched after her, up the battered stairwell to her apartment on the second floor of the old house, even though I knew that I just wasn't the sort of person who could straggle into a woman's apartment late at night without *something* going wrong.

I did, however, eliminate the worst possibility of disaster as soon as I'd made myself uncomfortable in her living room. *"Are you quite sure your husband is staying at Versailles tonight?"* I enunciated, clearly and distinctly.

"I have already told you so, Bart'olomew," she said shortly.

A certain constraint had arisen between us from the

moment we entered her apartment. To avoid catching my eye, she started wandering about, touching things.

"He's on a Supreme War Council committee," she said, smoothing the belly of a small ivory Buddha. "He said they will be sitting for some time yet, so he thought he would stay the night."

"Ah."

I relaxed a little more on the sofa, and looked around her second-floor living room. It was not nearly as luxurious as I'd expected, though she had managed to give it a certain untidy charm. The living-room walls were so colorfully decorated with pictures, wall hangings, and artfully arranged plants that you were quite prepared to forgive the cracked and rather grimy plasterwork beneath.

One of the pictures was an enthusiastically modern portrait of my hostess that made her look as if she were in the final stages of frostbite.

"Would you like something to eat?" she asked warily, as if she feared that food was the last thing on my mind.

It was. The thought of filling that gaping crater with nourishment made me quite nauseous. I settled for a glass of cognac.

"It's something to do with Russia," she said.

"What is?"

"Arser's committee."

"Oh."

"Some emergency or other."

"There usually is, with Russia."

"The blockade of Germany is almost ruined," she said stiltedly, "because now the Boche can get all the supplies they need from the Ukraine. Wheat and oil, and . . ."

"Coal?"

"Yes. So they are considering ways to, what's the word, recreate the Eastern Front."

"I see."

She lit a cigarette and inhaled unsteadily. "So the Allies

are thinking of sending troops. Of course, this is all very secret, you understand."

"What is?"

"What I've just been telling you, of course."

"Oh, yes," I said vaguely, and took a sip of cognac. I winced, and tilted my head sharply.

She looked at me in alarm.

"Did you hear something?"

"Eh? No, I'm just holding my head on one side to keep the booze out of the, where my tooth was."

She regarded me tensely for a moment, then slowly relaxed and smiled. She leaned back, putting an arm along the back of the sofa. Her red evening gown tightened over her thighs. I gulped the rest of my cognac.

"You know, I feel quite safe with you, Bart'olomew," she murmured.

"That's an awful thing to say about a fellow."

"I thought perhaps you'd come up here in the hope of sleeping with me."

I was too embarrassed to reply to this remarkably frank comment. Especially as it was true.

"I'm glad we can just be friends," she said impulsively, putting a hand on mine. "Because I've no intention of letting that happen, you understand? I've always been faithful to Arser, even though we've been married since more than a year."

"*Tiens.*"

"I am very fond of you, of course, but it can go no further than that, you understand?"

"Oh, sure."

She looked at me curiously. "You know," she said, "you are a personality, Bart'olomew. A lot of people at Madame de Hautcloque's asked who you were."

"They were probably wondering if I was planning another Latin revolution."

She continued to study me thoughtfully. A tendril of

cigarette smoke formed a wavery question mark beside her nose.

"You said some lovely things to me in the car, Bart'olomew," she said softly.

"I mean every one of them," I said, trying to remember what I'd said.

She leaned forward to stub out her cigarette. As she did so, her left breast rested for an instant on my right thigh, which immediately started quivering like mad.

"I 'ardly recognized the stiff, formal Anglo-Saxon of Flesselles."

"I'm stiffer than ever, now," I husked.

"But it's no good, Bart'olomew, Besides, I'm some years older than you."

Being a woman—adoring women so wholeheartedly, I really think I was beginning to understand them—she would expect me to deny that her age mattered one jot or tittle. How to do it without arousing that secret feminine scorn for patently untrue flattery?

"You could not be more interesting, more beautiful, and more desirable," I essayed, "were you twenty or fifty."

She looked quite impressed at this. So did I. In fact, I was so excited—by my own words—that I leaned forward to prove it didn't matter one jot or tit—tittle, that is. She drew back.

"No, Bart'olomew. In fact, I think you had better go. You have a long drive ahead of you."

Applying another lesson in feminine psychology, I replied, "Yes, perhaps I should. I'm already late. Witcomb will be very annoyed."

I passed the exam with top marks, this apparent acquiescence having the effect, not of speeding my departure, but delaying it.

"Do you really like me as much as you say, Bart'olomew?"

"When I look at you I understand for the first time those words about, with my body I thee worship. I could prove my love very well, that way. Though it's not entirely your face and form I find so lovely, but your sensual voice, your sly humor, your intelligence, even your bad temper. If you were mine, I would be ruined."

"Ruined?"

"Because no matter what you did I could not help forgiving you, and loving you just as much."

Even though I felt pretty sincere, I couldn't help admiring the way I was being so chick and swave about it all. By Jove, thought I, maybe I ought to take a whiff of N_2O more often.

We stared into each other's eyes. I swallowed, sounding rather like a damned pigeon.

"I suppose I shall never see you again," she whispered.

I couldn't help it. Flinging Katherine aside in all directions, I leaned over and kissed her.

She tasted of smoke and lipstick. As if of its own accord her tongue darted inside my mouth—straight into the dentist's excavation.

I jumped violently, as if all my reflexes had been stimulated simultaneously, and fell against her, clutching at her frantically in an effort to push her away, to get her tongue out of the crater.

"Oh, all right," she whispered hoarsely, her breath whistling up my nostrils, which were dilated with the pain.

She seized my hand and dragged me, half-fainting with nausea, to my feet.

"Come," she whispered. And before I knew what was happening, we were on our way to the front of the apartment, toward a room that I sincerely hoped was the bathroom. My brain felt as if it were being turned on a lathe. I was soaked in sweat. I was sure I was going to be sick at any moment.

There were two rooms at the front of the house. We

200

were just turning into the one on the right when a loud click sounded from the passageway downstairs.

We froze like two pillars of salt, staring at each other wildly in the dim light.

The front door opened; there was a rustling sound and a slight thump. It sounded like a body of a recently dispatched lover being deposited in the cellar. However, it's possible it was just a valise being set down in the hall.

Marguerite was digging her nails into my wrist.

"My 'usband!"

"It can't be. It only happens in plays."

"In there!" she breathed, pushing me toward the other door.

I started inside, then: "My cap! In the sitting room!"

Soames was already starting upstairs, calling out.

She gave me a uneceremonious push. "I'll get it," she whispered. "Hurry."

I staggered into the room, panting as if I'd just run a hundred feet. As my eyes accustomed themselves to the gloom, I perceived I was in some kind of a study. Books on shelves, a pile of papers and files on the radiator below the window. An old Remington typewriter.

Footsteps outside. Marguerite had left the study door open a few inches. I stopped breathing. A door squeaked.

"You went to the recital after all?"

"Hello, Arser. Yes. You didn't miss much. It was very boring."

There was some more of this, then: "Can you help me off with this dress. I'm having an awful time with it."

"You haven't unfastened it yet."

"Oh, haven't I? I thought you were staying the night at Versailles, Arser."

There was a silence, then a faint grunt. Did he suspect? Had he just sunk his fist into her solar plexus? No, his clipped voice clipped on—clippingly.

"The meeting broke up earlier than I thought . . . You left the light on in the sitting room."

"Oh, did I? I'll go and switch it off."

"I'll do it."

"No, it's all right. I have to tidy up anyway."

A bit more domestic-type dialogue. A rustling. Footsteps. A sigh. A throat-clearing. Their room was right across the passage.

I tiptoed to the window, my throat fluttering like a wounded bird. The curtains were drawn back, revealing a tiny, ironwork balcony overlooking the blacked-out street.

There were three casement windows, secured by brass catches. I opened the middle one. Cool midnight air wafted into my face, which felt as if it had been dipped in bronze, for posterity. Which seemed very close.

There was nowhere to hide in the study. If he came in, I was finished. Really finished, I mean.

"What are you doing here, Bandy?"

"Er—studying?"

More footsteps. A quick movement. My cap came flying into the room.

A few seconds later: "That mountebank Wilson was there."

"Who?"

"The C.I.G.S., of course."

"Oh, yes."

"I wish you wouldn't smoke so much, Marguerite. The whole apartment stinks of smoke."

Marguerite murmured something in reply, then started to hum an air from Carmen. She sounded hatefully cool.

But then I realized that she was covering up any sounds I might make. I started to climb through the window, inch by inch.

I was half-way through when I heard Soames mention my name. I stopped and listened with my leg cocked. Like a dog trying to demarcate its territory. Vainly. So far.

"Talking to Sykes. Air Minister. He's going to do something about it, right enough."

"But if his squadron is doing so well, Arser, I don't see—"

"I mean that business in Parliament. Damned frocks . . . Bandy put them up to it, I'm sure of it. Asking questions about parachutes."

"I don't understand why you always get so upset whenever parachutes are mentioned."

"I don't get upset! It's just . . . Oh, God."

"Chérie."

"I really thought we'd seen the last of him yesterday."

"Why? What happened?"

"He insisted on trying out one of the new parachutes. It snagged on the tail of the aircraft."

"What? . . ."

"He got dragged down behind the plane. You don't have to look like that; he got away with it. Naturally. Fell into a quarry. The only one around for fifty miles."

"My God," Marguerite whispered. "And he never even . . ."

"What?"

"Oh, Arser . . ."

There was quite a long pause, which of course I didn't interrupt. For the previous two or three minutes, I hadn't really been listening to what Marguerite was saying. But to the way she was saying it.

Though nothing she said seemed intimate, her tone was suffused with that unmistakable indulgence, warmth, fondness—of a woman in love.

I couldn't believe it. I listened, breathing rapidly through my mouth.

"Hold me, Arser . . ."

An unbearable pause. One of those wrenching sighs.

"Love you so much, Marguerite."

"Darling . . ."

She loved him? *Soames?* It was *disgusting*. But she did. There was no doubt about it.

I was absolutely furious.

As I swung my leg over the window sill, my lower lip was trembling with utter dismay at her inconstancy. The bitch! She loved him! I had been betrayed.

I was so agitated, my left shoe failed to see what it was doing. It caught the edge of a huge pile of papers on the radiator below the window. Half of them cascaded onto the little balcony beyond, and slithered through the gap between the balcony floor and the rusting ironwork that guarded it.

A shower of papers sailed off into the darkness before I could get my foot on them.

Simultaneously, a distant searchlight flickered on, and poked sullenly at the clouds, dimly lighting the street. The light revealed a perfect storm of paperwork, which drifted, glided, fluttered, and cascaded into the street and all over the sidewalk and far out over the cobbles.

"What was that?"

"What?"

"I heard something. In the study."

"It was just the wind, Arser."

Footsteps and agitated breathing, I flung myself over the ironwork, hurling myself frantically into space, clutching the ledge as I went over.

I was still hanging there and swinging about when Soames came into the study. I lowered myself until my arms were straight, holding on only by an inch of fingers, not knowing whether to hang on or let go. My head was pounding. I wondered if my nerves would ever recover from this holiday in Paris.

I heard Soames cry out. God, he must have seen my fingers in the glow from that *bloody* searchlight.

No. He was busy snatching at his papers. Luckily, because of the blackout, he couldn't switch on the light.

I still couldn't decide whether to let go or not. If I dropped, he was certain to hear the crash as I landed on the sidewalk—not to mention the crack of my bones. On the other hand, if I held on he was bound to see my fingers neatly arrayed along the edge of the balcony.

"My papers! Christ, they've blown out the window!"

As he cried out in anguish, I heard his voice coming nearer. I edged my white, straining fingers to the very edge, until I was holding on only by my fingerprints, desperately trying to remember if there were any sharp railings in front of the house. God, this was even worse than parachuting. Even confronting Soames was better than dropping onto an iron spear and becoming a shishkebab.

My arms were shaking uncontrollably by now. Above, there was a desperate clutching and crackling sound as Soames gathered up the few documents that remained. He was bound to see me now, any second. I was bathed in the reflected light from that sodding searchlight.

All this and I hadn't even had time to be guilty of anything.

Then, just as he was leaning out to gather up the documents that had scattered over the balcony, the searchlight went off.

"Damn it to hell, why did you leave the window open!" Soames was shouting.

Only, now his voice was receding.

He was going. He was probably rushing downstairs!

I uttered a fast, three-word prayer and dropped into the black void below, forcing myself to relax completely. It was fortunate I'd had some recent practice—but I hoped I wasn't going to make a habit of it.

It seemed like minutes before I hit the sidewalk. Once again my knees came up and cracked into my chin. Clouds of butterflies appeared as I sprawled backward into the gutter.

I was just picking myself up when I heard Soames scrabbling at the front door. Apart from that searchlight extinguishing itself just in time, there seemed to be no end to my bad luck that night; for my car was parked almost underneath the ironwork balcony, only a few feet from the door. It was madness to have parked so close to her house, whether I'd intended staying or not.

He can't have seen the car in the dark when he came in, but he was bound to recognize a service vehicle when he started hunting around for all that bumf of his. The damn thing was practically covered in squadron markings.

I did the only thing I could think of. I lurched forward, still pretty dazed after that uppercut, and just as the front door was clicking open I seized the big, tarnished door-knob and held on tightly with both hands.

I was only just in time. The door had just started to open. It thudded shut as I hauled on it. It started to heave open again. I held on tighter, my knuckles whitening until they seemed phosphorescent.

There was a muffled curse from the other side, about three inches away. The door heaved again. Suppressing the temptation to give up and accept my fate like a normal human being, I leaned back and put a foot against the door jamb, and pressed, holding on to the knob as before with both hands.

I heard his voice again, thick with frustration, from behind the door. ". . . damn . . . door . . . it's stuck . . . What? I said it's stuck!"

The door began to strain open again. The bastard was a lot stronger than he looked. I held on, putting both feet on the wall this time, now practically in a horizontal position over the sidewalk. I hoped a gendarme wouldn't come along. It might be rather difficult to explain why I was apparently walking up the wall of somebody's apartment in the middle of the night.

Soames again: "What the hell's . . . I'll have to go round . . . What?" His voice rose to a maddened shout. "I told you. Half the material for my bloody memoirs has blown out the window!"

Then, silence. I continued to cling on there, for several seconds. Then put my feet down and cautiously relaxed the counter-pressure. Nothing. He was no longer behind the door.

What had he said? "I'll have to go round . . ." Christ—he was going round the back!

I turned and ran to my car, and fell into it, almost gibbering by now. I stabbed at the self-starter, skinning a knuckle in the process. Thank the Lord, the motor was still warm. It fired immediately. I slammed it into gear and shot forward, wrenching at the wheel, missing an old Peugeot in front by the width of a hangman's rope. The Vauxhall hurtled away from the house. Even in the near-darkness, I could see Soames's precious papers strewn all over the road. I accelerated for only a few seconds, then switched off, snatching the gear lever into neutral. The motor died and the car coasted onward into the darkness, the tires shushing. The only other sound was the pattering of my perspiration on the papers that littered the seat and the floor of the car.

I was such a gibbering wreck by then that I was halfway to the Gare du Nord before I realized what they were. They must have fluttered into the open car from the balcony.

When, still feeling as if I'd been worked over by a gang of Algerian dockers and lightermen, I stopped the car to gather them together, I found that I'd made off with over a hundred sheets of the brigadier's raw material.

We were over half-way from Beauvais to Amiens, approaching a village called, according to Witcomb, Poicks, before I summoned up the energy to look through the papers in the light of the rising sun.

It all seemed to be pretty routine stuff: signals, official reports, copy letters, and the like, with only a few uninteresting personal notes and jottings, which made my decision to destroy the lot all the easier.

Well, after all, I could hardly return them, in the circumstances. Besides, I was in a thoroughly mean mood by then, and was quite looking forward to tearing them up and scattering the pieces along the roadside. In fact I was just starting to do so when the word *parachutes* caught my eye.

It was on the top sheet of a batch of War Office stationery, held together by a brass fastener, and was the subject of a memo dated December 16, 1917, from Soames to the Director General of Military Aeronautics.

The whole memo was of far more than routine interest, but it was the second paragraph that caught my attention most immediately. I almost fell to the floor of the car when I read it:

2. The E.R. Calthorp parachute ("Guardian Angel"): there are grave doubts concerning it practicability, as it has already caused a number of fatalities. The main problems are (a) that it restricts the freedom of movement in the cockpit and (b) when the pilot jumps and the parachute is plucked from its sack (which is attached to the aircraft) there is considerable likelihood of the canopy fouling on a projecting part of the aircraft. This is an inherent fault in this automatic design of parachute. Work, however, is continuing on this project.

It seemed that Soames had known for six months that the Guardian Angel wasn't a safe piece of equipment.

Why, the rotten dog! That's why he had given *me* the job of testing it!

Vamping

As soon as I got back to the squadron, I went straight to the hayloft without bothering with breakfast and, asking not to be disturbed, went over the memo for the third time.

War Office
Date: Dec. 16th, 1917

TO: Director General of Military Aeronautics
FROM: Asst. D.G.M.A.
SUBJECT: Parachutes
With regard to the upcoming Air Board meeting re the proposal that parachutes should be issued to pilots and observers of scout and reconnaissance aircraft as well as to KB observers, as requested I have investigated the subject in detail (see attached appendices) and respectfully submit a summary of my findings on the subject.
1. No Allied or U.S. authority has yet developed a satisfactory parachute for aircraft, as the difficulties seem insurmountable at the present time. There is no evidence of the enemy's having produced a workable design.
2. The E.R. Calthorp parachute ("Guardian Angel"): there are grave doubts concerning its practicability, as it has already caused a number of fatalities. The main problems are (a) that it restricts the freedom of movement in the cockpit and (b) when the pilot

jumps and the parachute is plucked from its sack (which is attached to the aircraft) there is considerable likelihood of the canopy fouling on a projecting part of the aircraft. This is an inherent fault in this automatic design of parachute. Work, however, is continuing on this project.

3. Some additional monies for research and development of manually operated parachutes have been allocated, but the scientific and technical manpower available to the Air Board is severely limited by the demands of many other fields of research. A separate technical department might have to be established. There are some doubts as to whether this is warranted in the light of para. 6.

4. The estimated cost of producing sufficient parachutes (see Appendices C and D) is unacceptable at the present time, particularly in view of the recent burden of financing to overcome the deficiencies of explosive ammunition.

5. Casualties are not such as to warrant issuance of parachutes (Appendix A).

6. There is no demand from the front-line squadrons for parachutes. In fact there is a marked resistance to the idea. Considerable time and effort would be needed to overcome these reservations.

7. The general consensus at the War Office is that the use of parachutes in aircraft would encourage the pilots to abandon their aircraft.

"I think," Soames had written in a covering note to his erstwhile boss, the D.G.M.A., "that it might be useful to distribute this material among the A.B. members before the meeting next week, to discourage any lengthy discussion. I think you'll agree that based on the facts as outlined, the large-scale manufacture of parachutes is neither feasible nor warranted at the present time."

There had obviously been some sort of pressure the

previous year in favor of parachutes. As Asst. D.G.M.A., Soames had obviously done his best to defuse the issue, and with what seemed to me uncalled-for determination.

For as I read through the sheaf of papers once again, it seemed to me that his supporting evidence had been moulded into the form of a preconceived prejudice. More: a determination to kill the issue once and for all. For instance, his statement, "Casualties are not such as to warrant the issuance of parachutes" was supported by an appendix that analysed the casualty figures, not over a significant spread of months, but over a mere eight weeks.

Moreover, Soames's contention that the enemy had failed to produce a workable design was either a monumental sample of clerical inefficiency in summarizing his own evidence, or a down-right fib, for among these very papers was a copy of an intelligence report dated the previous October to the effect that the Germans had not only developed a workable parachute known as the Heinecke type, *but were preparing to issue them to pilots.*

Soames did not appear to have included this information among his other 'evidence.'

The reports that the enemy was now starting to use these parachutes must have come as no surprise to him whatsoever.

One of his strongest supporting documents was a letter from the much respected and highly influential General 'Boom' Trenchard, a former G.O.C. of the Flying Corps. "While I have always supported the idea of parachutes for our balloon observers because of their defenceless state," Trenchard had written, "I long since came to the conclusion, after much soul-searching, that they should not be issued to the airmen, who must not be discouraged from making every effort to defend themselves."

Even Soames's use of this characteristically uncompromising statement had a certain deceit about it, for he had not quoted the letter in its entirety. "I do not like the implications in your letter," Trenchard went on "that

211

what I have to say on the subject is to be nothing more than a means of providing you with ammunition to help you oppose certain political pressures in support of the device, or to help you belittle the anxiety of people concerning the extremely high casualties in the R.F.C. (which I see you are still concealing from the public by incorporating them in the total Army casualties)."

Admittedly this omission did not alter General Trenchard's opinion; but it did reveal a certain suspicion on Trenchard's part regarding Soames's motives. If the Air Board had been aware of the suspicion from such a quarter, they might not have agreed to defer the discussion on the subject with as much alacrity as they apparently had done.

The truth was, the whole memo was riddled with half-truths, evasions, and inaccuracies. But it was that last paragraph that left me almost breathless with astonishment. Having parachutes would encourage pilots to abandon their aircraft? Though it was two or three years since Soames had flown at the front, he couldn't possibly have believed that any true pilot would jump out of his plane if there was the slightest chance of bringing it down in one piece.

The worst of it was, I couldn't use the information without incriminating Marguerite. And, more important, myself.

But the situation was even more frustrating than that. There was nothing I'd have liked better than to embarrass him with a glowing testimonial to the virtues of the Guardian Angel, and it is possible that, dismissing the accident as a fluke, I should have done just that, pointing out that the problems of its weight and bulkiness should be easily solved, if the designers really put their backs into it, literally and figuratively.

I couldn't do that now, in view of this memo. However much I wanted to, I had no reason to disbelieve his statement that the Guardian Angel was an inherently faulty design. It was a confirmation of what, deep down, I already knew to be true. The parachute was a dud.

So all my mild lobbyings had come to nothing. And to make matters even worse, there seemed to be no alternative in sight.

By the time I had finished the report, I felt like biting the rafters in my chagrin.

I was still in a pretty foul temper when I strode into the mess shortly before dinner. For some reason, the pilots were all in their best uniforms, a colorful display of pinks, khaki, navy blue, and sky blue. As I stamped in, there was a guilty stir, and they went into a defensive huddle at the far end of the room, as if enacting the scene where Penelope's suitors are caught in the act by an iron-faced Odysseus.

Derby was the first to recover. "Well, he's finally emerged from the pigeon loft," he said, coming forward a bit unsteadily. He seemed to be rehearsing for some sort of binge. "And how was Paris, *mon Commandant?*"

"A trifle hectic," I said.

"Yes, it looks like it."

I turned to the barman. "A large whisky," I said.

"Good Lord," Blackbourne murmured.

"Is he having a dwink?" Monty asked, wide-eyed.

"Course I'm having a drink," I snapped. "Why shouldn't I?"

There was a silence. "I say, what's wrong with the old man?" somebody asked.

"Oh, you know. These old chaps tend to get a bit crotchety at times," Middleton whispered back.

"What's the matter, Bart?" Derby asked. "Parisian girls not too willing, were they?"

Woofer Smith came up, all chin and concern, and put a hand on my arm. "Never mind, Maje," he said. "We can't all be irresistible. Just tell yourself, Maje, that there's more important things in life than girls."

I glared at him hatefully. It didn't do a bit of good.

"*You* know," he went on comfortingly. "Channel your frustrations into something creative, like making raffia baskets. Or maybe bury yourself in hard work, Maje, to keep your mind off it."

"I think you'd better go and console somebody else, Smith," Kiddell said warningly.

Smith looked at him, mystified. "I'm just cheering him up," he said. He turned back to me, but before he would open his mouth again, Blackbourne had taken one arm and Kiddell the other and led him away, protesting.

"Bloody right!" I shouted at his back, somewhat redundantly. "Go and console somebody else for a change! Waiter! I'll have another!"

"Good Lord."

"Tonight the drinks are on me," I shouted again. Everybody goggled. "Well, what're you waiting for, what the hell d'you think this is, a temperance hall? Come on, drink up. Waiter! Whiskies all round—or champagne, or whatever they like!"

I hadn't eaten since lunch the previous day, and by the third drink I was somewhat unsteady. I fell over a piece of furniture that wasn't supposed to be there.

"What's this?"

It was at the window, covered with cloth. I couldn't understand why I hadn't seen it before, as it was several feet long.

Jock lifted a corner of the cloth regretfully. "It's a pianer," he said.

"So it is. What's it doing here?"

There was silence. Blackbourne said, "We were hoping to keep you out of here until after the presentation. After dinner. But you came marching in too fast."

"What presentation? What are you talking about?"

"It's for you, Bart. It was for your birthday. It *was* your birthday yesterday, wasn't it?"

"A birthday present?"

214

"Yes."

I looked around at their youthful, dissipated faces. They were all smiling hesitantly, almost appealingly.

"For me?"

I was horrified to feel a lump forming in my thrapple. God, I was starting to crack under the strain of all the paperwork.

"Where—" I had to stop and clear my throat. "Where did you get it?"

"Where do we usually get our furniture?" Pash said carefully.

"Just a spot of looting, that's all," Derby said quickly.

I looked at them, as much impressed by their initiative as by their kindness. Only a couple of months before, I'd had great difficulty overcoming their reluctance to raid an R.E. supply depot for building materials and such. Now they were looting practically everything in sight with light-hearted abandon.

I looked mistily at the piano. It was a splendid Chapell upright, lacquered a brilliant Chinese red. There was even a handsome, padded piano bench.

"The men contributed that," Blackbourne murmured.

I looked at them, then slowly sank onto the piano bench. After a moment I poised my hands over the piano keys, blinking owlishly.

Then I started to play, delicately and emotionally, the hymn tune 'While Shepherds Watched Their Flocks by Night.' And I don't think I have ever played as well as I did that night.

As the pilots gathered reverently around the splendid Chapell, with spiritual looks on their faces, I opened my mouth and softly sang the immortal words,

> "The parson came home drunk one night
> As drunk as he could be.
> He saw a hat upon the peg
> Where his hat ought to be.

'My wife, my wife, my darling wife,
What is this hat I see?
This hat I see upon the peg
Where my hat ought to be?' "

One by one the pilots, looking all choked up at first, but with mounting fervor, joined in, as verse followed verse with rude inevitability.

"His wife replied, ' 'tis all right dear,
This object that you see
Is nothing but a rolling pin
To help and protect me.'
'I've travelled east, I've travelled west
Ten thousand miles and more,
But rolling pins with bollocks on,
I've never seen before.' "

Some of the new pilots hadn't heard all the words before, and by the end of the fourteenth verse they were rolling about helplessly. Then, as the whisky flowed and the Veuve Cliquot popped and ejaculated, I went on to play 'The Bells Are Ringing,' 'Any Time's Kissing Time,' 'Softly Awakes My Heart,' then, thumping faster and faster, but now with less accuracy, a medley of Harry Lauder songs, George Robey songs, Gertrude Lawrence songs, and,

Drunk last night
Drunk last night
Drunk the night before.
And we're going to get drunk again tonight
If we never get drunk no more.

As I launched into a dance tune, Monty Murgatroyd seized Middleton round the waist and they began to tango. They darted back and forth, whirled, undulated, pointed their feet, scuttled and slowed and swayed over backward, and the best of it was they did it seriously and intently, with the most sincere expressions and with movements as graceful as their alcoholic legs would allow.

Unfortunately one of the new pilots, Haworth, spoiled it by tripping them up. Whereupon Monty and Middleton, with howls of rage, seized him, upended him, and tried to dip his head in the Dolphin toilet, which Orville had brought down from the place of honor and was busy filling with champagne.

They must surely have heard the laughter in Hunland.

Not to be outdone by these Terpsichorean antics, Jock wrenched Pash's German propeller from the wall and executed a Highland sword dance, his feet tripping neatly among the four blades. He got really annoyed when Woofer Smith tried to join in. The sight of the gangling Canadian trying to imitate Jock's dainty footwork made me laugh so much I fell off the piano stool. While I was down, Haworth poured half a bottle of cherry brandy on my head.

I scrambled up and, seizing a chair, charged him, and would probably have ruptured his spleen if Monty hadn't reversed his naval tunic and waved the crimson lining at me and shouted, "Huh, *toro,* huh, huh!"

So I whirled and charged him instead. He executed a deft *verónica.* The chair smashed into the panelling and I rebounded right across the room and into the hall, frantically trying to regain my balance, legs buckling, elbows pumping, and I continued backward and crashed into the dining-room door, wrenching it off its hinges. Monty followed all the way, trying to take up a *pase de la muerte,* and shouting, *"Toro bravo, más, y más, y más!"* And, "Wait for the *matolo,* you silly bugger!"

Then they tried to carry me back inside on the splintered door, like a defunct Hamlet after the Act V slaughter; but I fell off, and bit Jock's leg.

Not even in the Camel squadron had I ever taken part

in such a maniacal binge. I tried to get Hibbert to read the Riot Act, but he was too busy trying to hold the Dolphin toilet aloft and drink the champagne out of it, as if it were a firkin, flagon, or outsized florid flask; but it was too heavy for him, and he skidded, and the champagne swashed all over the floor. Orville began to ice-skate with John Derby over the slippery parquet, their hands locked together behind their backs. I tried to crawl back to the piano to play 'The Skaters' Waltz,' but somebody had thrown my nice new piano bench through the window. I had another drink instead.

"Oh, my God, look at the teeth marks!" Jock suddenly yelled. He was so blotto it had taken about ten minutes for the pain to reach his central nervous system. "Ah'll get hydrophobia! Where's the M.O.? Fetch the M.O.!"

"Too late, Jock. You're already frothing."

"We'll have to cut off Jock's head and send it to the vet, in case it's rabies."

"It's that bloody carthorse over there! He didny have any teeth oot in Paris, the bugger—he had several sharp ones put in!"

Dinner utterly failed to sop up the high spirits. The binge became so frantic as to be heard at the S.E. squadron, all the way across the airfield, and several of their pilots came over and joined in, though some of them left rather hurriedly when Carson fetched his pistol and began to loose it off in all directions. He claimed to be bringing down several pairs of flies that were behaving indecently on the ceiling.

"Holy Jesus, get that gun off him!" Kiddell screamed. "He's just creased my ass!"

Finally everybody piled on top of Carson, and while he was being flattened under a six-foot heap of bodies, Blackbourne hurled the offending pistol into the night.

"Listen, Carson," I said, when he'd been released, "you're not setting us a very good sample, are you? Pull yourself together, and act like an officer and a gentleman."

"You should talk. You're lying flat on your back in a pool of champagne."

"I yam not. You're the one who's on his back. *I'm* leaning nonchalantly against the wall."

"Since when have we had a parquet wall?"

I turned my cheek and peered gravely at the wall, and found that it was indeed parquet'd. I'd never noticed that before.

"Someone ought to stop us," Hibbert said, running a curiously loose tongue over his dry lips, "before we get hurt."

"M'yes, it's becoming a trifle hectic," Derby answered in an awful whining sort of voice, that for some reason caused screams of drunken laughter.

Shortly after that, mindful of my responsibilities, I took Carson out for some fresh air, as he was no longer capable of standing.

"Come on, now, Carson, you've had quite enough for one evening," I said, stumbling slightly over the threshold. As we hit the night air we reeled back, half stunned by the blow.

"S . . . s . . . stop *buckling* that way, Carson."

"I'm trying not to, but you're so heavy, Major, leaning on me like that."

"You know, Carson," I said, suddenly feeling all sentimental and affectionate, "you know—you, Carson, are rude, vicious, ill-mannered, disloyal, intemperate, savage, brutal, insolent, and murderous. But, *au fong,* Carson," I said, *"au fong—you're all right."*

"Careful, don't trip over that body in the wheelbarrow."

"What wheelbarrow? No, but I'm, 'm, 'm mean it, Carson."

"It's this smile, Major. Do you realize it's turning me into an *optimist?*" he said despairingly. "God, I can't stand it—life is starting to look too damned *rosy.*"

I was awakened sometime during the night by a bombing raid. One of the bombs must have fallen quite close, because I distinctly remember apples and branches raining on me, and flames shooting up from a burning hangar across the field. I was re-awakened at four in the morning by a search party. They had been looking for me for nearly an hour. They finally found me under a tree, with a green apple clutched tightly in my hand, and the stem between my teeth.

"He probably thought he was pulling the pin from a Mills bomb," somebody murmured.

"Good job it wasn't. He forgot to let go."

At the Piano

I still had a mouth like the top of an old sauce bottle late the same afternoon, when the colonel rang up to announce that D.F.C.s had come through for no fewer than five members of the squadron: Captains Kiddell and Blackbourne, and Lieutenants Murgatroyd and France, and Major me.

"I'm sorry it's not the award I spoke of, Bandy," Ashworth said apologetically. "You understand, I put you in for it, but . . ."

I tried to thank him, but it emerged as a rather feeble moan. He must have thought I was sunk in chagrin, for he said sharply that it was my own fault, and that I was lucky to get anything, the way I'd been carrying on.

Another noteworthy episode that day was a letter from Katherine:

Darling: an epistle from you at last, which I clutched to that part of me that you once referred to in that droll drawl of yours as my pert bosom, and hurried off to gloat over it in my sitting room, only to find that once again most of the news was between the lines. You make it sound as if you cross into Hunland only about every second Sunday, and then only to make sure you can still fly. Then the next thing I read is about aerial free-for-alls where your 'stout' pilots (surely they can't all be stout—or have you a squadron of Billy Bunters?) bring down prodigious numbers of Albatroses and things, and you obviously know so much about it, it follows that you're in the thick of it yourself.

Come now, enough of this strong, silent rubbish. I'm not a plate of bone china, you know, or your maiden aunt. I really want the facts of life (the military sort I certainly know the other kind now—whoopee!), so from now on, so I'll *really* know what you're up to, pray raise your voice, dearest Bart, in blatant braggadocio. After all, you did enough swanking when you were a colonel, so why not now when you're a mere major? I do hope this letter arrives on the right day, darling. Very many happy returns of the day, my dearest husband (how exciting it still is, to write that word). I've already sent off your present. It's a magnificent gift: two tatty old American magazines. There. How's that for generosity? The other present awaits you at home: me.

I found the mags in a little book shop in Reading, after weeks of looking around. I think you'll find the articles I've marked rather interesting.

Forgetting my head, I yelled down to one of the clerks on the floor of the barn, "Entwistle! Have you finished sorting the rest of the mail?"

"Yes, sir."

"Anything for me?"

"A torn parcel."

"Send it up."

By now I suppose you'll have heard that Papa's radical friend, Miles Davenport, M.P., brought up the subject of parachutes at Question Time a couple of weeks ago, but I'm afraid he didn't get a very useful reply. Some jumped-up Parliamentary assistant answered for the Minister, and merely said they were looking into it.

Papa sends his apologies that this is as far as he's got so far. He also sends his bemused affection . . .

The rest of the letter was just loving remarks and news about mutual acquaintances. After I'd read the letter again with a silly smile on my face, and feeling glad all over again that I hadn't given in to the carnal man in Paris, I turned to the parcel that Entwistle had just dumped on my desk. It contained two copies of an American magazine, *Aeronautics,* dated April and October 1912. When I read the articles on pages 117 and 116 respectively—I was staggered.

Both articles were on the same subject, the Stevens 'Life-Pack' parachute. A man called F. R. Law had tested it from a Wright biplane that year. The parachute was described and illustrated in some detail. In its compactness and simplicity, not only was it far in advance of any other design I knew about—it was *manually operated.*

That meant there was no danger of the lines or the shroud fouling on the airplane when the pilot jumped, as with the Guardian Angel. The pilot could pull the 'ripcord' himself when he was well clear of his machine.

It was about half the weight of the Guardian Angel and about half the size as well.

And it had been available for six years.

I had just finished re-reading the articles, and was leaning back, staring up at the now pigeonless joists—it had finally been driven out by my pipe tobacco, Karpett's Thick Black Shag—when an agitated mess servant came hurrying into the barn to announce that our brigade commander had arrived, and wanted to see me straight away.

All the pilots were assembled in the ante-room when I strolled in, delightedly clutching the rolled-up magazines. Assuming that the brigadier-general had come to congratulate us on our host of awards, I strode forward with an it-was-really-nothing sort of smile.

Then I took another look at Soames's face.

Simultaneously I became aware that Colonel Treadwell was also present. And a major of the Military Police. And a frightened-looking R.A.F. corporal.

"That's the piano," Soames shouted, pointing a quivering finger toward the window at the far end of the room. "That's it!"

I looked around blankly. The pilots were all huddled together along the wall, looking as if they ought to be wearing blindfolds and smoking a last cigarette.

They were all staring at me fixedly, as if I might disappear in a puff of sulphurous smoke if they took their eyes off me for even an instant.

Carson was the only one who was smiling.

"Piano?"

"And don't you deny it! Don't you dare deny it!"

"Uh, no, I must admit I can't deny that."

"There! You see?!"

"That's a piano, all right," I said contentedly, feeling for my pipe. "I mean, it has a lid and little felt hammers and everything. But what's that got to do with the awards?"

"You took it! You stole it!"

I looked around again, frowning slightly. "But it's over there, sir. I haven't taken it. See, it's still there."

"I'm talking about *my* piano, you insolent puppy!"

"Oh, sorry, misunderstood," I said. "Thought you were —puff—talking about—suck—mine."

"It's not, it's mine, the very same!"

"Same make, you mean? Chapell? Yes, it is a common make. I should think half the pianos in the Air Force are by Chap—"

"Don't you answer me back! I'm saying you stole my piano! So what have you to say to that, before I place you under close arrest? Well? Well?"

I looked at the military policeman. He said formally, "A lorry-load of men in groundsheets, described as looking like officers, raided Brigadier-General Soames's headquarters under cover of darkness two mornings ago, and made off with his piano, while he was absent at Versailles. Do you know anything about it, Major?"

"Course he knows—because he stole it! And I have proof! You're under arrest!"

"Arrest? *Me?*"

"Well, don't you stand there," Soames raved at the major. "Arrest him this minute!"

"Excuse me, sir, if I might just put one question," the policeman said respectfully. He was an exceedingly tall, hawk-faced individual with a walking stick and a holstered revolver. He turned to the corporal. "Do you recognize this officer, Corporal?"

"I ... I ..."

"Come on, stop dithering," Soames said. "Speak up! Just say what I told—what you told me!"

"I ... yes, sir," the poor devil said.

"Yes, what?" the major asked. "You mean you recognize that officer over there as the one who led the raid on Brigade H.Q. from which a piano subsequently disappeared?"

"Y—yes, sir, Major Bandy, sir," the corporal recited, visibly trembling.

"How do you know that's Major Bandy?"

"Everybody knows him, sir."

Soames blared triumphantly, "There you are! And you can see they've painted it, to throw me off the rails! Desecrated it! Just look at it!" His face went all anguished as he considered the desecrated piano. He rounded on the major again. "Well, don't just stand there like a bloody drainpipe! Arrest him!"

The major moved uncertainly. Somehow Colonel Treadwell's broad shoulders got in the way.

"Are you going to arrest all the pilots, Brigadier?" he asked quietly.

"What? No, of course not."

"But if there was a whole lorryload of officers involved—"

"Bandy obviously put them up to it! I know these officers of old. They wouldn't say boo to a goose—until *he* came along! No, I'm holding Bandy solely responsible."

"I see," Treadwell said. "Solely responsible." He moved over to the window and looked out. "Just wanted to get it straight, that's all," he said indifferently.

"May I ask when this alleged piano was purloined?" I asked, phrasing it like that for the benefit of the military copper.

"In the early hours of July fourteenth," the major said.

"Oh, well, there you are," I said. "I *knew* I couldn't have stolen it."

I caught a glimpse of Derby staring at me in fright. He was obviously convinced I was about to throw him to the wolves.

"Because we've had this piano for, oh, seems like ages," I said.

"What? You're a liar," Soames shouted.

"Sir?"

The major said evenly, "You can prove that, can you, Major?"

"Sure. The brigadier himself must have seen it in the mess when he was here last."

"What?"

"Yes, don't you remember, sir? When you visited us, oh, sometime early in June."

"But I didn't come into the mess, then! I was down at the hangars only!"

"Oh, well, there you are."

"There I am where?"

"In the hangars. But if you *had* come into the mess, you would have seen our piano," I said, with the air of a Scotland Yard man clearing up a ridiculously simple case of mass murder.

"It's not your piano! It's mine, mine!"

"What did your piano look like, sir?"

"Plain—varnished!"

"Yes, I've got that," I said patiently. "It's plain varnished from sight. But what does it *look* like?"

"I've just told you!" Soames shrieked, almost jumping up and down. "It was plain, varnished mahogany!"

"Oh, well, there you are," I said. "*Ours* is red."

"Because you've painted it!!" the brigadier said, his mustache all knotted and bedewed, and his eyes bulging like a recently landed redfish on a rusty trawler deck.

"No, no, you've got it all wrong, sir," I said. I tamped fresh tobacco into my pipe, with strong, lean, reliable fingers. "Anyway, why would I take your piano if I already had one? I mean. Even *I* can't play two pianos at once. Unless," I added thoughtfully, puffing away, "I was playing, say Ravel's one-handed concerto on one piano, and vamping 'The Maid of the Mountains' on the other. M'm, yes, I suppose that might just be possible . . ." The brigadier opened his mouth to yell again. "Besides," I said, "I wasn't here on July fourteenth."

Soames's face bulged. But then suddenly sank like a deranged soufflé. "What?" he said.

"You weren't where?" the major asked sharply.

"Here. At the squadron. I left for Paris at 0300 hours that morning.

"So you see," I said, frowning slightly at my pipe—it was bubbling a bit revoltingly—"this is obviously one of those intriguing cases of mistaken pianos, Inspector—Major, I mean."

"You were in Paris that day?"

"M'm. Visiting a dentist. Terrible dentist he was, too. The G.O.C. recommended him."

Soames was looking about wildly as if hoping to find a fresh clue skulking in a corner. The military policeman looked thoughtfully at the corporal.

"We won't blame the corporal here, though," I said,

patting him on the back. "The poor chap is obviously so terrorized by all these pips and crowns he didn't know what he was saying."

The major didn't look as if he much blamed the corporal either. "Wait outside," he said.

As the corporal stumbled out, Soames said, his voice cracking, "I don't believe you. Then—then it was your pilots! You sent them!"

"You said yourself my pilots are the most circumspect gentlemen it's possible to meet."

I swear I saw red cracks appearing in the brigadier's eyes.

"Where did you get this piano, then?" the major asked.

That was the one question I was afraid of. But before I could answer, Treadwell strode forward and plonked himself in front of Soames.

"Is there any other way you can positively identify your piano?" he asked sharply.

"What? No, of course not. I wasn't likely to carve my initials on it, was I? But I don't need—"

"In that case, I don't think Bandy need answer any further questions," Treadwell said, overriding him. "I happen to know he's telling the truth—about Paris. Because we sent him."

"He's not getting away with this. It was he and his pilots—"

"You've already said you were holding Bandy solely responsible."

"I . . . I . . ."

"So that's the end of the matter. Now if you don't mind, Brigadier, I have more important things to do than listen to allegations that cannot be proved. The subject is closed."

Even the brigadier-general seemed reluctant to tangle with the G.S.O.1.

He looked around, his eyes like two air force roundels,

and with dew on his mustache. He caught sight of Carson.

"You! What's your name?"

"Carson."

"How dare you snigger at me! Wipe that smile off your face this instant!"

Captain Blackbourne, with perfect timing, said gently, "He can't, sir. That's the result of a recent operation on his face. He was wounded, you see."

A hideous silence fell, broken only by the rasp of Soames's unsteady breathing. The police major glanced at Soames, then looked down at his boots, far below.

To help Arser out of his awful embarrassment, I said brightly, "Still, I'm glad you've dropped in, Brigadier, because there's something I wanted to chat to you about."

"What?" He stared at me blindly.

"I bet you'll never guess what it is," I said archly.

"What . . . ?"

"Parachutes," I cried.

He began to feel his way out, blinking rapidly. I followed him into the hall, saying, "By the way, Brig, when I was at the Air Ministry, I heard—(I lied cheerfully)— that you told the Air Board back in December that parachutes oughtn't to be issued to pilots because it might encourage them to abandon their aircraft, and save their lives." He was scratching at the front door. He seemed unable to get it open. I took the opportunity to wag a forefinger at him reprovingly. "Now that wasn't a very nice thing to say, was it?"

He managed to claw the door open. Corporal Tomlinson, once again an oil-stained fitter, was just entering, whistling happily. He recoiled and banged his head on the doorpost at the sight of the red-tabs and matching face, and flattened himself hurriedly against the wall, as the brigadier fell out of the house.

"Another thing I can't quite understand," I continued, following him out, but being careful not to tread on his heels, as they were so nicely polished, "is why you told the Air Board that nobody in the world had come up with an effective parachute design. You really can't have done your homework, Brig, because, apart from the fact that the Germans not only have a good parachute but are issuing it to pilots—"

The brigadier walked straight through the flower bed in front of the house. "Quite apart from that," I said, "I have, right here—" I stopped to lick my thumb and open one of the magazines. The result was I had to trot to catch up with him again. "Look, it's in this American magazine, sir. And it's a proved, manually operated parachute. Look."

He seemed to have become a trifle disoriented, for instead of turning in the direction of his staff car, he lurched off toward the hangars. Realizing his mistake he turned back, and luckily ran into me. "Look, sir," I said. "Just have a dekko at these pictures, if you haven't time to read the text. This American Life-Pack looks like a— No, go on, have a look, sir. *There!* What d'you think of that?"

Arser didn't seem capable of thinking about anything. In fact, he was starting to whimper. As he ran around me, his chest was heaving and his eyes were lolloping around in their reddened sockets. He scuttled back across the front of the house, where the others had now gathered. They were watching open-mouthed as I trotted back and forth behind the brigadier, the magazine pages fluttering in the breeze. "And you said there were no workable designs," I said, just a trifle reproachfully. "Why, this one right here has been available since 1912. Believe it or not, 1912."

By now, great unmanly sobs were beginning to bubble from his lips. He was lurching through the long grass like a refugee from the chain gang. "No, but the interesting thing," I went on, "is that, well, I bet if you redesigned the pilot's wickerwork seat to allow this parachute to fit snugly, there'd be no problem of bulkiness whatsoever. In the Dolphin, for instance, just moving—sir, you're not listening properly—if you just moved the petrol tank back, oh, about four inches, there'd be plenty of room for the—"

I stopped. Soames had run into Malt's old outdoor privy, and slammed the door.

Naturally I had far too much taste to follow him inside. So I spoke respectfully through the keyhole. "While you're in there, sir," I called through, "it'll be a good opportunity to read the articles. Shall I slip them under the door, sir? Honest, they're very interesting and enlightening . . ."

I could hear him straining in there. Out of delicacy, I moved back a few feet to let him get on with it.

Treadwell and several others hurried up.

On an afterthought, I turned back and called through a crack in the door, "But perhaps the most significant part is, that if the Yanks could produce a parachute as good as this one six years ago, imagine how much better their designs must be by now. It's worth investigating, Brig, surely, instead of persisting with the Guardian Angel, which as I myself am now forced to admit, is absolutely rotten. And—"

"Bandy," Treadwell said. I stopped.

The M.P. major was tapping gently at the door of the ornate W.C.

"Sir?" he said.

"Go 'way."

"Sir, it's all right." There was no answer, unless you counted a queer sort of muffled sound.

The major looked worried. "Get him away, for God's sake, Colonel," he said.

Treadwell took my arm.

"I was just trying to show him these interesting articles, Colonel."

"Yes. Come on, Bandy."

"It's all right now. You can come out now, Brigadier."

"Won't."

"Sir. *Please.*"

"No—won't."

The major tapped on the door again. "But it's all right now, sir, he's gone."

"Hasn't."

"He has, sir. You can see through the keyhole if you like. Sir, please come out."

"Won't."

He did finally, though, and the major led him, blubbering, to his staff car. The chauffeur opened the back door and they both helped the brigadier into his seat. He seemed to have gone all to pieces, poor devil. Strain of command and all that. After all, he had eighteen squadrons to administer, nine scout and nine observation squadrons. It was sometimes too easy for one to forget that ours was not the only squadron to occupy his thoughts, though admittedly it often seemed as if it were.

No, I thought, as the car drove away at high speed, sending up great clouds of dust and gravel, and turning on screaming tires onto the Amiens road, no, on the whole, I wouldn't have wanted his responsibility, not for all the tea in China.

Down Behind Enemy Lines

The five Dolphins bobbed up and down like flotsam in an oily swell, as they flew back and forth, back and forth over the churned-up ground around Bray-sur-Somme.

It was boring work. I was yawning so hugely that at one point I almost turned myself inside out.

We were on a routine escort job that afternoon, having met the Harry Tate over Morlancourt at 1600 hours at three thousand feet. It was our job to protect it while it photographed the sector around Bray. We had been keeping it company ever since.

It was a glorious day, with fluffy cumulus clouds and lots of hot, billowy air. There were hordes of photographic and wireless machines around, most of them escorted by little packs of Camels. With so many targets to pick from, Archie had been giving us only a few scattered bursts from time to time.

The Dolphins rose and fell, rose and fell, hypnotically. I couldn't stop yawning. What with hayloft work, bombing attacks on us at night and the sun rising at about four in the morning, I hadn't had more than four hours sleep a night for . . . how long was it? Weeks.

Also, I was drinking too much again. It was because my nerves were starting to twang. All the same, I would definitely cut it down. Starting today. Definitely.

I peered blearily over the side, trying to see what was interesting the R.E.8 so much. The observer must have exposed about a thousand plates by now, of pillboxes and gun positions, zigzagging yellow trenches and dusty white roads. When the devil was it going to go home for its tea and crumpets?

There was nothing of any interest going on downstairs, at least not behind the German lines; though in our back areas there were hints that an Allied offensive might be coming soon. In August, perhaps. Tank-staging areas being prepared, surreptitious movements of troops at night ... and so forth ...

Nothing much happening aloft, either. No Huns had come anywhere near us, though we'd been stooging up and down for a whole hour, now. I wished I hadn't come. Getting bored with signing things, I'd joined Kiddell's flight on an impulse. But by now even the joys of flight were beginning to pall.

By and by, as more and more reconnaissance machines turned for home, Archie began to pay us more attention. Black puffs blossomed around the R.E.8 and in between the Dolphins. For a while, we darted about happily, feinting and changing height rapidly, to annoy the gunners. But as they got more accurate, and the dull thuds of the bursting shells turned to the bellowing cough of near misses, it got irritating. Blasted Archie, wasting thousands of quid worth of ammo, to no purpose.

I flinched as one of the shells burst with a metallic clang off to one side. I envied Jock and Pash all the more. They were the first to go on leave, and were now sampling the fleshpots of Newton Abbot and Ochterlochty, and places like that. But I still had another month to go.

I looked down again at the R.E.8. It was almost obscured by puffs of black smoke. God, who would be a reconnaissance pilot, having to fly in a straight line through all that hate?

But wait. They were waving. They were turning for home.

Immediately Kiddell, who was leading, started to climb at full throttle, toward a cluster of dots far to the east, a small group of Albatroses that were busily patrolling their own back areas.

I'd also been keeping an eye on them for the past half-hour, and wondering what the hell they thought they were accomplishing. They'd been chased away by Camels several times, but had kept coming back.

They saw us while we were still miles away. They climbed higher. When we finally clawed up to their altitude, twelve thousand, they turned away.

I hoped Kiddell now realized what they were trying to do: to lure us under those fleecy clouds over there, farther to the east. Just above the clouds was a large pack of Fokker Triplanes.

Kiddell must have seen them. Nevertheless he continued to dog the Albatroses. I worked the interrupter gear and cocked the loading handles of the Vickers, and warmed them up with a short burst, beginning to feel annoyed with Kiddell. He was always doing things like this. He took too many risks. Triplanes weren't all that harmless; and there were so many of them that even the few Camels that were still stooging in the neighborhood were treating them with caution.

However, the Tripes stayed up there, jiggling about indecisively as Kiddell gave up and turned back. The Triplanes, two dozen of them, were being led by a biplane of an unfamiliar design. It looked like the one that had shot down . . . What was the name of that new pilot . . . ? In appearance, it looked more British than German.

The Albatroses turned west again. Kiddell continued to frig about underneath. I had a feeling there was going to be a fight, and felt all shivery, as if I had a touch of flu. There was a lot of it around; 19 Squadron (Dolphins) had it bad. I knew because they'd invited me along and then had to cancel the binge, because half their pilots were in hospital with the Spanish influenza. Naturally the doctors called it something else. Pyrexia of unknown origin, or something.

Even Archie knew something was going to happen. He'd stopped firing. I felt simultaneously cold with excitement and hot with annoyance at Kiddell for putting the flight in unnecessary danger. He seemed so desperate to get at the Albatroses he was making no attempt to climb above the Fokkers, though he could easily have done so.

I was sweating cobs, and was glad I'd left my fox fur behind on this warm, sunny, dangerous day. Not that I'd had much option. The pilots had nailed it to the wall the night before, as a war trophy.

I was just about to draw alongside Kiddell and stab my finger at the heavens, when once again he turned and dived toward the Albatroses. This time, about half the Fokkers came tumbling down in a ragged swarm.

The air was almost immediately criss-crossed with tracer. I'd have no opportunity to be fatherly on this trip. It was every man for himself. There was a dry chatter of guns from above. A Tripe hurtled past a few feet away in a flash of purple and green. I flung the Dolphin about, turning on rudder, dipping, zooming, sideslipping in a far-from-pukka Gosport manner. A Tripe banked ahead. I pressed the levers. The tracer went nowhere near him. I dived away again as another popped at me from behind. I managed to shake him off, and fired the Lewis gun at another, above. The slow stutter of the Lewis was heartening. But then it stopped. Jammed.

Somebody else fired from the side. As it passed overhead, I kicked viciously at the rudder bar and fired back, but missed again, and it dipped out of range.

I looked around quickly. One of the Dolphins was circling with the enemy biplane. Even as I watched, the Hun maneuvered almost casually onto the Dolphin's tail and fired a short burst. The Dolphin toppled and went into a vertical dive. Who was that? He had no streamers. It was either Middleton or that new man, what was his name? And where was Carson?

236

Then I saw another Dolphin going down, spinning far below.

Orville was lucky. It was his day off. It looked as if he would be the only survivor of A Flight.

I turned toward the solitary Hun biplane, but had to sheer off as another tripe came at me from ahead. Holes brailled across the wings. As he passed below, I half-rolled and fired after him at extreme range. His dive increased until he was going down vertically on full engine. No sane Triplane pilot would do that voluntarily. Tripes had a habit of shedding their wings in a dive. I zoomed and looked around again. That biplane was now circling with Kiddell. There was no sign of Carson's machine. God, it looked as if Kiddell and I were the only two left.

Most of the Triplanes seemed to be watching the flight between Kiddell and their leader. When I tried again to get over there, two of them dived on me, and kept me busy.

Whoever was flying that biplane knew his business. Kiddell was trying every maneuver he knew to shake him off, but the other continued to dive and zoom on him, harrying him with snapshots, driving him down remorselessly.

It didn't last long. In desperation, Kiddell tried to emulate the other's incredible climbing ability. He stalled. His wings were barely level again before the biplane nipped onto his tail and fired a long burst.

The Dolphin's heavy nose, with its yellow spinner, dropped slowly, and the plane plunged downward, to crash beside the Somme River somewhat near the battered remains of Cerisy.

Then the biplane turned toward me.

As the Tripes sheered off to watch the fun, the other machine fired a short, careless burst from the side, as if to see what I'd do; sort of to study my form, I guess. He can't have found it very stimulating. I turned toward him, dived underneath, zoomed, rolled off the top in much the same way as I'd got onto the tail of that Albatros on the occasion when Orville had fired his first balloon. But when I started to dive, the biplane was nowhere in sight.

I changed direction hurriedly, just in case he was behind. He was. He was only thirty feet away. For a second, his Maxims sounded awfully loud.

I held the stick back on full power, trying to gain height. But that machine, whatever it was, could rise like a lift. It shot up at twice my speed. I persisted, climbing and turning, putting the wing over whenever he fired from above, to present him with a smaller target.

Then we were circling at the same level. I looked across, feeling calm now, or perhaps resigned. I stared across at him. There was nothing fancy about the other bus. It was decorated in the standard camouflage pattern of blue, green, pink, and yellow lozenges, with a plain black cross on the stabilizer. Unusual top-plane extensions. Radiator in front, suggesting a stationary engine rather than a rotary, which was surprising, considering his ability to turn like a summer gnat.

It was the Fokker D.VII, all right. There'd been nasty rumors about this new design. It looked as if they were true.

Luckily the Dolphin could turn just as well, and I was still managing to keep away from a lethal burst. After a while, two of the Tripes hanging about upstairs got tired of watching and came down. As one of them fired and passed by, I fired a quick burst after him, and he went into a wild spin. Almost simultaneously, I turned toward the other Tripe and fired again, just as he was banking to turn head on. There was a burst of flame from his engine. He shot past only a few feet away, leaving an untidy path of smoke.

The pilot jumped out by parachute.

I was still watching in fascination when there was a bang and a shower of glass, a thunk! and a brief display of sparks. Holes appearing in the side of the cockpit. Metal flying from the radiator. The biplane had used the distraction to good purpose. That parachute seemed to have finished me off. The Dolphin fell.

I let it go, on full power, looking hurriedly over the damage. The altimeter had been hit and was in ruins. There was ragged metal on one of the steel cross members, the Lewis-gun barrel was buckled. There were holes and tears everywhere. But as there didn't seem to be any holes in me, and as the engine still sounded healthy, though going through a considerable strain at the moment, perhaps things weren't as bad as they seemed.

There was no time for further inspection. The biplane was following, and not only following but keeping up, though the Dolphin was going down at nearly 200 m.p.h.

I could tell he was keeping up because tracer was corkscrewing past and there was the dry crackle of guns right behind. There was nothing for it but to pull out. I zoomed, the wings bending, the wires shrieking in pain. The other bus zoomed higher. I banked. He banked sharper. I climbed, he rained lead on me from above.

Then he did something I'd never seen done before and wouldn't have believed possible. Getting bored with firing at me on the dive and zoom, he suddenly dropped below and hung on his prop, and with his rudder bent like a bruiser's nose, simply followed me around from the centre of the circle, below, taking potshots.

It was incredible. He seemed to be hanging there without losing height while I ring-a-rosied round him helplessly, trying to bob and wiggle away from his tracer. I couldn't straighten or turn away, he would have riddled me in a second. I had to keep circling, twisting the plane about on rudder, as I peered, pretty wide-eyed by now, straight down into his flat nose. I could plainly see his Maxims flashing, or Spandaus, as they were usually called; incorrectly, I believe.

I'd never see the end of the war now, I thought. (And in fact I never did.)

I was a goner this time. He was a better man than I was, Gunga Din.

Another pair of Triplanes intervened. One of them darted in from the side, his tracer wavering about through my starboard planes. For a split second as he passed, he got in the way of the biplane. I straightened and fired. Then the Vickers stopped. I was out of ammunition.

The biplane caught me as I was starting to turn again. An interplane strut splintered, wires parted and thrashed, the radiator on the left side of the fuselage flung off bits and pieces. Something lashed at my left foot, jerking it off the rudder bar. I let the bus fall naturally into a spin, hoping to fool him. The ground whirled into view.

I was astonished to see it was only about two thousand feet below. The D.VII had driven me down ten thousand feet.

The Triplane I'd just shot at was also spinning. As it whirled into view again, its wings folded and tore free. The colorful panels started to dance and flit gracefully in the sunlit air. But why wasn't the pilot jumping? Why had only one of the four Tripe pilots used a parachute?

Well, I'd soon be able to ask, in person. For, as I pulled ever so cautiously out of the spin, the Hispano-Suiza spluttered and died.

Several miles inside Hunland with a dead engine. Oh, well. At least I was still alive.

The Fokker appeared overhead, firing on the dive. I sideslipped, but didn't dare put the stick any farther forward. It didn't look as if the port upper wing would stay on. It was pulling away from the struts. The whole plane was riddled. For the first time, I became aware of the stink of petrol.

I hurriedly switched off. The Fokker was now behind. I crossed the controls again, without much hope, my back crawling. He didn't shoot, though.

The ground was only a few hundred feet below.

There were a couple of green spaces ahead, to one side. I pressed the rudder gently, turning in that direction, sinking fast. The biplane was now drawing alongside, also gliding. I looked across. The pilot was jerking his thumb down, insistently. He was ordering me to land. I don't know what else he expected me to do, with a stationary propeller.

I faced front again. The horizon tilted and straightened as I aimed into the narrow field on the left. There was rough ground and a wire fence in front of it. I hoped I'd be able to coax poor old D.4141 past the fence.

The field rose, the grass a vivid green in the sunlight. It looked flat enough, though rather narrow. As I raised the nose slightly, the biplane, on the right, pulled ahead. Over the whistling of the wires, I heard its engine open up. Somewhere over to the left, soldiers in field grey were running over a hill.

The field rushed up. At the last moment, I tugged back on the stick, relaxing in case the wheels caught in the wire fence. It whipped past, a few inches below. The grass sharpened and the plane dropped, and bounced joltingly. The field sloped toward the woods at the far end. The Dolphin bump-bumped down it, and came to a stop about half-way down the field.

There was a blast of sound as the D.VII roared overhead, then climbed steeply and circled round again, at half-throttle.

The sun seemed hotter on the German side of the lines. Birds cheeped. Somewhere over to the left, behind a hill, there was a faint clamor of voices. I unfastened the lap belt, fumbled around in the cubby-hole behind the wicker-work seat, and brought out the flare pistol. Petrol was sloshing about over the floor of the cockpit. The main tank behind the seat must have been holed. Thank God he hadn't been using explosive or incendiary ammunition.

Some three hundred yards away, the soldiers appeared on the brow of the hill, hollering at each other, their rifles held high. I climbed onto the lower wing and fired the gun into the cockpit and jumped. There was a woof! and a burst of flame, and in a few seconds the Dolphin was blazing.

Corporal Tomlinson would be very unhappy about that. He'd spent many an hour, sometimes working devotedly far into the night, to keep the engine of my bus in the best condition it was possible to keep a Hispano engine in.

I retreated from the heat and waited for the soldiers to come up, wishing I'd brought some chocolate on this trip. It wasn't likely to be available in prison camp, at least until the Red Cross parcels started to arrive.

There was a faint whirring sound in the sultry air. I looked up and saw the biplane sideslipping toward the adjoining field, beyond the narrow wood that separated the two strips of field. As I watched, he dipped from sight, behind the trees.

No doubt he was coming down to greet his latest victim in person. I wondered why he hadn't landed in the same field, but then realized that it was too narrow for him to roll into it without hitting my bus. The chancy landing had carried me only about three hundred feet down the narrow field.

I wondered if German pilots still invited downed flyers to their messes. Or perhaps that gesture had long since been discontinued. Still, he'd been chivalrous enough not to shoot when he finally noticed that my engine had stopped.

I would be quite proud to meet that German. He had

shot down at least three highly experienced pilots with effortless ease.

I waited, looking toward the wood, thirty feet away on the right, expecting him to emerge at any moment. But it was pretty dense. He'd probably prefer to walk back up the field, then around the promontory of woodland, rather than risk tearing his flying gear—

My heart began to thud painfully as an idea came to me.

By now, his machine must be stopped almost opposite, on the other side of the wood. If he walked around, it would take him a good two or three minutes to reach me.

There was nothing to lose. The soldiers were running down the hill now, only 150 yards away. I could hear them shouting excitedly. Under cover of the smoke from the blazing Dolphin, I dashed for the wood and hurled myself into it and started beating my way through the undergrowth, leaping over rotten logs and through dense shrubbery, heedless of clawing branches and thorns.

A branch slashed me across the face, a glove caught and was wrenched off. I left it in the bushes back there. It seemed to be waving good-bye. A strand of rusty barbed wire slashed at my best coat, ripping it.

I was making a noise like a charging rhino as I crashed through the dense wood. On and on, through thicket and thin, crackling over dry wood, splashing through wet bog, panting harshly. And also giggling a bit hysterically at the absurdity of it. It would never work, of course. But it was better than just standing there, waiting to see who claimed me first, the pilot or the soldiers.

From the air, the promontory of trees had looked narrow and not particularly overgrown, but I must have charged across the widest and densest part of it. It seemed like hours before the light brightened ahead. If that marvellous Hun pilot wasn't walking around the trees, I would be meeting him any moment.

He was bound to have a pistol. However friendly his

intentions, he wasn't likely to approach an opponent otherwise. I should have brought my own automatic. I usually did. Too late now.

I was tripping every five feet with exhaustion by the time I finally struggled free of the wood.

And there, only forty feet away, stood the enemy biplane, sunlit, stationary, brand-new—and deserted.

I tottered up, gulping in great lungfuls of air, and flung myself at the cockpit, hauling myself up and, still hanging over the side, staring wildly into the interior, panting so hard I feared I might faint from sheer hyperventilation.

It had a fairly simple interior compared with the Dolphin. Just the basic instruments. The stick was decidedly queer-looking, but, at the moment, that interested me least. Where was the ignition switch? Quick, quick. I could hear the voices behind me. O Lord, help me to make sense of it in time. I didn't want to end up in jail.

Keep calm, now. No gibbering, please. Take your time —so long as it's no longer than ten seconds. Now.

There was the altimeter, registering from 4 to 16. Or was that revs? Shut up. Never mind, it didn't matter. Below it, a two-position switch. Fuel-tank selection. Below that something called *Höhe* in km.

On the left, oil pressure, below that, temperature. Compass on the floor. On the same side, below the starboard Spandau (or Maxim) butt, a switch, below that a knife switch. Between the tank selector and the *Bosch Anlass Magnet*, a pump handle. Fuel pressure? Interrupter gear? Never mind, pump the bastard.

The ignition, though. There. On the right. A push-pull switch. It was pulled out.

So I pushed it in, and reversed the knife switch.

Bloody hell, I couldn't find the throttle lever! It was ridiculous. I couldn't see it anywhere. Damn it to hell, they were *bound* to have a throttle! It didn't make sense.

Giving up, and hoping that wherever it was it was in

the right position for starting up, I dropped back to earth and staggered round to the front of the aircraft.

The engine was ticking as the metal parts contracted. There probably wouldn't be any need to suck in, but which way to swing the prop—clockwise or otherwise? The Dolphin's prop swung clockwise, the Camel's counter-clockwise. Think, think! Yes—the biplane's left-hand turns had been much sharper than its right-hand turns. So the prop probably swung the same way as the Dolphin's.

There wasn't, literally, a second to lose. I could hear men shouting quite close by. Teutonic vituperation, I imagined, as they lacerated themselves on the vegetation. I stood with one leg back, carefully balanced, the way I'd seen the mechanics do it, and pulled the prop down until it was horizontal; then took a deep breath and swung down, leaning back hurriedly.

The engine coughed and stopped. Naturally the pro-peller would have to stick vertically. I wasted precious seconds bringing it horizontal. Hurriedly doing the balanc-ing act again, but not *too* hurriedly—not a few mechanics had been sliced up when they fell into the propeller—I swung again. The engine phutted derisively, and failed to catch.

I levelled the prop again, gasping and shaking all over, and feeling the sweat bouncing down my ribs and the knobs of my spine. The shouting was close now. And, looking down the fuselage, I saw a bulky figure running alongside the wood from the top end of the field. The pilot. He had his helmet in one hand and something else in the other. I could guess what it was. If the engine didn't start this time, that was it. I doubted if he'd invite me back to his mess now. Also, I'd be lucky to escape a kick or two, or worse, from the soldiers, when they emerged from the wood, hot and angry, scratched and torn and thoroughly bad-tempered.

Putting all my remaining strength into it, I hauled down on the blade. The engine cleared its throat, hesitated. For an agonizing moment, I thought it had died on me again. Then it roared. I stumbled. The plane began to move. Forward. Toward me. God, the swine was trying to run me down.

I couldn't get out of the way in time. I threw myself backward and lay flat. The wing passed overhead. The plane began to trundle down the field, faster and faster.

I jumped up and started running after it, followed, about two hundred feet farther back, by the pilot. The plane was heading for the trees where they swept outward from the woody promontory. Christ, after all this, the plane was going off by itself, weaving from side to side as the wheels encountered bumps and hollows in the ground. It would be miserable bad luck if I'd gotten this far only to have the plane itself defeat me.

With a desperate, flying tackle, I hurled myself forward and just managed to get my fingers round an interplane strut. My boots doubled over, digging grooves in the grass as the plane dragged me along. But the braking effect was swinging it around. As it turned, it slowed. I scrabbled along the wing and gripped the top of the cockpit. Somehow I managed to fling a foot sideways onto the top of the fuselage, then another, and hung there like an inept hider on a runaway ostrich.

The plane was still turning. Now the sod was heading for the trees again.

I could hardly see foɪ sweat. I still don't know how I managed to get into the cockpit. I seem to remember flinging myself astride the top decking and dragging myself in by the gun butts, but for all I knew I could have gone in head first.

At any rate, I found myself in the cockpit. The trees were only a few feet away. I still couldn't find the throttle. My hand slashed repeatedly down the left side of the cockpit where it ought to be. The soldiers appeared from the trees and stopped, gaping. Where in God's name did they keep the F!¢%$n(*) throttle!! The stick! There was a lever on it. I pushed it. The engine bellowed and the plane jumped forward. I lashed at the rudder. The plane whirled round. I only just got the tail down in time.

The pilot swung into view beside the great, jutting radiator. He raised his pistol, but thought better of it when I pointed the nose at him and shoved the lever right forward. I got a better grip on the strange hand-piece on the right side of the control column. The tail came up. The grass started to blur. I was travelling across the field, straight for a ravine. Beyond it, more trees. They were only a hundred feet away and looked impossibly tall. I held the plane down until the wheels started to skip over the edge of the ravine, then hauled back on the stick. The plane reared almost vertically. A desperate forward heave. The plane staggered through the treetops, lurching as a branch lashed at the wing. Then it was diving, regaining flying speed just as the wheel crashed with a neck-wrenching jolt into the field beyond. Then up again, vertically, and another near stall.

The engine howled in protest, but managed to keep a grip on the situation. The plane began to climb. A road filled with transport and a column of marching troops crossed underneath. They hardly even glanced up. Even from three hundred feet they looked despondent. The poor buggers were probably going back into the line.

I was at six thousand before I regained even the slightest degree of composure. My legs were shaking uncontrollably, and I was foul with sweat. I'd lost my goggles and one glove, and my face smarted. I touched my cheek and felt dried, gritty blood.

After a while, I began to think to some purpose again, the purpose being to find out how to fly this thing. I guess I already was flying it, but I hadn't yet worked out how. It had all been blindly instinctive. I loosened my hold on the hand grip—it was shaped to fit the palm of the

247

right hand, and was much easier to hold than the British spade grip. I wiggled the stick experimentally from side to side, then forward and back.

The plane was as sensitive on the controls as the Dolphin, and, my gosh, it seemed able to shoot straight up without losing air speed. It couldn't be anything else but the new Fokker design. The rudder seemed a bit stiff, but that might be because it was a new machine. It smelled new, and the grey paintwork on the metal parts was unscratched.

Fuel. Odd's teeth, I'd better check that. I peered numbly around all the plumbing. There wasn't likely to be much left after flying for two hours.

But then I remembered that this wasn't my machine. It had probably been flying for only half that period, as it was probably no more than a dozen miles from its home airdrome.

Next, the compass, to make sure I was going in the right direction. It was just settling down at around 260, so that was all right. Anyway, there was the sun, straight ahead.

My legs continued to tremble, though the rest of me had grown calm enough. I still felt clammy and horrible inside the leather coat, and my lungs ached. I felt a wreck. But a cheerful enough wreck. I hadn't really fancied spending the rest of the war behind barbed wire.

I must confess I felt kind of sorry for that pilot, in an insincere sort of way. I guess he'd landed with the intention of walking over to say howdy to his latest victim. He must be one of their aces. He'd certainly made Kiddell and me look like amateurs. It was too bad that, after all that skilful work aloft, he would now have to trudge home and report that some *Schweinhundt* had stolen his bus. I don't suppose he'd find that very amusing, him coming over to congratulate me on a lucky escape, pat me on the back, offer me some Rhine wine and tell me zet for me zuh war wass over, and then have his ungrateful guest run off with his brand-new plane. I wondered if the Herr Generals would make him pay for it. In the same circumstances, ours probably would. I'd hate to be two thousand pounds in debt. On our side, there was hell to pay if you even forgot to remove the eight-day luminous clock after a forced landing. You were supposed to unscrew it from the instrument panel to keep it safe from thieving fingers. Aircraft watches were much sought after by Tommies and peasants. You had to hand it in, and sign a form and everything. So what would they do if you lost a whole aircraft, without the excuse of being shot down?

I realized I was still flying at full throttle. I thought the engine had sounded a bit noisy. I eased back on the lever that was attached to the control column. There were a couple of other levers there, as well. Those would be the triggers. You obviously had to pull them toward the hand grip, rather than press them, which was curious.

Suddenly remembering there was a war on, I looked around quickly, to make sure there were no Huns creeping up on me. But there was just a flight of S.E.s passing high overhead, and some Camels frisking about among the black Archie bursts far over to the left. That was all right, then. I peered over the side. The front lines were just appearing under the squarish front of the plane. Shells were bursting around a yellowish mound that had once been a village, sending up puffs of smoke that streamed away quickly in the wind.

I wondered if my dear friends Karley and Craig were down there somewhere, burning the lice out of the seams of their shirts with candle-flames, or sipping scotch from chipped enamel mugs. I was glad I was out of all that, and was able to take off my boots at night and sleep more or less soundly, except when there was an air raid. Air raids were becoming a nightly occurrence, now. Yet, even when the bombs were falling quite close, it was nothing like being in the trenches, and having that sort of thing happen all day long as well.

The line drifted underneath. I was safe. *For he shall deliver thee from the snare of the hunter: and from the noisome pestilence. He shall defend thee under his wings, and thou shalt be safe under his feathers.* Now all I had to do was find out where I was safe at.

It took about three seconds. The Somme was just below. I recognized the bend in the river near Vaux. I'd be home in a few minutes. Not a very happy homecoming, though, the only survivor out of an entire flight. What on earth would I do about that? I'd have to ask for new flight and deputy commanders, and at least one other experienced man as well.

Anyway, I'd worry about that when I got down.

The first indication that this might not be too easy was when somebody coughed. Archie. Two more bursts, dead ahead.

I dived instinctively, and darted off the straight and narrow. But the bursts were greyish-white, not black. What on earth? My own side was shooting at me, the curs!

There was another bellow from alongside. For heaven's sake, how come they were shooting at a friendly chap? I glared indignantly over the side. It didn't do a bit of good. Several more white Archies thudded about. It was only then that I remembered I was flying a Jerry aircraft.

I turned rigid. My head snapped around. Sure enough, thousands of S.E.s and Camels were hurrying up from all directions. They'd been attracted by the Archie. They were coming after me. Good Lord, after surviving that massacre, I was going to be shot down by my own side.

Those S.E.s must have seen me some time ago, but because the Heinies rarely crossed over to our side of the line, they'd probably assumed I was a friendly aircraft. Of course I was a friendly aircraft, but they weren't to know that. Good Lord, I thought.

They were hurtling down on me. And S.E. 5a's were almost as deadly as Dolphins.

Their leader was well ahead of his squadron, and he opened fire at long range. I flapped the stick about in considerable alarm, the throttle quadrant whacking my left knee, and dived. The ground drove up, a spinning, yellow-ochre blur, stained with dark green. Now all the S.E.s were shooting at me, spinning a web of tracer. Oh, grief, no, they were Camels. The air was thick with S.E.s and Camels. I'd never get back. There was still a dozen miles to go. I'd have to get down. And pretty damn fast.

The messy silhouette of Amiens was far ahead. After sideslipping away from a couple of Camels—they almost collided in their eagerness to get at me—I dived for the ground at full throttle. The long straight road from Amiens to Albert flashed by underneath, then familiar open country. There was a Bristol Fighter field somewhere near here: Allonville, not far ahead. I'd go there. Perhaps.

The popping sounds got loud again. I shot down the side of a hill, the wheels practically swishing through the crab grass. A woodland ahead. I looked back, wide-eyed. Good God, I was being chased by at least sixty aircraft. They were all over the horizon, dipping and contour-chasing. The Camels were falling behind, but the S.E. men were well up. Two of them were actually ahead of me.

A straight gap had been cut through the wood, possibly in preparation for a new road, or for a telegraph right of way. It was a little wider than the plane, but not much, but I didn't dare climb. I ruddered into the gap, and hurtled along it, trees swishing past only feet beyond the wingtips. The trees sent back great blasts of sound, mimicking the engine. Then out in the open again.

Right rudder, a touch of bank, toward an avenue of poplars. The S.E.s flung themselves skyward. I fled down the avenue, two feet up, at about 130 m.p.h. A staff car coming the other way, the occupants gaping over the windscreen. It dodged off into the ditch. I eased the left wing over it.

Then, cottages. Allonville. A pond, women with cloth on their heads, a dog nosing around.

I had to lift over the village. I knew the airfield was just beyond, so I snapped back the throttle lever. This took the leading S.E.s by surprise, and several of them overshot. I risked a quick, steep climb to lose speed, then dropped down over an orchard. The field spread out on all sides, the hangars at the far end. The speed continued to drop, but I was still going at quite a lick. Nevertheless I sure wasn't going round again. I held off. A Bristol Fighter was just taking off on a converging course. I was landing downwind, right in front of it. That wasn't going to help—going downwind, I mean. I caught a glimpse of the Bristol ground-looping. It leaped onto its nose, sending up clods of earth.

The Fokker's wheels touched down, bounced, and banged down again. I watched helplessly as the hangars loomed up. Hard back on the stick, the skid jittering and jumping in the grass. A Camel with two streamers hurtled past, a few feet up, then zoomed vertically over the hangars. Mechanics were leaping around like fleas. I was headed straight for the middle hangar. Why the hell didn't they give us anchors or something, to throw out at critical moments like this.

I sailed straight into the hangar. A mechanic threw himself under a tarpaulin. There was a partly dismantled Bristol on the right, and a work-bench on the left, deep in oily rags, tins of paint, dope, wire-splicing spikes, leather palms and hammers, tensionometers, Abney levels and cable and thimbles. The biplane rolled neatly between the plane and the bench, the left wing sweeping everything off the bench, a great shower of paint and tools. The Fokker slewed and stopped with the prop thrashing against a stack of oil drums. There was a splintering crash and the engine screamed. I grabbed at the push-pull control. One of the small drums sailed over the naked Bristol and smashed against the far wall.

Then, a blessed silence. But not for long. An officer, without wings but with an ample tummy, came rushing into the hangar, trying to disentangle the lanyard from his Smith and Wesson.

"Get out of there," he squeaked. "Come on, get out!"

I peered out at him blankly.

"Hoch der hands into zuh bloody air, you Hun!"

There was a rush of bodies. The plane was surrounded by gaping Bristol Fighter merchants, mechanics, a cook in a white apron. Through the entrance of the hangar, I could see the sunlit field. Camels and S.E.s were landing from all points of the compass, the air loud with the rasping blip of their engines. Also the hollerings of the portly officer.

"Get out when I tell you! Hands up, I say!"

"I can hardly get out and still keep my hands up, now, can I?" I said peevishly.

Everybody grew amazingly still. A handsome major with a walking stick pushed through the mob and stared up at the cockpit.

After a moment, he snapped something in German.

"Eh? You'll have to speak English, old bean. Don't understand that lingo. Except *Donner und Blitzen,* and Dasher *und* Prancer, and a few odd words like that."

As I climbed out, wondering how I'd ever gotten into the cockpit without a ladder, the hubbub started up again as Camel, Bristol, and S.E. pilots poured into the hangar by the hundred, or so it seemed.

"Who the hell are you?" the major said.

Before I could answer, somebody said, "It can't be . . ."

"What?"

"It's that fellow *Bandy* . . . But it can't be!"

"Got shot down," I explained. "Pinched this plane. Flew back," I said. "Say, you wouldn't happen to have a drink on you by any chance?"

Yes. I would definitely give up drinking. Tomorrow, though.

Looking Shopsoiled

The reunion with Katherine was joyous, but the home-coming was kind of melancholy. As the Rolls burbled up the driveway of Burma Park, the white Georgian mansion seemed to have lost its air of serenity, as if it were aware that the Lewises were leaving it in the lurch.

It looked positively glum under the grey and sultry August sky, its curtainless windows staring hollowly at the furniture that was stacked at the edge of the great lawn, ready for the next Pickford's van.

Most of the staff were already installed in the Kensington house, except for poor old Burgess, who, like so many millions of people all over the world, was down with Spanish influenza.

Katherine's mother and father were in the echoing entrance hall, arguing about whether or not to leave their sixteeneth-century sideboard behind. "I have always considered it an extremely ugly piece," Mrs. Lewis was saying, "and I don't care what good Queen Bess says. Moreover, it is ostentatiously heavy. The workmen are complaining about becoming embedded in the side garden because of its weight; and I do not wish to leave our side garden behind dotted with cloth-capped proletarians. Such socialist statuary might give the next tenants the impression that we were of an eccentric mind, or worse, that we had been reading Mr. Bernard Shaw. No, William: give me something modern in the way of furniture; for instance, Regency. You would never find a Regency sideboard causing Pickford's to sink up to its ankles in turf."

"At the very least, we ought to take it along for fire-wood," Mr. Lewis said, his face lighting up at the sight of his daughter. "They say there is a shortage of kindling at the moment, in London . . . Ah, my darling. And Bartholomew."

As he pressed my hand, he studied me keenly. "You look decidedly shopsoiled, my boy. Notoriety seems to have a wearing effect on you."

Mrs. Lewis was adorned in her travelling bonnet, the one with all the veil, that made her look as if she were swathed in ectoplasm. Her voice, however, was far from spiritualistic.

"Bartholomew," she thundered. "You are here."

"Mother!"

"There is no need to be formal, Bartholomew. You may continue to address me as Mrs. Lewis if you wish."

As I kissed her lined, haughty face, Katherine linked arms with her father and they both smiled and waited, as if settling down to enjoy a bout of amateur theatricals featuring two performers who were sufficiently well-loved for their thespian deficiencies to be overlooked.

"You seem, Bartholomew," Mrs. Lewis said severely, "to have a habit of coming home early."

"You can't get away from me that easily, Mrs. Lewis."

"Then we shall just have to put your premature arrival to good purpose. You may help move the furniture."

"Certainly, Mrs. Lewis. I have room in the car for either you or the Elizabethan sideboard."

"I hope, Bartholomew, that you are not implying that I take up as much space as the end product of a four-hundred-year-old oak tree. Incidentally, I gather you have been attracting attention to yourself again, in the public prints. Pray what vulgar display of self-advertisement have you been indulging in this time?"

"You know very well why he's in all the papers, Mama," Katherine said. "Incidentally, Bart has to go to Canada in a few days."

"Just as I feared; he *has* been disgracing himself again." She looked at me severely. "So you are being sent back to Canada, are you? Well, if you will steal, Bartholomew, you must be prepared to suffer for it."

As the kitchen had been cleaned out down to the last cockroach, and as the dining room was also stark naked, we had lunch among the roses in the west garden, using a bench dragged from the greenhouse by Katherine and her father (with me, of course, supervising the operation).

It was a delightfully frivolous picnic that even Mr. Lewis' news could not spoil. He had been in touch with the American Embassy, he said, to enquire about the Stevens Life-Pack parachute.

"Ah!"

"It's not very good, Bart. The U.S. Army evaluated the Stevens parachute some time ago, as well as the Broadwick Safety Pack, along with one or two others. They found none of them suitable for aircraft use."

"Ah."

After lunch, Mrs. Lewis went off to hound and chivvy the moving men, and Mr. Lewis went back to the library to finish packing his books, where he was found, two hours later, walled in by still uncrated tomes and reading a particularly sordid passage from Walter Pater.

Meanwhile Katherine and I went for a last stroll across the sward. The air was hot but sunless. Swallows dived and zoomed over the grass.

"Don't know how you can look so happy, leaving this place," I said dismally.

"It's not the end of the world, darling. We'll have just as much fun in London."

"Won't be the same at all."

"You gloomy old thing," Katherine said affectionately, squeezing my arm. "You'd think it was you who'd been born and brought up at Burma Park, not me."

The heat billowed around us as we tramped onward across the enormous lawn.

"I suppose all the furniture's out of your rooms upstairs as well, is it?"

"M'm," she said, flicking a mischievous glance at me. "Including the bed."

"Huh. And we won't be settled into the other house until tomorrow night, either."

"Papa's booked us a room at the Ritz for tonight."

"That's hours away."

Katherine whistled a few bars from Stravinsky, then said off-handedly, "You said before you left you wondered how you'd be able to hold out. Did you—" She took an unsteady breath, trying to look as if it didn't matter in the least. "Did you manage?"

"It was quite a struggle."

She glowed, and took my hand as we turned onto the trail through the east woods. The air among the trees was hot and heavy, and we had to keep stepping off the path to avoid all the dogfighting gnats.

We stopped and kissed among the ferns, murmuring daft endearments.

"Oh, darling, why do you have to go away again?"

" 'S only for a short time."

"I suppose you'll receive quite a hero's welcome back home."

"M'yes. They want me to help restore morale on the home front."

"If they only knew what they were letting themselves in for."

"Howjamean?"

"The idea of you restoring morale. You're more likely to cause a riot."

"I better take your mother. She'd soon quell it."

We walked on again. As the path narrowed, Katherine moved ahead. She was wearing a long grey dress, the thin material stroking and caressing her flanks as she moved. I felt myself becoming engorged with desire. My heart started sending out jungle messages.

"The *Express* says you'll probably be getting the Victoria Cross. I was pasting that bit in my scrapbook last night. They said it was perhaps the greatest *coup* of the war."

"*Coup* lummy."

"Tell me about it again," she said, as we drew abreast once more. She hugged my arm to her excitedly.

I caught sight of a mossy bank over to the left, beneath an oak tree. It was surrounded by ferns, and had a suggestive hollow in the middle, which looked perfect for a pair of hips. Two pairs, in fact.

"I've already told you twice," I said.

"What's the matter? Your face has gone all red."

"Katherine. Let's go over there."

She looked at me wide-eyed. "Here? In the open?"

"Yes. Why not?"

She began to breathe faster, and turned red as well. "Oh, Bart," she said, shivering in the heat.

"Come on. Come on."

In fact she was already hurrying through the crackling ferns. I was panting by the time I caught up with her. I squatted down to feel the moss.

"It's wonderfully springy," I husked.

"What if somebody comes?"

"We can pretend we're rooting for truffles."

She snorted breathlessly and started to remove her dress; but then: "I'm shy."

I kissed her for as long as I could hold my breath, then sank down and rose again, my hands full of hem; then spent a frantic half minute wrenching at my Sam-Browne, kicking off my shoes, and unsticking my shirt.

* * * * * * *

* B. W. Bandy left instructions that these asterisks should be left intact, in spite of editorial pressure for the usual filthy sex scene.

It was all over in about two damn minutes. As we lay panting and twitching on the moss, a bunch of gnats came over to see what all the hubbub was about, and hovered over our gleaming forms.

"That was short but sweet. Oh, darling, I do love you."

"Me, too."

"You certainly have been saving up."

"Lots left in the bank, too."

"Oh Bart . . . I feel so lucky and so happy. I love you with all my heart."

"Did you know there was an earwig in your navel?"

A shriek, then faces contorted with laughter, slowly softening into barrierless love.

"Oh, hell, I've lost my shoe."

I'd kicked it so far into the woods it took us minutes to find it again.

"I wonder," Katherine said as we walked back, "what it would be like, doing it up a tree?"

As we strolled back across the lawn, bumping gently against each other, Katherine asked me to tell her all about it again. "Specially the bit where you turned up at your squadron and they were so overjoyed to see you again."

So I told her about it once more, but making an effort, this time, to recount it as it happened, rather than in the way it had been described in the newspapers.

I had related the story so often, to sundry pilots, staff officers, and war correspondents, and had subsequently read so many differing versions, that it was already getting quite hard to sort out what had actually happened. For the benefit of their readers, i.e., for dramatic purposes, the correspondents had melted down and recast the untidy shape of the action in a neater and more symmetrical mould. In particular, they had reshaped the basic fact, which was, of course, that I'd merely been making desperate efforts to save my own skin. The fact that I'd saved it in a plane that the authorities were particularly anxious to acquire was purely accidental. But at least one newspaper said I'd deliberately lured down the new Fokker with the express purpose of acquiring it for the Allies, basing this on the assumption that no pilot who had shot down twenty-two e.a. in three months could possibly be vanquished by one miserable Jerry.

Odd's blood.

"It must have caused a tremendous sensation when you came back in a German plane," Katherine said, her dark eyes alight with anticipation, though I'd already told her twice about the reception at R.A.F. H.Q., and about being congratulated by Haig's Chief of Intelligence, and getting a telegram from the King, and being photographed for the *Illustrated London News*.

"Go on, tell me what they said when you got back to your squadron."

"I honestly don't remember too well, Katherine. I'd just had a decidedly blotto session at Wing."

"No, go on. About them all cheering like mad.'

"They were really applauding my luck."

"Oh, don't make me sick."

"It's true. Pilots appreciate good luck much more than feats of derring-do. Mind you, I pretended all the praise and plaudits and stuff was only my due. I was very lordly and casual about it all . . ."

The squadron hadn't been informed that I had got back safely, and the mess was so hushed as I staggered up to the house I thought they'd all gone to bed.

They were nearly all there, however, including Carson. He had managed to get back, after crashing on the front lines. Some Tommies, he said, had counted eighty bullet holes in his machine before giving up and going back to their game of bezique.

When I walked in, putting one drunken foot carefully in front of the other, they couldn't believe their eyes.

Carson had hold them about the flight, and Artillery had confirmed his account. Under the perfect weather conditions prevailing, their spotters had watched the whole show through field glasses. Three Dolphins had gone down, they reported. The fourth, after disposing of four of the enemy, had disappeared behind a hill. Two minutes later, dense black smoke had rolled into the sky.

They had all thought me burned to a crisp, or badly wounded, but in either condition, quite definitely in enemy hands.

"How could you possibly have escaped?" Derby asked; and when I told him, he laughed so much that tears poured down his cheeks.

"The men have been coming up to us all evening, asking if we'd heard any news of you," Orville said. "The colonel came too, even though it was after dark. He said we'd never see your like again."

"I bet he looked relieved."

"He managed to conceal it pretty well."

"Hell, we ought to've known you'd get back somehow," Derby snorted, "and make a profit on it, into the bargain."

"And the next day," Katherine said, "you were called to Canadian H.Q."

"Yes. And—"

"And the Canadian Minister for Overseas Forces told you you were going home on leave."

"Yes. And—"

"And they were in process of forming the Canadian Air Force, and you were to be given a wing."

"That's right. Go on, I'm dying to hear the rest."

"No, you tell it, darling. About how excited they were in Canada about your exploit, and they wanted you to make speeches at Peace Bond rallies, and the Prime Minister was anxious to meet you, and everything."

"M'm."

"Well, go on! Tell me!"

"We had great difficulty in persuading the R.A.F. to give you up," the Minister confided over lunch that day. "They must obviously have thought very highly of you, Bandy, even before that exploit of yours. You've no idea what determined and subtle efforts the British made to keep you in the R.A.F."

"Really?"

"The Air Minister was particularly crafty about it, in that sly British way of his. When I told him we wanted you transferred, he acceded to our request with alacrity."

"Natch—eh?"

"It was their devilishly clever strategy, my boy. They were attempting to lower your value in our eyes, by simulating relief and satisfaction. Hoping, you see, that we would begin to wonder if you were really worth having. You know, to make us feel insecure. They're always trying to make us feel insecure, you know."

"I must confess that I did in fact experience a faint twinge of doubt in the face of their apparently overwhelming relief at the prospect of losing you. But don't worry, I saw through their crafty strategy in time and immediately rendered it abortive by the simple process of pretending not to see through it. I reaffirmed our determination to have you, Bandy, and nothing the Air Minister could say would change my mind. So the whole matter," the Minister said triumphantly, "was concluded in a matter of minutes."

Well, at least the pilots had been flatteringly reluctant to lose me. At the farewell dinner at Montonvillers, attended by the C.O.s of about half a dozen squadrons, and honoured once again by the presence of the G.O.C., Captain Derby had made one of the best drunken speeches I'd ever heard—especially as it was all about me.

"When he first arived, we all felt certain," John said, standing at the head of the table, grave and spifflicated, "that no good could come of a C.O. who looked like a pantomine horse that had strayed by mistake into the nearest abattoir. And we were—hichug—right. We used to be simple, loyal, dutiful offishers, utterly honest, obedient an', an' upright. Now look at us: half of us look as if we'll never be upright again.

"There are so many stories about Major Bartholomew that one doesn't know whether one is faced with an embarrassment of riches or a richness of embarrassment. The time he and Lieutenant France, for instance, joined the men's football game, riding a couple of motor bikes, and ended up charging each other with the goalposts, like demented knights of yore—or should I say gore; or the time he jumped on a certain prize peacock; or the time he wangled several new Nissens from the Royal Engineers, after presenting them with a chit signed by none other than D. Haig himself—Lance Corporal Dougal Haig, that is, one of our engine fitters . . ."

He mentioned one or two other incidents, but after he referred to me as Major Foxfurs, by the time the screeches of laughter had died down he had forgotten where he was.

"Major Bandy," he went on, turning owlishly to the G.O.C., "has had a simply shocking effect on this squadron, General, I'm sorry to tell you. Among other things, teaching us to be so considerate to the other ranks that now the blighters won't work more than twenty-one hours a day on those frightful Hispano-Suiza engines . . . but above all, encouraging us circumspect chaps to emulate his example of being so frightful in battle that I hear the Jerry Air Force is seriously thinking of adding hair dye to their standard equipment—their flying helmets, blood sausages, pipeclay, whips, monocles and the like—the dye being for the benefit of Hun pilots whose hair has turned white overnight after meeting our redoubtable C.O. . . ."

When the cheers had died down, he ended gravely, "All the same, I know there is not a single pilot who is not deeply chagrined at the thought that we are no longer to

263

be stricken by the sight of that often dishevelled figure in fox furs and bicycle clips, surmounted by that insurmountable face that can only be described as indescribable, as he lurches about the airfield inspiring the men to devoted labor and the pilots to a martial determination that does not entirely deny the possibility that they are perhaps a little more than mere cannon-fodder. Major Bandy may be the most infuriating, tactless, undignified, deplorable, larcenous, and mulish individual on the face of this earth —but, by God, he's offensive!"

"I tried to explain what Derby meant," I said to Katherine. "He just meant I was a bit aggressive in combat; but the fellows were making so much racket I don't think they got that bit."

Lording It in London

Two hours later, we left Burma Park forever.

I was the only one to look back, as the huge Georgian house sank slowly into the Berkshire foliage. The others were too busy quarreling about who had sat on the tomatoes.

Mr. and Mrs. Lewis were staying the night with friends, and so Katherine and I put up at the Ritz. It was pretty expensive: 15s. 6d. incl. bth., but as I explained to Katherine, the Spartan Hotel, where I'd always stayed before, just wasn't good enough for me any more.

We were given a room that was said to have an excellent view of Green Park, but somehow we never got around to confirming this, as Katherine was so anxious to make up for lost time. She acted almost as if sex were quite natural, if occasionally rather comical and absurd, and was even willing to try some of the unforgettably shocking variations I'd read about in *Fanny Hill of Sunnybrook Farm*. Or was it *Rebecca*?

Finally, however, we were driven out of the bed, the armchair, and the bathtub by starvation. As we floated bonelessly into the restaurant, there was quite a stir among the guests, and a craning of necks.

For an awful moment, I thought they were gawking like that because they could divine, through some subtle dishevelment in our manner, that we had just been making love. Before dinner, too, my dear. However, I told myself firmly that this reaction was merely a tribute to my renown. To my surprise, this was confirmed a couple of minutes later when a tall schoolgirl, all teeth and elbows, came blushing up for my autograph, and the headwaiter presented us with a complimentary bottle of Bulmer's Cider.

It was pleasant enough being famous, but I'm afraid I couldn't restrain a certain cynicism during those few days that remained before I sailed for Canada. It was only about four months since I had been just as much an object of public attention; only then I had been regarded with fury and loathing.

Nobody seemed to remember that scandal now. One couldn't help reflecting that fame was sure to be just as fleeting as notoriety. In some ways, the two were hard to tell apart.

Not that I failed to take advantage of the new esteem. I swanked modestly in the approved R.A.F. manner throughout all the subsequent interviews, dinners, and other social occasions. I particularly enjoyed the deference shown me during the demonstration at Martlesham Heath, where the new Fokker was dismaying the experts with its advanced, tubular-steel construction and its exceptional maneuverability, speed, and climbing power.

There was also the visit to Drury Lane, where an adaptation of Bach's cantata *Phoebus and Pan* was being repeated, owing to lack of popular demand, and where my presence in the audience was announced from the stage just after the intermission.

This drew an enthusiastic round of applause from those members of the audience who had not already left. Following the show, Katherine and I were invited backstage to meet the conductor, Sir Thomas Beecham.

"I perform on the pianoforte myself, occasionally," I smirked.

"You perform *what* on the piano? Hand stands? Card tricks?"

"No, no, Sir Thomas. I mean I tickle the ivories on occasion."

"If you mean you play the piano, why the devil don't you say so?" Sir Thomas snapped.

I could see the conductor was in a bad mood, because of all those empty seats. Still, I couldn't let him get away with that. After all, I was a great man, with my picture in the papers and everything, while he was just another conductor, with no future to speak of, judging by *his* reviews.

"That's all right, Sir Thomas," I said. "You can snap at me all you like, old man. I mean, it's not my fault if one of your clarinets squeaked during a particularly ill-rehearsed *pianissimo* passage. But if it relieves your feelings, you go right ahead, I don't mind," I said, looking extremely indulgent.

Sir Thomas turned his basilisk stare on me for a moment before wheeling on his concert-master, who was looking quite frightened. "Who did you say he was—former music critic of the Ramsbottom *Gazette?*" Which I must admit was rather a neat way of pretending not to know who I was. Unless—no, no, he was *bound* to have heard of me, absolutely bound to.

It was just like old times, being back in the Air Ministry in the Strand. Even the general attitude to the Secretary of State was familiar: he was just as unpopular as the last one had been.

However, he greeted me, initially anyway, with such affability that for a while I thought he really had called me in merely to offer his congratulations.

"Yes, it was a very dashing exploit, there's no doubt about that," the Minister said, sketching airplanes on his desk pad with a Ministry of Works pencil.

" 'M'kew."

"Nor must we overlook the work you did with the

squadron, Bandy. The G.O.C. waxed most eloquent on your work in turning an exceedingly smart and dutiful squadron into the most thoroughly disreputable collection of bandits operating on the Western Front."

He uttered a brief laugh to show that he was just indulging in a little verbal playfulness.

"No, but seriously, though your methods were perhaps a trifle contumacious, there's certainly no doubt about the result. The G.O.C. informs me that in July your squadron accounted for the third-highest total of kills, after 43 and 56 squadrons."

He started to sketch a French guillotine, complete with a basket of heads. "In a separate dispatch, by the way," the Minister continued, intent on his work, "he asked that something be done about the parachute situation, pointing, among other things, to their increasing use by the enemy.

"I told him, Bandy, that it's not quite as simple as that. Our production facilities are already strained to the utmost. Now that we and the French are supplying the Americans with air equipment, we're having difficulty in keeping up even with the demands for aircraft, let alone ancillary equipment."

I cleared my throat and started to speak, but the Minister continued firmly, "However, in spite of the difficulties, and in view of the growing concern in, ah, certain quarters, I have informed him that I have given orders for the Guardian Angel to be put into production forthwith, with the intention of distributing it in quantity among the front-line squadrons later this year."

"That's very interesting news, sir," I began.

"Yes, I thought you'd be pleased, Bandy. You know," he said heartily, "you've given us a good deal of trouble over this business. Causing dissension among your superior officers, and the nervous prostration of at least one brigade commander, and instigating questions in Parliament, and so forth. And now I see you're using this temporary fame of yours to make outspoken comments on the subject to the press.

"It may be unreasonable of us, Bandy, but we don't particularly enjoy being accused of indifference to the lives of our airmen." He started to shade in the guillotine blade. He also added another head to the basket. "I must remind you, Bandy, that whatever your government's future plans for you, you're still in the Royal Air Force, and subject to our discipline. So—" He glanced up with a smile. "I'd be personally obliged if in future you would desist from giving interviews to the press on other than personal matters."

He screwed up the paper and dropped it decisively into the waste bin, and leaned back, smiling again. "Anyway, now that something is being done about it, that should be a satisfactory conclusion to the affair, don't you agree? Let me see, now, is there anything else . . . ?"

"The only trouble, sir . . ."

"What's that?"

"The Guardian Angel is almost as dangerous as the situation it's designed to alleviate."

The Minister's smile froze solid. "What?"

"Your Chief of Air Staff's assistant was good enough to let me see that fat file on the Guardian Angel, sir. With all those unfavorable reports, which I heartily endorse—" (Gad, I was getting quite good at High-Grade Civil Servantese) "—after having tried it out for myself, I don't see how you can send a parachute like that to the squadrons."

The Minister seemed able to change his racial characteristics at will. His face turned quite black. "But it's as a result of your damned interference that I've ordered it to be rushed into production!" he shouted.

"Can't help that, sir. It's no good, and it never will be. It'll put the pilots at an impossible disadvantage.

"You see, sir," I said, crossing my legs and delicately

269

folding the crease of my trousers sideways over my knee, "while it may get a pilot out of difficulties, its constricting effect in the cockpit will in many cases contribute to those difficulties. The pilot won't be able to move the controls freely enough.

"By Jove, sir, there's irony for you, isn't it!" I exclaimed, smiling like anything and even giving a little laugh. "The very apparatus designed to get a pilot out of a crippled aircraft, is likely to be the very thing that causes the aircraft to be crippled in the first place. By Jove, what irony," I said with an appreciative twitch of the head at the sheer irony of it.

The Air Minister was now starting to keen like a darkie as well, and clench and unclench his fists in a rather impotent, speechless sort of way.

"However, Minister, don't despair," I went on soothingly. "I've just learned about another British parachute, the best design I've ever come across, called the Prentice parachute. It—"

"Get out!" the Minister shouted. "Get out!" He sounded uncannily like his friend Soames.

"No, but sir, just let me tell you about the Prentice parachute. It's been designed by a man who, by some amazing coincidence, is called Mr. Prentice. It—"

But the Minister just wouldn't listen. In fact, he was already calling for the entire corps of commissionaires to come up and manhandle me out of the building, so I had no alternative but to get up and run for it.

Really. The brass were a terribly unreasonable and illogical lot, when you got right down to it.

I'd learned about the Prentice design only the day before. Mr. Lewis' M.P. friend, Mr. Davenport, had rung up to say he was sending along a man called Prentice, who had something interesting to add to the parachute controversy. In fact, Davenport said, he was thinking of using Prentice as a fresh weapon with which to belabor the government.

Mr. Prentice arrived at the Lewis house in Kensington while I was upstairs making myself spruce and smart for another portrait sitting.*

When I came down, it took me a minute or so to find him and Mr. Lewis, among all the books stacked several feet deep in the library.

"Mr. Prentice is with the Vickers design staff," Mr. Lewis murmured.

"It's a great honor to meet you, Mr. Bandy," said the visitor, gazing at my face as if glimpsing Canterbury Cathedral or the Hammersmith Underground Lavatory for the first time.

"Course. I mean, yes, thank you."

"I won't keep you more than a few minutes," Mr. Prentice said ingratiatingly. "I can see I've interrupted you in the middle of your nap."

Eh? I looked uncertainly at my best uniform. Surely it didn't look as if I'd been sleeping in it?

"I've read all about you, of course. I've been particularly interested in your comments about parachutes."

"Mr. Prentice has been working on a new design since 1916, Bart," Mr. Lewis said.

"Oh?" I sat on a pile of encyclopedias and looked interestedly at Mr. Prentice. He was an elderly little man—well into his thirties—in a crumpled suit, and he had a peculiar habit of making tentative, clutching motions at his unspeakables, as if he'd recently caught crabs and was trying to remember not to claw at them in mixed company. And Mr. Lewis and I were certainly mixed company.

"My work is really in aeronautical dynamics," he said, his blue eyes apologetic yet determined, as if he expected

---

* This portrait of Bandy, by Sir Alfred Munnings, who specialized in horse pictures, can, with some persistence, be seen at the National Portrait Gallery in London, where it has been carefully stored in the cellars. Ed.

to be thrown out of the house but was going to have his say beforehand. "But, as Mr. Lewis indicated, I've had some interest in parachutes for quite some time, and, well, I've done a fair amount of work on a design of my own."

"Manual or automatic?"

"Oh, manual, of course. Automatic types are just too risky. I've . . . I've brought one along, as a matter of fact, in case you had a moment to . . ."

"You've brought a parachute?"

Mr. Prentice struggled up and looked around anxiously. "Let me see, where did I . . . ?"

He eventually found it behind a stack of display cases in which Mr. Lewis kept his prize ferns. Ferns were Mr. Lewis' hobby.

I looked at the parachute in astonishment. "That's a parachute?"

"I know it's unusually small, but it's the way the silk is machine-sewn, and the way the shroud lines are arranged, you see . . ."

I hefted it. It weighed only about twelve pounds, including the harness. It was smaller than a hiker's rucksack and a good deal flatter.

I was tremendously excited—until Mr. Prentice opened it. It required only a sharp tug at a wooden ring to spill the parachute onto the carpet.

I looked at his creation blankly for a moment, then backed away cautiously. The man was a lunatic. The parachute was only two feet wide.

"M'yes, very interesting," I said, wearing a carefully inscrutable expression so as not to send him completely over the edge. "M'yes . . . but don't you think—" I cleared my throat. "Don't you think it's a trifle, well, small, to support the weight of a 160-pound pilot?"

Mr. Prentice smiled. "Oh, no," he said. "That's just the . . . Well, I'll show you." And he gathered up the parachute and started to back away. As the shroud lines of the teeny parachute tautened, other material appeared, and swirled over and around the stacks of books that littered the library floor. He stopped after several square yards of white silk panelling had been exposed.

"This little parachute, you see, is held by elastic bands, and when it's released it shoots out and drags out the main parachute with it. I can't show you its full size in here, of course. It's much too long. The canopy is about sixteen feet wide."

"The little parachute is there to drag the main one out quickly?"

"Very good. Yes, that's its main purpose."

I leaned forward so fiercely that the little man recoiled. "And does it? Has it been tested?"

"Oh, yes. Several times."

"And found to be workable?"

"Yes," Mr. Prentice said with a faint smile. "Or I wouldn't be here."

"You . . . you don't mean *you've* tested it?" I asked incredulously.

"Well, I couldn't let some young man risk his life with an untried and in some respects rather revolutionary design."

Mr. Lewis and I looked at each other, then back at the crumpled little man.

"Perhaps it is hard to believe," Mr. Prentice said. "So I've brought along some photographs."

He took out an envelope and extracted a score of photographs. They were all dated and signed on the back by the various photographers.

The first photo was an air-to-air shot, showing a bundle of old clothes falling sideways from a Sopwith three-seat biplane. "That's me," Mr. Prentice said apologetically. "You can just see the, the dragging parachute, as I call it, streaming out under the aircraft. There, see?"

"I'll be double-danged . . ."

"That was taken over the Sopwith works at Weybridge."

"Why Sopwith? Didn't you say you were with Vickers?"

"Well, you see, they wouldn't let me try it out at Vickers. Said I was too useful to them. Anyway, it was my own private project, you see, and . . . Actually I had to sneak over to Sopwith's at weekends without telling Vickers. I got Tom Sopwith to fly me."

I stared at him open-mouthed before turning back to the rest of the pictures. The first few were in sequence, from the first leap to the touch-down, though not all taken on the same occasion. The next was a ground shot, clearly showing Mr. Prentice drifting below the graceful canopy over a ploughed field, though at a somewhat alarming angle to the ground.

"That's the first time I sprained my ankle," he said. "I still haven't quite solved the problem of keeping the parachute completely stable. The air spills out circumferentially, you see, setting up a turbulence that tends to swing the parachute in circles as it descends."

"I've found that, too," I said faintly. "A corkscrewing effect . . ."

"Exactly. But an agile young man shouldn't have much difficulty compensating for it, on landing," Mr. Prentice said, looking at us anxiously, as if fearful that we would condemn a device that might just possibly endanger a pilot's ankles after it had saved his life.

Hs showed us another photograph of himself being dragged across a field on his back. "It was pretty windy that day," he said.

Mr. Lewis took a deep breath. "Mr. Prentice," he said firmly. "Would you care for some of my very best brandy?"

"Oh, no, thank you, Mr. Lewis. I'm sorry, I have an ulcer, you see."

"Bartholomew?"

"No, I've . . . given up drinking . . . Getting into training for Canada, you understand . . . But listen," I cried, turning back to Mr. Prentice, "a pack like this, even a

Camel pilot could wear it easily! What do the brass say about it?"

Mr. Prentice's tale was pretty astonishing. He had first approached the authorities in July of 1917. Months went by, while he was shuffled from one department of the War Office to another, dealing with literally dozens of staff officers. Some of them had reacted to his samples and his authenticated pictures as if he were a door-to-door salesman with an inferior line of merchandise, or as if he were just another crackpot with a scheme for milking cows by electricity, or refuelling aircraft in the air, or some such impossible dream. A few of them, however, were interested enough to take a sample of his parachute, promising that it would be tested at the first opportunity.

"And?"

"They said they'd be in touch. But weeks went by, and nothing happened. When I went back again I saw a completely new set of people, and not one of them knew a thing about it. I never even got my parachute back. They just said they already had a parachute, the Calthorp design. Do you know that one, sir?"

"The Guarian Angel. It's useless."

"Yes, I'm afraid I was rather tactless and said much the same thing myself, which didn't help my cause very much. They just kept saying that the Calthorp design was the one they were committed to, and that was all there was to it."

"The man to see was the Director General of Military Aeronautics. Did you get to see him, Mr. Prentice?"

"Yes, I did finally, He was quite interested, but he also said they were interested only in the Calthorp.

"By this time, I must admit I was getting rather discouraged. Even though a lot of people had admitted that it was superior to the Calthorp, they just kept on making excuses about not changing horses in midstream, and that sort of thing.

"Finally I decided to make one last attempt before giving up—my health was starting to suffer, you see—and go and see the Air Minister himself."

"What did the Air Minister say?"

"I don't know."

"Eh?"

"I never got to see him. I couldn't even get to meet his military aide, let alone get past him to see the Minister. It was that military aide who finally defeated me. I just couldn't go on after that."

"Some jumped-up, pompous, interfering bonehead, I've no doubt," I said bitterly. "Oh, yes, I know the type."

"M'm. As I say, I never even got to meet him. A rather odd Canadian, by all accounts."

Mr. Lewis looked up slowly.

"Wait a minute," he said. "You *are* talking about the *present* Air Minister's military aide, aren't you?"

"No, his predecessor's. Lord Rackingham."

There was a simply awful silence.

"Lord—" I began. I had to clear my throat and start again. "Lord Rackingham's military aide refused to let you see the Minister?" I faltered. "When was this?"

"Last February."

Mr. Lewis looked at me. I looked at one of Mr. Lewis' ferns.

It was I who had been the Minister's military aide at that time.

It seemed that it was I who had killed off the only good parachute design the Allies were to produce in the entire war.

There's Me, Among the Ruins

Five minutes after the rusty freighter had braked to a halt at a ruined wharf half-way along the stream, a Canadian naval lieutenant came clattering down the gangway outside my iron bedroom. He stuck his head through the hatch. The hatch was so small it looked as if it had been designed to admit only undersized deep-sea divers with the bends.

"Hey," he called in. "Where will I find this flying fella?"

I gazed up at him emaciatedly.

"Quick, man, I'm in a hurry. Which cabin is he in?"

"Flying fella?" I croaked. "That must be me. I've been flying all over this cabin for days."

"No, I mean the Flying Corps man."

" 'S me."

"You're Colonel Bandy? Gee whizz."

I stood up, and immediately lurched sideways all the way across the cabin—it was a good four feet wide—and clanged against a bulkhead. My feet hadn't yet noticed that the ship had stopped yawing and pitching.

The smart young lieutenant stepped deftly into the cabin without even having the decency to smash his cranium against the top of the hatch. I was pretty annoyed at that. I'd hit it nearly every time I'd dragged my tail back from the head.

"Welcome home, sir," he said in his quick, enthusiastic voice. "My name's Toogood, port admiral's aide. Admiral Byrd-Kustard wishes me to welcome you back to Canada,

Colonel, and extends an invitation to put up with him."

"Is he hard to get along with, then?" I asked numbly.

"I mean, he wants you to be his guest, during stay in Halifax." The bright-looking lieutenant stood to attention and added formally, "Him and his old lady. Okay?"

"There was some talk——" I stopped to clear my throat and scrape some rust off my voice. It had become eroded from disuse and neglect, because nobody had talked to me for such a long time; throughout most of the voyage, in fact. They'd been put off, I suppose, by the sound of my retchings, which had been echoing throughout the ship for days on end. "Some talk of my staying with the Lieutenant-Governor," I finished.

Toogood inserted eight fingers into his tunic pockets and said smoothly, "There must be some mistake, sir. We have a room all prepared for you at Admiralty House, and we're supposed to be looking after you, seeing you get to the civic reception on Friday, and so on and so forth. The admiral and his wife would be deeply disappointed if you turned them down, sir." His thumbs, hanging over the edges of his pockets, wiggled enthusiastically. "They, and in fact everybody else, are looking forward very much to meeting the hero of Morlancourt. The papers have been full of your splendid action, sir, that single handed battle against more than thirty enemy aircraft when, after all the rest of your men had been lost, you not only emerged triumphant but, in one of the most remarkable demonstrations of quick thinking, enterprise, courage, and devotion to——"

"Oh, shut up."

"Sorry," he said. "Thought you'd enjoy me piling it on. Most of our important guests can't get enough of my nauseating flattery."

"I don't mind the nauseating flattery. It's your voice I can't stand. It's so cheerful."

"I know how you feel," Lieutenant Toogood said sym-

278

pathetically. "I always get seasick myself, hence my present job as the admiral's megaphone.

"We can take it, then," he added, "that you accept his invitation?"

"I guess so."

"Very good. We'll have a car waiting for you as soon as you've cleared the health authorities."

"I doubt if I will clear them. I've been at death's door for fifteen days."

"A prescription of terra firma will clear that up in no time," Toogood said briskly. "By the way, there's a few reporters waiting for you outside the dock gates."

"What, in the middle of the night?"

"It's not the middle of the night, it's broad daylight."

"It is? It's been so dark down here . . . What time is it, anyway?"

Just then, eight bells rang.

"There you are," Toogood said. "Eight bells."

"How much is eight bells?"

"Eight, of course."

"Yes," I croaked patiently. "But what time does that indicate?"

"Ah. See what you mean. Let's see, now . . . eight bells. That would be . . . Don't prompt me, now. They told me all about it at Dartmouth . . . That would be, oh—about eight in the morning?"

I gave him a look, then, clinging tightly to the nearest cock, began to draw my clothes from a rusty steampipe where they'd been hanging up to dry. I had just finished packing, wondering dully why my undies had orange streaks across them, when there was a thump of boots on the gangway outside. Somebody else was fearlessly following the naval lieutenant down to my iron maiden, laughably described by the first officer, before I boarded, as a first-class cabin amidships.

He must have meant it was first-class in comparison

with the stoker's accommodation. It was amidships, all right, but so deep in the ship they had to climb *down* from the engine room to reach it.

The newcomer turned out to be a middle-aged Canadian Army captain. He peered in, looking like a speleologist who'd just discovered an unusually sordid cave.

"Is it Colonel Bandy?" he asked, panting.

"Too late, Mac," Lieutenant Toogood cried. "He's accepted the admiral's invitation."

"Damn."

The Army captain glared in through the hole. "You knew he was supposed to stay with us," he snapped.

"First come first served, Tommy."

"It's the second time in a row you've done this! It's too bad, Toogood!"

"What's all this?" I asked.

"You were supposed to stay with the Lieutenant-Governor," the captain shouted, looking at me as if I were a traitor to the country.

In fact, I'd received a very indefinite invitation, through the High Commissioner's office in Victoria Street, London, and had assumed, when the subject wasn't mentioned again, that they'd had second thoughts about it.

I tried to explain this to the Lieutenant-Governor's private secretary, Captain McCann, but he wouldn't listen. "His Honor isn't going to be very pleased when he hears you've turned down his invitation," he said loudly.

"His wife isn't, you mean," Toogood said smugly.

"What's it got to do with his wife?" I asked. Then, wearily: "Look, I'm in a sufficiently debilitated state as it is, without all this mystery. I've hardly eaten a thing for fifteen days except dog biscuits and glasses of milk," I said, "and I'm in no mood . . ." The rest died away in what sounded alarmingly like a death rattle.

"Three weeks ago, it was the Overseas Minister," McCann said, turning back to Lieutenant Toogood. "You practically kidnapped him. Now you've done it again!"

"Well, you took that famous American poet, whatsis-name, off us. *And* the C-in-C, Atlantic."

"Look here," McCann demanded, glaring back at me. "Do you or do you not intend to honor your promise to stay with the Lieutenant-Governor and his wife?"

"You heard the colonel, Mac. He didn't receive a firm invitation from you—"

"I wasn't talking to you!" the Army man shouted.

The two of them continued to fume, glare, snap, and bicker for several minutes. Under the developer of their polemic, the picture gradually emerged, a trifle fuzzily, but clear enough for me to discern that it was the spouses who had issued the invitations rather than the bigwigs themselves. I gathered, with a sinking heart, that the wives had been vying with each other for some time to see who could entertain the larger number of important visitors to Halifax.

"So," I said to Toogood, after McCann had stormed back up the ladder, "you've landed me in the middle of a contest between the leading lights of Halifax society, is that it?"

"I wouldn't exactly call it a contest, sir," Toogood said cautiously.

"What would you call it, then?"

"A feud."

"Thank you. Thank you very much indeed."

Toogood waved away my thanks with a cheerful smile.

He'd been honest about it not being the middle of the night, though. Upstairs it was bright daylight.

Gratefully, I sucked in tremulous lungfuls of the first fresh air I'd imbibed since the ship had just missed col-liding with Ireland, a couple of weeks ago.

A cool Maritimes breeze was competing with the hot August sun. Dockyard cranes patterned the cloudless sky. As I tottered across to the gangway, oily debris sucked and swirled between the ship's side and the battered wharf.

At the gangway, the first officer said heartily, "Well,

haven't seen much of you this trip, have we?"

"And it's the last time you ever catch me on a boat again."

"Ship."

"*Or* a ship. From now on, I'll never voyage across anything wider than an old mill stream. Rotten tub . . ."

"That's no way to talk, Colonel. We gave you a cabin all to yourself, didn't we?"

"Only because there wasn't room for anybody else. There wasn't even room for me, and look how much space I take up, after fifteen days."

"M'm, you do look a trifle wasted . . . By the way, what was that Army chap in such a huff about? He stormed off the ship as if someone had called his mother a socialist."

Toogood jauntily told him about the mix-up over the invitations.

"Oh, God, are they at it again? I hope you picked the right side, Colonel. The Lieutenant-Governor's wife, Mrs. Capon, can be pretty mean when she's crossed."

"Wonderful," I said.

There was a sizeable crowd outside the docks. As I lurched through the gates, accompanied by Lieutenant Toogood, a few of them clapped, albeit a bit self-consciously.

Most of them, however, just stared, as if finding it hard to believe that this emaciated land-lubber with the face like a collapsed tent could possibly have done anything more heroic than volunteering to taste the food in an Army cookhouse.

The newspaper reporters, looking equally unimpressed, were good enough to ask pretty much the same questions as had their European confreres, so I was able to trot out the same answers without having to think too coherently.

After telling them I'd had an awful voyage, thank you, so it was doubly good to be home, I described the action once more, then settled down for the usual interrogation.

This one here, with the purple stripes? A new medal, called the Distinguished Flying Cross . . . No, I hadn't heard a word about the V.C. . . . I didn't know exactly how many confirmed victories. I kept careful score the first time, but somehow the second time . . . No, not nearly as many as Billy Bishop . . . Yes, I'd met Bishop a couple of weeks ago at the Air Ministry—the greatest marksman of them all . . . No, my wife wasn't *enceinte*, and yes, I believed she was related to an earl, through her mother (that was in response to a lady reporter) . . . No, I still felt like just plain folks (liar) . . . I found the Prince of Wales charming, no hot air about him at all (the lady reporter again) . . . I didn't expect the war to end for a long time yet . . . What latest attack? . . . Oh, I hadn't heard about that, I was on the high seas at the time, and my God were they high. What happened? Don't tell me the attack was successful?

So the press interview ended with me asking them the questions, about the Australian, British, and Canadian advance on August 8, on the Amiens front, in which six German divisions had been overwhelmed, many of the German soldiers surrendering with every sign of relief and satisfaction.

"They say it's the first time that's happened in the war, the Heinies giving up so easy," the Halifax *Mail* reporter said, "and it may be the beginning of the end."

"No," I croaked authoritatively. "Don't delude yourselves, gentlemen—and lady. The war will last at least until 1920; 1920 at the very least."

When they'd finished taking pictures—Toogood managed to get into several of them in spite of my efforts to elbow him aside or stand in front of him—a naval rating drove up in a gigantic Pierce-Arrow Vestibule Suburban with brass door handles.

"We used to have a Ford Touring," Toogood said as we embedded ourselves in the upholstery, "until Mrs.

Capon got her husband, the Lieutenant-Governor, to buy an American-Broc Brougham. So the admiral's wife persuaded her husband to retaliate with *this* sumptuous vehicle."

The ladies had been competing with each other for as long as he'd been in this job, Toogood said. "Mrs. Byrd-Kustard is ahead at the moment. Her last catch was the Minister for Overseas Forces, a couple of weeks ago. He was passing through Halifax on his way to London and was supposed to be staying with His Honor, Mr. Capon. But I met his train further up the line, and somehow he got the impression I was from the Lieutenant-Governor's office. By the time we had him ensconced in Admiralty House, it was too late for him to do anything about it without offending the admiral as well. Mrs. Byrd-Kustard gave me a sterling-silver mustard pot as a reward for that little *coup*."

"You should have got a good biff on the boko," I muttered.

"Sure. And I'd have deserved it, sir," Toogood said in that disarming way of his. "But what else can I do? I'd lose my job if I displeased the old girl, and I'm sure as hell not in any hurry to get back to my proper job, getting seasick on over-age destroyers, if I can help it."

I could understand that, anyway.

"Even so," he went on, drawing down a silk shade to keep out the sun, "our *coups* barely make up for Mrs. Capon's last triumph, when she not only lured the admiral's own superior officer to the Lieutenant-Governor's mansion, but organized a state dinner for him, knowing that Mrs. Byrd-Kustard was down with the flu.

"Mind you, Mrs. Byrd-Kustard attended the dinner anyway, and deliberately breathed germs all over Mrs. Capon. Their husbands have tried to persuade the ladies to share important guests on a rota basis, but they're too far gone in enmity for that. It's quite painful to see the way they smile at each other whenever they meet by accident."

"What are they like?"

"Mrs. Capon is like an aging actress who isn't getting enough good parts. Though, come to think of it," he added thoughtfully, "she already has two or three good parts . . . As for Mrs. Byrd-Kustard, she's like one of those lamplighters' poles: long and thin, with a flicker of flame at the top.

"Oh, yes," he added, "and she hates to be touched."

"Touched? Ah, I see. You mean she's totally unreceptive to appeals to sentiment, and cannot abide romantic or tender exchanges of any sort."

"Eh?"

"I'm explaining what you meant. That there is a certain cynicism to her outlook, and cloying sentimentality is abhorrent to her basically realistic attitude to life. That's what you meant, isn't it?"

"I just meant she hates to be touched, Colonel."

"That's what I just said, wasn't it?"

"Oh, forget it," Toogood said.

We were half-way to Admiralty House before I remembered to feel the exhilaration of the returning traveller.

It was over two years since I had left. As we drove through the narrow streets under the squinting sun, I gazed at the dingy Victorian edifices with gratitude and some emotion.

I even found the sound of the trams affecting, as they screeched and swayed around the telegraph-tangled corners, and the clop and groan of the slovens that plodded over the cobbles, loaded with barrels, sacks, and cloth-capped drivers.

Although the grey city of Halifax was more like a British than a Canadian port, there was still enough of a difference to make it feel like the threshold of home, particularly the accents, the cleaner air, and the bustling, optimistic pace. The most gratifying impression, though, even in that huddled town, was the sense of space. In Europe, everything seemed so crowded and constricted, with no room to move on the sidewalks, and little feeling of elbow room, even in the small towns; and always the sense that beyond the next hill was another crowded place. When I caught my first glimpse of the glorious sweep of forested horizon beyond the Bedford Basin, and sensed the scale of the land beyond it, I felt relief and freedom. This really was where I belonged, after all.

"Home," I croaked, taking a deep, proud breath of Narrows mud, rotting fish-heads, oxy-acetylene smoke, and the pong from the refinery near McNab's Island. "Even if it does look a bit run-down." I cleared my throat noisily. "The docks look as if they've been bombed. And all these boarded-up windows—is there a shortage of glass or something?"

"That was the explosion."

"Eh? Oh, yes . . ." I said, looking around again. "I heard about that."

"You'll hear little else while you're here. People are still talking about it, nine months later."

"A munitions ship, wasn't it?"

"Last December. The *Mont Blanc*. It was loaded with TNT. Another ship ran into it. When it went up, it damaged towns sixty miles away." Toogood's two gold rings gleamed in the sun as he turned to point at Citadel Hill. "It was only the hill that saved the whole city from being devastated. You should see the north end of town. It's completely destroyed. They still don't know how many people were killed. Over a thousand five hundred, anyway."

The car bounced and rumbled as it sped along a cobbled street between hordes of sunburned girls on bicycles, all shamelessly showing their ankles. We passed what had

286

once been a row of wooden houses, their walls leaning, splintered and scorched.

"The *Mont Blanc* was also carrying benzol, and it rained fire for minutes on end. Houses were still burning in the snow three days later."

As we reached the centre of town and were puttering slowly along crowded Barrington Street, a car came racing down one of the steep intersecting streets, its horn parp-parping urgently. Toogood and I watched uneasily as it hurtled toward us at a reckless pace, the front wheels wiggling wildly. It was being driven by a woman.

She looked remarkably unconcerned, even though her vehicle was about to plough into the side of one of the trams. The tram, as if in anticipation, was already screech-ing. Beside her in the swaying vehicle was a maid, who, to make up for her mistress' unconcern, was looking dis-tinctly apprehensive.

At the last moment, the tall, narrow vehicle swung away from the tram, rising perilously on two wheels as it did so. Missing a pair of gentlemen in black serge by a good eight inches, it screeched to a halt transversely across the prow of our Pierce-Arrow.

One of the black-serge gentlemen shouted angrily and shook his fist. A helmeted policeman started portentously toward the offending vehicle, but stopped when he caught sight of the driver. He turned away to tie his bootlace. When nobody was looking, he hurried up the nearest alleyway.

"Mrs. Capon," Toogood murmured.

The lady's face, now seen to be slightly flushed, was only about six feet away. Toogood leaned over to open the window on my side. Simultaneously Mrs. Capon flung open the high, narrow door of her brougham, just as a cloth-capped cyclist was shooting between the two cars. He ran into the door and fell under the mud-guard with a cry of alarm, his wheels spinning and scraping.

"Do look where you're going," Mrs. Capon cried irritably, projecting remarkably well over the din of bicycle bells, grinding trams, hooting cars, and pedestrian exclamations.

The cyclist stared up groggily from under the mudguard. Mrs. Capon paid no further attention to him, but addressed us across the six-foot gap.

"I thought it was you, you hooligan," she said in her extremely loud voice. "I thought I recognized your motor car, and I said to myself if that's that son-of-a-bitch Toogood, I want a little word with him."

Beside her, the maid whimpered at this shocking language, but for some reason covered her nose rather than her ears.

"Oh, do stop blubbering, Olive," Mrs. Capon exclaimed impatiently.

"I've banged me nose, Mam."

"Well, you should know to hang on properly," Mrs. Capon shouted. She had a Canadian accent, garnished with Irish, delivered through a slack mouth that didn't quite cover several dangerous-looking teeth. Though she was expensively attired in a light silk dress, there was a certain air of dishevelment about her. A tendril of Celtic hair hung from under her theatrical hat.

"Always delighted to have a little word with you, Mrs. Capon," Toogood called back, touching his cap in a rather nervous salute.

She pushed the door wide open for a better view. "You won't be so delighted when I've finished with you," she shouted. "I've just this minute heard from Captain McCann, and I was just on my way to tell that woman just what I thought of her. But now I've seen you, Mr. so-called Toogood, I'll give *you* a piece of my mind instead. I'm going to ask my husband to lodge an official complaint about your conduct, you gold-ringed maggot. You've done this sort of thing once too often, my lad, and I've half a mind . . ."

The rest was lost in an outburst of hooting and raving from a growing line of frustrated drivers behind us. A fair crowd of morning shoppers were also clustering at the street corner, whispering and nudging. Even the seagulls seemed excited by the *brouhaha,* as they planed and complained over the rooftops.

Mrs. Capon's castigations continued under the uproar, most of her words being inaudible, which was probably just as well, as there were several sailors nearby, as well as a gang of urchins.

Her voice bridged a lull in the vehicular racket ". . . not going to get away with it this time, my fine featherbrained friend," she hollered. "Even if he is only half a colonel." Her little green eyes, arranged on a stave of wrinkles, flicked suddenly to me. "That's you, is it?" she asked scornfully.

"I'm really sorry about this, Mrs. Capon," I wheedled hoarsely. "But honest, I didn't realize it was a definite invitation from the—"

"Some warrior you are, letting yourself be bullied into staying with that stuck-up length of drainpipe," she interrupted. "Well, all I can say is, don't expect any help or favors from the Lieutenant-Governor. And don't expect us to attend your reception either. Seeing you now, it'll probably be as dull as ditchwater anyway."

There was a lot more of this, but we missed most of it because of a renewed bedlam of bellowing and parping. By now, the traffic behind us was backed up as far as the Bedford Basin.

That didn't seem to trouble Mrs. Capon in the least. "Anyway, I've read all about you between the lines," she shouted across the gap between the two cars. "And you're no great catch anyway. From what I've heard about you, and by God your face confirms it, her ladyship'll be sorry she ever landed you, that's all I've got to say. And another thing: I remember you were in the papers a few months ago as well, about some half-witted speech you made

289

about Sir Douglas Haig. I wonder if her ladyship knows about that." Her voice went all upper-class British. "She just *adores* dear Sir Douglas." Her flushed face rearranged itself again into a scowl. "Maybe I'll tell her and she can find out what kind of a snake-in-the-grass she's landed, you simpering carthorse. Good day to you, *Colonel* Bandy."

So saying, she slammed the door and backed her electric car rapidly out of the way of the southbound traffic, scattering pedestrians as she did so. A moment later, she was shooting back up the hill again, on the wrong side of the street.

"Trifle fiery, isn't she?" I whined, as we drove on. "Gee, I certainly wouldn't want to get in *her* bad books."

After a wash and brush-up in a room that was as chilly, even in August, as it was overfurnished—it contained a huge hearts-of-oak bed with about fourteen layers of bedclothes, all of them damp—I came downstairs to meet the other half of the feud.

As I was crossing the panelled hall, past an artistically arranged display of naval mementos, battle standards, musical instruments, and the like, I heard her saying in precise but approving terms, ". . . done splendidly, Toogood. That will teach her to confiscate the admiral's very own superior officer, right from under our noses. She was furious, was she? Wonderful. You must tell me all about it."

She broke off as I rolled, Jolly Jack Tar-like, into the Admiralty House drawing room.

"Ah, Colonel," she said regally as I approached, wearing my upper-class face. "How very pleased we are that you were able to accept our invitation. Welcome to Admiralty House."

Toogood's description hadn't been overly exaggerated. Mrs. Byrd-Kustard was very nearly as tall as I was, and even thinner, with fanatic eyes and a nose you could have used as a cheese-cutter. She held herself as if her stays were made of reinforcing rods.

She looked a good deal more rigid a moment later. This was after I'd lurched forward to seize her flipper, and wring it as if pumping out the bilges of a side dragger.

"Darned glad to meet you, Mrs. Byrd-Kustard," I exclaimed enthusiastically. A moment later I was forced to seize her shoulder as the drawing-room floor heaved like the deck of a 70-gun ship of the line off Ushant.

"Sorry," I said, shifting my grip to her forearm until the house had settled itself on an even keel. "Still a bit unsteady on the pins, you understand."

Mrs. Byrd-Kustard had suddenly developed lockjaw—all over. There definitely seemed to be some sort of internal struggle going on there.

However, after swallowing a few times and taking several quick, shallow breaths, she managed to say, "Yes . . . Well . . . perhaps you'd better be seated," and showed me how to do it by dropping onto a *chaise-longue,* suddenly, as if someone had just kicked her behind the knees.

I looked around for a seat. She immediately arranged the folds of her dress to each side of her, to make it plain that I was not expected to plonk myself beside her.

"Toogood," she said in an unnaturally high voice, "would you hurry and inform the admiral that Colonel Bandy has arrived."

Toogood murmured and withdrew, glancing back a trifle anxiously as he did so.

After a while, Mrs. Byrd-Kustard began to regain her color.

"As I say, my husband and I are pleased you were able to accept our invitation to stay with us for several— for a day or so," she said, watching me through perceptibly narrowed eyes as I felt my way into the nearest upholstered receptacle. "We're looking forward very keenly indeed to hearing all about that heroic exploit of yours, against the Heathen Hun."

We smiled at each other. It was hate at first sight.

"It was nothing really," I said. Mrs. Byrd-Kustard nodded approvingly at this correctly modest response. "It was merely," I went on, "a typical example of my brilliant flying, shooting skill, quick thinking, opportunism, and outright panic."

I settled myself more comfortably into the armchair. "Though in fact," I said, "all I was doing was looking after my own skin."

Mrs. Byrd-Kustard didn't seem to like things like skin being mentioned. "There must have been a little more to it than that, Colonel," she said, steepling her fingers. They were trembling only slightly, now. "For I believe you had the honor to be personally congratulated by none other than Sir Douglas Haig himself."

"I'm not sure whether he congratulated me or not," I said with an equally hypocritical smile. "His Chief of Intelligence introduced me, but all I heard from the field marshal was a grunt."

"Indeed? That's strange. I remember him as invariably expressing himself very clearly indeed."

"Who? *Haig?*"

"But if in fact his response was a trifle lacking in clarity or enthusiasm," she said, smiling in a way that suggested she was receiving an enema, "perhaps he also was beginning to doubt whether all he had read in the papers was true."

Touché, thought I. "As Haig is responsible for half the lies published in the papers," I said, flexing my own *épée,* "I should hope he *would* have some doubts."

"I happen to know personally," she said, sitting even more erect, were that possible—and it weren't—"that Sir Douglas is a man of the utmost honesty and integrity."

"So was Czar Nicholas the Second, and look what's happened to him."

"I met him and his charming wife before the war," she

said, as if I hadn't spoken, "when he was commander in chief at Aldershot."

It was no good. She was obviously one of those who preferred to see war in Tennysonian terms, rather than in those of, say, Siegfried Sassoon.

"Oh, yeah?" I said.

"We were invited more than once to his select dinner parties, and I must confess I developed a particular admiration for his methodical qualities and attention to detail. You only had to see him on the fairway to realize that. My husband played golf with him, and told me all about it later: the infinite pains Sir Douglas took over every single stroke—bringing to that game those qualities of dedication and painstaking care that have since made him such a success as commander in chief in France. My husband was so impressed, he has never played since."

It seemed like hours before the admiral joined us. He came in rapidly, puffing distractedly at a cigarette. I arose, with almost as much alacrity as relief. Unfortunately, the sudden motion caused me to lurch slightly, the result, as before, of fifteen days of nautical disequilibrium.

Mrs. Byrd-Kustard flinched. It was almost as if she thought I might grab her again to support myself—perhaps this time by the throat.

"Ah," the admiral said, after Toogood had performed the introductions. "So this is the young aviator whose heroic exploits have so enlivened the pages of the newspapers of late."

"Yes, that's me all right," I said, essaying a light laugh. It came out like the rattle of an anchor chain.

The admiral started slightly, and puffed more furiously than ever at his dog-end. I looked at him in some surprise.

All the admirals I'd met at the Air Ministry had autocratic beaks and ferocious voices. Admiral Byrd-Kustard, however, had a squashy sort of nose, and tended to mumble, a fault that had led to some confusion on the bridge of his last ship. A remark to the effect that a passing sea-gull was a "speedy tern" had been interpreted as an order for full speed astern, with the result that his battleship had run into a lighthouse; hence his present job in this outpost of the Empire.

"We've been having a most interesting conversation, Bertram," his wife said. She seemed to be making some kind of signal to him. "Especially about our acquaintance-ship with Sir Douglas."

"Oh, God, yes," the admiral said. Whatever her signal meant, he didn't seem to understand it either. He puffed hurriedly at his cigarette again, and winced as his upper lip sizzled. "You must tell us all about your exploit Bandy," he mumbled. I opened my mouth to do so. "Per-haps at dinner tomorrow night. We're having one or two people in. I'm sure they'll be most interested to hear all about it first hand."

His initial wave of enthusiasm had already drained away into the scuppers. When nobody said anything for a few seconds, he looked longingly toward the decanters.

His wife said quickly, "I suppose you'll be looking for-ward eagerly to seeing your parents again, Colonel."

"Yes, Ma'am. I'll be leaving for Ottawa right after the reception on Friday."

"Oh, splendid," Mrs. Byrd-Kustard exclaimed, smiling genuinely for the first time that morning.

The admiral started chunnering again. I couldn't make out what he was saying, and had an impulse to call out sharply, "Speak up, man, you're not on your battleship now!" But having failed dismally to earn his wife's ap-proval, I was all the more anxious to recoup the situation by making the best possible impression on the admiral; so I just said, "Eh?"

"Toogood says you bumped into Mrs. Capon on the way over."

"That scandalous woman," Mrs. Byrd-Kustard said.

"The Lieutenant-Governor would have got rid of her long ago had he not his position to think of. What a common person she is. She is a disgrace to Halifax society. Mrs. Cross tells me she created a most disagreeable scene at the flower show last Wednesday, stumbling over a display of the Honorable Mr. Harvard's prize gladioli. So we will not discuss her if you don't mind, Bertram. Others may gossip about her abandoned behavior and deplorable habits, but we must be above that sort of thing."

"Mumble," the admiral said.

In the leaden silence that followed, he glanced around distractedly. Seeing no empty glasses, he said, "Toogood, this isn't very hospitable of you. What about a spot of sherry for our guest?"

"No!"

We all turned and looked wide-eyed at Mrs. Byrd-Kustard.

"That is . . . isn't it a little early in the day for that, Bertram?"

"Oh, is it?"

A moment later, I caught her shooting urgent frowns at him again—and darting her eyes in my direction.

It was only then I understood why she'd been looking at me with such suspicion since I first floundered into her drawing room.

It was all that swaying about I'd been doing, because my legs still didn't believe they were on dry land again.

She thought I'd been tanking up at some dockside groggery.

Another View of Halifax

Dinner the following evening, attended by some of the poshest people in Halifax, was initially something of a strain. Mrs. Byrd-Kustard not only remained convinced that I was addicted to alcohol but had obviously had a word with the servants about my problem, with the result that when I signalled for a second glass of wine, they avoided my vicinity with such badly acted preoccupation that some of the guests also began to regard me warily, as if I might at any moment pull up my pant legs and start tap-dancing on the sherry trifle, or drool into the nearest cleavage. But I would never have done that. There were no cleavages around. The ladies all wore gowns determinedly secured at the throat.

However, I wasn't going to let a little misunderstanding get me down, so to show that I was as sober as anyone, I launched into a suave, polished, but restrained account of my nautical adventures, as befitted the dignified occasion; and in fact held the company spellbound for nigh on twenty minutes with my tales of the sea.

"The sea" (the old salt related) "more than lived up to its reputation as the bounding main. It wouldn't have been so bad if the Atlantic had been battering along anywhere near the Plimsoll line, but the ship was riding so high even some of the barnacles were sticking out of the water."

I looked around brightly. Everybody was listening most attentively, without even blinking. After a moment, Mrs.

Byrd-Kustard said faintly, "Surely that's not possible, is it, Bertram?"

"I assure you, Ma'am," I said. "We were returning empty, you see. Our only ballast was a few tons of brine that poured in when the seacook opened the seacocks somewhere off Saltee. That's in Ireland," I explained to a little old lady who was listening in a catatonic sort of way. "They said the seacook was demented, you know. *I* thought he was behaving very sensibly."

As the guests sat there in rapt silence, I leaned back in a lordly fashion, pleased to hear that my voice had returned to its normal, piquant whine. "It was just as well there was nobody on board with artistic pretensions," I said, "for my green face must have clashed revoltingly with the ocean blue. Quite apart from all the wallowings, which prevented me from keeping anything down except several litres of saliva, I hardly slept for more than nine and a half minutes at a time."

There was a faint clink as somebody pushed away his pudding.

"This was mainly because the marine noises keep changing every hour on the hour. I was enclosed in an iron cabin deep in the ship—I'm sure it was below the bilge, Admiral—and I'd just be getting used to one aural rhythm—the rusty grindings of the engine, the beatings of the generator, the gurgling of the bilgewater, the ravings of the cook, and so forth—and would be drifting off into a dehydrated slumber when, after exactly one hour, the rhythm would alter itself in some subtle way, just enough to drag one back to wild-eyed wakefulness. The machinery would still be thumping away, of course, but now it would be grinding its teeth as well; the pumps might still be clanking, but with a greater urgency; or the hum of the air-conditioning might die away altogether, to be replaced by queer tearing and splashing noises, as if corpses were being slid into the sea down nail-studded planks.

"By then I was so debilitated that my uniform looked

as if there were nobody in it; so starved, parched, dazed, battered, and feeble as to make even retching a formidable but not entirely inefficacious effort.

"And that," I said, "was only my second day out."

After a moment, the admiral said, "Weren't you supposed to be staying with the Lieutenant-Governor?"

I'd been particularly anxious to make a good impression that evening, because, as well as being convinced that I was a common drunk, Mrs. Byrd-Kustard had also got it into her head that I was also a common lecher.

What had happened was this: that morning I'd been taken in charge by the mayor's wife, who, as if under the impression that I was the head of a trade delegation, had dispatched me on a tour of Halifax industry: steel mills, biscuit and confectionery factories, and a fish-curing plant; and, in the afternoon, on a sightseeing trip through the worst parts of Halifax, to see the damage.

She had organized these activities through a women's club. I spent about seven grueling hours in the company of dozens of twittering ladies, every one of whom had her own personal anecdote to relate about The Great Explosion. One had seen a horse and cart flying over her house. Another, a Mrs. McAndrews, had been blown out of bed and had hit the ceiling. "My," she said, wideeyed, "you should just see the great dent I made in my bedroom ceiling."

She was one of the good-looking ones. "Can that be arranged?" I whispered, under suggestively arched eyebrows. She looked pretty flustered at that, and for the rest of the tour had remained hidden behind some of the burlier members of the throng.

I'd only said it for fun, of course, and to relieve a momentary boredom. In fact, I'd been almost as taken aback as she was. It hadn't sounded like me at all. I couldn't help wondering at the changes that had come over me since leaving the country twenty-five months before with a moral outlook that would have made John Knox seem a dirty old man by comparison. Now look at me: flirting with comely widows.

The trouble was, Mrs. McAndrews was among those who had been invited back to Admiralty House for tea, and she had told my hostess about it instead of keeping decently quiet, the bitch.

So, even before dinner, Mrs. Byrd-Kustard's manner had been pretty arctic. To top if off, and entirely ruining the memorable impression I'd made during that monologue of mine, as we were strolling back to the drawing room, I tottered again.

I'd just finished congratulating myself on once again re-establishing a working relationship with the earth, too. Mind you, it was a very minor totter, hardly more than a teeter, in fact, and normally it wouldn't have been noticed by anyone who wasn't on the lookout for further symptoms of inebriation and debauchery.

Unfortunately, in tottering (or teetering), my foot clacked against the bottom exhibit of the admiral's artful display of fifes, drums, and battle-tattered ensigns salvaged from some of the Royal Navy's more notable defeats. The whole works came down with a reverberating crash. But that wasn't the worst of it. I had to grab at somebody for support, and of all people, it would have to be Mrs. Byrd-Kustard.

The result was so awful that I had split nerve-ends for the next twenty-four hours. She uttered a piercing scream in which fright and fury were so mixed as to be inseparable outside of a psychoanalytical centrifuge, were there such an apparatus. Turning on me with gritted eyes and staring teeth, she clawed at my hands with nails that I'm sure had been specially sharpened for the occasion.

Everybody stood transfixed, nay, petrified, all their muscles bunched up like cauliflowers. There was not a sound, except for the patter of blood from my lacerated veins, and the ticking of a side drum as it rolled across the floor. We all watched blindly, until it had settled down with a final, wincing clunk.

It really didn't seem worthwhile explaining that I hadn't quite got my land legs yet.

Not more than ten minutes after the last guest had departed in disorder, I accidentally overheard her talking on the telephone to her arch-enemy, the Lieutenant-Governor's wife. Well, I didn't exactly overhear by accident—I emerged from cover to listen the moment I heard my name mentioned.

"No, no, not at all, Mrs. Capon," Mrs. Byrd-Kustard was saying. She was holding the telephone receiver as if it had recently fallen in the exercise yard of a dog pound. "He's a most delightful person, quite dashing, with a most stimulating way of describing his experiences. The admiral was just saying to me that Colonel Bandy was a most . . . Yes, I realize we've had our little differences in the past, and that's what I'm calling about, Mrs. Capon. I do feel we have an obligation to set an example—noblesse oblige, as they say—and much as we should like to keep him, one cannot help but feel a certain moral obligation to . . . Would that be possible? Oh, thank God—that would be . . . a splendid start to a new era in our relationship, don't you . . . ? . . . Oh, no, not at all. As I say, he's a most intriguing man, quite overwhelming in fact, and we're *most* reluctant to part with him, but I really do think it's high time we ended this undignified conflict that . . ."

Anyway, it was *much* more comfortable at Mrs. Capon's.

At first Mrs. Capon's manner was not particularly cordial. In fact, she seemed to view the transfer with a good deal of suspicion. I wondered uneasily how long it would take some busybody to whisper the reason Mrs. Byrd-Kustard had suddenly become so terribly reasonable and unselfish.

It took about three and a half hours. To my surprise, when Mrs. Capon heard the gossip her eyes lit up like headlights.

"Why didn't you tell me you were a common drunkard?" she cried gayly, after lunch. "Why, I'd have been much more friendly this morning if I'd known."

"But I hardly drink at all, Mrs. Capon."

She laughed as if I were joshing her.

"Admittedly I was starting to imbibe rather too much in France, but ever since then—"

"I know," she said, touching my arm and smiling at me approvingly. "Captain McCann's told me all about you getting fuddled at their swank dinner last night, and talking wildly about vomit."

"But I was stone cold sober!"

"Oh, sure. That's why you smashed all their hall furniture and clawed at Mrs. Byrd-Kustard's corsets."

"I *didn't!* I—"

"Oh, I'd have just loved to have seen her ladyship's face when she discovered you were a confirmed boozer. So that's why the old trout was being so accommodating. Well, don't you worry, son, I'm not one to look down on a fellow just because he's a thorough souse."

"But I'm not! I—"

"I'm not averse to a spot myself now and again," she said, and, after a quick glance around, poured each of us about eleven fingers of rum. She drank half of hers in one go. "And what's this I hear about you forcing your way into Mrs. McAndrews' bedroom and getting so enthralled with her that half the ceiling falls onto the bed?"

"Good grief, does everyone in Halifax know what everyone else is doing?"

"Yes—you dirty bugger," she said, giving me a sly nudge and a remarkably coarse wink.

"Honest, Mrs. Capon, it wasn't like that at all," I protested, just as the Lieutenant-Governor came in with

Captain McCann and found me clutching a glass so brimming with rum that the slightest tremor sent rivulets of the stuff coursing down my ivory knuckles.

A distinguished-looking gentleman, much aware of the dignity of his position, Mr. Capon was not at all pleased to find us busily transfusing alcohol at two in the afternoon. He looked bitterly at his wife. The poor woman almost cringed, obviously only too aware that she wasn't good enough for him.

After confiscating the bottle, he took me aside and said, "I hope you don't mind my saying this, Colonel, but I wish you wouldn't encourage my wife to imbibe quite so early in the day."

"But I—"

"Please don't think I fail to understand. The hardships of war, and so forth. I know a little of the appalling conditions at the front, the bottle frequently being your only recourse and comfort."

"No, 'tisn't, Your Honor. I—"

"But as you may already have gathered, my wife also tends to look for solace in that quarter, with not nearly as much excuse."

"But I—"

"Well, we won't say any more about it," he said, ordering his quadrate muscle to deliver a tolerant smile to his lower lip. It made him look as if he were auditioning for the part of Dracula. "Mrs. Capon is a cross I have to bear, but all I ask is that you not add a further burden by giving way to your own alcoholic tendencies."

God, being back at school couldn't have been any worse.

That evening, the Premier of the Province and an Honorable or two of the Legislative Council came to dinner. Either they were unmarried or word had gotten out that I was an unprincipled cad, for their wives failed to turn up.

That was one difference between North America and Europe, I thought. In Europe, hearing I was a sex-maniac, the women would have come to dinner in droves.

As soon as Mr. Capon and his visitors had retired to the study for some political haggling (taking the brandy with them), Mrs. Capon sashayed into her private sitting room at the back of the house, and after firmly closing the door and cutting off my escape, took a fresh bottle of rum from behind Law Society Volume XIV.

I hurriedly started yawning, stretching, and mumbling excuses about being a trifle weary. As it was still only half after eight, my excuses weren't overly convincing.

"What's the matter with you? You don't want me to think you're reluctant to keep me company, do you? Come on, sit down and stop babbling. Anyone would think you were a damned Temperancer instead of an old soak, the way you're going on. Here, that's not enough to drown a flea. Pour us a decent snort, will you, for God's sake. That's more like it, now."

I suppose, being rather more determined than I used to be, I could have acted firmly, and told her that I'd no wish to reel around with her in drunken debauchery this particular evening. Unfortunately, feeling sorry for somebody invariably immobilized my shindy instincts. Besides, I was more than normally anxious to avoid any kind of scene, and still determined to make a good impression on my fellow countrymen, especially people like Capon, on whose peacetime influence I might one day have to rely; if I survived to call upon it, that is.

So I just sat there in a sulk. This made Mrs. Capon tremendously friendly.

"You're a man after my own heart," she said, leaning over unsteadily and squeezing my arm. "I knew it the minute I clapped eyes on you. You don't belong either, do you, even if you are half a colonel. It's because you're not smart enough to show the bastards respect when they don't deserve it. Whereas with me, it's because I've been too smart. I've shot up the elevator of life so fast I've passed my own floor—the one where all the commercial travellers are, and freight agents and publicans and the like . . ."

She was sloshing back the rum as if another Great Explosion was due at midnight—and it probably was. As for me, it was a good job I'd had a good dinner that evening, to help soak up the liquor. Even so, after two of her snorts my eyes seemed intent on swishing sideways and lodging somewhere behind my ears. I was looking around desperately for somewhere to pour the stuff when she wasn't looking.

The only convenient receptacle anywhere near my chair was a Singer Sewing Machine. It had five drawers, two of which were within easy reach. I wondered if they would be sufficiently leak-proof.

I could hardly check to make sure, though. "Pardon me, but are your drawers leakproof?" No.

Gosh, though, I had to do something. If the Lieutenant-Governor and his mates came in and found me genuinely blotto, I'd lose what little reputation I still had in these parts.

I was really dismayed at the mess I was making on the doorstep of home. It was no good telling myself defensively that everybody seemed to have a surplus of decorum and a deficit of humor. I ought to have remembered that, however worthy your average Canadian was, a gay, lighthearted, abandoned attitude to life was not one of his attributes.

Somehow I had to salvage the last remnants of my reputation before they got to hear about it in Ottawa, and started cancelling all the free dinners. I considered letting my hand drop casually to the floor and pouring the fire-water into the imitation Axminster. But then visualized the Lieutenant-Governor coming in and seeing a wet patch under my chair. He would almost certainly conclude that I was incontinent as well as alcoholic.

The simple fact was, there was only one feasible place to dispose of the rum, as an alternative to admitting I'd had enough and causing a scene. And Mrs. Capon certainly knew how to cause a scene. So, watching her carefully—at the moment, she was staring resentfully at the wallpaper, a dense, vinous design with bamboo trellises, calculated to drive *anyone* to drink—I inserted two fingers into my left boot, to pull the leather away from my trousers, and, with a heavy heart, poured the rum into the gap thus created.

Only just in time, too. Mrs. Capon was looking at me again, her lips sagging away from her formidable teeth.

"Have you ever been to Ireland?" she was asking.

"I once went there by mistake," I said dejectedly, feeling the liquor soaking my sock.

This statement failed to rouse any interest, except as a stepping stone into her own stream of thought. "I came to Canada by mistake," she mumbled.

"Oh, yes?"

"My father abandoned the family when I was thirteen, and came out here, leaving us to fend for ourselves. But, a couple of years later, he wrote to my sister Siobhan— she was always his favorite, the green-eyed cow—asking her to join him and look after the house for him.

"But he got our names mixed up, you see, and I came instead. Father wasn't at all pleased, I can tell you, specially as he hadn't the ready cash to send me back, even though he was a puisne judge at the time and getting all of six thousand dollars a year."

"M'm, most judges do seem to be puny and undersized," I said, wiggling my toes dispiritedly.

"Puisne, you daft bugger. P-u-i- . . . whatever the sod it is. That's how I met my husband, Mr. Capon. He was up in court for reckless driving at twelve miles an hour along the public highway.

"I only married him," she said, swishing her rum around, "because he was going to have a baby."

"Ah. Eh?"

"He'd given it to his private secretary."

"What, Captain McCann?"

"Oooh, don't be so silly. How could Captain McCann have a baby? His secretary, you great carthorse. My husband was attorney-general of Nova Scotia then, and in line for this job, so he couldn't afford a scandal. So the idea was I'd marry him and take over her baby."

"About my remark about Captain McCann," I said firmly, "I naturally didn't think *he* was capable of having a baby, I just thought you meant he intended to hand—"

"Pass us your glass, for God's sake, and stop interruptin'. Anyway, it turned out she wasn't having a baby after all, and I was stuck with an attorney-general, when I could have married a publican . . . Tom Swift his name was . . . Oh, he was lovely . . . chest like a barrel of ale, eyes like two bungs . . ."

Two tears coursed down her right cheek. The other, for some reason, remained dry.

"Made the best whisky in Truro, he did, until the government caught him for back taxes . . ."

I was in a pretty unhappy state by the time the second glassful of rum had gone into my boot. I'd paid several quid for those boots in London. I tried not to think what it was doing to the leather. I'd probably turn up at the civic reception tomorrow with one brilliantly polished boot and one crinkled like a corrugated shed.

Now she was commiserating with herself. "I've no friends, do you know that?" She glared at me as if it were my fault. "I've no friends!"

"No friends. I see."

"I'm too low for His bloody Honor's acquaintances and too high for the ones I'd like to know. Nobody invites me to their homes any more, since I was sick on Mrs. Graham's cat. Is it any wonder me only consolation is the demon rum?

"You're not drinking," she said suddenly.

"I am. Look, my glass is empty, Mrs.—"

"Well, you don't look like you're drinking to me."

"I'll drink to you anytime, Mrs. Capon," I said gallantly.

"You don't look like a boozer, either. What are you, some sort of fake?"

I had to pour us another drink before she would calm down again. That emptied the bottle.

I raised my glass, trying to look as if I were having a real beano. Luckily her eyes glazed over long enough for me to get the glass into position for the next insertion into my boot.

"Tell me a confish," she said.

"What?"

"Tell me one of your con-confidences and I'll tell you one of mine."

"You mean, tell you a secret?"

"Don't you understand plain English? Tell m' one y'r confish, and I'll tell one, one of mine . . ."

"Ah. Well, let me see, now."

"You know what? My father's letter to Siobhan. He didn't get the names mixed up at all. I instep—intercepted's letter, and let on it was me he wanted. Tha's how I came to Canada. There. Never told anyone else that. I ins—insepted his letter, an', an', know what?"

"What?"

"I made him think he'd made a mistake with the names, see. Oh, I was always the smart one, right enough . . ."

"M'm. Well, I think I'll go to bed now," I said firmly.

"Shaddup and siddown. What's . . . what's happened to your drink?" She glared at me accusingly. "I din't see you drink that drink. You know what you are? You're a hypocrite. Don't believe you're a drunk after all."

"You're the only person in Halifax who doesn't, then," I said gloomily, feeling the rum sloshing between my toes. God, how did I always get myself into these situations? Captain Blackbourne would never have been mistaken for a chronic drunk. Derby would never have poured rum into his boots. Why was it always I that was forced to do things like that?

It was my face, that's what it was. I should have gone to that plastic surgeon of Carson's. If I'd looked like Katherine's brother Robert, with his strong, uncomplicated physiognomy, I would never have been suspected of being an habitué of low taverns, or of raping members of the Women's Guild. But my huge face, with its expanse of bland incredulity, invariably caused others to believe the worst of me. Dogs barked instinctively, parrots bit me, children kicked me, senior officers instantly diagnosed dumb insolence, and little old ladies hit me with brollies; whereas I was really the most normal fellow it was possible to meet, utterly temperate in manner, attitude, habit, and outlook.

The whole situation was enraging. Then, suddenly, it was alarming again, when I heard the door to the Lieutenant-Governor's study open, and voices sound in the hall. He had concluded his business. Any moment, now, he would enter and find both of us sitting in a stupor, hers alcoholic, mine of despairing fury at the sheer injustice of it all.

With abrupt, teeth-gritted resolution, I got up and started for the door, my boot squelching hideously, as if I had one foot in a cowshed.

"Where you going?" Mrs. Capon mumbled.

"Bathroom!" I hissed viciously, and peered out into the hall. The Lieutenant-Governor was in the doorway of the study, chatting to his cronies.

The telephone rang inside the study. As soon as Capon had gone to answer it, I charged toward the circular staircase and shot up as if pursued by shrieking chimeras, and scuttled into my room, where I hurriedly removed the boot from my drenched foot, poured the rum into the only available receptacle, a certain domestic utensil usually kept under the bed, and wrung out my sock, then stood and screamed and cursed silently in the middle of the room, jumping up and down flailing my arms, and imagining myself with a broadsword, laying into everybody I'd met in Halifax, chopping off heads wholesale, and Mrs. Capon's twice over.

The worst of it was, I really needed a drink, now.

Half an hour later, I was still sitting on the bed in my bare feet, mumbling and softly pounding the bed post with my fist, when there was a tap at the door, and a maid came in and said timidly that His Honor would like to see me in his study as soon as possible.

I marched truculently into the study, expecting to be blamed, after all, for getting his wife drunk again. But after a searching glance to make sure I was sufficiently in control of myself to take in what he had to say, he spoke on an entirely different subject.

"You were leaving for Ottawa tomorrow night, weren't you, Bandy? After the civic reception?"

"Yes."

"I'm afraid you'll have to change your plans. I've just had a call from Ottawa. The Prime Minister is arriving tomorrow. He wants to meet you."

"He's coming to Halifax just to see me? Gee."

"Of course he isn't. He has several engagements in Nova Scotia next week. He's the Honorable Member for Halifax."

"Oh."

"But the reason I've summoned you, Bandy, is that . . . well, Sir Robert is to be my guest during his sojourn in Halifax."

"Ah. That makes you one up on the admiral, eh?" I said archly. I was beginning to feel like my old self again, now that I knew I wasn't on the carpet. Except that I was, as I was wearing carpet slippers. "Congratulations, sir."

He regarded me crossly. "I have no interest in whatever unseemly rivalries my wife might see fit to engage in," he said. "I offered to be his host, he accepted, and that's all there is to it."

"Yes, of course, Your Honor," I said sycophantically.

Somewhat mollified, he opened his mouth to continue.

"Though," I added, "it certainly is one in the eye for Mrs. Byrd-Kustard, eh?"

"I'm not the least interested in the admiral's wife," he said sharply.

"I don't blame you. She's no Gertrude Lawrence. Still, there's no getting away from it, Your Honor, it'll be quite a feather in your cap."

"Why should I care whether it's a feather in my cap or not!" he shouted. "I don't want a feather in my cap!"

"Caps look quite good with feathers."

"Damn you, I don't even have a cap!"

"How about a feather in your Homburg?"

"Will you be silent! I didn't call you in here to discuss my headgear!" he shouted. "I called you in to tell you *I shall need your room!*"

Well, it was nearly as comfortable in the Shubenacadie Hotel.

The following afternoon, Friday, August 30, I delivered my speech at the Town Hall. The mayor got a bit restless when I went on, perhaps a trifle too lengthily, about my favorite subject, but the rest of it went down really well, especially the part where I praised Halifax to the skies. So I was in quite a jaunty mood again by the time I arrived back at the Lieutenant-Governor's mansion for my meeting with the P.M.

There were several others waiting in the hall to see him. The Prime Minister was giving audience in Mr. Capon's study, and streams of visitors were going in and out, as well as aides, equerries, secretaries, and the like. A single mounted policeman stood guard.

Excited servants peeked from doorways, and the hall

buzzed with muted conversation. Even Mrs. Capon seemed impressed by the occasion. She saw me loitering beside the staircase and came over, her face flushed and her largish teeth glistening.

"Not that I care a damn, but this'll show her ladyship who gets the really important visitors," she said triumphantly. Then: "By the way, darlin'," she whispered, squeezing my arm, "I take back everything I said about you not being a true drinker. By God, you must have been knocking it back. When I went into your room this morning to supervise, the maid showed me your pisspot. It was filled with almost pure rum."

When I went into the study, The P.M. was complaining to his private secretary about the crush of people streaming away from the Town Hall. "Some damn fool was making a speech." He had had considerable difficulty maneuvering his bike through the crush, he said. To make matters worse, some oaf had stood on his carbuncles.

"Still," he added, "it helped to take my mind off my phlebitis, lumbago, rheumatism, and sciatica."

Cycling was Sir Robert Borden's sole eccentricity. In Ottawa, he always rode a bicycle to work on Parliament Hill.

He gave me a nod. Thus encouraged, I put in, "Bike riding doesn't seem at all a good idea, if you have all those ailments, Prime Minister."

"I need the exercise."

"Don't believe in it myself. Never stand when you can sit, and never sit when you can lie down, as Lloyd told me."

"Lloyd?"

"Lloyd George. Or was it Winston?"

"Winston?"

"Churchill."

Borden looked at me with a new respect. "Yes," he said. "Well, what is it you want?"

"Want? I don't want a thing, Prime Minister."

"Everybody who comes to my office wants something."

"You've got it all wrong, Sir Robert. I'm the intrepid birdman all the fuss is about."

"What fuss? I'm not making a fuss. Are you making a fuss, Fred?"

"This is Colonel Bandy," the private secretary explained, looking me over coldly. "He's come to pay his respects—"

"Hasn't paid many so far, has he? Bandy . . . Bandy . . . Are you that corporal that Sam Hughes promoted to assistant paymaster general? The one who immediately gave all his mates a raise?"

After these initial misunderstandings, however, I got on so well with this thick-set, modest man that the five minutes allotted to the interview stretched to nearly six.

"I sure would like him to meet Sam Hughes," Borden said, grinning at his secretary.

Hughes was Borden's former defence minister, the Orangeman from Lindsay who had done good work mobilizing the Army for war, but who had ultimately been kicked out of the government for trying to foist an inferior rifle on the infantry, and because of some scandal involving the shell-purchasing commission. "It would be quite a meeting, wouldn't it, Fred? He reminds me of Sam."

"He's a quiet, gentlemanly sort of chap, is he?" I asked.

"He's erratic, intemperate, mulish, and more than a little crazy. But I will say this for him, he knew how to stand up to the bigwigs. At the beginning of the war, when the great Lord Kitchener informed Sam that he intended splitting our Canadian divisions among the British units, Sam told him to go to hell; he had other plans for the Canadian Army. Nobody had ever talked that way to the Field Marshal before, but Sam got away with it, all right.

"Yes," he mused, "a lot of people said I should've gotten rid of Sam years ago, but I'll tell you why I didn't, Bartholomew. I needed his terrible temper. You ever flown off the handle, Bartholomew?"

"No, I don't think . . . Oh, wait. Yes, I did, once. At an English garden party."

"I've only lost mine once, in my entire political life," Borden said, removing his boots with a sigh of relief. "You know, for years I've been running myself ragged, doing everything I possibly could for the imperial war effort. Working sometimes eighteen hours a day on their behalf, and ruining my health in the process. I've given them a hell of a lot of money and material, and about half a million men, and I've just about torn this country apart in my efforts to go on supplying them with men."

"Conscription and all that."

"Yes. And you know what? For years, I never knew what was going on, except what I read in the papers. The British never told me a darned thing, Bartholomew. And when I finally confronted that Deputy Prime Minister fellow, Bonar Law, about it, you know what he told me? It wasn't convenient to keep us colonials informed, and that I had a durn cheek even suggesting they should. I should mind my own business.

"That's when I went up like the Halifax explosion. I told the government over there just what I thought of them. I said that if they'd all been German agents they couldn't have run the war more effectively—for the benefit of the enemy. I said they were a bunch of durned incompetents, and in fact I'd been secretly relieved until now not to know what was going on, so I'd be able to sleep at night; but when some arrogant expatriate Canadian like Bonar Law tells me to mind my own business, I'd had enough.

"And it got immediate results, Bartholomew. They've been buttering me up with floods of secret dispatches ever since, and keeping me meticulously informed about a great many perfidious deals I now find I'd much rather not know about. But at least they no longer treat me as if I were a quartermaster-sergeant.

"The point is, Bartholomew, all my life I've been gentlemanly and easygoing—the perfect example of Anglo-Saxon reserve, and the only time I've ever really got anywhere was when I blew up like that. That's made me realize a lot of things, Bartholomew, principally that you can talk all you like in praise of protocol, reason, and diplomacy, but it's emotion, Bartholomew, *emotion* that makes people sit up and take notice and get the lead out of their boots. So, from now on, bang, it's outburst of temper from me, whether I feel like it or not."

His private secretary leaned over and whispered in the P.M.'s hairy ear.

"Oh, yes," Borden said. "He's the one, is he?" He looked at me guardedly. "Bartholomew?"

"Yes, sir?"

"I have some interesting news for you."

"Yes, sir?"

"Your tour over here will have to be cut short."

"Oh?"

"They've got a job for you. Know anything about Russia?"

"I . . . met a Russian spy once. He sold me a samovar . . . Russia?"

"That's where you're going, Bartholomew."

"Russia? But it's full of socialists!"

"It's purely voluntary, of course."

"In that case, Prime Minister, I think I'll just go to Ottawa instead."

"But if you don't volunteer, I gather you're likely to end up defending the Outer Hebrides," Borden said, leaning over and regretfully drawing on his boots again. "Well, you asked for it, didn't you?"

"I didn't ask for anything," I cried indignantly. "Specially not Russia!"

"Now, now, don't lose your temper. That won't get you anywhere. What I meant was—" He stopped and looked up at his secretary. "What did I mean, Fred?"

The private secretary looked at me as if I were a common species of hornet. "You gave a final interview to the press just before you sailed from Liverpool," he said curtly. "About parachutes."

"What about it? All I said was there was a first-class parachute available that was being ignored, though it would need almost no development work whatso—"

"You said all that," the secretary interrupted, "in spite of the fact that the Air Minister had just announced that they were putting the Guardian Angel into production."

"Of course. That's *why* I said it."

"You made him look like a durn fool, Bartholomew," the Prime Minister said, a shade reprovingly. "They've been on our backs ever since."

"They're incensed about it," the secretary said. "With good reason, in my opinion."

I opened my mouth.

"Further," he said, "you went on to announce your intention of airing the subject as soon as you got back to Canada."

"And I see," Borden said, drawing a sheet of foolscap toward him and glancing at it sorrowfully, "that you did just that, Bartholomew, this afternoon."

He shook his head. "There are certain reasons why we don't wish to upset the imperial government at this time, Bartholomew," he said. "We're beginning some very delicate negotiations, you see, regarding foreign policy. It looks as if, in that regard, and in the not too distant future, that we'll be able to gain control of our own destiny."

"Yes, we're obviously ripe for independence."

"Now, now, Bartholomew, let's not be bitter. Anyway, it's not as if you haven't had a nice change, is it, getting home like this. After all, you've seen Halifax. What more can you ask?"

"I want my mummy."

The snotty secretary ignored this, perhaps because I hadn't said it loudly enough.

"Now, if you don't mind," he said, "Sir Robert's a busy man." He picked up a sheaf of bumf, paper-clipped together. "You're booked to return on the *Star of the East,* which is now loading at one of the piers opposite Upper Water Street."

"The *Star of the East?* Oh, my God."

"You're lucky," he said. "They say they'll even be able to give you back your old cabin."

Back Again

After several years of enemy submarine activity, the admiralty had finally been persuaded by one or two far-sighted, frustrated fellows in Whitehall that the enormous shipping losses might be minimized if the ships travelled in convoy.

It worked fine as far as our convoy was concerned—only five ships were sunk—but it was chaos when the survivors reached port, where too many vessels were trying to nudge into too few berths.

This was at Liverpool (known, I believe, as The Athens of the North), where over twenty of the ships had to anchor in the Mersey, ours among them.

It looked as if we'd have quite a long wait before it was our turn to hitch up to the nearest bollock. Or—bollard, was it? So I was really pleased when the first officer told me that they were sending a boat for me, to take me ashore immediately.

I thought it was because I was so important, but it turned out that they had an urgent message for me from London. Katherine was down with the flu.

As the hospitals were overcrowded with war casualties and victims of the Spanish influenza, she was being nursed at home, so I didn't think she was too seriously ill. But when I spoke to her father, he said she'd been taken to the Kensington and Fulham General.

Mr. Lewis sounded so alert and clear-headed, I was frightened. "How soon can you get here, Bart?" he asked.

"There isn't a train to London for nearly three hours. Is she worse this morning, then?"

"I'm afraid she is. She had a temperature of over a hundred and five. Bart? Hello? Hello?"

"Yes?"

"Her mother's with her now. I'm just going back there.

"She keeps asking for you, Bart," Mr. Lewis said clearly.

I thought I'd be clever and get down there by air. But it took two hours to reach the nearest airdrome and talk the C.O. into giving me a ride to Croydon. By the time the aircraft actually set off, two and a half hours had elapsed. Then the plane—a D.H.9 again—had engine trouble and had to land at the R.A.F. field at Castle Bromwich.

Fortunately I knew somebody there and managed to get a lift onward, without delay, in a reliable old 504K. But it was another four hours before I got to the hospital, and by that time she was dead.

It was three days before I could really believe it, which was strange, because I was experienced; I had lost quite a few friends.

It was like being concussed. I couldn't show any grief, because I felt nothing. For that reason, I didn't want to be with her family. But there was Mr. Lewis. He had been her friend as well as her father. She had always gone to him for comfort when she was really troubled.

He smiled whenever I caught his eye, but he looked as if he were suffering some physical pain that he wanted to keep from us. I was afraid he would see through my unfeeling callousness.

I was lucky. The one and only time there was anything to hear, he heard it, and came into the spare room where I was sitting on the bed, holding her favorite cartwheel hat. He put his arm around my shoulders, and we just sat there in silence, more or less.

It was a glorious day, the day of the funeral, a beautiful September day. There was a balloon crew in an unused corner of the cemetery. They seemed to be having trouble with the winch. The balloon was stuck at two thousand feet, its silver flanks rippling in the sun.

The padre was a full colonel. Robert Lewis, in a simple air-force tunic of the maternity type, was standing as far away from him as possible. He had taken an instant dislike to the padre. I don't know why, except that Robert tended to take a violent dislike to people before he even spoke to them. He was still staring at the padre, his eyes burning. But I don't think it was really the padre that was enraging him.

Mrs. Lewis looked old, though she held herself erect, her long, lined face turned upward defiantly. Some mourners looked at her resentfully, because she had disdained to wear the veil, traditionally used to conceal a lack of grief.

The coffin was lowered into the hole just as the balloon started to soar upward.

When she smiled, she smiled with all her heart, holding nothing back.

The last time I saw her was on the front steps of the Kensington house. The ship was leaving from some out-of-the-way pier, with no visitors allowed, and she didn't want to say good-bye in a far-off railway station, among grimy pigeons and sour smoke and chipped railway cups abandoned on gritty ledges.

To bring her up to my lips, I put one arm behind her knees and the other round her waist, and picked her up. My arms never seemed able to remember how light she was, and I very nearly heaved her over the park railings.

In that civilized London way, the passers-by pretended not to notice. She had laughed, only slightly embarrassed, and kissed back enthusiastically.

That was what I remembered best about her for a long time afterwards: how extraordinarily light she was

Mrs. Lewis was in the sitting room, gazing into the fireplace.

"Well, I'm off to the Air Ministry," I said.

"You are always off somewhere, Bartholomew,' she boomed. "I hope you are not making all these journeys under the impression that travel broadens the mind. In my experience, it merely subjects one to a great many discomforts that one could suffer just as easily at home. Besides, I have never discerned any virtue in bemusing one's eyes with unfamiliar and invariably disappointing sights."

"You've travelled widely, have you, Mrs. Lewis?"

"I have. When I was a gel I once visited Marlborough. And also, I believe, Cheltenham, though naturally I would never admit to the latter. A very rowdy sort of place, as I remember."

"They want me out of the way," I said, compressing my lips in a mulish manner. "I'm an embarrassment to them."

"You are an embarrassment to everybody, Bartholomew. That is one of the things I have always liked about you. You have never given way to the self-effacement that is currently so fashionable among one's more arrogant acquaintances. Only two weeks ago I had great difficulty in distinguishing young Howard Quinzy from one of his own servants; and indeed, I only clarified the situation by holding out my umbrella half-way between them, to see who took it."

"And who did?"

"Lord Quinzy, of course. The footman only accepted hats—and cloaks, if he were in a particularly good mood."

She turned and regarded me severely. "But I am sure that you, Bartholomew, will not allow them to walk rough-shod over you."

"No."

After a moment, she looked away, then said in tones I had never heard from her before, "You were good for Katherine, Bartholomew. We are most grateful for the joyous turmoil you brought to the last two years of her life."

I was surprised to see it was raining outside. The windows were swimming.

She put a hand over mine. Her hand was cold as the grate in the fireplace.

"Now she is dead. But *you* will not give way to despair."

"No."

"No—my dear Bartholomew."

The meeting this time was in the office of the new Chief of Air Staff. As well as the C.A.S. and the Minister, there were two senior advisers present, and an observer from the Foreign Office, who obviously didn't have much pull, for nobody had given him a chair.

They seemed to be settled in for a lengthy discussion, but the matter was concluded swiftly enough.

"This proposal," the Minister began, squinting irritably through the window at the cloudless sky, "to send an Air Force officer to advise the counter-revolutionary govern-ment in North Russia on how to employ the aircraft that have recently fallen into their hands—"

"Yes," I said. "I'm ready to tell them what they can do with their aircraft."

"Now look here, Bandy," the Minister said, flushing.

"I mean I'm willing, sir."

"Most people would consider it a signal honor to be selected for such a task. It demands a man of initiative, with the ability to improvise, and you've amply. . . . Damn it, man, can't you see we're doing you a favor? It's not as if we were sending you to some barbarous spot like the Persian Gulf or, or Texas. The Russians are fairly civilized—they drink almost as much tea as we do. The fact is . . ." He was starting to run down, but the momentum of his prepared argument was such that it took up quite a bit of extra track. "The fact is, Bandy, that though we've asked you to volunteer, we could just as easily order you to go. You haven't officially been transferred to the Canadian . . . What did you say?"

"I agree, sir."

"And . . . and in spite of a few successes lately, the war is obviously . . . You agree?"

"Yes, Minister."

The Minister was now beginning to look as if he'd put his money on a thoroughbred and had just noticed that it had only three legs.

"You mean you're prepared to actually go?"

"I'm ready to leave any time, sir."

"Oh," the Minister said—doubtfully.

The Dreadful Shore

Nobody seemed to be quite sure why the Allies intervened in the civil war that followed the Russian Revolution. At least, *I* never met anyone who knew what he was doing in Russia.

The right-wingers said we were fighting for ideological reasons. (Mr. Winston Churchill, the main driving force behind intervention, hated the Communists enough to have attacked them single-handed.) The left-wingers believed that intervention was a plot, by the international financiers, to overthrow Lenin and Company because they had repudiated Russia's foreign debts. The Canadians supported the anti-Bolsheviks in the hope that this might give them a post-war trade advantage. The Czechs fought in Russia for political reasons, that the Allies might look favorably on the establishment of their new state, Czechoslovakia. The Japanese, who provided most of the manpower for the Siberian expedition, were mainly interested in getting a solid foothold on the Asian mainland and in snapping up choice pieces of China.

As for Mr. Wilson, the American President, it was his uneasiness about that same Japanese expansionism that drove him into dispatching several thousand U.S. soldiers to Siberia, following this up by sending several thousand more to Archangel, because everybody else was doing so; and then trying to pretend he wasn't intervening at all.

Initially, though, the basic motive for intervention was military. Even at the end of August 1918, it looked as if the war would last well into the following year, and the Allied brass considered it essential that the Eastern Front should be reactivated.

It was only later that the Allies, principally Britain and France, turned their guns on the Communists for more personal reasons. It was bad enough that the Reds had failed to fight the good fight to the bitter end; the bounders had also announced their intention of overthrowing the Western democracies by world proletarian revolution. The Allies couldn't allow that sort of thing to go unchallenged. It might give their own lower classes ideas.

Though they made a considerable investment in troops and material, the Western Powers hoped to crush the Bolsheviks mainly by backing the forces that were already opposing the Red take-over.

These included the White Russians, who seemed to be doing quite well in the south, where they had recently captured Ekaterinodar, the capital of the Kuban region. However, it was the Czech Corps that had done the most effective fighting so far. Formed of men from the Slovakian part of the Austro-Hungarian Empire, the Czech Corps had fought staunchly on the Russian side throughout the war. When the Peace Treaty of Brest-Litovsk was signed by Russia and Germany, in March 1918, the Czechs had asked to be transferred to France in order to go on fighting for the Allied cause.

Their way westward, of course, was blocked by the German Army, so they had turned east, with the intention of sailing back into the fight from Vladivostok, at the Pacific end of Russia. In the process, they had been forced to battle the Bolsheviks. They had done so with such astonishing success—within weeks they had seized control of about half the Trans-Siberian Railway, a certain Captain Gaida so distinguishing himself in the process that he had been promoted to general—that the Allies decided the Czechs would be of even more use in Russia than in France, and ordered them to remain and support the Whites until the Americans and Japanese could come to their aid, through Vladivostok.

The Allies never did come to the aid of the Czechs. Most of them were so busy keeping a suspicious eye on each other, they never even got past Vladivostok.

In northern Russia, where I was sent, the action had begun as a purely military adventure, to deny the northern coastline of Russia and Finland to the German submarines. The establishment of British units at Murmansk had amply justified itself by holding down a substantial German army in Finland that might otherwise have been deployed on the Western Front.

The occupation of Archangel, however, was purely interventionist. The Royal Navy had fought its way into that port at the beginning of August, kicked out the local Bolshevik administration, and replaced it with a Provisional Northern Government under the leadership of a Mr. N. V. Chaikovsky.

Mr. Chaikovsky, I was told, had a number of aircraft at his disposal. I was to be his Air Assistant. Somehow, though, I had the feeling that the Air Minister didn't really care whom I assisted, so long as it wasn't he.

I sailed, as violently anti-Bolshevik as any red-blooded crusader in the cause of Motherhood and Profit, with a quarrelsome collection of Russians, British, French, Americans, Japanese, Serbians, Italians, and a volunteer party from the Canadian 16th Brigade, an artillery outfit. I spent most of the voyage trying to learn the rudiments of Russian.

Not since my third-year anatomy exams had I worked with such intense concentration. I sat on my bunk from morning until late at night, hunched over my grammar books, dictionary, and notebooks. A few times, when I couldn't sleep, I even got up in the middle of the night to resume my studies.

It was as good a way as any to distract myself, I suppose; and it was effective enough; I was quite distracted. By the time we reached Archangel, I had familiarized myself with the alphabet and had memorized all the numbers up to a hundred, a few common verbs, and two or three hundred nouns, and was able to repeat quite fluently such phrases as 'We wish to visit theatres, museums, and cathedrals' and 'Do you know of anyone who can mend my socks?'

The only trouble was, the Russians I shared the cabin with couldn't understand a word I said.

It was some time before I realized that the secret of that strangely constructed language, with its absence of articles and its double negatives and the like, lay in its tone. Where other civilized tongues had particles, Russian had inflection. Unless one learned to give their words the right lilt, one might just as well have conversed in Cree or Old Norse.

One of my cabin mates was an infantry general. He was very seasick indeed. He spent the first week lying on his bunk, groaning and muttering and occasionally biting a ship's biscuit in a melancholy way.

Knowing from recent experience what it was like, I did my best to make things as comfortable as possible for him, keeping him warm and bringing him cups of tea, damp cloths, and buckets. He wasn't at all grateful, though. The only time he evidenced any gratitude was when the ship yawed with more than usual violence, so that his head rolled against the ship's iron ribs with a mushy thud. He was obviously hoping to be battered unconscious, or, better still, killed outright.

I was quite surprised when I saw him standing up for the first time. Lying prone, he had looked so scrunched up and frail. Arranged more or less vertically, he turned out to be as substantial as he was hairy: he had unusually broad shoulders, and what I had taken to be an extra blanket proved to be a massive brown beard shaped like a bent spade.

I never did find out for sure what his name was. When he pronounced it, it sounded like *Brzhtvh;* but he may just have been retching.

Our other cabin mate was completely immune to the succession of storms we encountered in the North Sea. This was surprising, considering that this was his first real voyage. He had been a life-long court official at the Imperial Palace at Tsarskoe Selo.

Count Anatole Snetkov was a man of about sixty, with a face that looked as if it had been injected with a permanent local anaesthetic. A member of the White Russian Council in Paris, he was on his way to Archangel to put the White Russian point of view to the new political regime there.

He was unlike his compatriot in every way. The general was like a bear that had just struggled out of a garbage dump, and smelled like it, too. He was pessimistic, indifferent to discomfort in the field, and violent. He had first come to our attention while we were waiting for the train to Dundee from King's Cross Station, in London. He had struck one of his soldiers for repeating Communist propaganda, knocking the man unconscious with one blow.

Though the other members of the expedition, particularly the Americans, had been outraged, nobody among the Russians appeared to find this summary discipline the least disconcerting, and I must admit it had its effect. By the time he had recovered from the concussion, the soldier was quite converted to the ways of democracy.

By contrast, the count was slender, dapper, and stilted in his relations with ordinary people. He dressed fastidiously and was a devil for perfume. As soon as he'd finished dressing in the morning, he took out a cut-glass scent spray from his inlaid toilet case and sprayed himself practically all over, until he smelled like an acre of sodden lilacs.

For the first few days, the count made no effort to converse, beyond the stiff apologies our close confinement made necessary. One evening, however, he returned from one of his marathon bridge games in the brown Windsor wardroom that served as a salon on that drab ship, to find me trying to sew on the expedition shoulder patch, a white star on a blue background. After watching me for several minutes with mounting impatience, he snatched the needle and thread and sewed the patch on for me, neatly and quickly.

"Thank you very much. That's very nice."

A smirk wrenched desperately at his frozen features. "The Grand Duchess Tatiana Nicolayevna herself taught me to sew," he said, biting off the thread and handing back my tunic between thumb and forefinger, as if passing over an angry cat.

After a moment, he went on stiffly, "I see you are an aviator, *Monsieur*. You are to fly in Russia, then?"

"I'm to be air assistant to your Mr. Nicholas V. Chaikovsky."

"Nicholas V. Chaikovsky . . . ?"

"Governor of the Archangel Administration."

"Oh, yes? Dear me, I cannot keep up with all these new people who are springing up like weeds."

"Isn't he the man you're supposed to advise, Count?"

"Perhaps," Snetkov said vaguely, and, changing the subject, went on to complain about the British. It seemed they had been unable to make room for the count's personal servants.

"That's too bad."

"I told them I had not been without servants for fifty years. They continued to refuse, even though I offered to keep my servants *en arrimage*."

"In storage? With labels on them, Count? 'Not Wanted on Voyage,' that sort of thing?"

"Of course not," he said, looking at me with a frown. "What an absurd notion, my dear Colonel." He flapped his wrist and sniffed. "They would have been safe enough in the hold *without* labels."

Over the next day or two, he told me quite a bit about his life in the Alexander Palace, near Petrograd (or St. Petersburg, as he still called it). It appeared that he had spent almost his entire life in the imperial palace.

He gave the impression that his duties had been onerous but stimulating. I noticed, though, that he was careful to avoid defining what his position was. I began to suspect that he hadn't had an official title, but was just one of the vast number of courtiers whose energies had been applied exclusively to the service of the Tsar and his family.

This impression was confirmed one morning when, perhaps not properly awake and on guard, he let slip the information that it had been his job to arrange the royal correspondence.

"You mean, that's all you did?" I asked. "Sort the mail?"

He looked at me like an offended catfish, and wouldn't speak to me for the rest of the day.

I learned later, though, from a former royal official in Archangel (*his* job had been to summon the yamshchik, or imperial troika-driver), that I hadn't been far wrong. Snetkov wasn't high enough in the hothouse hierarchy even to *open* the correspondence. All he did was shuffle it into neat piles—letters from relatives, invitations, threatening notes from anarchists, ads for corsets and the like, and dump all the invoices in the jewelled Fabergé waste bin.

He was so annoyed with me he spent the next two days on the lookout for ways to put me in my place. The following evening, for instance, when I used the word *Tsar,* he replied witheringly, "What is this *Tsar* and *Tsarina* you are always talking about? My dear Colonel, except to historians, the words are entirely unknown in Russia. These titles are the products of ignorant journalists. One never hears them in Russia."

"Oh."

"His Majesty the Emperor Nicholas is referred to as *Godusar Imperator,* never as *Tsar*. Similarly, Her Royal Highness is *Imperatritza*. And that poor boy of theirs is not *Tsarevitch* but *Nadslyednik. Tsarevitch* indeed!"

"Thank you, Count. By the way, what exactly is wrong with the *Nadslyednik?* Is it true he has haemophilia?"

"Nadsly*ed*nik," he said, wearily correcting my pronunciation. Then, dismissively: "You will forgive me, Colonel, but we do not discuss the state of health of His Royal Highness outside the royal circle."

It seemed to me that, for a government adviser, he was slightly out of touch. He talked as if the imperial court were still in existence. When I asked where the Royal Family was now (their whereabouts were still unknown, though there were rumors that they were incarcerated, under harsh conditions, in Siberia), he looked at me as if to say, My good man, where else would they be but making their rounds of the palaces at Tsarskoe Selo, exercising their dogs, and sacking their ministers.

He didn't actually say the Royal Family was still reigning at Tsarskoe Selo, for then he would have had to explain to himself what he'd been doing in exile, as a member of the White Russian Council; but his whole attitude seemed to deny all that had happened in Russia since March 1917.

However, if he wanted to live in the past it was all right with me. Maybe he was a lot better off back there.

All the same, when he went on to talk as if the whole of Russia were still in raptures of affection for the Royal Family, I couldn't help murmuring that events seemed to suggest the opposite.

"That is nonsense," he said sharply. "The Russian peoples love their Little Father." There was not a time when His Royal Highness went out, to hunt, for instance, that his entourage did not return with breathless accounts of the almost mystic adoration in which he was held. "You are a foreigner, of course, my dear, so you cannot understand the almost religious devotion to the Royal Family that permeates the soul of the Russian people. Once, His Royal Highness was approaching a village that was in danger of being washed away during the unusually wet autumn of 1911. The *Imperator,* of course, had braved the elements regardless, refusing to alter his schedule merely because of a temporary inclemency in the weather —conditions that would have sent any ordinary man scuttling for shelter— Ah, what courage he has! Alors, just as he was riding along the hill overlooking the flooded village—the rain stopped. The rain stopped—just like that! The very moment he appeared! As they floated past on their houses, the peasants realized it was a miracle, and would undoubtedly have prostrated themselves before their Little Father, had the configurations of their roofs permitted it."

By then, Brzhtvh had started to recover. He was sitting up on his bunk, listening wanly to the count's babblings. I waited expectantly, for I knew that the general was exceedingly hostile to Nicholas II and Alexandra.

He had told me so only a couple of nights before, while I was tucking him up after a particularly severe bout of vomiting. "At one time, Bandyeh, I would have given my life for the Emperor," he croaked. He brought a couple of huge hands from beneath the blankets and held them up shakily. "I personally, Bandyeh, personally strangled the first man in my regiment to raise the red flag. With these very hands I throttled that man until his eyes fell onto his cheeks." His hands fell limply onto the bed. "But now, though I will kill every one of those Soviet swine if given the opportunity"—his face flushed as rage stirred up

331

his blood—"I realize that all our troubles have come from the Emperor and that German bitch of his, with her priests and lickspittles. If I met them today, I would spit at their feet."

So I expected him at any moment to start pounding the count's anaesthetized face in the berserk fury he was noted for, crying, "If everybody loved the Emperor so much, then how, you cut-glass ornament, do you account for the revolution?!"

But all Brzhtvh did was to listen somewhat inattentively and nod, and occasionally smile vaguely through the undergrowth.

I couldn't understand Brzhtvh's indifference, unless he was even more demoralized than he looked. As soon as the count had left, I said as provocatively as my mood would allow, "The count talks a lot of sense, don't you think?"

"Ha?"

"About the Tsar."

Brzhtvh shrugged, looking at me with a queer, speculative sort of look. "He's strange fellow," he said in English. "He reminds me of schoolteacher, when I was in kindergarten . . . Used to tell us wery good stories when he wasn't hitting us."

"What kind of stories?"

"Fairy tales, I suppose . . ."

"Ah."

He was still looking at me in that strange way. He said suddenly, "You like me, eh, Bandyeh?"

"H'm?"

"You have fancy for me?"

"Eh?"

"A fancy for me?"

I gazed back at him, equally interrogatively. "Fancy? How do you mean, sir?"

"You have been good to me, Bandyeh. Bringing tea.

Mopping the brow. Cleaning up the sick. Tucking me into bonk. Come, I understand."

He lifted the corner of his blanket a trifle resignedly, as if he wasn't really in the mood for exposing his grubby sheets but felt that he should reciprocate for all I'd done for him.

Except—why should he think I was interested in his grubby sheets?

"You have been wery tender, Bandyeh."

That word tender made me feel kind of uncomfortable. It seemed rather a soppy word for him to use. "Oh, I wouldn't say that," I mumbled.

"So? Now I am better, Bandyeh. We are alone, yes?"

"Eh?"

Brzhtvh smiled. A tooth glinted through his brown beard.

"I'm sorry, I don't know what you're talking about, General."

His tooth winked. "You are wery delicate, Bandyeh. I like that. You are nice man."

To my annoyance, I felt myself flushing. Well, it was those mushy words, and that sort of mushy look on his face. I much preferred his usual lethal expression. Also, I don't know why, but the drift of the conversation was making me decidedly uneasy.

"Don't know what you're on about," I muttered, kicking the count's luggage. "Much rather you didn't talk like that, General. Humph. Think I'll go up and get some fresh air."

When I looked at him again, he was staring.

"But—"

"See you later."

"Wait. Bandyeh? You mean—you do not have fancy?"

I drew myself up—as far as the deck overhead would allow—and said a bit coldly, "Your English is quite good, General, but there are certain words that really should be avoided when talking to a chap. *Tender,* and . . . *nice,* and dreadful words like that. You're not really supposed to use them, you know. At least not to another fellow, you know."

Having set the record straight. I went out, leaving him, for some reason, a bit open-mouthed.

When I got back, he was still looking pallidly puzzled. However, I assumed this was because he was having to listen to the count again.

Snetkov had also returned, and already had his mani-cure equipment spread all over the place and was filing and polishing his nails and talking to Brzhtvh in French about the time he had accompanied the *Imperatritza* on a visit to a Red Cross hospital at Pskov.

Snetkov remembered the occasion well, he said, be-cause it was only the second time in his life that he had been away from Tsarskoe Selo. He was enthusing almost girlishly. "Ah, my General," he was trilling, "if you could have seen the expressions on the faces of the common soldiers when their Little Mother appeared by their bed-side in that hospital. They looked up at her with such anxiety that one could not help but be moved almost to tears, almost to tears. Moreover, Her Majesty was in a simple nurse's uniform. Just imagine it, she had come as an ordinary nurse!"

"What happens then?" Brzhtvh asked with a simple smile.

"Alors, as she questioned the soldiers—in her astonish-ingly good Russian as, strangely enough, none of the soldiers spoke French—their anxiety gave way to looks of the most touching perplexity—almost as if they couldn't understand a word she was saying."

He emitted a little giggle, and flapped his wrists in a way that deepened the suspicions of him still further. "Though of course they were merely torn between be-dazzlement at the Presence and humbled by the awareness of their own insignificance." He glanced at me coquettishly.

"The Russians, you see, Colonel, have a profound religious sense of humility. One of the soldiers was so affected that he tried to struggle up, his face contorted in an expression of almost frightening humility. He tried to answer her, though it must have cost him an effort, for his teeth were clenched. A less perceptive man than I could quite easily have mistaken his passion of loyalty for one of incoherent rage and hatred. Even Her Imperial Majesty could not help looking slightly uneasy.

"Unfortunately, on that same occasion, the imperial visit was marred by the scandalous behavior of one of the hospital doctors—a selfish request that the *Imperatritza* might wish to appear at a parade of the local School of Cadets, so that the young lads might be inspired by a glimpse of their Empress before their departure for the front. But of course her itinerary could not possibly be altered." The count's lips tightened. "In spite of which, the doctor had the effrontery to allow the boys to line up along her route, behind a railway fence. The Empress would have been entirely justified in ignoring them completely; and in fact had a perfect excuse for doing so, as little could be seen of the boys behind the fence boards apart from pairs of wide-open eyes and the occasional nose. Nevertheless she nodded at the fence most graciously as she sped by."

Over the previous few days, I'd had a growing suspicion about the count. It increased still further as he flapped his hands about, to dry his nail varnish. I was certain that he was one of those people I'd heard about who were not entirely, well, sexually normal. *You* know.

To confirm my suspicions, I asked casually, as I leaned against his trunk—his luggage, I mean—I wouldn't have come anywhere near his actual trunk—"By the way, Count —you're not married, I suppose?"

"Pardon?" He seemed to be having difficulty adjusting to this change of subject. "But yes . . . ?"

"You *are?*"

"Certainly. Why do you ask that, dear?"

"Oh . . . just, just wondered," I said.

But perhaps his marriage was a cover for his sordid leanings. "Got any children?" I asked subtly.

"As I said before, *Monsieur,* you make some very strange remarks . . . I have eight children."

"You do?"

"Certainly. Olga, Vera, Petya, Nina, Maria, Elizaveta, Sonya, and Gladys."

"Gladys?"

"Such a beautiful English name, don't you think?"

"I . . . yeah," I said, wondering how I could have been so wrong. He was obviously as normal as Brzhtvh.

On the second-last day of the voyage, a wireless message for the general was delivered to the cabin. After ten hours of Russian studies, I needed some fresh air and offered to deliver it to him.

I found him at the stern of the ship with his batman. They were huddled closely together behind a life raft, with their arms around each other.

Brzhtvh seemed an unusually democratic sort of chap, I thought.

As Brzhtvh read the signal, the batman, pale and shrunken inside his British khaki, leered and vanished into the gloom.

"I knew that already," Brzhtvh muttered, and tossed the signal into the White Sea, which of course was grey. "I am to join Slavo-British Legion in Archangelsk."

"M'm."

"If they have not already deserted to Reds."

"Ah."

"Still, as we Russians say, *If a man has many kopecks in his pocket, he jingles as he walks.*"

I gazed dully across at the dreadful coastline of northern Russia.

"Tyem nyeh myenyeh, na Moskvu."

"I hope so," I muttered. "I don't like the look of this place at all."

The White Sea coast was as leaden as the dusk. No houses, no sign of cultivation, just miles and miles of melodramatic forest.

"Don't go, Colonel. Talk."

"What about?"

"I am puzz-led, Bandyeh. I have asked about you. I have learned that you are great hero of British Air Force. You have more than fifty air victories, yes?"

"M'm."

"You were also fine infantry officer. They say you should have received Wictoria Cross."

I shifted uncomfortably.

"But you are so unhappy, Bandyeh."

"No, no."

"Is because you are going to Russia?"

"I volunteered."

"How do you feel about Bolsheviks?"

"Viciously."

"Is not good to be unhappy alone, Bandyeh."

A chill, damp breeze flapped his long, grey greatcoat, and riffled his whiskers.

"You think I am too coarse to understand, Bandyeh?"

"No, no."

"You think I am great, hairy, disgusting Russian."

"Why on earth should I think that?"

"Prove you do not disapprove of me. Confide, Bandyeh. Confide."

I had no alternative, unless I were to seem cold and hostile. I told him much more than I'd intended, and when I'd finished he put an arm around me and wept, to keep me company.

It was my first experience of that aspect of the Russian soul: that wholehearted willingness to lessen the anguish of others by sharing in it.

"I love you, Bandyeh. But in good way, you understand."

I turned away, to wipe my face.

"Come, Bandyeh. Let us end it all in the cabin."

I thought he was proposing a suicide pact. But he was only referring to the whisky.

We reached Archangel on September 24. I had orders to report first to the Allied commander, General Poole, but when I finally managed to ease a way through the importunate throng of merchants, refugees, civil servants, and high Russian officers at Army H.Q., the harried British major who seemed to be dealing with the mob single-handed said it wasn't much use consulting Poole, because he had been replaced. General Ironside was taking over as Commander-in-Chief of the Allied and White Russian Forces. He wasn't due in Archangel for several days. However, the major would make a note of my name, and in the meantime I should just carry on to my unit, next please.

"I'm not with any unit. I'm attached to Chaikovsky."

"Yes, sir, and I'm quite fond of Chopin, but I don't quite see what that has to do with it."

"Mr. Nicholas V. Chaikovsky, the chief of the new government."

"What new government?"

"The new White Russian Government. Up here in Archangel."

"Oh, them. They were thrown out last week."

"Thrown out?"

"Another *coup d'état,* I suppose."

"What's happened to Chaikovsky, then?"

"Shot, I imagine. He was a socialist, you see."

As it happened, Chaikovsky hadn't been shot but had suffered an even worse fate: he had been made President.

As such, he had even less power than when he was Governor. A British First Secretary told me so, and advised me to seek fresh instructions from the Air Ministry, which I did very promptly after meeting Mr. Chaikovsky.

He was seventy years old, with a yellow-and-white beard, and spent most of his time in pointless administrative wrangling and in issuing proclamations that nobody read, because everyone knew it was the British who were running the show.

Naturally he hadn't been told I was coming, and knew nothing about me. He began to look interested, though, when I brought up the subject of aircraft, and he was half-way through a declaration of White Russian air policy before he discovered that I wasn't offering him aircraft but asking where *his* were.

"I'm supposed to advise you on the best use of your equipment, sir."

"Mon cher," he quavered, "there appears to have been some slight misunderstand. We have no airplanes at all. You are quite sure you have no *escadrilles* to offer us? No matter; we have no need for such frivolities. A few regiments of our splendid White Russian soldiers are all we shall need against the dastardly Bolsheviks, who are quite plainly on the point of collapse."

As he rose to signify that the audience was at an end, there was a faint phut, and another bullet hole appeared in the window behind him. "It's nothing," he said, watching me in amused disdain as I crouched behind his desk. "Just one of our dear boys in the barracks across the street, having his little amusement."

As nobody would admit responsibility for me, I had some difficulty in obtaining official accommodation. Brzhtvh solved the problem by getting me a room in a requisitioned house occupied by White Russian officers. It was next door to the technical school that served as American headquarters.

The other occupants were high officers of the Russian Army, all of them wearing prodigious numbers of medals that rang like field telephones whenever they took more than two steps (usually toward the bar). They accepted my foreign presence with admirable complaisance. As for me, I was happy to be in their company, partly because I was becoming very fond of Russians, but mostly because it afforded me an opportunity to continue practicing my Russian on people who were too well-bred to cringe at my pronunciation.

Days later, I was still in Archangel, waiting for fresh instructions to come through from London. In the meantime, between baffling conversations with the senior officers, some of whom had taken to sneaking back to their rooms as soon as they heard me pronounce the words *dobroye ootro,* I went sightseeing.

Archangel was, in normal times, a city of forty-eight thousand souls, clinging narrowly to the shore at the mouth of the Dvina River. I was drably surprised by its appearance. I'd visualized something like a Canadian arctic settlement with a few Russian touches: droshkies, samovars, Cossacks in tcherkasses, *alfresco* church services with deep-voiced choirs, and people getting excited about metaphysics as they knouted their serfs, with others lying around on stoves complaining about life. Well, they always seemed to be doing that sort of thing in Russian novels.

But if you'd seen them scuttling along Sparks or Wellington Street in winter, you couldn't have distinguished the Archangel citizen from the Ottawa resident. The city was similarly full of contrasts, a queer mixture of substantial villas and frame or log hovels, of minarets and the blackened chimneys of jobless mills. There were sophisticated buildings as massive and ugly as you'd find in any civilized spot. Right next to them, open sewers with an almost visible miasma.

Dominating the city, and indeed the whole countryside, was a splendid cathedral with a blue-and-gold cupola and four graceful spires. Not many paces away, the Café de Paris, where the whores teemed.

The main street of the city was the Troitsky Prospekt. Curving around the bay, parallel to the shoreline, it was macadamized for most of its length; a busy, bustling thoroughfare, loud with wheeled and pedestrian traffic, trolley cars flashing and swaying, gaudily attired officers and a few well-dressed ladies strolling and gossiping and haughtily acknowledging salutes under the electric lamps with their misty halos.

A few yards behind this sophisticated thoroughfare were streets so wet and muddy that even the stepping stones were hard put to it to keep their heads above water.

The old Russian tricolour hung limply in the muggy air from every flagpole in the city—except in the industrial suburb of Solombala, at the northern end. There were no flags visible there, though judging by the hostile attitude of the factory workers, I had an idea they had plenty of red flags tucked away for future use.

The crowds were just as varied as the city: refugee peasants from outlying towns, many of them pinched and penniless, humbly stepping off the wooden sidewalks for the local toffs; plump, well-to-do merchants and their families from as far away as Petrograd, hoping for passages on Allied ships before the White Sea froze over and the Red Menace engulfed the peninsula; dock-workers with sullen, downcast eyes; worried, discontented diplomats—the foreign diplomatic corps had recently moved here from Petrograd; and thousands of Russian, British, French, and American soldiers and sailors who were just as strongly contrasted as the setting: the Russians bewildered and disheveled, the British war-weary, the French cynical, the Americans bright-eyed and interested (except when they looked at the native girls, who were all uncommonly dumpy, with large behinds and no waists).

Sightseeing soon palled, however, and gradually I found myself doing what all the other officers did: I paced up and down the Troitsky Prospekt, stopping here for a coffee and there for a vodka. I certainly had lots of aimless company. There were hundreds of unemployed Russian officers in the city, and they and the wealthy citizens and senior government employees seemed to be having a frenziedly good time in Archangel, dancing, gorging, gossiping, crowding the cafés in loud-laughing parties, staggering away from all-night drinking sessions, joshing and preening. After three days, I was desperate to get away from the place.

My hopes soared when I met a British 2nd-lieutenant pilot and his observer, and learned that they were on their way to an airfield that had been established at a place called Obozerskaya.

I knew the Navy was operating seaplanes in the area, but it was the first time I'd heard that the R.A.F. was also in northern Russia.

"What are you flying?" I asked eagerly.

"Strutters."

"Sopwith Strutters? Oh. Still—is there any room for another pilot?"

"I shouldn't think so," the pilot said, looking at me curiously. "They already have too many."

There were only five aircraft at Obozerskaya, he said. They were machines that had been found at Murmansk, still crated, though they had been delivered to the imperial Russian forces nearly two years before.

The Russians had never got around to unpacking them.

Unfortunately, there were about twenty Russian and British flyers competing for these five aircraft. Obviously the C.O. wasn't going to welcome yet another pilot, especially a thoroughly shopsoiled colonel with a face like a despairing camel.

That same afternoon, I encountered General Brzhtvh again, just as he was coming out of Army H.Q. He had been upriver at Kholmogori for the past few days.

He was in one of his elated moods, and greeted me with a spectacular embrace right there on the street, as if I'd been in the Château d'If for twenty years. Seizing my arm, he hurled me into the nearest café.

With one look, he swept a table clear of five sky-blue cavalry officers.

"Vodka!" he shouted jovially, smashing the table with his fist. As a waiter scuttled up with a bottle and glasses: "And tell me, Bandyeh, what you have been doing."

I told him, in a frightful mixture of Russian and French. He listened, gripping his beard between his thumb and finger. He was always trying to straighten it in this fashion, but it continued to remain bent.

"Good," he said. "Good!" He banged the table again. "You would be wasting your time with these lapdogs. As we say in Russia, *Only a foolish crane flies north in the winter.*"

He drilled me with his fierce, fierce eyes. "Tell me, Bandyeh. Would you be interested in joining Slavo-British Legion?"

I stared back at him. *"Eta mozhna?"*

"Da!"

"The Air Ministry said I was now to consider myself under General Poole's orders. Can you arrange it with him?"

"General Poole agrees to everything I say. He does not care, he is leaving in few days."

Before I had a chance to change my mind, I said in my very best Russian, *"Ya k vashim oosloogam."*

"Eh?"

"I am at," I said, "your service.'

Disguised as a Bear

The training base for the White Russian Army was forty-two miles up the Dvina River from Archangel, at Kholmogori. It was a seaport threatened by grey forest and muskeg, with clouds to match.

Even the numerous tall churches seemed to have difficulty holding up the leaden sky. Somebody told me that the golden onion domes and spires were gilded that way in order to provide the town with a spot of celestial street-lighting. At this latitude, the sun was barely able to heave itself above the horizon in winter, and the domes and spires were supposed to help illuminate the town during the four or five hours of winter daylight, by catching and reflecting stray helpings of vitamin D.

If that was the idea, it was a sheer waste of gold paint. All the time I was there, the sun shunned northern Russia as if it had orders not to relieve the monochrome with even the most watery of beams.

The centre of town, with its churches, military establishments, and administrative buildings, was in fairly good shape, but it seemed to me there was a certain indefinable air of neglect about the dock area: toppled cranes, collapsed warehouses, crumbled quays, piers buckling at the knees, and sunken barges protruding slimily from the silted harbor.

"As a seaport," I remarked to my adjutant, Major Poupychev, "Kholmogori would seem to leave something to be desired."

"Has not been used as seaport for two hundred years."

"Oh."

"Not since Archangelsk became deep-sea port for northern Russia."

"I thought it was just a bit run down, like everything else in Russia."

Major Poupychev looked at me in rather an offended way. He was a ponderous, pessimistic man of about forty-five, with bright, wet lips set in a plump, heavy face. He looked as if he had just been sucking red lollypops, or chewing betel nuts. His lips glistened like crimson slugs. Rather amorous slugs, when he compressed them, as he was doing now.

Though not too prepossessing, Poupychev was a reasonably good administrator, when forced to rouse himself from his lethargy.

"Your orders, Bartalamyeh Fyodorevitch?" he asked stiffly. (My father's Christian name was Frederick, so they called me Bartholomew Fyodorevitch—Bartholomew, son of Frederick.)

"Same as today. Exercises by company and platoon. We must get the men used to moving fast across country. And at the risk of being tedious, I must also say it is important that they learn not to throw away their equipment when it becomes too heavy, Vladimir Petrovitch."

"It is impossible to move fast at this time of year, Colonel. There is too much mud." He looked at my boots. "As you have already found." His own boots were brilliantly polished.

"We must try nevertheless, Vladimir Petrovitch," I said with an encouraging scowl.

Since the beginning of October, I'd been in charge of four decidedly under-strength companies of White Russian troops, spending most of the day slogging about with the men on training exercises, and most of the night reading old infantry training manuals to find out what I'd been doing during the day.

Though they were supposed to be half-way through their advanced training, half the men still didn't even know how to aim their long Russian rifles properly, let alone grasp the idea of military discipline as a means of getting individuals to act in concert. They skylarked about at target practice, pricked each other for fun at bayonet practice, fell asleep during lectures, and marched like girl guides with chapped thighs.

Taking into consideration the time we had at our disposal and the kind of terrain we would have to traverse, I had decided to eliminate any kind of physical training or drill, or technical instruction except of the most rudimentary kind, and to concentrate on encouraging them to aim their rifles instead of just shooting them off a hundred feet above the target, and in teaching them only the most basic tactical lessons: how to establish advance, flank, and rear guards, how to circle around enemy positions, how to co-ordinate their attacks, how to give each other covering fire, and how to take up defensive positions once they'd attained their objective.

Everything else in the book I threw out, from saluting to march discipline, and all the hundred other details a knowledge of which helped to compose the well-made infantryman. Apart from anything else, there was no time for more. General Brzhtvh had ordered his regiment to be ready to join in the attack on Emtsa and Plesetskaya about the middle of October.

Emtsa and Plesetskaya were respectively 100 and 120 miles south of Archangel on the Archangel-to-Vologda railway. At Vologda, this railway intersected the Trans-Siberian Railway, and there was the entire explanation for the Allied strategy: to get astride the Trans-Siberian at Vologda and use it to link up with Czechs and White Russians in Siberia. This accomplished, and with General Denikin pressing up from the south toward Moscow, the Bolshevik Government would be completely encircled, and would stand little chance of surviving.

The men didn't seem to mind my crude efforts, but the officers were pretty upset about it. Though there were a handful of British officers in other Slavo-British units, in mine they were all Russians, and they remonstrated haughtily against the abandonment of all conventional discipline, especially saluting. The ex-Tsarists particularly enjoyed being saluted. They had been brought up in the old tradition, and still seemed to think that saluting was their main responsibility; though occasionally, if their mornings were clear of hang-overs, they were prepared to make brief appearances on parade, to get the latest gossip from the sergeants.

Major Poupychev personified the strange attitude to life that seemed to smother the soul of officer, soldier, and civilian alike. He expected nothing of the future but misfortune and calamity. There wasn't a single ounce of hope in his bulky frame.

"It's no use trying, Colonel. It is impossible to make our Russian Army efficient."

"Why not?"

"We are too badly organized."

Like the others, he saw no point in even trying to shield himself from fate. "Take our last commander, our much revered Pavel Pavlevitch. He tried for *days* to get the men to march in step, but always they would end up in convulsions, like caterpillars with many sore feet. Finally he went back to bed, and was run over by a vehicle."

"In bed?"

"He made the mistake of getting up again you see. He went to visit his lady friend in Archangelsk. On the way, he was run over by a droshky. On purpose, we heard, by one of those Bolshevik curs from Solombala. We thought of investigating the incident, but . . . However, we did complain very bitterly to the British about it."

The officers were capable of sudden bursts of sublime enthusiasm, and would work energetically for several hours, or sometimes even for a day or two, with joyous expressions; but as these moods were invariably succeeded by deeper passivity than before, I came to dread their energy almost as much as their inertia. I had difficulty enough coping with my own depression.

Not that *they* suffered in silence, sensible fellows. The mess was usually loud with vitriolic criticism of other people, inspired self-disparagement, and violent analyses of the world's ills (for which, of course, they saw no cure). How they could spout, those handsome, elegant, beautifully mannered officers, with bitter eloquence and cynical, theatrical laughter; continually contradicting themselves, but always ready with an illogical but brilliantly argued justification of their own contrariness. I quite enjoyed these tirades, until it occurred to me that if they put their rationalized inaction into action, I would be the one to get the blame.

"All the same," I said one day in the mess, during a discussion on the virtues of being an intelligent cabbage, "even if one's destiny is unavoidable—and I don't believe that for a moment—it would be much more exhilarating to try to circumvent one's fate, rather than just do nothing."

They all looked quite intrigued at this novel thought, and to give them their due they considered it quite carefully before dismissing it as an example of the strange ways of thinking of the Mysterious West.

"No, my dear Bartalamyeh Fyodorevitch," elegant, drawling Lieutenant Togonidze summed up, "there is nothing to touch the intellectual satisfaction in rationalizing one's inertia, or the sheer emotional joy of having one's worst forebodings come true. As we Russians say, *He who drinks from a horse trough must also eat oats.*"

(I was always being brought up sharp by these Russian proverbs of theirs. *Only a hungry wolf will eat a lawyer. A cottage built from old wood is an old cottage. Many a snowflake lands on the coat of a fat woman. Even a rabbit can bite the ear of a sleeping bear.* By the time I'd worked out the relevance of their proverbs, I'd forgotten what the subject was that they were supposed to be illustrating.)

As it turned out, though, while details irked them, and while they were congenitally incapable of understanding the needs of their men, the officers proved themselves more than ready to fling themselves into battle—preferably armed with something dramatic and useless, such as a cavalry sword. They were all brave men when faced with death. If they had had half as much fortitude in the face of life, they would have been invincible.

"The snow feels colder to the peasant whose thatch is afire," as Lieutenant Bodrov summed it up.

Though I grew very fond of them, officers and men, I found their fatalistic attitude extremely annoying; until one day it occurred to me that perhaps the difficulty lay in my attitude, not theirs.

One Sunday, I attended one of their Russian Orthodox Church services.

Actually it all seemed extremely unorthodox to me— quite unsettling and totally unfamiliar. There was no pulpit in the church, nowhere to sit and fidget, not even an organ. Furthermore, it was so dark that five minutes elapsed before I realized I was standing behind a pillar.

Things weren't much clearer after I'd shuffled into the open. There were hundreds upon hundreds of people in the great cavern of the church, but they could be felt (and smelled) rather than seen. It was only gradually that I felt my senses brushed by impressions of almost uncivilized opulence: the gold and silver and ornate brass gleaming faintly in shivery patterns, illuminated by thousands of candles; precious stones, winking like stars, set in barbaric, breath-taking icons; marble columns soaring into a darkness so profound that it seemed, up there, like the day of creation minus one.

It was when the choir boomed into that startling harmony of theirs that I began to understand. The hymn was so dramatic, so strange, so orchestral, the boys sounding like violas, the men like double basses, so totally, completely beyond one's experience—it was then I began to realize that I had been thinking of the Russians as rather odd Europeans living on the eastern extremities of Western Civilization. But—was it not more likely that, far from being the most easterly of Westerners, they were, in fact, the most westerly of Easterners?

By Jove, I thought—they're really Orientals!

From then on, their fatalism and blind acceptance of destiny began to make sense. And I was more or less able to cope with it, not by argument or reason, but by convincing them that, in all my impulsiveness and lack of logic, *I* was their destiny.

This made them gloomier than ever.

After several twelve-hour days of field exercises by sections and platoons, we set aside a day for three companies—the fourth was a shrunken headquarters company —to play the roles of attacker and defender in one large exercise.

The result was awful. Two platoons of attackers got lost in the woods, one platoon misread its compass and went downriver instead of up, and the remainder got so excited by the colorful display of furious Very lights, they forgot that the purpose of the fireworks display was to co-ordinate their attacks. When they finally shambled forward to the attack, they did so piecemeal and at five-to-ten-minute intervals. In battle, they would have been leisurely wiped out.

As for the defenders under the command of Captain Kisselev, they dug in along the river efficiently enough, but after several hours of rain and discomfort, half of them sneaked back to their barrack stoves. The ones who remained, crowned the shambles by standing up for a better view, as soon as the attackers started ambling forward (in, of course, small, good-natured parties).

Tiny little Captain Kisselev was very annoyed. I had

some difficulty in getting him to put away his Nagent revolver. He had threatened to shoot several of the temporary deserters personally.

He finally saw reason. "Then I shall have them flogged," he compromised.

I persuaded him just to give his men a good talking-to. I had an idea that would do the trick, as Kisselev had considerable force of personality, in spite of his stature. He was so short I could look straight down into his dandruff. He was barely four feet eleven in his knee-high boots.

He was also extraordinarily good-looking, a miniature Lothario, and equally 'haughty, gallant and gay.' His splendid black eyes were shielded by the longest eyelashes I'd ever seen on either a man or a woman, and they were so spiky that when he lowered them it looked as if he had black lines painted below his eyes. These features, along with his tiny but perfectly proportioned figure, must have roused his women friends into a perfect frenzy of maternal lust. He looked more like a doll than an infantryman.

He was also the most ruthless and efficient man in the battalion, perhaps because his mother had been German. A baroness, somebody said. Prussian.

I tried to set him an example the next morning when I packed all three hundred men into the largest barracks room available. As my interpreter, a civilian appointed by the Archangel administration, had gone absent without leave (we never saw him again), I was forced to address the men in Russian. After weeks of constant and devoted practice, my grammar and accent were now merely contemptible.

"Men," I croaked, "you did fine, just fine."

I was still hoarse from shouting and groaning the whole of the previous day, and still damp from the downpour and from wading through various swamps. "However," I went on, "I'm sure you will agree we've all learned a few lessons from yesterday's exercise. Can anyone suggest how things might have been improved?

"Anyone? Speak up, lads. Is there anything we didn't do that we should have done, or anything we did do that should have been done differently. Anyone?"

They just sat there like steamed puddings. I tried several times to get a response—*any* response—but they all seemed to think it had all gone off quite splendidly.

"For instance, the attackers: do any of you think that it might have been better if you'd kept your blank cartridges until it was time to use them during the exercise, instead of shooting them off at each other as soon as they were issued?"

No answer was the stern reply. They just shuffled and snickered, picked their noses and nudged each other. A couple of the officers, who didn't like the proletarian odor, tried to sneak out.

I was on the point of giving up when I caught the eye of one of the headquarters runners, Ufan. He was a thin, ungainly fellow with such wide gaps between his teeth that he looked like an unkempt tower, with battlements. The day before, while waiting in vain for position reports at battalion H.Q. (a ditch at the edge of a pine forest), I had overheard a rib-nudging exchange between a couple of the men that seemed to indicate that Ufan had spent more than one night on the stove with a local lass named Vera Petrovna. I wondered if Vera's home was one destination than Ufan *had* managed to locate.

In desperation I said, "What about Ufan there, lads. Does anyone think the day might have gone even more successfully if he had delivered his messages *before* he went off to visit Vera Petrovna?"

For a moment, I thought I'd got it all wrong and was making a dreadful fool of myself. Then somebody tittered, and when I affixed a wry smile, a shout of laughter went up. Some of Ufan's pals started pounding him on the back. Ufan smirked sheepishly, and shuffled, showing his gap teeth, which further increased the merriment.

After that, seeing I wasn't in an accusing mood, the suggestions started to come in; haltingly at first, then in a rush. Most of them were useless—one chap suggested that next time we should pick a fine day instead of a rainy one—but there was enough self-criticism left over to make it unnecessary for me to underline more than one or two of the most important points.

As a result, morale soared from the depths of melancholy to the heights of pessimism, a great improvement; and, among others, Ufan took to saluting me every time we met, thinking it would please me.

I told him and a cluster of others that if the Bolsheviks could get along without saluting, so could we. It was much more important for them to learn to obey orders instantly, for their own safety.

"Excuse me, Your Excellency," Stefan said, "but a lot of orders are stupid. How, then, can that be for our own safety?"

"Well, Stefan, it's like your mother and father. They sometimes gave you orders that seemed to be stupid, didn't they?"

"I hear you, Bartalamyeh Fyodorevitch."

"But," I said, "they obviously knew what they were doing, for look at the fine fellow you've become, eh?"

Actually Stefan was a pretty hideous sort of person, an unpleasant peasant with sly, slitted eyes, a thief and troublemaker; which I guess is why the others laughed so heartily at my description of him as a fine fellow.

(Later I heard he was one of the ringleaders in a mutiny in which eleven officers were murdered and an entire White Russian unit deserted to the Reds; but, then, that kind of thing was quite commonplace in the civil war.)

That was the day we received orders to proceed seventy miles upriver to Seletskoy. As this was the supply base for the offensive, it was a confirmation that in spite of our total unpreparedness, we were still to take part in the attack. General Brzhtvh was already at Seletskoy with the other battalion.

Seletskoy was on the Emtsa River, which was a tributary of the Dvina. We found the wooden town packed with American soldiers, and I was pleased to run into an engineer I'd met in France, a boyish lieutenant by the name of Lin Halver.

However, things were moving so fast I didn't have a chance to chat with him for more than a few minutes. I had to rush off to Brzhtvh's H.Q. There were only three days to go before the attack.

His H.Q. was in a peasant log cabin. Even though he was sitting on the hot, tiled stove, the general was in a chilly mood that day.

"Your battalion is ready, Bandyeh."

"No, sir. The men haven't even learned to aim their rifles properly."

"Is all right. The Bolsheviks haven't either."

"We're hopelessly unprepared, General."

"So is everybody."

"It would be crazy to expect the men to—"

"I was not asking if your battalion was ready, Bandyeh. I was telling you."

"Oh."

"Is essential the Russians take part in this attack with the British, French, and Americans."

"I see. All right."

Brzhtvh nodded curtly, looking at me with his blazing eyes as if daring me to assume that our shipboard camaraderie entitled me to rely on his indulgence.

"Then let us get down to business." He spread out his map on the stove. The main thrust, he said, was to be along the wide road from Seletskoy through Kodish, toward Plesetskaya. It was to be made mainly by units of the American 339th Infantry Regiment, with Brzhtvh's other battalion in support, Brzhtvh commanding. My battalion, however, was to move not south but west, against the town of Emtsa, which was above Plesetskaya, on the railway to Vologda. Simultaneously, the Americans and the French would be fighting down the railway toward Emtsa from the north.

Our battalion's part in the affair was to be principally diversionary, to unsettle the Reds in Emtsa while the Americans and the French were driving southward into the town. The enemy strength in Emtsa was estimated at three thousand. Units of the Kazan Regiment had been identified there.

I indicated the road we would have to take, from Seletskoy to Emtsa. "What kind of opposition will there be along here, sir?"

"There are no reports of Bolshevik troops. Obviously, though, the road will be guarded. You will just have to probe ahead of your main force."

"What condition is the road in?"

The inevitable samovar was hissing softly in the corner of the cabin. Brzhtvh shoved himself off the stove and went over and drew off a cup of dreaded Russia tea. "Is passable," he grunted.

"It must be the only road in this area that is, then, after all this rain. Can I see the reconnaissance reports?"

"We don't have reconnaissance reports here, Bandyeh. We ask peasants. They said the road is good all the way to Emtsa."

"H'm."

His shoulders bunched up. "Please do not hum to me, Colonel Bandyeh!" he shouted. "Is best I can do!" He drove his badly bent beard at me. "This attack has been ordered in too much of a hurry! Attack, they say! But they cannot even bring up supplies on time!" His eyes were puffy with fatigue and exasperation. I could see that quite clearly, as his eyes were only two inches from mine. "I have machine-gunners without machine guns, mortars without enough shells, runners without boots, ponies without fodder, and now, battalion commanders without brains, it seems! Perhaps you would like me to walk all the way to Emtsa, to make sure is safe enough for you! Ah, what nonsense it all is!"

"That won't be necessary, sir," I said huffily. "I'll take a look for myself."

He stared at me for a moment, then leaned wearily against the stove and rubbed his hairy face in a hopeless way. "Just be ready to move west toward Emtsa on time, Bandyeh," he said, as if addressing an adolescent whose recent behavior—drooling, lip-strumming, having fits, and exposing himself—hinted at the faint possibility that the lad might not be quite all there. "I don't expect you to get more than a few versts along the road, but perhaps that will be enough to upset the Bolsheviks." He started to get angry again. "But please do not also worry me! You have little enough time even to reach the river north of Kodish where you will start from, without all this strange talk that you will see for yourself."

"I can do it in a few hours, General. You see, I have one advantage."

"That you are deranged?"

"That I can fly."

Brzhtvh glanced around quickly for a defensive weapon. Yes, it was true: I was deranged.

"In an airplane, General."

"Ha?"

"There are suitable British aircraft at Obozerskaya. If one of them can land at Plesetskaya, I can arrange to fly along our route within the next few hours."

"A reconnaissance by air? But—that is wonderful idea, Bandyeh. Is brilliant!"

"We've been doing it on the Western Front for four years."

Brzhtvh's expression iced up again. He didn't like being reminded that their Russian methods weren't quite as up to date as ours.

"Do you want me to reconnoitre your line of advance through Kodish while I'm at it?"

"That will not be necessary," he said curtly, burying his beard in a map. "I have all the information I need here. It was drawn by Peter the Great, so it is accurate." He glared up at me, daring me to deny that a map drawn by Peter the Great could be anything but accurate.

As we clumped unceremoniously into the Y.M.C.A. hut at Seletskoy next morning, an unsettling hush descended. About a couple of dozen doughboys were scattered around at crude tables. They had been chawing, smoking, and sipping soft drinks when we came in. At the moment, their mouths were open and stationary. I couldn't tell whether they were staring in resentment at this sudden interruption of officers into their refuge from army madness, or whether they were just looking mightily impressed at the sight of the fat, morose major, the blank-faced colonel, and the tiny, handsome captain, all in their plutocratic coats—the two Russians in scarlet and grey, and the other foreigner in a giant, moth-eaten fur coat purchased in Archangel from an Armenian banker who had lost all his money in a card game.

Gradually the conversation swelled back to its former boisterous level, mixed with politely suppressed laughter. I peered through the fug with watering eyes. The air was so layered with smoke it was several seconds before I located Lieutenant Halver. He was four feet away, democratically sharing a bench with several of his men.

After weeks of spine-cracking labor, flinging up blockhouses all over the landscape, Halver's particular engineering company had been inactive for several days.

When he saw the three of us lurching through the maze of benches and bodies, his pleasant, alert features brightened welcomingly.

"Well, hello there," he cried, standing unsteadily. He looked flushed, and the top of his tunic was unbuttoned. As he and his men appeared to be drinking only ginger ale, I assumed it was the heat that was mottling his face. It was stiflingly hot in the canteen, and hazy with cigarette smoke and wood smoke from the stove.

"Hey, come on over and join us, Colonel."

"Just what we were hoping to do, Lin."

"That's great. Hell, I thought you'd be miles away by now. Move over fellers. It's that guy I was telling you about."

His men looked me over cautiously.

"Lieutenant, I'd like you to meet Major Poupychev. Major Poupychev, Lieutenant Halver."

"Hello, there."

"And Captain Kisselev."

"Howdy," Lin cried, his face flushed with ginger ale. "Gentlemen, let me introduce you to Dave Swadge, Gil Leng, Art Stendardo, and Sergeant Bill Fine. Hey, Dave, see if you can rustle up another three glasses, huh? Say, this is great."

As we crushed onto the bench, the canteen manager, a young civilian with a pale, unformed face, watched suspiciously as Private Swadge weaved back to the table with his fingers stuck in three empty glasses.

"These gentlemen are American engineers," I explained to Kisselev in English. Kisselev smiled, though he hardly understood a word of the language. "And it's a well-known fact that American engineers are the best in the world."

"Oh-oh," Lin said. "Better fill 'em to the top, Bill. He wants something."

Sergeant Fine was clutching a bottle under the table in his huge, chapped hands. With extremely unconvincing nonchalance he glanced across at the manager. The manager happened to be looking away. Sergeant Fine drew a handful of glasses out of sight. There was a clinking and gurgling noise.

"All we got is ginger ale," Lin said, and winked solemnly as he pushed the half-filled glasses toward us. "Rules of the house, right, Bill?"

Major Poupychev looked mystified and uncomfortable. He wasn't used to hobnobbing with private soldiers.

Also, he was still in something of a tizzy, a pother and a stew over the new orders I'd been forced to issue immediately after returning from the aerial reconnaissance.

I'd made the trip early that morning in a Sopwith 1½-Strutter, a fine reliable 1916 aircraft flown by an equally fine pilot, an ex-Royal Naval Air Service toff in a white silk scarf.

It had been a triumph of airmanship, plucking the Strutter out of the mud at Seletskoy. He had flown there from Obozerskaya to pick me up, and had to make four attempts before he finally staggered into the air with about thirty pounds of Slavonic gumbo plastered to the under-surfaces of the wings and fuselage.

Thus encrusted, we had flown along the route that our battalion was supposed to take. But it had hardly needed more than a glance to determine that we sure as hell weren't going to get anywhere near Emtsa along *that* road.

Even under a badly-lit sky, you could see the light reflected in the troughs and potholes. The waterlogging was confirmed when we dipped down to 100 feet. The road looked, as the pilot expressed it, about as firm as a whore's mattress.

In places the outline of the road had disappeared completely in wild scribbles of mud where carts had got stuck and had had to be hauled out by brute force. A few miles past the theoretical front line, just west of Kodish, the water from a marsh had made things even worse by seeping onto the road, creating a sausage-shaped lake.

That was where the Reds had established themselves, and there was no way around them. There were about 200 of the enemy. They could have held the road with five cooks and a veterinary officer.

There was no way to get at them without wading straight into their guns. And I certainly wasn't going to do that.

However, while I was up I thought I might as well take

a look at Emtsa. I bawled at the pilot and he banked the aircraft over the Red positions and continued along the road.

Emtsa was about twenty miles further on. It was easily identified as it was near the intersection of the Emtsa River and the Archangel-Vologda railway.

We circled the town at 1,200 feet, just under the clouds. From the back seat I hung over the side in the chill slipstream, studying the town and then the bridge a mile south, which was being held by a unit of Red Guards; then back along the forty-mile stretch of river to Seletskoy.

After three trips up and down that river, I decided that that was the way we were going.

"Is too shallow," Kisselev had protested.

"It's deep enough for the method I have in mind."

"The water flows the wrong way—we would have to travel up-stream," Lieutenant Togonidze exclaimed.

"It's slow-moving even where the river narrows into channels."

"There are no boats available," Lieutenant Bodrov shouted. "Your Navy has withdrawn from the waterways, and the few barges and paddle steamers we have are needed to ferry the troops across the river at Kodish!"

"That's why we're going to see the Americans."

"You cannot countermand General Brzhtvh's orders!" Poupychev cried, in a panic.

"I haven't been able to get in touch with him. He's already left for the Kodish operation."

"It won't work!" Poupychev shrieked. "It is hopeless! We must do things the correct way!"

"This is the correct way. So cancel the move, please, and send the men back to their billets," I said, though I was well aware of the awful job I was giving him. It is extraordinarily difficult to get an Army machine to overcome its inertia.

The officers continued to remonstrate heatedly. Many

of them already distrusted me because I was not only a mad foreigner but a pilot, i.e., somebody frivolous and irresponsible, fit only for bombing, machine-gunning, and drinking himself silly.

I finally had to stamp my foot at them and order them formally to undo all their good work.

I had acted like the very worst kind of despotic commanding officer, but it had worked. After three years in the Tsarist Army, they had grown used to autocratic nincompoops.

I became aware that Halver was nudging me.

"What's the matter with that gloomy major of yours?" he whispered loudly.

His men leaned over to listen, their faces looming sweatily out of the smoke and heat of the Y.M.C.A. canteen.

"He's in a huff," I whispered back, "because I've cancelled the general's orders for our attack."

"My guard."

"Just temporarily, mind you."

"Jesus."

"You see, we were supposed to be attacking along the road to Emtsa."

"Yeah, I know."

"But it's impassable."

"You're impassable too, Colonel. My guard, you can't just countermand a general's orders, just like that," Lin said excitedly. "Even if he is only a Russian." He looked around. "I told you he was crazy!"

"You didn't say he was crazy, Lieutenant. You just said he was kind of eccentric."

"That's right. Absolutely crazy."

"The thing is," I went on, sweating inside my tatty furs, "it would take a week to reach Emtsa by that road."

"Yeah?"

"Even if there wasn't a force of Reds half-way along it."

"Uhuh." Halver looked at me more calmly. "This leading up to something?"

"The point is that not only is the road impassable but so is the forest and marsh on either side."

"My, my," Dave Swadge said. He had a dark, cynical sort of face with a three-day growth of beard that made him look like a rather vicious gollywog. "You don't mean to tell me it's just like all the rest of this goddamn countryside?"

"Yes."

"Gee, I'm really amazed."

There was a pause. Sergeant Fine, who had been studying Kisselev appreciatively for some time, suddenly put an arm round him and gave his shoulders a friendly squeeze. "Say, you're a neat little feller ain'tcha, Cap'n."

Kisselev looked at me enquiringly, but I didn't know how to translate this. Major Poupychev, who knew some English, stared bewilderedly at the big American.

"Ain't he the cutest, handsomest little doll you ever seen, though? Jeez, would my kid sister love him for Christmas."

"Put him down, Sarge," Halver said. "The manager's watching."

Captain Kisselev raised his eyelashes and his glass.

"Is visky?" he asked.

"That's right, little feller. Scotch.'

"Scotch," Kisselev said. He gestured politely at the sergeant with his glass, breathed out noisily, brought the glass to his lips and drank the contents in one open-mouthed gulp.

"Ha!" he shouted, and raising himself to his full height of four feet eleven inches, flung the glass at the stove. It struck the pot belly with an alarming crash. Silver splinters flew through the air and pattered against the far wall.

"Uh . . . as I was saying," I said, after the manager, looking more suspicious than ever, had come and gone, "so—the road is out."

362

Wrenching his eyes off a now angelically smiling Kisselev, Lin said, "You're not thinking of moving your men upriver, are you?"

"Yes."

"Well, in that case you've substituted an impassable road for an impassable river. It's too shallow, even if there were any boats around, which there ain't."

"That's true."

"So?"

"It's a real pity, because it's flowing quite slowly. And it's almost unguarded, all the way to Emtsa."

"Sure. The Bolos know darn well they've nothing to worry about from that direction."

"Because it's too shallow for gunboats?"

"Yeah."

"Or steamers?"

"Sure."

"Or even barges?"

"Right."

"How about rafts?"

There was a silence. Kisselev looked around alertly at the staring faces.

"Rafts? Rafts? What is rafts?" he said.

"You told me most of your work is in building blockhouses and winter quarters for the 339th?"

Lin nodded, regarding me unblinkingly.

"Out of all the fine, straight pine trees around here. You said they were great for building blockhouses."

"Uhuh."

"I don't suppose you'd be equally adept at building rafts, I don't suppose?"

He stared up at the rafters with unfocused eyes.

After a moment, he said slowly, "You sure it's navigable enough?"

"Quite sure. It narrows to ten or twelve feet in places, but the water is continuous all the way."

After a moment, Halver said slowly to Bill Fine, "It would be a change after all those lousy blockhouses . . ." He looked back. "How many?"

"Enough for three hundred men."

"Jesus H. Christ."

"In the next twenty-four hours?"

There was an uproar from the engineers. Sergeant Fine got up, walked around the bench, then sat down again, expelling his breath. "You're right," he said. "He's crazy."

"Colonel Bartholomew W. Bandy . . ." Halver took another breath and leaned over. "Look," he said. "We'd have to fell about two hundred trees. We'd have to get them down to the river, size them, trim them, lash them together, caulk them—you'd need over twenty big rafts to move that many men and supplies. You expect us to do that in twenty-four hours?"

"I guess it is asking a lot."

Halver looked at his men. They looked back at him.

"Here we go again," Dave said hopelessly.

But there was a gleam in his eye.

Halver didn't manage it in twenty-four hours. He did it in sixteen, in one, sustained, backbreaking shift, working far into the night by the light of campfires. He decided that if the men didn't mind being a trifle cramped, we could manage with fifteen rafts, each approximately twenty feet long.

The last raft logrolled into the river above Seletskoy almost exactly sixteen hours after the first axe chunked into the first tall pine. And he threw in forty punting poles as well.

A Tinpot Generalissimo

By the middle of the night of October 14, we had reached the jumping-off point for the attack, just north of Kodish.

Though the main force, composed of units of the American 339th Infantry, of the Canadian 16th Field Artillery Brigade, of the Royal Scots, and of Brzhtvh's regiment, were not due to cross the river until dawn, we were supposed to have started westward from this point some hours earlier, as we had much farther to go, and theoretically were not supposed to be in touch with the enemy for the first ten or so hours.

So I instructed everybody not to stop but to keep going, giving as an excuse the fact that we were well behind the official schedule. My real reason, however, was to avoid a loud scene with General Brzhtvh. He would have read my message by then, and I feared that he might try to strangle me until my eyes fell out when he found I'd changed all his orders.

I realized later that he couldn't have cared less which route I took. He was just testing an amateur battalion commander to see how much of foozle, bungle, or boggle-de-botch he could make of things. I don't think he really expected us to accomplish anything, but it would be useful experience for us.

Safely past Brzhtvh at Kodish, I pulled to the side of the river and counted the moonlit rafts as they poled past, to see how many men had deserted. Fourteen of them gurgled past. I was very pleased.

"We've only lost one raft," I said, drawing my head down into my fur coat. The temperature had dipped below freezing. "Fourteen out of fifteen. Not bad, eh?"

"We are standing on the fifteenth, Colonel," little Kisselev said with an even littler smile.

I cleared my throat. "M'yes, of course," I said gruffly.

We pushed off again. Two hundred feet farther upriver we passed the empty barges on which the main force would be ferried across the river for the Kodish attack.

For the first few hours, we made quite good progress. By four A.M., I reckoned we had reached the bend of the river north-west of Avda.

From there on, though, the going was much slower, as it took time to maneuver the nine-foot-wide craft through the increasingly narrow channels. In places, the river was only a few inches deep. It needed only one raft to ground on the bed to hold up all the following rafts in a series of geometrically progressive delays. Between four and five in the morning we travelled less than half a mile.

It could have been worse, though. By seven A.M., we had reached the clear stretch of the river, where we were to assemble the platoon that was to deal with the Red outpost I'd seen from the air. The outpost, a simple log hut perched on a bank above the river, was occupied by only a handful of Red soldiers. It was one and a half miles ahead.

It was starting to get light as the last raft yo-heave-ho'd into a preselected clear stretch of water, and tied up along the densely wooded north bank.

It was quite a sight, as the sun rose somewhere behind the mist and cloud. The entire stretch of it seemed paved with wood, the rafts sparkling with frost. The air was sharp and still. Early birds darted silently in and out of the trees. A snowy owl on reconnaissance flapped across the river and was mobbed by a feathery dawn patrol.

The men seemed exhilarated by the adventure as they prepared a hot breakfast. (As it was misty, there seemed no reason why fires should not be lit.) As they waited for the hot tea, soup, and black bread, they cavorted about the rafts, talking softly but excitedly, and pretending to push each other overboard. They were obviously well rested, and in high spirits. Quite a contrast from the previous evening.

Part of the delay in reaching the jumping-off point had been caused by their unwillingness to venture aboard the necessarily crude craft. They hadn't liked the idea, at all, of teetering forty miles upriver on twenty-foot logs. They became even more reluctant when, at Seletskoy, they saw two of the rafts break away and start to drift downstream with about fifty of their comrades aboard, all of them lying flat on their faces and embracing the logs and wailing, too petrified even to stick in the poles and thrust themselves back to the river bank. The American engineers on the bank had laughed so much that one of them had choked on his chewing gum.

By the time we'd convinced the men that floating on a river was much more fun and much less arduous than floundering through mud and swamp, it was almost dark, and we were faced with the task of maneuvering fifteen rafts upriver with only the most rudimentary system of communication, i.e., by a system of hoarse whispers.

"Hello, raft just behind, this is number twelve, what number are you?"

"Twelve."

"How can you be twelve, we're number twelve.'

"No, you're not, we're twelve. His Excellency said.'

"His Excellency is *nyemsky*. He said *we* were twelve.'

"Tell you what, comrade. You be twelve and we'll be twelve and a half."

We had hoped to creep up on the outpost by river, under cover of darkness, but it was almost full daylight before the platoon was ready to move.

As the outpost had a clear view down half a mile of river eastward, these tactics were no longer feasible, so we had to take to the north bank. It took over an hour to get through the last half mile of forest.

I'd put Captain Kisselev in charge of the assault platoon, emphasizing that I was just going along as an observer. So I brought up the rear, just in case some of the men decided to vanish into the arboreal gloom. They were showing marked signs of nervousness at the prospect of a fight.

As it turned out, only one shot was fired. When I went forward to join Kisselev I found that he had reached a shallow gully. It was all that separated us from the hut, which was barely a hundred feet away. The only enemy in sight was sitting on a rock at the edge of the river bank, shaving.

He was obviously supposed to be a look-out, but all the time we had him in sight he raised his napper only once from the pieces of metal he was using as a mirror.

It was my first close look at a real Bolshevik. He was wearing a greyish-green *rubashka,* something like a combination shirt, blouse, and tunic, and ragged grey breeches. There was a red star sewn on his sleeve. Apart from that last item, he was indistinguishable from most of the White Russians, including the ones in the Slavo-British Legion, who, though they had been outfitted in British khaki, had gone back to the usual cast-offs and rags. I think they were keeping the khaki as their Sunday best.

One of Kisselev's men excitedly aimed his rifle. Kisselev hissed and glared at him. The man lowered his weapon, grinning self-consciously.

As we watched from the blackness of the forest, another man came out of the hut, carrying a bucket. He went to the edge of the river and pitched the yellowish contents over the edge, yawned, stretched, called something to the sentry, then slouched back into the hut, scratching himself with the bucket.

Kisselev gathered his thirty men together, and whispered instructions. It was quite a touching sight, somehow, the tiny little captain surrounded by the hulking moujiks. Any one of them could have tucked Kisselev under his arm and still had plenty of strength left for his pack, rifle, and loaf of black bread.

As he finished whispering, Kisselev glanced across at me interrogatively, his long eyelashes spraying out from his alert, black eyes. I just gestured. It was his show.

We crept cautiously down into the gully, glancing repeatedly at the sentry until he dipped out of sight. His profile slowly appeared again as we rustled up the far side of the gully and crouched along the rim. The sentry was wiping his face with a rag, now, and humming to himself.

Kisselev looked along the line of men, took out his revolver, then stood up and swept his arm over as if slow-bowling at a rather boring cricket match. He climbed out of the gully, straightened, then strolled casually in the direction of the hut. As one of his men started to rush forward, Kisselev snatched at the man's sleeve, forcing him to a walking pace.

We were almost at the hut before the sentry turned and saw us. He gaped. Nobody moved for several seconds. As he snatched up his rifle, one of our men fired. The crack of the rifle echoed down the river.

As usual, the bullet went nowhere near the target, but it upset the sentry no end. He took a step backward and fell into the river.

Kisselev turned to face the hut, his revolver held out at arm's length. A few seconds later, six men ran out. When they saw thirty rifles pointed at them, they stopped dead and flung up their hands. They had all rushed out without their weapons.

A couple of minutes later, Kisselev, keeping the barrel of the Very pistol as low as possible so as not to attract attention upstream, fired a flare. The bright green light curved shallowly over the water and dropped into it with a puff of green smoke. It burned for a few seconds, then winked out.

It was the signal for the rest of the force to proceed. Five minutes later, the first raft cautiously peeked round the bend of the river, half a mile away. At the same moment, the faint thud of guns sounded from the east. The main attack through Kodish was under way.

Three hours later, we were in position for the attack on the railway bridge south of Emtsa.

Three of our companies, with Lieutenant Bodrov scouting ahead with a section, had taken to the north bank about a mile short of the bridge, made their way across a swamp, and occupied the wood just short of the field where the Red unit was still busily preparing its defences.

Simultaneously, Lieutenant Togonidze, who was in charge of the mortars, led a party along the south bank to a clearing about two hundred feet back from the river and more or less opposite the enemy camp. As soon as I fired the first Very light, they were to open fire, with all five mortars, for exactly one minute. The moment they stopped firing, the rest of us were supposed to come charging out of the wood on the north bank, with fixed bayonets.

As a plan of attack, it was simple to the point of idiocy, and the officers, knowing I'd been nowhere near a staff college and was totally ignorant of the finer points of tactics and strategy, were plainly uneasy, especially because I'd no alternative plans to meet unforeseen contingencies or setbacks.

It was true I knew nothing of staff-college stuff—military history and geography, economics, military law, and the like—but I had learned from a certain Captain Craig the value of speed and surprise in an operation of this sort. So I wasn't too worried about my dispositions. Provided the men, spread out in the wood on either side of me, clearly understood that they were not to move forward until the second Very light went up, the action, I felt, had a good chance of success.

The only thing that was worrying me was whether they would attack at all.

I wasn't at all confident about it. Even General Brzhtvh had admitted that there was little sign of dedication to the White Russian cause among the rank and file of the Slavo-British Legion. Moreover, there were not a few Bolshevik sympathizers among them, ready to exploit the situation at the first hint of hesitancy or failure.

Major Poupychev tried to reassure me. "The men would not dream of letting you make the charge all by yourself, Bartalamyeh Fyodorevitch," he said. "Already they would follow you anywhere.

"They like your jokes," he added gloomily.

But, then, adjutants were supposed to say encouraging things like that.

He was right, for once. It turned out quite well. A suspenseful half-minute after I'd fired the first red light high into the air, mortar bombs whistled over the river and started to explode all over the field in front of us.

The mortars did no damage whatsoever—I hadn't expected them to—but they had the Reds running around in panic within seconds. Their disorientation was complete when, as the mortar fire ended and the second flare went up, they saw nearly three hundred men charging out of the trees to their right, and slightly *behind* their trenches. For, of course, anticipating an attack from the north, their defence works were all pointing the wrong way.

They dropped everything and ran. As I scampered forward with automatic in one hand and Very pistol in the other, I was relieved to see that they were making instinctively for the protection of the town up ahead, instead of retreating toward the bridge and making a stand there.

So we secured the bridge without opposition.

The men were elated, and hugged and slapped each other on the back, bellowing like mad. One huge bearded fellow called Seriozhka rushed up and embraced me, and gave me two great smacking kisses, one per cheek.

"I say," I said.

More and more men crowded up to the bridge for their share in the celebrations. While waiting for the right moment to get them in order again, I fired the green flare to bring up the supply rafts, sent off a runner—Ufan—to tell the mortar party to get up to the bridge as fast as possible, and called a hurried conference of officers and NCOs. As they reported in, we were astonished to discover that we had suffered only two casualties, including one fatality, a man who had been hit in the head by a stray bullet, probably one of our own. The Reds had hardly fired a shot.

One hundred seventy-one of the Reds had surrendered. Like the White Russian soldiers, most of them were young peasants who had been more or less forcibly conscripted. They were obviously just as inadequately trained as our men. They talked quite readily when Poupychev questioned them.

Among the captured stores were two Maxim machine guns on wheeled mountings. Until then, we had had no machine guns at all. I had them placed at the far end of the bridge, in case enemy reinforcements appeared from the south.

Meanwhile, I thought, we might as well push on while the enemy was still in a state of shock and disarray, so as soon as the festivities had petered out and some sort of order had been restored, I set off along the railway track at the head of a patrol, cautiously, in case any of the fleeing troops had been rallied by their commissars and were lying in wait for us. There were no Reds visible, however, until we emerged from a shallow railway cutting and Emtsa came into view.

It was about a quarter mile farther on, just beyond a large, flat field of long, yellowish grass. The town looked even more drab and scattered than it had appeared from the air. A few stone buildings were visible, huddled around the railway station. The rest of the town consisted of churches, log houses laid out with no discernible plan, and a large cemetery.

Carefully folding and laying aside my fur coat, I climbed to the top of the railway cutting and crawled forward for a better view.

The Reds had obviously been warned. Gangs of them were hurriedly digging holes and trenches along the southern edge of the town. There appeared to be many hundreds of them.

Through the glasses, I could also see additional hundreds of soldiers milling around the railway station in the centre of town. I wondered why. A Compagnie Internationale des Wagons-Lits express was hardly likely to come along.

Just how many men were there in Emtsa? One of the prisoners had said that fewer than a thousand of their comrades remained, the others having troop-trained northward the previous day to meet the attack of the Americans and French at around Verst 455. (Locations on the railway were marked in distances from Vologda, apparently; Verst 455 was therefore 455 versts from Vologda, or about three hundred miles.)

Even a thousand Reds, however, were several hundred too many for us. Also, there was some very ominous activity going on among those birch trees about two hundred yards to the left of where the narrow-gauge track drove into town.

The Reds had a battery of guns half-hidden among the trees.

By then, our main force was straggling up the line behind me. Kisselev and Lieutenant Bodrov came scrambling up the embankment, followed by a panting Poupychev. Bodrov was one of the more enthusiastic officers, a young, rosy-cheeked fellow with bright blue eyes above a little snub nose.

As they wriggled alongside and aimed their field glasses, I said to Kisselev in a low voice, "On the left—take a look will you, Alexander Nikolayevitch?"

His glasses jiggled about, then stilled.

"What kind are they?"

Kisselev looked again through his glasses, then: "They are fifteen-centimetre howitzers," he said calmly. "Very good guns when properly used."

"What did he say?" Poupychev said as he crawled up, breathing like an asthmatic buffalo. "They have field guns?"

"Howitzers. Five of them."

"Oh, shyit," Bodrov said. He had learned this word from one of the Americans—certainly not from me.

The Reds were busy hauling the guns around to face us. Until a few minutes before, the howitzers, narrow and thin-looking weapons with unusually long, slender barrels, had been pointing in the opposite direction.

We watched anxiously. The Reds were being pretty efficient about getting the guns turned around. I estimated that we had about fifteen minutes before they were ready to open fire.

I looked over the town again and tried to put myself in the enemy's shoes. They must still be in a state of considerable perturbation down there; otherwise they would have organized a patrol by now, to probe our position and estimate our strength. But they hadn't. Therefore they would have no idea what kind of threat they were facing.

All kinds of rumors would be circulating as well, and the rumors would be frightening, because inevitably the facts would be grossly exaggerated.

The Reds would also be feeling trapped. Psychologically adjusted to the idea of an attack by bands of aggressive foreigners from the north, they would be totally unprepared for a sudden onslaught from the opposite direction. They would be all the more alarmed because we had also cut off their line of retreat.

Yes, if I were the enemy, I'd be in a frightful froth.

I looked at my watch. There was still a couple of hours to go before dark.

"Well," I said, taking a deep breath, "if we're going to attack, now is the time to do it."

"Oh, shyit," Bodrov said.

Five minutes later, the men started trotting out of the railway cutting. They spread out left and right over the soggy field with a discipline and dispatch that I wouldn't have thought possible twelve hours before. As they passed, they shouted and waved, their soiled, whiskery faces alight with pride, and bifurcated with vodka.

They had no right to look up at me like that, with such affection and confidence. I was sending them in on a frontal attack.

I'd been in several frontal attacks myself since 1916, and every one of them had been cruel and disgraceful and useless, reflecting the utter paucity of imagination of the Western leadership. I had sworn long before that if, by some dreadful error or circumstance, I ever found myself in command of numbers of men, I would never, ever send them in on a frontal attack. Never.

But, gosh, it was amazing how one's perspective altered, once one became a brass hat oneself.

Of course I told myself that if there had been the slightest sign of organized opposition I wouldn't have sent them in so precipitately, with such shocking lack of preparation. Nevertheless, now that I was a great captain of men myself, suddenly frontal attacks seemed the perfectly normal and sensible thing to do.

I didn't even feel much humility or concern. All I felt was hypocrisy. For as I stood up there on top of the railway cutting, smiling and waving back in a sovereign fashion, I was simultaneously working out what action I would take if half of the men were cut down before they reached the town and the rest turned and bolted.

Now 4 Company was trotting up the track. This was the headquarters company, in action for the first time, under Captain Sysojev. They were to attack straight down the railway track. I halted them at the cutting and waited for Lieutenant Togonidze to finish setting up his mortars over to the right. He was doing so with a care and thoroughness that at any other time I'd have found most praiseworthy. But I was now in a great hurry to get the attack going before that battery of guns opened up. Howitzer shells were not particularly alarming if you were familiar with them. With their high, slow trajectory, they always shouted out plenty of warning. If the audience was experienced, that is. But many of the men had never heard any kind of shell rushing through the air, and I was apprehensive that it might unsettle them enough to make the attack falter. Any sign of hesitation would encourage the defenders to resist with greater determination.

At last, Togonidze was satisfied with the siting of his weapons. He then spent another two damn minutes adjusting the sights, to range on the howitzers.

I forced myself to stand calmly in the open on top of the railway cutting, expressionless and motionless, but jumping up and down inside. As the men spread out over the field, a few shots were fired from the town. One bullet buzzed quite closely overhead.

That, at least, was heartening. Not the stray bullet, but the fact that the enemy was jumpy, shooting off their rifles at long range.

One of the runners tugged at my sleeve, chattered, and pointed. The men on the right were starting to move forward without waiting for the signal. I could hear the thin voice of their officer, shouting and trying to wave them back.

Now the men on the left were starting to shuffle forward prematurely.

Well, I'd just have to make it official. I hurriedly pointed the Very pistol at the darkening clouds and pulled the trigger.

The red ball of fire left a curiously erratic white trail against the dark-grey clouds. The hundred or so men concealed in the railway cutting started to rush forward, their boots crunching on the loose gravel under the tracks. "Walk, walk, don't run!" I shouted. "Save your strength, lads!"

I wished I was going with them. But I had to see what was going on, and I certainly couldn't do that if I were down there in the long, yellow grass.

I wondered why the lenses of the field glasses were distorting the picture. Or, Good Lord, was my vision going, was I starting to faint from sheer nerves? Then I realized it was raining.

I wiped the lenses hurriedly and looked back at the howitzers. One of them seemed ready for action. Its long barrel was rising. Just as I was about to give Togonidze an imploring shout, one of his mortars fired with a sharp, hand-clapping sound.

One of the loaders, who hadn't covered his ears fast enough, stumbled about, holding his head and cursing.

The shell burst well short of the line of guns, sending up a billow of grey smoke. Togonidze ambled across and adjusted the next mortar, still taking his time about it. But his next burst was right in front of the guns.

Now Togonidze moved faster, and quickly adjusted the sights of the remaining three mortars. He stood back and shouted. The three mortars fired almost simultaneously. As Togonidze trotted back to the first mortar, smoke swirled among the trees a quarter-mile away.

By then the troops had covered over half the distance to the town. They were still tramping steadily forward over the wet, yellow grass and around the birch trees. The fire of the defenders didn't seem to be getting any fiercer. Through the glasses, I could see one party of Reds shooting from behind gravestones.

They hadn't had time to dig trenches. As they were in a cemetery, they were probably glad about that. As I watched, one or two of them jumped up and started to run off, deeper into town.

For a moment, a curtain of drizzle obscured the others. When I focussed on the cemetery again, it was deserted.

The mortar fire stopped. "Keep firing, keep firing," I shouted.

"We are now out of ammunition, Bartalamyeh Fyodorevitch," Togonidze called back, smiling and shrugging.

My heart bounced as machine-gun fire sounded from the town. A flat phutting sound, like damp firecrackers.

A few of our men were falling. But then the firing stopped, as suddenly as it had begun.

Twenty seconds later, the first platoons were level with the log houses on the southern outskirts of the town. On the left, Captain Kisselev's company was charging through the trees on both sides of the deserted howitzers. I could see him waving his men on, past the guns, deeper into town. He disappeared behind a house. We were in Emtsa.

Only one party of Bolos held out, and that for only half an hour. They had barricaded themselves into the grey stone administration building near the railway station, and as the first of the attackers appeared in the cobbled square, they fired through the windows with rifles and machine guns. Captain Sysojev was killed instantly.

Just as I got there, Kisselev, learning that one of the defenders was a commissar, stormed the building from the rear, using stick grenades. Like all the White Russian officers, he had a ferocious hatred of the hard-core Bolsheviks. His former colonel, a friend of the family, had been tied to a tree and disemboweled by several of them, while their commissar, a former ensign in the Imperial Army, had stood by, grinning.

Two minutes after Kisselev went in, half a dozen of the enemy ran out the front door with their hands up.

Kisselev ran out after them and threw a stick bomb. As they lay screaming and writhing over the crimson cobbles, he went up to the one in the black uniform and systematically shot his face to shreds.

I don't know if it was because they were free of their hard-driving commissar—the Bolshevik commissars were a tough, ruthless, and dedicated lot—or because they thought Kisselev might start putting *them* out of their misery as well, but most of the thirteen hundred prisoners we took promptly offered to support the White Russian cause. I thought the howitzer battery commander went a bit far, though, when he not only volunteered to join us but to turn his guns around once more and bombard his former comrades farther up the line.

The Reds were no more constant than the Whites, it seemed.

On our side, we had thirty-one casualties, including eight dead. The booty was quite impressive. As well as the 15-centimetre guns, we captured thirty-eight machine guns, several mortars with ammunition, numerous Mosin-Nagent carbines, which were hotly competed for, a shedful of food, clothing, and vodka, a motor car, a large sum of Bolshevik currency discovered on the person of an absconding supply sergeant, and about one hundred thousand leaflets signed by somebody called Trotsky, apparently one of the more energetic leaders of the Red Army.

The Train

The following morning. Six forty-one A.M. in the Emtsa
Municipal Building. A cluster of candles on an iron stand
burning a yellow hole in the morning darkness.

So far, about half the officers had gathered in the entrance hall, murmuring hollowly and drifting about aim-
lessly like hung-over ghosts. Major Poupychev seemed
the only substantial person present, his bulk further in-
flated with pride in the White Russian achievement in
capturing Emtsa before the Americans and French were
even half-way there. He kept thumping and clinking back
and forth across the tiles, splashing merrily every time he
crossed the wet spot where the freezing rain had blustered
in through a broken window.

"But of course," he was saying, "our success was only
to be expected. These Bolsheviks are obviously much inferior to our own troops. This Lenin of theirs will end
up back in Switzerland, I assure you, if we do not hang
him first. As we say in Russia, *The shoemaker should not
make boots for his ox.*"

I was getting a bit fed up with these damned Russian
proverbs. "Don't you also say," I riposted, *"Where is the
hunter when the reindeer has its hoof in a pool of lava?"*

Poupychev stopped pacing and looked at me. "What's
that got to do with it?" he asked.

I peered around, trying to count the uniformed wraiths
around us. "Where are the rest of the officers?" I snapped.
"I thought you called this meeting for six."

Poupychev, still looking at me a shade suspiciously, waved. "Oh, I'm sure they'll turn up sooner or later," he muttered. "They have a good excuse, Colonel. They were up all night, you see, drinking and playing cards.

"Yes," he went on, stroking the hilt of his sword, "there is not the slightest doubt that we shall be in Moscow by January, just in time for Christmas."

His eyes double glazed to keep out the chill of reality, he immediately transported himself to some Moscow mansion to gorge on imaginary caviar, strawberries, and kirsch, or swirl to the music of galleried minstrels, with ladies with bosoms indented with diamonds.

I looked at him in resigned curiosity, as he dreamed back and forth, back and forth across the tiled floor, his lips gleaming like two slices of calves' liver. Poupychev was wearing his best Imperial Russian Artillery uniform that morning, complete with spurs, sword, and gleaming steel scabbard, and three and a half rows of medal ribbons, including the Russian Orthodox Church Good Conduct Medal (very rarely awarded). He might just as well have been wearing a loin cloth and spats. He had no useful knowledge of artillery whatsoever.

I'd discovered this the previous evening when I asked him to take charge of the battery of 15-centimetre guns. He had smiled forbearingly and explained that as a staff officer he had been concerned only with grand strategy. "The picayune details," he said, "I left to others."

"But all I want you to do, Major," I'd said, stupid with fatigue, "is to lay the guns and see they are fired roughly in the right direction. You don't have to actually *hit* anything, you know."

"Lay them?" he asked suspiciously.

It finally got through to me: he hadn't even *seen* a gun fired from close quarters since sometime last century.

What with him and people like Count Snetkov, it was no wonder the revolution had come as a bit of a surprise.

It was after seven before the rest of the officers assembled, yawning and bleary-eyed. Whereupon Poupychev, believing he knew what the situation was, proceeded to summarize it.

Skipping such sordid details as supply, transport, communications, and reserves, he talked at great length about our strategic intentions. I listened quite interestedly. I hadn't realized we had any, until then.

Poupychev droned on and on. He was enjoying himself so much I was reluctant to interfere . . . No . . . to be truthful, I was beginning to feel the dreaded Russian inertia enveloping me . . . as if I'd been given lumbar anaesthesia . . . A few more weeks in this brooding land, with its fearful forests and fatalistic humidity and I'd be lying on a stove like a skillet, rusting away in melancholy, saying, "What's the use . . . If *Gospod* had meant me to survive, He would never have set my mattress on fire . . ."

With his inspiring words about a consummated counter-revolution, Poupy would have made a fine hypnotist . . .

It was a relief when one of the officers interrupted him. He did this by falling off his English shooting stick.

He sprawled in an icy puddle of water, which made him very annoyed.

"Yes, my dear Major," he snapped, plucking fastidiously at his wet breeches, "but I believe you have some orders for us. Well, let's have them and get it over with, my dear Vladimir Petrovitch."

Thank goodness, I thought, for at least one realist.

"So we can get back to our bridge game," the officer added. Then, indignantly: "I was having a run of luck, you know."

"I was coming to that," Poupychev said. "However, first: our immediate objective is to wipe out the Bolsheviks who are now trapped between us and the Allied forces to the north. Accordingly, as soon as all is ready, possibly even within the next two or three days, we shall move north to link up with the Westerners."

Next two or three days? Surely he meant hours?

"Thus, with our help, the Westerners will be able to continue their offensive southward. We shall, of course, greet them in Emtsa with a parade, and with our glorious Russian tricolor flying triumphantly above this very building."

There was an approving murmur. Somebody started to clap, but desisted when the others winced and held their heads.

"What is the situation to the south?" Kisselev asked.

"The local bureaucrats have informed me that there are no Bolsheviks to the south of us within thirty versts," Poupychev said, a shadow of impatience flitting across his moonscape. He didn't much approve of little Kisselev. Kisselev could be so un-Russian at times, so darned practical. "However, as soon as I get round to it, I shall send out a patrol to make quite sure that there is no danger from that direction."

"It is true, my dear Major," one of the platoon officers said, biting a yawn in two, "that we should have no difficulty in linking up with these Westerners. But surely that won't be necessary? One of the local girls, I forget her name, the daughter of some paltry official, tells us that the Americans have already reached Verst 445."

"That's a god idea," said another. "Why don't we just wait for them to arrive? No need for *us* to stir, is there?"

There were sounds of approval. The ones without hangovers nodded emphatically.

"That is a good point," Poupychev said. "We shall certainly take that viewpoint into consideration."

"Well, if there's nothing else, I think I shall turn in, now," another said, yawning so exorbitantly that his jawbone crunched.

"Good idea, Mishka. Me too," said a friend.

"Er," I said.

They all turned and smiled with polite condescension, obviously bracing themselves for another of my encouraging pep talks.

Before I could ruin the general mood of euphoria, somebody else beat me to it. Ufan, his ragged greatcoat sparkling with ice, came stumbling into the hall, panting urgently.

He stopped, momentarily abashed by the stares from twenty pairs of bloodshot eyes; then thrashed his way up to me and wrenched at my furs, and started to stutter incoherently.

He was so agitated I couldn't understand what he was saying. Major Poupychev was kind enough to repeat it for me slowly.

Ufan's message was simple enough, heaven knows: an armored train was approaching from the south.

After a moment, somebody said uneasily, "Nonsense. There are no Bolsheviks within thirty versts. I have it on the highest authority."

"But I saw it," Ufan shouted, scratching himself frenziedly. "A big long train, with great huge guns!"

"It's just as I thought," Poupychev said. "It's hopeless. We are doomed."

Because of the outrageous condition of the late commissar's almost new Renault, I had no compunction about driving it at top speed over the fields and crashing it ruthlessly over hillock and ditch. I found Lieutenant Bodrov and his sergeant at the south end of the bridge, near the Maxim machine guns. Bodrov was looking anxiously through his field glasses. The sergeant was looking for the nearest exit.

Ignoring a hubbub of frightened queries from the machine gunners and the pleading looks of the sergeant, I trained my glasses down the track. The locomotive was still about five miles away. It was headed straight toward us, so all I could see, fuzzily, through the draperies of rain, was its smokestack and the red flags crossed over its round boiler.

"There are twelve cars, Bartalamyeh Fyodorevitch," young Bodrov said, trying to sound nonchalant. "All of them are heavily armored. There are two big guns."

"Thank you."

"Shall I blow up the bridge, Excellency?" the sergeant asked.

"Just a moment."

"But we must do something quick, Your Excellency! It is coming very fast! There is no time!"

I looked back at the train, chewing my lip. I turned to Bodrov. "Is that true, Petya?"

"I agree. We have only a few minutes. The charges are laid."

"I mean, do you agree that the train is travelling fast?"

"The fuses are ready to light," the sergeant said helpfully.

"Yes," Bodrov said. He sounded short of breath. "I saw it clearly when it came round the bend. It is coming up at full speed. It will be here in perhaps twelve minutes."

"Listen, Petya," I said. "Are you listening?"

Bodrov took a deep breath, came to attention and thumped the heels of his boots together. "At your orders, Colonel," he said, his eyes wide-open and brilliant.

"Petya, if the train was expecting trouble, do you think it would go fast or slow?"

Bodrov stared as if I were trying to start a discussion on the merits of the Maryinsky Ballet. "If it were expecting trouble?" he said. "But of course it is."

"Then would it go fast or slow?"

Bodrov started to reply, stopped, then said, "It is true . . . They would not take risks with a valuable train."

"Does that not suggest that they are not expecting immediate trouble, if they are travelling fast? That they may not know we have captured the bridge—or that we are in Emtsa?"

"But they must," he replied bewilderedly. "Or why else are they here?"

"We must blow the bridge," the sergeant said angrily. "I ask permission to blow up the bridge immediately."

"Shut up." I turned back to Bodrov. "They may just have been sent up to reinforce their comrades north of Emtsa."

A soldier manning one of the machine guns nearby, started to run back along the bridge. I stepped in his way. "Get back to your post, you great, lousy bundle of rotting, evil-smelling rags," I said in English, but smiling and nodding at him encouragingly at the same time. The soldier hesitated, shuffled, then went back, trying to look as if he had merely been stretching his legs.

"You are going to assume they do not know we have captured Emtsa?"

"Sergeant Pazelsky was smart enough to cut the telegraph wires as soon as we took the bridge, Petya."

"It . . . it is a great risk," Bodrov said shakily, his fresh cheeks pink and hot enough to melt the ice that had formed on his fur hat.

"The other way is worse, isn't it?" I pointed down the track. "If we blow up the bridge, they will still be there. The train will dominate the town and the railway as far north as its guns can range. Also, blowing the bridge would be to their advantage. We wouldn't be able to get at them. What do you say, Petya?"

"It is a great risk, Colonel."

"I'm going to try it, Petya. Especially as *you're* the one who's going to take the risk."

Ten minutes later, from the safety of the railway cutting three quarters of a mile back, I watched through field glasses as the train reached the bridge, or, to be exact, a point about a hundred yards short of it. By dipping the glasses slightly, I could see our machine guns in place. But now they were both under the bridge. They were covering the hundred or so ex-Bolsheviks who were pretending to dig trenches in the field below the bridge.

I was having them covered just in case any of them got the idea of running for it and giving the game away, or warning the train that they were no longer loyal little Red soldiers.

The moment the train stopped, a dozen soldiers jumped off, holding their rifles clumsily at the port-arms position. They were surrounding an officer in a grey greatcoat.

At least I assumed he was an officer, though his only insigne was his red star. From this distance, he looked about sixteen years old.

Bodrov, also wearing a red star on the sleeve of a *kittel* that he had hastily borrowed from one of the former Bolos, walked forward to meet the newcomers.

The view jiggled as Ufan clutched at my arm and whispered excitedly. I turned on him, hissing fiercely, then turned back to the train, agitatedly refocussing.

I couldn't locate Bodrov. For an awful moment I thought they had already seen through his bluff and promptly liquidated him. But then one of the Reds shifted aside and I saw Bodrov talking to the officer.

Everything now depended on Bodrov's not losing his nerve. I watched tensely, holding my breath.

Bodrov admitted later that he had been sweating and quaking so noticeably that he had to pretend he was suffering from some unspeakable disease. He said that luckily he hadn't needed to persuade the colonel in command of the train (after abolishing all commissioned ranks for several months, the Reds now appeared to have restored them) that Emtsa was still in Red hands. The colonel was so convinced that his enemies were still many miles away that he had asked only the most perfunctory questions about the local situation. His main concern was to get on up the line as fast as possible.

He had shown only a momentary suspicion. That was when he mentioned a name unfamiliar to Bodrov.

"Avilov, Comrade Colonel?" Bodrov faltered.

"Avilov. Surely you know the name of your own adviser?" the colonel asked with a frown.

Bodrov managed to conceal his momentary confusion. Avilov, apparently, was the name of the commissar Kisselev had killed.

In the meantime, I took the opportunity to study the train. From this angle I could see its entire length. The locomotive was apparently not Russian-made, for it lacked the usual tall smokestack. It was drawing a dozen cars, every one of them heavily armored with crude steel plates.

The second and third cars bore long-barreled guns. They looked like naval guns. In addition, there were several heavy machine guns on swivelling mounts on top of six of the remaining ten cars. The rear three cars seemed to be passenger coaches, the doors being almost undiscernible openings in the armor plating.

A formidable weapon, that train. With the doors secured it would be impossible to get at the occupants without a giant tin-opener.

Unless, of course, they were so obliging as to open them voluntarily . . . ?

We arrived back at the railway station only eight minutes ahead of the train. As the Renault squealed to a halt on the weedy ground alongside the track, a dozen officers ran up, shouting questions. Then swarms of NCOs and men surrounded the car. They were all looking at me as if I were Moses in a Red Sea that had failed to part.

On the far side of the cobbled square, Poupychev was also surrounded, in his case by equally disillusioned-looking civilians. The fattest and best-dressed of the civilians—he was wearing a sort of beaver hat, so coated with white ice from the freezing rain it looked like the first prize in a loony-bin baking contest—hurried over, waving his arms.

"Now you see what you have done!" he shouted, stamping his foot and wringing his mitts. "We shall all be murdered by the Communists, or worse, robbed of all we have in this world!" He stamped his foot again. "What a calamity it is! What have we done to deserve it, that's what I want to know. It's disgraceful, that's what it is! Oh, what nonsense it all is!"

The rest was drowned in the panicky hubbub. I stood up on the front seat of the car, holding onto the windscreen. "Listen, lads," I bellowed. "Listen! The enemy doesn't know we have captured Emtsa! No, listen! Silence! Quiet! Shut up!"

"Listen to the comrade Colonel, boys," somebody called out—presumeably a former Bolo. "Let's give him a chance, eh?"

"The Bolsheviks don't know we have taken Emtsa," I hollered, trying to sound calm as custard about it. "So listen to me, lads: we're going to make them think we are Bolsheviks! I want you all to line up along the track! You understand? Do just what you usually do when there is a train coming. Stand along the track and wait for the train to stop. Wait for them to open the doors."

The men fell silent, gaping. It took an effort not to jump up and down on the seat in exasperation at my own stumbling words. I'd had a thumping headache for days now, from concentrating so intensely on the language. Many times, I'd had to give up and let Poupychev translate.

But I had to get across to them now, and very quickly. I could hear the train. It was already chuffing into the southern part of the straggly town. Its smoke was visible, too, billowing up as if half the town were on fire.

Maybe it would be, in a few minutes.

"Isn't that right, Alexander Nikolayevitch," I bawled across to Kisselev. "It will seem more natural if the station is crowded? Is it not so that Russian *vauxhal* are always crowded with people, waiting for a train?"

It was elegant Lieutenant Togonidze who got it first. "That's right," he shouted, addressing the huge throng. "Our colonel is right, my dear fellows. He means that we must not hide and shoot at the train, but stand and wait

389

for it, as if we are Bolsheviks ourselves. Then, when it stops and they open the doors, we will rush in, and kill them!"

The moujiks stared at him stupidly for a moment, then back at me, as if it were now my turn to talk incomprehensible gibberish.

Events were simply moving too fast for the poor old peasants. They were still looking apprehensive and uncomprehending as the quicker-witted among the NCOs started pushing and shoving and pummeling them into position on both sides of the narrow railway line—the only narrow-gauge track, I believe, in the whole of Russia.

The men were still thrashing around in hopeless confusion as the armored train appeared round the final bend, sending up clouds of dense, black smoke.

The train men, though, must have been reassured by the typical scene of Russian disorder. At least, there was no sign of hostile intent from them. Yet. And the train was perceptibly slowing.

As he leaned out of the cab, one hand on the controls and the other gripping the side, the engineer's face bore the usual expression of lofty contempt for the townspeople.

Meanwhile I was scuttling back and forth along the track, whispering, hauling, and shoving men into position, hoping nobody on the train would notice the few inches of khaki below my burly furs.

I found myself shoving the adjutant into position as well, and angrily asking him where the hell he'd left his rifle.

"Oh, it's you, Poupy. Where's your pistol?"

Poupychev waved it resignedly. "I shall give my life, of course," he muttered. "But it will never work."

"All the same, Poupy, *mon vieux,* you be ready to jump inside as soon as the doors are open— No, no, Doubevitch, no grenades! You'll just kill your own men. Damn it, you, don't point your gun! We must not look hostile! Oh, good Lord . . ."

I ran smack into Private Seriozhka and reeled back, cursing.

"But Your Excellency," he said bewilderedly, "if we just stand here they will kill us."

I explained again, hurriedly, between great shuddery gasps of apprehension and excitement. Seriozhka looked blankly at the train as it loomed out of the rain, spitting sparks. The great driving wheels grinded past, inches away. A gout of steam blew sideways, melting the ice on Seriozhka's *kittel*.

The train squealed onward through the jam of bodies, vast and ponderous, its brutal steel sides seeming to blot out the entire sky. I saw a set of grimy fingers wiggling through one of the slits in the side.

On top, the gunners were looking around, huddled over their machine guns. I couldn't tell whether they were on their guard or not. I glanced around quickly, to find out where Poupychev had sited our machine guns, but couldn't see them anywhere.

A few yards farther on, Lieutenant Doubevitch was talking quietly to an apprehensive platoon. At least *he* seemed to know what was expected of him. He was passing out bloodthirsty advice as he gripped an unsheathed sword. He looked quite pleased at the prospect of hacking off a limb or two.

A thought occurred to me. Seriozhka was still shifting about nearby. I grabbed his arm, "Kolya," I said. "Listen. Run to the steam—the—the engine! As soon as it stops, climb up and cover the two men there with your rifle. Do you understand?"

"I hear you, Your Excellency."

I could have kissed him with gratitude for this alert response. "Don't kill them, though. We need them."

"Yes, I understand, Excellency."

"Good. Go. Run."

Seriozhka lumbered up the track alongside the train, barging through the huge crowd. By now, the train had almost stopped. There was no sign of any of the iron hatches opening, though. God, it had to work now, or we'd be slaughtered. I looked around again for our machine guns. They might be desperately needed any second now, to deal with the gunners on the roof of the train.

I saw two of the machine guns. They were on the roof of the municipal building, two hundred feet away across the cobbled square.

I also saw something else. The tricolor was still floating above the roof.

The bloody idiots had failed to haul down the imperial flag.

"Oh, Jesus Christ."

Surely the enemy gunners had seen it. They were looking in that direction. It was too late to do anything about it now. The flag was plainly visible, flapping heavily in the freezing rain.

The train stopped with a prolonged nerve-twisting shriek of brakes. The soldiers on both sides of the track pressed back instinctively against the crush of bodies behind them, their faces tense as they fumbled with their weapons and stared wide-eyed up at the train, which seemed so utterly impregnable.

An agonizing pause. Nothing happened. Then, all at once, as if they'd rehearsed the action for a French bedroom farce, the kind where lots of doors open and shut simultaneously, the steel hatches all along the train started to gape. Faces and dim figures appeared in the openings.

The men around me remained frozen. I caught a glimpse of Doubevitch's sword, gleaming dully in the miserable light. Shouting, he ran up the steps opposite him, slashing away like a madman, and disappeared into the train.

Nobody was moving at the hatch nearest me. I forced my way through to it, through the men jammed against the steel sides. They were just standing there, as if waiting for an engraved invitation to board. I managed to get on the steps and forced my way into the interior, clutching an automatic. Then I was inside.

It was a converted cattle truck, packed with men. They retreated slowly to the far end, mouths agape, eyes stretched wide. Tired, bearded faces, little suggestion of a uniform, just an odd variety of torn, grimy blouses and filthy coats, dozens of different sorts of hat, boots, shoes, or just rags on their feet.

We looked at each other. The sound of firing farther along the train was muffled. Men shouting. A muffled bang from somewhere and a shocked silence, then cries of pain. Somebody using grenades.

"Out!" I said. "Out!" Nobody obeyed. I fired at the ceiling. The Reds cowered, too frightened to move. For something to do, to impress them, I kicked at a teepee of rifles, scattering them into the straw.

Men crowded behind me. There was a deafening bang. One of the Reds shrieked and clutched at his chest. The rest flung up their hands and started babbling in terror.

It took minutes to fight my way off the train again. The machine guns on top of the municipal building were firing. One of them had tracer. As usual, they were aiming too high. I could see the wisps of smoke far overhead. The enemy machine-gunners were wrenching their guns around on the swivels.

Men were struggling along the entire length of the train, yelling. Guns banging, bayonets stabbing, grenades exploding among friend and foe. A stream of blood poured through one of the open hatches and splashed onto the icy gravel. Some idiot was firing his rifle at the inch-thick turret of one of the naval guns. The bullets howled off into the icy rain.

An iron ladder led to the roof of one of the cars. "Follow me, follow me!" I shinned up the ladder. The armor plating ended a foot from the roof. The wooden roof was more or less flat. There was a machine gun ten feet away.

The gunners were trying to depress the muzzle to fire into the packed crowd on the far side of the train. I aimed. "Hands up!" The machine gun started to swing around. I pulled the trigger. The gun was empty. I couldn't understand that. I only remembered firing one shot. The machine gun was pointing at me. A soldier was wrenching at the loading handle. It had iced up in the freezing rain. It wouldn't fire. I threw my automatic. As it clanged against the gun shield I followed up, trying to get around the shield. I skidded on the icy roof. I cannoned into one of the Bolos. He rolled off the roof. Another Bolo picked up a belt of ammunition and flailed it. A couple of dozen 7.62-mm. cartridges clouted me across the head and I went sliding across the roof and over the edge, unable to hold on. Everything was coated in ice. I landed on Poupychev.

I was quite glad about that.

"Don't just lie there—get in there and shoot!"

"It's all over, Bartalamyeh Fyodorevitch."

" 'Tisn't! Don't be so bloody pessimistic!"

"I mean we have won," Poupychev said dazedly, and gestured—with some difficulty, as I was still sitting on him.

All along the train, in both directions, I saw arms held high in the air. Other Reds were still being hurled bodily out of the hatches.

The shooting had stopped. Men were shouting and cheering, waving. Whiskery moujiks were embracing each other, spitting joyfully.

It appeared that Poupychev was right. The fight was over.

Unfortunately, when I went forward to the locomotive, I learned that several of the men, maddened with excitement and blood lust, had stormed the locomotive, and despite the fact that Seriozhka was covering the crew with his rifle, had bayoneted the engineer and the fireman, killing the former and seriously wounding his mate.

So now we had a train, but among our fifteen hundred supporters, and this latest batch of about seven hundred volunteers, there was not one competent to drive the train onward.

Another View of the Train

"What happened then?" General Ironside asked.

"Yes, yes, tell him, Bandyeh, tell him!" Brzhtvh cried, shaking all over with excitement and bending his beard.

Ironside looked really interested, though he had already heard most of the details from the official reports, as well as personally (a talented linguist, he had picked up Russian in about three weeks) from several of the officers and men who had taken part.

I think he had insisted on first-hand reports of the action because of a perfectly understandable suspicion that most of the accounts he'd heard so far were products of the overheated Russian imagination. Brzhtvh's generous and enthusiastic version, for instance, had sounded pretty improbable, even to me.

"Well, there we were," I said, daintily heaping four teaspoons of sugar into my tea, "with a splendid armored train at our disposal and nobody to man it."

My lips pouted over the delicate rim of the Dresden chinaware. Forgetting I was back in civilization, or at least, Archangel, I sucked up a couple of mouthfuls. As the slurping sound splashed around Ironside's regal office with its curtains of purest silk brocade flouncing against fourteen-foot-high windows, I winced and tried to make up for the lower-class clamor by raising my pinkie; but had to fold it again when I noticed that there was dirt under the fingernail.

Ironside put a hand to his chin and turned to glance

at Brzhtvh; but the view in that direction was just as unrewarding. The great hairy Russian was trying vainly to insert the pipe-wrench of his forefinger through the handle of his tea-cup. Ironside swivelled away again, his handsome features twitching, and gazed out the window.

Outside, snowflakes were busy smothering the cupolas and onion domes of Archangel. It had been snowing heavily for two days, and though it was now midday, the sky was the colour of a gun barrel. Above the ermine roofs, the clouds wore a black lining, as if sending out invitations to mourn the passing of the sun. On the Troitsky Prospekt the trolley cars flashed startlingly in the deranged gloaming.

Even half an hour after arriving I was still looking in some awe at the Commander-in-Chief. Ironside was even larger than Brzhtvh, a magnificent giant of a man, at least six foot four, and weighing about 270 pounds, most of it brain and muscle. To make it all the worse, he was virilely handsome.

Nobody had the right to look like that, and be greatly admired by the rank and file into the bargain. I'd heard quite a bit about him in France. He was the only general, apart from Plumer, to have earned both the affection and respect of his troops, not least because he had frequently visited the front line, usually accompanied by his pet bulldog.

When he faced us again, he was still trying not to laugh at the two of us. "But you brought the train up to Verst 455, trapped another Bolshevik train, and linked up with the Americans," he said, looking at me as if in eager anticipation of a *risqué* story, familiarity with which would not diminish his continued enjoyment of it. "Then turned south again, to rout the enemy at Plesetskaya. So you must have found *someone* skilled enough to drive the train."

This time I managed to draw up a mouthful of tea with scarcely a sound.

There was a brief silence. General Brzhtvh suddenly

sprang up, and with a laugh that Peter the Great might have uttered as he tortured his favorite son, smote me on the back.

"It was Bandyeh," he shouted. "Bandyeh himself drove the train!"

Time was still the crucial factor in this foray of ours, and that's what the others never seemed to grasp. When they learned that the enemy had thoughtlessly failed to provide a back-up crew for the train, the officers were immediately resigned to abandoning the whole idea of turning it against its former masters, and proposed instead a game of whist and a few parties before pressing on up the line on foot.

"Besides, we must reorganize, Bartalamyeh Fyodorevitch," Poupychev explained. "After all, we now have a considerable force to administer. With these latest volunteers from the train, we have nearly twenty-five hundred men. A real regiment!" And he went on to babble about logistics and a properly appointed regimental or even a brigade staff, a signal corps, a quartermaster's, an artillery staff—

"And perhaps a regimental band?"

"A band?" Poupychev pouted his bright red lips and thought about it—with growing enthusiasm.

"I used to play the drums, Bartalamyeh Fyodorevitch," Bodrov cried, his eyes lighting up. "I once had several tin drums, with which I used to accompany my collection of lead soldiers. I became so skilled that my grandfather, Prince Fomin, put an entire wing of the house at my disposal, so that I could practice undisturbed. Ah, what a good man he was. A real saint . . ."

"I myself play the balalaika quite passably," Togonidze drawled.

"Yes, well, perhaps we can talk about that later," I said hurriedly. I turned to Kisselev. "In the meantime, would you be good enough to select about eight hundred men you can rely on, Alexander Nikolayevitch, to man the train. And if Major Poupychev would divide the rest of the force between the town and the bridge?"

"But, my dear Colonel, you have just finished shouting that the train is now useless," Poupy said with a smile.

"I'll try and drive it myself," I said.

There was hearty laughter. Togonidze slapped me on the back and squeezed my shoulders affectionately. "You are a card [*dyestvyooshyeh*], Bartalamyeh Fyodorevitch," he said. "There is no doubt about it."

"Thank you. Please be ready to move in about an hour," I said, and lurched off up the track, my feet crunching loudly in the sudden silence.

A couple of minutes later, the officers appeared outside the cab and gaped up into it. I was already busy up there, looking knowledgeable.

I should like to have explained to them that when I was a boy I had often ridden the footplate of the CPR freight train that meandered daily from Ottawa to Mississippi Lake, and thence eastward to join the Grand Trunk Railway along the St. Lawrence near Brockville. The trainmen always stopped at the water tank outside my home town, Beamington, to swing their great fat hose over the tender. Sometimes they had allowed me to ride with them as far as Smith's Falls—where I sometimes had an awful job getting a lift back to Beamington. (For some reason, the engineer of the eastbound freight was rarely as accommodating as his westbound colleague.)

As I say, I should like to have explained this, but communication still took an inordinate amount of mental energy and I needed what little I had left to try to make sense of the controls that I was now gazing at so intently.

"It is impossible," one of the officers called up, looking irritated at this latest sample of occidental presumption. "It is quite plain from the superior way they behave that even real engine drivers do not understand the workings of a locomotive. Come down and have a drink with us, my dear Colonel, and stop all this nonsense," he said, gesturing around at the war.

"Besides, one should not tamper with fate," another said. "Look what happened to that fellow in Pushkin's *The Queen of Spades*. The officer in that story tampered with the unknown, and look where he ended up."

"Where?" somebody asked.

"I'm not quite sure, my dear fellow. My English nanny read it to me, but her accent was nearly as bad as Bartalamyeh Fyodorevitch's."

"I know that story," another put in and started to describe the plot. The officers all gathered round to listen with childlike interest.

"Seriozhka," I said.

Thirty minutes after that unfortunate bit of bayonet practice, the huge, lumbering peasant was still standing forlornly on top of the piles of wood in the tender, gripping his rifle helplessly. He looked miserable, as if he had been banished to Siberia . . . Except that, actually, he came from Siberia.

"You will be . . ." I didn't know the word for *fireman*. I picked up the stoking shovel and used it to swing the fire doors open. "Wood. Put wood on the fire."

"Then you are not angry with me, Bartalamyeh Fyodorevitch?" he faltered.

"I will be if you don't get a move on. The fire is nearly out."

His eyes shone. He scrambled joyfully from the tender. For a dreadful moment, I thought he was going to start smooching again. I hurriedly passed him the shovel and turned back to the controls, trying to ignore the growing audience of officers and men who were crowding the track on both sides of the cab, all making loud and unhelpful comments, except the one who was giving away Pushkin's plot.

The locomotive was obviously one of the few pieces of foreign aid that the former government had bothered to unpack. It was an old narrow-gauge engine, made, I think, by Baldwin, a U.S. firm, with six huge driving wheels and several smaller ones acting as hangers-on. Though it was old, it still had a great many levers, valves, wheels, and gauges, most of them scarred and bent as a result of repeated blows and knoutings. In fact, it looked not unlike the cockpit of a Dolphin, on a vast scale—and I couldn't immediately identify any of the controls, except the regulator handle.

Trouble was, though the Ottawa engineers had sometimes let me work the controls, I'd never really understood what they actually controlled. The regulator, for instance, that long bar sticking out sideways in the midst of the clutter: I knew it was the principal driving control, but what did it actually regulate?

Presumably, the steam entering the cylinders at the front of the loco. Let me see. The fuel, in this case large hunks of hardwood piled six feet high behind us in the tender, went into the sloping fire-box. The hot gases travelled around several miles of boiler tubing, and superheated the surrounding water to steam. This, under tremendous pressure, was allowed to enter the two driving cylinders. The steam exerted force on the pistons and piston rods. The rods were attached to the massive crossheads, which in turn were connected to the centre driving wheels by the main rods.

The power was thus transmitted to the wheels in a bicycle-peddling kind of operation, that is, by eccentric cranks. (And, having served in the 13th Bicycle Battalion, I was thoroughly familiar with eccentric cranks.)

So that was how a loco moved forward. To reverse it, the steam would obviously have to be admitted by the valve to the other side of the piston, pushing it forward rather than urging it back.

Right. Now. What was the right pressure for the steam?

Seriozhka was already stoking with vast enthusiasm, grinning all over his stubbly face. So the pressure would

401

be rising fast. But to what? Think. It would be rather humiliating if I blew up the boiler before we even got under way.

Look, there was the pressure gauge, high up on the extreme right of the cab, above the car-heating steam-pressure gauge. Thank the Lord they hadn't changed the Western measurements. I'd have difficulty enough remembering the figures without having to transpose them from poods, or whatever system the Russians used.

Eighty, was it? Ninety pounds per square inch?

I put that problem aside for the moment, and turned to the cut-off indicator, marked in percentages. What percentages had the Ottawa engineers held it at? I couldn't remember that, either. Twenty-five per cent? Forty? And percentage of what? And what, in addition, did it cut off?

Then there was the reverser. There, the screw-reversing handle low down on the left. In spite of its name, though, it didn't necessarily do any reversing, did it? I seemed to remember that the Ottawa engineers had always set the lock in full gear before starting off forward. Yes! They'd told me once. It governed the timing and admission of the high-pressure steam in the cylinders. Subsequently, the engineer would turn the handle of the reversing gear to adjust the exhaust sound to his liking.

Perhaps that, then, was the cut-off, the percentages indicating the proportion of high-pressure steam being allowed to enter or exit the cylinders, to adjust for an economical pressure.

Then there was the water level indicator. The water had to show in the glass but neither fill the gauge nor drop out of sight. There wasn't any water in it at the moment. What did that mean?

"Anyway, this chap Hermann—or was it Tomsky?—makes his way into the countess' boudoir," a voice was saying excitedly from the track alongside the cab, "and watches her from behind a screen as she undresses. The sight almost makes him sick—I remember that part—

because the countess is over ninety years old. Anyway, as soon as she flings herself into bed . . ."

Seriozhka was still hurling tree trunks and things into the fire with joyous abandon, his ragged blouse already soaked with sweat, from exertion, and the increasing heat of the fire. But most of the wood was going into the nearer end of the fire-box.

"You have to throw the wood far inside," I explained hurriedly. "It has to cover the floor of the . . ." Fire-box. What was the Russian for that? "I'll show you," I said. And showed him by showering a shovelful of wood all over the floor, after completely missing the fire-door opening.

Red-faced—from the heat—I tried again, and wasted another two minutes straightening the edge of the shovel after it had clanged against the iron door.

"Yes, well . . . carry on," I said, and stared woodenly at the isolating cocks for the vacuum ejector, and wondered what the hell *they* were for, as well.

Several of the officers, who had presumably lost interest in Pushkin, were now crowding the steps of the locomotive, peering squeamishly into the sordid interior.

"Listen," I shouted exasperatedly. "You have fifty minutes left to get the men onto the train. Move! Quick-quick!" And to show them I meant business I yanked at what I thought was the whistle stop valve, to sort of underline the gravity of the situation with a dramatic ululation of steam. But all that happened was that a glass jar of scalding water emptied itself onto my foot.

I danced round a bit. However, they must have thought I was throwing a tantrum, for after a final, stupefied look into the proletarian interior, they started to retreat back along the track, whispering to each other in a mystified sort of way.

I stopped prancing as I suddenly remembered the water-supply valve in the tender. In a panic, I darted my eyes all over the place, looking for the valve. Maybe that was

403

why the water wasn't showing in the glass. I was firing up a waterless boiler? No, there it was, on the tender. It was on. And the pressure was rising. Good God, it was already over 170 pounds!

I started to clutch at Seriozhka, then looked again. Of course! The pressure at which the Ottawa train men had maintained the boiler while it was drifting was 196 pounds. Higher only if they were approaching a gradient.

Good. That was one major problem out of the way.

Seriozhka was still stoking with undiminished enthusiasm, grinning hugely whenever he caught my eye. Steam was starting to wisp and snort from sundry valves, cracks, and crevices all over the locomotive. I leaned out of the cab, wishing I had an oily rag. Train engineers always had an oily rag to wipe their hands on. A couple of dozen tattered soldiers were still hanging around, though some of them were starting to retreat as the loco spat at them and dripped boiling water.

One of them was the sergeant who had had the presence of mind to cut the telegraph wires as soon as we'd taken the bridge. He was a former member of the crack Preobrazhensky Regiment and had still not got out of the habit of receiving orders without organizing a friendly debate on whether they should be obeyed or not.

"Sergeant Pazelsky!" I shouted. "Undo the engine! Unjoin the engine! I want to try it out, understand?"

He nodded, and instantly seized two of his men by the scruff of the neck. Bellowing orders and pointing at the coupling, he hurled them in between the tender and the first armored truck.

They immediately ran out the other side, and scuttled off in the general direction of Siberia. Cursing, Pazelsky had to unhitch the engine himself.

The pressure was now at 185 pounds, and the water was filling the glass gauge. I tried the reverser, but couldn't move it. For some reason, the designers of steam locomotives always made the controls stiff and heavy to operate, except for the regulator. The Ottawa engineers had spent half their time belaboring everything in sight with their picks. So who was I to go against tradition? I hit the reverser with an axe, and chipped away at it until it was at full lock.

Well, this was the great moment. I reached for the regulator, and taking a deep lungful of burning wood smoke—two lungfuls, in fact—pressed it down gently.

Seriozhka stepped back in alarm as the loco shuddered. There was a screeching sound. But nothing else seemed to be happening. I peered at the ground outside, to see if it was moving. It wasn't. I pushed the regulator down a little farther. The screeching got worse, and the loco vibrated alarmingly.

The engine started to move, grinding horribly, but at only one mile an hour, though the regulator was now nearly half-way down. There was something wrong somewhere. I felt sure that even a loco as old as this was bound to do more than just 1 m.p.h. at half speed.

Seriozhka had stopped feeding the fire. He was now looking decidedly apprehensive as the loco shuddered and squealed in agony. He had left the fire door open. The glare from the box showered him in brilliant yellow light. He had his hands over his ears and was looking ready to abandon ship.

I was ahead of him. I was already poised on the outside steps, with one leg in the air.

I couldn't understand what was wrong. The noise was terrible. It sounded and felt as if the loco had abandoned the rails and was trying to drive through a scrap metal yard on square wheels.

Down below, soldiers were gathering in multitudes, looking as if they felt they ought to be paying to watch.

The brakes, for gosh sakes!

Quick, where the hell were the brakes? One of the small wheels on the left of the cab had a steam valve above it. That might be it. I took the axe and hacked at it. The squealing started to die away. As the wheel jerked around under the hail of blows, the loco rumbled and picked up speed. In a few seconds, the driving wheels spinning and the exhaust beating like a thousand hang-overs, it was soon doing five miles an hour. Then seven. Then eight.

The axe fell from my shaking hands. But, by George, we were moving. I leaned exhaustedly out of the cab, face flushed, forehead beaded, eyes staring, to make sure there was nobody on the track.

There wasn't. But about a hundred yards ahead there were switches, where the siding joined the main line. My God, if they were open . . . I jumped back to the regulator and knocked it up, then grabbed the reverser. Having got the beast moving, I was now desperate to stop it.

The reverser was immovable. I wrenched at it until my veins stood out like blue snakes. It wouldn't budge. I looked around frantically for the axe. It had fallen off the footplate.

I leaned out of the cab and shouted down the line, "Axe! Axe! Get me axe!" Then staggered back to the brake, and, making perverted keening noises through clenched teeth, wrenched at it again. I could just see us hitting the switches, now only a few yards away, and continuing on over the track for a while, the loco bumping a bit as it left the rails and sliced a few ties in two, before finally keeling over in a dead faint, with me underneath.

Sergeant Pazelsky, meanwhile, was chasing after the loco, brandishing the axe in much the same manner as he'd chased his company cook after he caught the son of a yak spitting into the borsht for good luck. The loco was coasting quite slowly, but the momentum was still carrying it toward the switches.

Then we were over them. Apart from the usual rhythmic clatter, nothing happened.

So I continued to panic. It was like the first time I ever flew the Sopwith Camel. The moment the wheels left the ground, all I could think about was getting safely down again, so I could abandon aviation for something comparatively placid, such as submarine warfare. In much the same way, I just wanted to get that train stopped so I could lie down and tremble uncontrollably for a while.

Abruptly I was thrust aside. I almost followed the axe overboard. Then Seriozhka was grasping the brake wheel and twisting it in his huge hands.

There was a spiteful hiss, then a grinding, and the loco began to slow.

It stopped with a protesting yell about two hundred yards past the switches; which, of course, had been in the right position all along.

Getting back was much easier. I was very careful to operate the power reverse mechanism, take off power, loosen the reverse wheel, and apply the brakes in plenty of time. I certainly wasn't going to disgrace myself by driving too fast and damaging our precious train. So we crept back to the armored coaches at a ridiculous speed. It seemed like 1 in.p.h. The loco connected neatly with the bumpers.

There was an ear-splitting crash. The impact knocked over four hundred men, causing quite a few bloody noses, and sent me flying into the woodpile.

However, after removing the splinters and after some more practice along the rails, I was sure I was getting the hang of it. I ought to have known better. While it was not all that difficult to move a ten-wheeled monster by itself (once one had the brakes off), it was a totally different matter moving it with twelve enormously heavy cattle trucks, converted flat cars, and passenger coaches attached. With the pressure just right, at below 200, and with the brakes firmly off, and the water just so in the glass gauge, the train refused to budge an inch.

Even with the more delicate adjustment of regulator, reverser, and live-steam injector, the six huge driving wheels merely spun impotently on the rails.

I simply couldn't get the swine to move. To make it even more exasperating, the men, who had taken an hour getting onto the train, kept climbing out again and walking forward to see what I was going to do next. Also, half the population of Emtsa turned out to watch as well.

They probably hadn't had so much fun since the 1905 executions.

To top it off, the freezing rain continued to fall, making it just that much harder for the wheels to grasp the icy rails.

I tried reversing. Naturally this worked splendidly. The whole train clanked backward quite effortlessly. But that wasn't the direction we were supposed to be going in. But when I braked, then tried to move forward again, the wheels did their spinning act once more.

Finally, by backing the train nearly half-way to the bridge, I found a slight gradient, just enough to get some kind of forward momentum. By teeny little movements on the regulator and with the reverser just off full lock, the speed gradually rose, and we were doing a good 4 m.p.h. by the time we reached the railway station again.

Twenty yards past, the wheels started spinning, the train stopped, and the passengers got off for lunch.

"Altogether," I told General Ironside, "it took three and a half hours to travel thirty feet. I thought I was doomed to remain in Emtsa for the rest of my life. I didn't particularly fancy that, as the local mayor, or whoever he was, was trying to present me with a bill for all the damage we'd done to his admin building."

"How did you finally manage it?"

"After the men had had a hot meal, I got some volunteers to collect everything they could find—ashes, gritty slush, cinders, stones, even pieces of cloth and fur and broken glass, and got them to lay the stuff on the rails in between the wheels, and ahead of them. And after some more jiggling, the locomotive finally got moving.

"Some of the men didn't get back on the train in time. I think we left about ninety of them behind. But I was darned if I was going to stop for them, or even slow up. I just kept on going, opening up an inch at a time. We got to Verst 445 in about an hour."

There we ran into the Red Guards, literally. Poupychev's information, of course, had been incorrect. The Allies were still at Verst 455. However, the appearance of the armored train in the wrong hands had its effect. My trainsmanship helped considerably. I collided with their troop train with such force that their forward cars were derailed. With their transport out of action, some of the Red Guards, following a brief skirmish, fled into the pine forests, and the remainder ran to surrender to the Americans, farther up the line. Apparently, after one look at the wild, blackened face staring at them from the cab, they thought they'd be safer in American hands.

"Unfortunately," I said, "hitting their train that way blocked the line to Archangel, so we couldn't go on. We had to go the other way."

"So you resumed the offensive southward, and continued on for about forty miles."

"Yes, sir."

"And took Plesetskaya the same day."

"Well, I thought we might as well. There was nothing in the way until we got there."

Ironside jumped up and strode up and down excitedly, smacking a fist into his palm. "Their main base—the only remaining strong point guarding the Trans-Siberian. You could have been astride the Trans-Siberian Railway in another day!"

"There wasn't enough follow-up support. We'd have been cut off."

"I know, I know. The usual story."

"I could not get past Kodish," Brzhtvh said, looking guilty. "The road was too bad."

"And all together," Ironside said, sitting down again, "counting the attack on the bridge, the capture of Emtsa, and the storming of Plesetskaya, you had, I believe 222 casualties?" He looked at Brzhtvh, shaking his head; "222 casualties. After a sixty-mile advance over the most difficult terrain I've ever come across. Four thousand prisoners, most of them on our side. A huge amount of war supplies. A battery of howitzers. An armored train, a troop train—all in four days. With three hundred men."

"I told you he was not ordinary man," Brzhtvh shouted. "Ha?"

"No," Ironside said, looking at my horse face, as I snorted faintly and pawed the carpet with a Shackleton-booted hoof.

"Even though he disobeyed my orders, the devil!" Brzhtvh bristled, wrapping an arm round my shoulders and grinding my scapulas together. "Eh, you devil?"

"It was a superb achievement," Ironside said. "Tell me, Bandy, how do you account for it? Are you a student of military history and strategy, perhaps?"

"Heck no, sir, I don't know the first thing about all that stuff. I've just been around enough to notice that if there's one thing an army can't stand, it's somebody who moves at anything faster than a snail's pace. I don't think there's much of an achievement in realizing that. We just kept surprising them, that's all."

A couple of days later, I was back in Ironside's office at Army H.Q.

"Bandy?"

"Sir?"

"If you were in command in this peninsula, how would you conduct future operations against the Communists?"

"Eh?" I said. Then: "I don't want the job, sir, thank you very much," I said quickly. "But thank you very much for offering it, sir."

"I wasn't offering it. I was asking for your opinion."

"Oh," I said. "Well . . ."

"Bearing in mind," Ironside said, leaning forward and looking at me with hard eyes, "the supply difficulties, the obdurate attitude of the White administration, the approach of winter, political reservations at home, the fact that half the Americans are down with flu and three quarters of the White Russians are down with mutiny—I want your unbiased opinion about my decision to go on the defensive. What would you do in my place?"

I tried smiling at him obsequiously. When that didn't work, I said, "I'd attack."

"You'd continue the offensive deeper into Russia?"

"Yes."

"Like Napoleon?"

"These Bolshevik swine," I said, "may be good at slaughtering civilians—at Plesetskaya we found some people who'd had their hands plunged into boiling water, so the Reds could amuse themselves by stripping off the skin—"

"The Whites have committed atrocities as well."

"Not just because their victims were property owners."

"Go on," Ironside said grimly.

"The Reds obviously haven't the fervor to fight for their ideas," I said, with the first certainty I'd felt since arriving in Russia. "State ownership indeed. They'd make civilian life even worse than the army."

"Anyway, I'm sure the whole rotten Russian Revolution will collapse within the next few months. And we can help it along if we keep up the pressure. I'm quite sure of it."

Ironside glared for a moment, then suddenly smiled and came round the desk and drew up a chair. It groaned pitifully as he sat on it. "Well, I'm glad you see it that way," he said mildly, "though I don't necessarily agree with you." He studied his boots for a moment, then: "I've been in contact with the Air Ministry, by the way, about that appointment . . . They seem—well, pretty ambivalent about you, Bandy."

"Ah," I said, looking pleased about it—but not too pleased, just in case 'ambivalent' meant something uncomplimentary.

"On one hand they seem curiously disappointed over your success, and thoroughly annoyed to be hearing about you again. While on the other hand they seem to find it equally difficult to let you go."

"Like a piece of flypaper."

"Rather like a hunk of metal," Ironside said, "and they can't decide whether it's made of lead or gold." He regarded me unblinkingly. "Which is it, Bandy?"

"It just looks like gold. Actually it's brass."

"M'm. Yes, that's just the kind of answer I was expecting. Do you know, Bandy, I may be the first person ever to see through you."

"Oh, crumbs."

"I think you've spent your entire career trying to make people think the very worst of you. Presenting yourself in the worst possible light, out of a profound sense of the absurdity of human endeavor."

"Absurd? Me?"

"And naturally people have taken you at your own estimation, and believed most of the things you've said about yourself. But whatever its true—shall we say extrinsic?—value, your achievements in this war have obviously been considerable. In many ways, you're a great man, Bandy." He paused. "Do you believe that?"

"Indubitably, sir."

"I see you don't, but I've taken the trouble to look at what you've actually done, rather than listen to what you say you've done. You have many flaws, of course. But in the—"

"Flaws? What flaws? *I* haven't any flaws."

"Obsessiveness, arrogance, narrow-mindedness—"

"Oh, *those* flaws."

"Blind, stubbornness, vindictiveness, deceit, disobedience, eccentricity—"

"Eccentricity? I think I resent that."

Ironside laughed. "Anyway, that's enough of Ironside's fireside homilies," he said. He got up, his smile fading. He glanced at his watch, his voice turning dismissive. "The appointment is confirmed, by the way. I'm giving you the so-called 2nd Slavo-British Division . . . though it's hardly more than a brigade at present . . . You'd better see Major Wedge about your orders and warrants . . ."

His voice trailed away as he busied himself shovelling papers off his desk and into his briefcase.

I stood to attention, then trudged toward the door.

"General?"

I looked over my shoulder before realizing he was talking to me.

"Eh?"

"Are you still interested in the Guardian Angel?"

It took me a moment to adjust to this. "The parachute? Yes?"

"Just thought you might like to know about it. I gather you had some interest in the subject at one time. They're issuing to the squadrons on November fifth."

"Next year?"

"This year. November 1918."

"Ah," I said.

And, for the first time, it occurred to me that what Ironside had said was true: that human endeavor is pretty absurd, after all.

Home

As I stepped off the train at Ottawa, a brass band crashed into triumphant melody. As the introductory chords oompahed among the girders, a cloud of goitrous pigeons whirred through the steam and grit, defecating in panic.

An important-looking khaki-clad figure stepped forward. I put down my emaciated valise and drew on a world-weary and rather bored expression appropriate to my military eminence. Feeling very august, though it was only May, I straightened my shoulders and started to bring my hand to the salute, but faltered a bit when I noticed that the chap wasn't wearing any trousers.

Not only that, the fool was going in the wrong direction. He was headed toward some other passenger, at the far end of the railway car.

Then I saw he was, in fact, wearing pants—short pants. He was a boy scout—a fifty-year-old boy scout—with his whistle dangling—and the band was also in shorts and kneecaps.

It was the Manotick, Munroe and Hildasville Boy Scouts Band, and they were greeting the new Dominion Commissioner, Mr. J. W. Robertson, C.M.G., LL.D.

I cleverly converted my salute into an arthritic sort of wave, and sidled past through the mob, gazing far afield, feet and eyebrows raised and mouth slightly agape, to suggest that I'd just caught sight of my friend in the distance —obviously a rather shy and retiring friend, as he had retired half a mile down the platform to skulk behind several crates of live chickens.

As soon as I was out of sight, I resumed my normal expression, and, thus scattering farmers' wives in all directions, hurried for the exit and Constitution Square.

For, of course, there was nobody there to greet me, behind the poultry or anywhere else. This time there would be no newspaper reporters, women's clubs, civic receptions, and small boys goggling. Which was perfectly understandable, as it was 1920.

Everybody else in the Armed Forces had long since been demobilized, had settled down in civvy street, and had conceived about a quarter of a million howling kids, if it is possible to conceive of a quarter million howling kids.

Even the Militia and Defense representative on the new Air Board didn't know who I was.

"You've just come from Russia? What on earth were you doing there?"

"Intervening."

"You don't seem to be on the strength of the Canadian Air Force. In fact, we've no record of you whatsoever. Can you explain that?"

"I don't know anything about a Canadian Air Force. I was in the R.A.F. Then attached to the British Army. Though, before that, of course, I was in the Canadian Corps. Before I was in the R.F.C., that is. Except for the time I was with the White Russians."

"Haven't you forgotten the Navy?"

"Funnily enough, an admiral did say once that he just wished he could get me in the Navy. Matter of fact, he said it twice. That was when I was at the Air Ministry."

"You were with the Ministry too, were you?"

"Just before I joined the 13th Bicycle Battalion."

"And just what was a pilot doing with a bicycle?"

"Peddling."

"I see. I see. Excuse me a moment ..."

"Just stand there, will you, Corporal. No, I don't think that will be necessary, but keep it handy, just in case . . . The fact is, nobody's ever heard of you, Bandy—if that's your name. Can you prove who you are?"

"I could ask my father, I suppose."

"I mean, who you are in the Services?"

"There's that letter from the High Commissioner in London. Everything else, my Identification Card, paybook and so on, was taken from me in Rush—"

"All that letter proves is that you told them in London the same story you're telling us. They're rather a gullible lot over there."

"Excuse me, sir."

"What is it, Mitchell?"

"Miss Arsenault has just found these newspaper clippings in the archives."

"In the what?"

"That tin box, sir."

"Oh, yes."

"There's quite a lot about a Colonel Bandy."

"H'm . . . You seem awfully young to be a general, Bandy. You only look about thirty-five."

"Actually I'm twenty-six."

"Are you sure this is you, in these clippings? You don't look like this now."

"Well, I . . . I was seasick."

"H'm. It's all very irregular, Bandy. Surely, you must have *some* idea where your service records are?"

"Whatjamean? That's *your* responsibility, not mine. Look, all I'm interested in is getting demobbed, like everyone else."

"Demobilized? Why didn't you say so? That's an entirely different matter."

"Oh, good."

"That clears it up entirely, my dear fellow."

"Fine. So—demobilize me."

"Certainly not. You'll have to see the Soldiers Settlement Board, or somebody. That's not our department at all."

I'd gotten home so late that even the military were reluctant to get involved in the aftermath of the war—and I was an aftermath if ever there was one.

As for civilians, judging by the looks I received from the bowler-hatted veterans, the impatient glances of the young women as they rasped past in their fascinating black and white silk stockings, and the annoyed hootings of the motorists on Wellington Street in their unfamiliar designs of motor cars, the country was determined to forget the European catastrophe utterly, and get on with the important things, such as mortgages and sex.

I was a nasty reminder of the conflict, for I was still wearing the all-too-familiar cloth the color of horse-dung; worse, it was the conspicuously ornamented uniform of the class that had made such a shambles of the war: bloody red tabs and overbearing braid, and the pip and crossed sword and baton of my rank rank.

No wonder the civvies glared. It must have looked as if I were flaunting my martial proclivity. They were not to know that, having returned from Russia in rags, I had been forced to outfit myself in a new uniform to avoid being conscripted into the London County Council Refuse Collection Department.

One straightbacked civilian on Albert Street even reacted aloud, muttering and snorting contemptuously as I strolled by, as if to say, "Bloody twit—staying on in the Army when he could be free to enjoy the promised rewards and benefits of peace."

I didn't mind, especially as he was almost at the end of the unemployment line-up.

I didn't mind. The main thing was I was home. And home was beautiful: a perfect May day in the national capital, the sun shining from a sky clouded only by the smoke from the Eddy Match Company across the river,

417

the sunlight beaming onto tulip and daffodil (one of each in the Capital Commission gardens), and upon the verdigris towers of Parliament. There was hardly a sign of snow, except for a trickling, dirt-speckled heap of the stuff along the wall below the hill.

Though my heart was fluttering about helplessly in its cage of ribs because I felt so breathless with joy and anticipation at seeing my folks again, I forced myself not to hurry, in order to savor the once so familiar sights and sounds, to help convince myself that after four years of combat, politics, death sentences, and other *contretemps,* I really was home again.

There was so much nourishment for the senses, they felt quite bloated. I stared, I sniffed, I tasted, I listened with eye-prickling emotion to the clear, bell-like tones of the North American speech, after one and a half years of the Slavonic rhapsody. "What in tarnation," "Sakes alive," "You ain't kiddin'," "Be seein' ya."

So much was unfamiliar, so much had changed, visibly and invisibly: some new buildings, entirely new fashions, new Prime Ministers—Borden was still P.M., actually, but would be giving up in a few weeks—another blue-blood Governor-General had taken over since I first left, in 1916, Laurier had died while I was in the Peter and Paul Fortress in Petrograd. The newspapers were filled with unfamiliar names and references to incomprehensible events—there was talk of a Radio Station to be opened in Pittsburgh. What did that mean? Was it going to broadcast morse code? And there'd been some general strike or other, that had taken place in Winnipeg a year before. And expressions of detestation of the United States, especially now the goldurn Yankees were claiming to have won the war single-handed . . . In spite of which, the country seemed less British and more American. People wore American clothes, drove American cars, whistled American songs—I heard Ted Lewis singing a new hit called *When My Baby Smiles at Me,* on someone's Edison

Phonograph—and American business firms were flooding in—possibly to escape something called Prohibition.

The prices had changed, too. The raincoat I had bought for $5 was now $14; a kitchen range, formerly $26 was now, I saw by the shop windows, $40; Chambray dresses were as much as $2, corsets had doubled, cinema prices had soared to 10¢, and you couldn't get a Studebaker for less that $885, or even a Ford for under $530. It was really shocking.

But I wouldn't really have cared even if corsets had risen three times. I was home.

Nearly there now, pale and thin as a poor excuse but joyful as a lark, as I picked my way through the garbage cans in the narrow back street where my parents lived.

A couple of years after my father's *alfresco* cavortings in the barley with a girl called Denise, my parents had come together again, though in somewhat reduced circumstances. In place of the Ontario gingerbread house in Beamington, they now shared a frame house near the Rideau Canal. It was in rather a shabby district, i.e., in the vicinity of Parliament. In fact, it was no more than three minutes' walk from Parliament Hill.

'We finally prevailed on your mother to take him back,' my Aunt Barbara had written—Aunt Barbara was the only forthright relative I had—'And though she says she has neither forgotten nor forgiven, your father doesn't appear to notice much difference in her attitude. But then she was never one to flaunt her feelings, as you know.'

The Reverend Mr. Bandy had, of course, long since lost his stipend. Since being told by the Church to go unfrock himself, he had been eking out a living by writing articles for ecclesiastical journals (under a Latin pseudonym) and adapting his old sermons for sale to other ministers (under a Greek one).

'At the moment,' Aunt Barbara went on, 'they are living in a district in Ottawa where they are least likely to meet any of their former acquaintances. As for how such a man as your father could have come to topple off those high moral principles of his, you will have to work that out for yourself. If you manage to find out, however, please don't tell me, as I now live in Toronto, where we prefer not to hear about animal husbandry and all the other sordid things that go on in the country.'

As a matter of fact, that was one reason I was so anxious to get acquainted with my father, to try to understand how he had come to abandon his belief that words speak louder than actions. I suspected, from my own experience, that he must have had a lot of excess passion locked away behind his dickey and, like the time he tried to drown the deacon's cat in the rainwater barrel, had not had sufficient strength to hold down the lid.

When I first heard about it, my reaction had surprised me. Denise, an exceedingly pretty and quite honest girl, one third my father's age, had figured quite prominently in my own shamefully lascivious dreams. I couldn't understand how father had managed to dandle her on his lapse. She'd never even let *me* see her garters.

I hadn't been so much shocked—as jealous.

And there it was at last.

Home sweet home.

It was hideous. Grass was growing out of the sagging gutter, great flakes of whitish paint curled their lips contemptuously from every clapboard.

Still, in the back garden, glimpsed along a narrow side passage, a glorious magnolia tree exploded out of the backyard clutter, the flagstones strewn with its white, pink-tipped petals.

Heart thudding away like billy-ho, I marched bravely forward—not much of a march, as the front door was only two steps away from the sidewalk—my eyes darting eagerly from window to window, in case mother was looking out for me. I'd telegraphed from Montreal telling them

I was arriving that morning. But the blinds were down against the sun.

I raised a shaky hand to knock. There was a large lady standing in the next doorway. Her hair was all over the place. She looked like a giant sea anemone.

"The meter's round the side," she bellowed. "You lot oughter know that by now."

"I'm not the meter reader. I'm their only begotten son."

"I'm danged. I didn't know they had none," Mrs. Danged said.

"But then, of course," she added, "they never tell me nothin'."

A small child with a bare bum appeared from behind her skirts. I looked away squeamishly, and taking a deep breath, rapped on the door.

"You back bein' a soldier, then? What's the matter, couldn't ya get a job?" When I didn't answer—my throat was too constricted—she muttered, "All right. Stuck-up-back stud. Just like his old man . . . Airs and graces . . . Fuggen wing-collar . . ."

She went in and slammed the door. Locked out, the child started to holler, looking at me in panic.

Mother opened the door.

"Oh, it's you, Bartholomew," she said.

"Mother."

She peered around cautiously. "Were you talking to Mrs. Gore?" she asked. "I wouldn't do that, Bartholomew. It might encourage her."

Safely inside, she embraced me so warmly I felt quite choked up.

"It's wonderful to see you again, Bartholomew."

"Me, too . . ."

The living room was as dark and stifling as the hot room in a Russian *isba*. Father was sitting by a large coal fire in his shirt-sleeves, holding the Bible in a domineering way.

421

"There's your father," mother said, in case I hadn't noticed him. Then, before the old man could say anything: "When did you get in? I thought you were arriving early this morning?"

"I had to go to the Air Board, Mother."

"That's nice," mother said. "You finding a spare moment to see us."

"Yes, we're very honored, Bartholomew," father said heavily. He was obviously put out because I'd caught him without a collar.

We shook hands. After a warm exchange: "Well, I'll show you your room, Bartholomew," he said. "I expect you'll want to look neat and tidy for dinner."

"Sit down first and have a cup of tea," mother said.

Within a few minutes, I was sweating like a cistern. Even father was plucking a bit moodily at his shirt. Mother's pores, however, remained undemonstrative. Her skin remained as dry as a diploma.

"You don't seem to have gained much weight since you left," she said. "Don't they feed you in the Army?"

"There's a famine in many parts of Russia," I said, and started to tell her about it.

"Why didn't you write?" she asked. "We were worried about you."

"After all, he's a general now, Mother," father said.

"I'm still a lieutenant, really. The rest was just kind of acting temporary."

"I'm glad to see there is still a shade of humility left in you, Bartholomew," said father. "Always remember that in the eyes of God you are less than nothing."

"It's funny," I mused, after a moment. "You remember the last time I was in church, in—" I stopped, not knowing whether to mention Beamington or not. It might be considered a rude word, now. "In your last church? In 1916. You remember, Mother? When I sat between you and Mabel House?"

"I remember you sang very loudly, Bartholomew,"

mother said with what I was absolutely certain was a fond smile.

"M'yes," I whined. "Anyway, you know what I was thinking about? I was a brand-new sub-lieutenant at the time, and there I was, only just starting out on my military career, already dreaming of becoming a general, and having tea with the Archbishop of Canterbury and everything. Actually, I never met him."

"In that case, Bartholomew," father said, "why are you relating this story?"

"But I did meet the King," I finished, beginning to slump a bit. "The point is, you see, I was also daydreaming about meeting . . . uh . . . him . . . Anyway . . ."

I started to pluck at my wound stripes; but then thought, "Dammit, I'm Major General Bandy, C.B.E., D.S.O. and bar, M.C., D.F.C., et cetera. I sat up straight again.

"That seems rather a pointless sort of story, Bartholomew."

"M'yes," I muttered. "Well, you know what they say in Russia, Papa. *A wet cabbage weighs less than a dry samovar.*"

"Don't be foolish, Bartholomew," Papa said.

Afterward, we sat around the dinner table with what remained of the best silver and linenware, sipping coffee. When I told mother that after that eighteen months in Russia it seemed the best coffee I'd ever had in my life, she leaned over impulsively and tapped me twice on the wrist with her fish fork.

"It's so nice to have you back, Bartholomew," she said tenderly. "I've missed you . . . So much has happened . . ."

"Yes," I said, thinking about those four years.

"You know that Mabel has three children now."

"Ah."

"And your Aunt Beatrice choking on her teeth."

Throughout the meal, father, grown more at ease now that he had his wing-collar on, kept stealing glances at

423

me when he thought I wasn't looking. Despite himself, he was quite plainly filled with wonderment. He was obviously trying to suppress his awe at the remarkable achievements of this son of his, this Knight of the Air and leader of men who had hobnobbed with generals and prime ministers and aroused the ire and admiration of thousands.

I looked back at him, erect and beribboned, sworded and batoned and pipped, authoritative, commanding, ready at the drop of a hint to strip my sleeve and show my scars and say, "These wounds I had on Crispin's Day," or words to that effect. I waited agog.

He continued to sit there for the longest time, marvelling at his progeny; this noble, modest, circumspect lad of his who had always been clean-thinking, right-minded, God-fearing, and moved his bowels regularly.

There it was again, that piercing look. Now he was rubbing his temples with thumb and middle finger, one for each temple, and muttering. It sounded like, "Certainly not from *my* side of the family . . ."

"What?" mother asked flatly.

"I just don't understand," he said at length, shaking his head and staring at me openly this time, "where on earth the boy got that face."

I looked around the room, at the chocolate wallpaper and the colorful picture of 'Moses in the Bullrushes,' then down at the early-nineteenth-century library wheelbarrow that my father had used for carting his sermons around the study; and I knew I was home.

IF YOU ENJOYED READING DONALD JACK'S

IT'S ME AGAIN

THEN YOU'LL BE SURE TO ENJOY READING

THE PAPERJACKS BOOKS

ON THE FOLLOWING PAGES AS WELL . . .

THE BANDY PAPERS

VOLUME 1

THREE CHEERS FOR ME

'Keep your feet in good condition . . . don't forget you're
a minister's son and kill a few Huns . . . spurn the trium-
virate of evil intoxicants, gambling and the opposite sex'
. . . With this advice in mind and his bible in his old kit-
bag, Lieutenant Bartholomew Bandy leaves his home in
Ontario and marches off to the trenches of the Western
Front. His small-town puritanism, extraordinary face and
potentially lethal naïveté don't go down too well in the
officers' mess, and when he manages to capture his own
colonel in a dashing raid on his own lines he is promptly
transferred to the Royal Flying Corps, where life expect-
ancy is little more than a month . . .

Bandy learns to take things in his stride in this outrage-
ously funny story of the first volume of THE BANDY
PAPERS, which record the adventures of this delightfully
clumsy hero who, without ever learning from his mistakes,
always seems to profit by them.

Canadian author Donald Jack won the 1962 Stephen Lea-
cock award for humour when THREE CHEERS FOR
ME was first published. The book was also serialized on
CBC radio and went on to become an underground classic.

AT YOUR LOCAL BOOKSTORE, OR

SIMPLY FILL OUT THE ORDER FORM

ON THE LAST PAGE OF THIS BOOK.

THE BANDY PAPERS

VOLUME 2

THAT'S ME IN THE MIDDLE

"The most lethal secret weapon of the First World War . . ." That's Canada's Bartholomew Bandy. Whether demonstrating his skills in a Sopwith Camel or bicycling deep behind enemy lines with a kamikaze commando brigade, he wreaks havoc wherever he goes.

But unfortunately, havoc has become a way of life. Although Bandy crosses the paths of people like Winston Churchill and Lester Pearson, his brief career in politics almost ends with the collapse of the government. He gets lost flying to Portsmouth and ends up in a Dublin pub with gun-running rebels. A Bolshevik spy is found in his wardrobe and a randy war-widow in his bathroom. Even on his wedding night he manages to fall out of bed at a crucial moment.

However, his luck holds out, and Bandy's hilarious, hair-raising exploits leave only one thing to be desired . . . more adventures.

FILL OUT THE HANDY ORDER FORM

FOR THE BOOKS YOU WANT TO READ . . .

CHARLIE FARQUHARSON'S HISTRY OF CANADA

A saucy, hilarious interpretation of Canada's history as only Charlie could tell it. Written in that madcap "Parry Sound farmer" style, Charlie romps through a million years from "yer prehisterical times" to the reign of "Premier Trousseau".

THE GOLDEN AGE OF B.S. by Fred C. Dobbs

Fred C. Dobbs' answer to THE CANADIAN ESTABLISHMENT . . . "Many's the time I have rolled helplessly on the floor while Dobbs-Magee regaled me on national and international affairs, and now he's put out this book, which is great . . ." — Doug Collins, *The Vancouver Sun.* "It does a remarkable job of transferring the raucous, scurrilous old curmudgeon's disreputable character and outrageous opinions to the printed page, and says things even Dobbs wouldn't try to get away with on radio or T.V." — Bob Blackburn, *The Toronto Sun.*

A DIVINE CASE OF MURDER by Charles Dennis

Murder was not meant to be this funny! What would you do if you were plagued by the voice of an Irish priest . . . if you were being followed by a one-armed man who thought you were a god from outer space . . . and most of all, if a gorgeous young widow kept throwing herself at you in public? Rabbi Jerome Feldman is a man whose troubles begin where others' end . . . a sensuous, loving man whose tale of woe is a ribald, hilarious, unconventional one.

ORDER FORM

MAIL SERVICE DEPARTMENT
PAPERJACKS LTD.
330 STEELCASE ROAD EAST
MARKHAM, ONTARIO   L3R 2M1
CANADA

No. of copies	Order No.	Title	Price
_____	671-80373-5	THE HOWLING ARCTIC	$1.95 _____
_____	671-78857-4	TALES OF THE FOREIGN LEGION	1.75 _____
_____	7701-0003-1	THE DIFFICULT DAYS AHEAD	1.95 _____
_____	7737-7115-8	THE MEMOIRS OF A SURVIVOR	1.95 _____
_____	7737-7117-4	PRETTY LADY	2.50 _____
_____	7737-7103-4	THE CASE OF THE COLD MURDERER	1.95 _____
_____	7737-7036-4	A CHOICE OF ENEMIES	1.50 _____
_____	7737-7133-6	MURDER ON THE HOUSE	2.50 _____
		TOTAL:	_____

Please add 25¢ for handling charges.

Please enclose cheque or money order.

We cannot be responsible for orders containing cash.

(Please Print Clearly)

NAME _____

ADDRESS _____

CITY _____

PROVINCE _____ CODE _____

ORDER FORM

MAIL SERVICE DEPARTMENT
PAPERJACKS LTD.
330 STEELCASE ROAD EAST
MARKHAM, ONTARIO   L3R 2M1
CANADA

No. of copies	Order No.	Title	Price	
_____	7737-7075-5	THREE CHEERS FOR ME	$1.95	_____
_____	7737-7076-3	THAT'S ME IN THE MIDDLE	1.95	_____
_____	7737-7118-2	CHARLIE FARQUHARSON'S HISTRY OF CANADA	1.95	_____
_____	7701-0035-x	THE GOLDEN AGE OF B.S.	2.25	_____
_____	7701-0050-3	A DIVINE CASE OF MURDER	1.95	_____
_____	671-80367-0	GOOD-BYE SIBERIA	2.50	_____
_____	671-80718-8	YELLOWKNIFE	2.50	_____
			TOTAL:	_____

Please add 25¢ for handling charges.

Please enclose cheque or money order.

We cannot be responsible for orders containing cash.

(Please Print Clearly)

NAME _____

ADDRESS _____

CITY _____

PROVINCE _____ CODE _____